Jon Fordham, a retired building society general manager and county cricket executive director, has followed up his two successful non-fiction books with his debut crime novel: *Too Clever for His Own Good*, the first in the D.I. Steven Hardcastle trilogy.

Born and bred in south east London, Jon is married with three grown-up sons. He is a life-long supporter of Charlton Athletic Football Club and a keen follower of Kent County Cricket Club.

This book is dedicated to five wonderful people who sadly are no longer with us.

To Patricia and Donald Smith, my wife's parents, who we lost during the first lockdown of 2020. I could not have asked for better in-laws.

To Jean Cryer and Carly Philips who helped make the 11 years I spent at Kent County Cricket Club the best years of my working life.

And to Barry Moore, a good friend and fellow Charlton Athletic fan with whom I travelled across the country following the Addicks.

I miss you all very much.

Jon Fordham

TOO CLEVER FOR HIS OWN GOOD

AUSTIN MACAULEY PUBLISHERS™

LONDON • CAMBRIDGE • NEW YORK • SHARJAH

A CIP catalogue record for this title is available from the British Library.

ISBN 9781398434691 (Paperback)
ISBN 9781398434707 (ePub e-book)

www.austinmacauley.com

First Published 2022
Austin Macauley Publishers Ltd®
1 Canada Square
Canary Wharf
London
E14 5AA

Prologue
Three Years Earlier

The man stopped and looked at his iPhone. It was 1:18am and the temperature was a very humid 18C. It would be the longest day in six days' time so darkness would give way to daylight in around three hours. This wasn't a problem. He would be home, tucked up in bed, in well under an hour.

He had been planning this night out for several weeks and had carried out a couple of dummy runs at this precise time in the morning to make sure he hadn't overlooked anything; he was satisfied that all would go according to plan. After all, it wasn't as though it was the first time he had done something like this.

He had also walked the route several times in daylight and on each occasion, to blend in with the surroundings, had borrowed his sister's dog; a very docile and slightly overweight six-year-old black Labrador called Buster.

He knew from experience, having once owned a dog, that passers-by were more likely to remember the dog than the owner.

After careful consideration, he had chosen to approach his target, a small cricket pavilion, from the rear via a fairly narrow public footpath that ran behind it.

Dressed in a black polo shirt and black tracksuit bottoms, and with a black balaclava stuffed into the black holdall he was carrying, he would be virtually invisible to any insomniacs that may be walking the same route as him at that time of night, although he knew this would be highly unlikely as the footpath neither began nor ended near any residential or commercial buildings, although it did skirt the back of the village hall at one point.

He looked at his phone again. It was now 1:23am.

Nothing had stirred, and not a sound could be heard, apart for a lone dog barking somewhere way off in the distance.

He walked round to the front of the building and stopped for a minute or so. All was quiet now—even the dog had stopped its barking.

He tapped the first window very gently with the rock hammer he'd bought some 18 months earlier. On the fourth tap, he both heard and felt the window crack. Another tap and he was through.

Using the gardening gloves he had brought with him, he picked carefully away at the glass until there was a hole large enough to shove a hose through.

Moving to his right, and passing the front door of the building, he came to the second window, and repeated the exercise.

It was now 1:30am, just as he had planned.

Reaching inside the holdall, he pulled out a short length of garden hose and a green 5-litre plastic jerry can which was full to the brim with the petrol he'd siphoned out of a two-year-old Volkswagen Golf a few nights earlier.

He very carefully poured half of the petrol through each window. He then put the hose, the can and the rock hammer back into the holdall, and zipped it up.

He was almost done.

He took out a packet of cigarettes from one of his pockets and a disposable lighter from another. He took out two cigarettes, lit them both and dropped one through each window. In an instant, the petrol ignited. The building was very old and had been constructed mainly in wood. From past experience, he knew it would be completely ablaze by the time he was back on the footpath to the rear.

Because of where the building was situated, there was every likelihood that the fire wouldn't be discovered until daylight.

But if, by chance, someone noticed the glow of fire, the building would almost certainly be burnt to ruins by the time any fire engines arrived on the scene.

As he walked quickly along the footpath, he didn't bother to look back.

Usually, it was the thrill of the fire that gave him pleasure, but not on this occasion.

This time it was the thrill of revenge.

His job was done.

He was ready for bed.

He would sleep well.

The Present Day
Sunday 5pm

"HOWZAT!"

As the ball thudded into the batsman's front pad, eleven men of the fielding side shouted out in unison, including the two standing on the third man and fine leg boundaries some sixty yards or so away from the action.

Despite not having the slightest clue where the ball had hit the batsman, their enthusiasm to join in the appeal with their teammates was understandable, since the batsman in question was the home side's best player by a country mile. Getting him out so early on in the innings would give the visitors a crucial advantage over their long standing rivals.

"That's out," responded the umpire to the appeal, putting up the index finger of his right hand.

However, the batsman didn't budge.

"You have got to be joking, umpire," he said. "The ball hit me a good six inches outside the line of the off stump."

"Sorry batsman, but you moved your front foot after the ball hit your pad, so you are definitely out."

The batsman held his pose for a few seconds more, all the time glaring at the umpire; or at least the umpire assumed it was a glare. His eyesight wasn't as good as it used to be, and the batsman's protective helmet made it even harder for him to see his face.

Finally, realising that he had no choice other than to accept the umpire's decision, the batsman took off his helmet, put his batting gloves inside and gave the umpire one last lingering look.

If looks alone could kill, the umpire was a goner.

As the batsman began the lonely walk back to the pavilion, he stopped for a few seconds to exchange words with the other umpire who was standing at square leg, before continuing his slow walk back.

As the wicket had fallen on the last ball of the over, the umpire turned to his left and walked away to take up his position at square leg so he would be ready for the first ball of the next over.

The brief exchange of words with the departing batsman had unsettled him and he couldn't help thinking that these days the hassle of umpiring wasn't worth the few quid he would receive for his troubles at the end of the game.

In his Own playing days, which admittedly were more than two decades ago, whenever an umpire had made a poor decision, a batsman would just walk off and keep his mouth shut, or at least keep it shut until he was out of the umpire's earshot.

If he'd edged the ball into his pads, but was given out leg before, he might walk off rubbing the edge of his bat to make the point that he'd actually nicked the ball, but that was as far as it went.

These days though, players seemed to have lost all respect for the men in white coats, and batsmen and bowlers alike would sometimes behave in a way which suggested they were trying to intimidate an umpire into giving a decision their way.

"Why do I bother?" he said out loud, although softly enough to be certain that no-one overheard him.

However, one of the consolations of this particular game had been the food served up by the ladies of the home team who were well known in cricketing circles for the quality of their teas.

Instead of the usual cricketing tea of fish paste and egg sandwiches, followed by a dry Victoria sponge washed down with lukewarm tea and coffee, the range of food served up in the village hall during the tea interval had been a sight for sore eyes.

On offer for players and umpires alike had been jacket potatoes, roast potatoes, spicy chicken wings, a large tureen of chilli con carne and a couple of very decent pasta dishes, as well as a variety of homemade sandwiches on a par with those usually available from upmarket food halls such as Marks and Spencer.

On top of that, there had been a large lemon drizzle cake, a chocolate sponge and a selection of individual fancy cakes.

There had also been a decent collection of fresh fruit on offer, but faced with a choice between cake and fruit, as far as this umpire was concerned, the former won every time. And as a widower, at least he wouldn't have to cook himself a meal when he got home.

And the umpire had certainly eaten well today; so well in fact, that he had had to undo the top three buttons of his trousers as his stomach was pressing uncomfortably against the waistband. Thankfully, nobody had noticed this as his three quarter length white umpire's coat completely covered any potential source of embarrassment.

Tea aside though, he really wished he had never agreed to umpire this particular game. But when the secretary of the village league rings up to ask you to umpire a match as a personal favour, it's really difficult to say no.

Over the past few years there had been a bit of bad blood between the two teams involved in today's match and the secretary had said that he needed two strong-minded umpires who wouldn't be intimidated and who would be able to retain control of the game if things threatened to get out of hand.

He had reluctantly agreed to this request; even though he had seriously considered politely declining the invitation.

Lately, he'd been giving a lot of thought as to whether or not to continue as a village league umpire. Only his deep love of the game was stopping him from hanging up the white coat once and for all.

Just at that precise moment, and not for the first time of late, he felt a sudden painful twinge in his abdomen, which really made him flinch.

He dismissed it as a touch of indigestion. After all, he had made a bit of a pig of himself with the tea.

His stomach felt full and with the sun beating down, at that precise moment in time he really wished he was having a snooze in his garden, and not standing at square leg waiting for the game to restart.

He hadn't been feeling at his best for some weeks now and had decided to visit a doctor sometime during the coming week.

The sound of the other umpire telling the fielders "New bowler, left arm over, six to play" put an end to his musings and brought him back to earth with a jolt.

The first two balls were tapped back to the bowler by the batsman. But he clipped the third off his legs and now the ball was coming straight at the umpire, at knee height and at a fair rate of knots.

Just in the nick of time, he lifted his right foot and the ball missed him by a whisker, on its way to the square leg boundary. But with most of his weight now on his left side, a fall was inevitable.

Toppling over with the grace of a three-legged baby hippopotamus, as one player later described it, he hit the ground with quite some considerable force.

However, as he was not exactly the slimmest person in the world, his natural padding cushioned most of the impact.

A lot of men his age and size might well have done some serious damage to themselves, possibly breaking a hip, a wrist or a forearm.

Fortunately, a few seconds after hitting the ground, he realised he'd gotten away with it. The only damage done was to his pride. *I bet they're all having a good laugh at my expense*, he thought to himself.

However, lying on his back, looking up at the cloudless sky, he sensed an opportunity—an opportunity to cut short his involvement in the rest of the game, as long as he played his cards right.

The idea that had come to him was to make everyone think he had twisted an ankle when he fell and that the pain was far too severe for him to continue umpiring.

And, as it happened, there was a ready-made replacement in the form of the league secretary who he knew had also done a fair bit of umpiring in his time.

I could let him have my white coat and my ball counter and then limp slowly off to the pavilion and shut myself in the umpire's room for a couple of hours, he thought to himself. *And perhaps I could also persuade someone to bring me a cup of tea and then I could settle down for a nice nap.*

He was suddenly jerked back to reality when he realised that two of the younger players from the visiting team were now standing over him.

"Can we help you up, umpire? Do you need a doctor?"

"I'll be fine, lads, just give me a hand up," he replied.

They each took an arm and with a bit of an effort they eventually got him back on his feet.

By now, his fellow umpire had joined them.

"Are you OK?" he asked.

"Yeah, I'm fine," was the reply. "Ouch, no, sod it," he added quickly as he put his weight onto his left foot. "Bugger it. That stings a bit."

"Are you going to be OK to carry on, old chap?" enquired his colleague.

Those words were music to his ears.

After a brief conversation with the league secretary, who had come on to the pitch to see how he was, he readily agreed to call it a day and was already hobbling back to the pavilion as the secretary, now in a white coat several sizes too big for him, took his place at square leg.

The limping umpire wasn't expecting too much sympathy from the home players sat in front of the pavilion.

Sadly for him, he was spot on.

"Are you going to get your glasses, umpire?" asked one of them.

"Forgotten your white stick, mate?" said another.

"Specsavers is that way." This from the batsmen he'd given out just a few minutes ago.

"Very funny," he replied, "and very original. I've not heard any of them for at least a fortnight."

He knew that it wasn't the wittiest of ripostes, but by that time, he couldn't care two hoots. *No chance of any of them getting me a cup of tea now*, he told himself. *I won't even bother asking.*

He walked down the short corridor which led to the umpire's room on his left. He tried the door handle, found the door locked and then remembered he'd put the key in his right hand trouser pocket.

He paused; relieved that he hadn't left it in the pocket of the white coat he'd just given to the secretary.

As the senior of the two umpires, he'd locked the door so that they could leave things like mobile phones, wallets and keys safely in the room whilst they were umpiring—not as though there was much chance of them being pinched today, even if he'd left the door unlocked.

"At some grounds I've umpired at, they'd have your false teeth in the blink of an eye if you left them lying around," he had told the other umpire before the game.

Despite that, through force of habit, he still went straight to his sports jacket that was hanging on the back of the door to check that his own keys and wallet were still there. They were.

He did own a mobile phone, but had bought it for emergencies only, and had recently made up his mind to cancel his contract, as he rarely used it.

Today, he had decided to leave it at home.

As expected, his keys were in the right hand front pocket of the jacket, and his wallet was in the inside left.

The fairly spacious umpire's room obviously doubled up as some sort of meeting place with a fairly decent table and eight chairs the centre piece. There were also a couple of armchairs which, like the umpire, had seen better days, and he plumped himself down on the less careworn of the two. He found it deceptively comfortable and he knew he would have no trouble getting off to sleep.

He was one of those fortunate people who could fall asleep anywhere and at any time, and it normally only took him a minute or two to doze off.

Looking around, he saw there were a few framed cricket prints on the walls and a notice board with fixture lists and an out of date Health and Safety notice pinned to it.

One thing missing from the room was natural light as there were no windows. Rooms with windows made it easier for yobs to break into buildings, or even set them alight.

He picked up a year-old copy of a cricket magazine from a small table to his right, flicked through it, and then put it back down. His eyes were already beginning to feel heavy.

He could feel himself nodding off when he heard a noise, which he recognised as the squeak of a door knob turning.

He opened his eyes and gave them a quick rub. It took a couple of seconds for them to focus, and he half rose out of his chair, ready to greet whoever was coming into the room.

Looking down as he went to get up, he noticed that the top three buttons of his trousers were still undone.

Bugger me, he thought to himself. *Did I really walk off the pitch with my flies undone like that? In the old days, we used to say that someone was 'flying without a licence' if they'd forgotten to button up.*

That rather obscure reflection was the very last thought to pass through the mind of the umpire.

The first blow felt like a massive firework exploding inside his head. By the time the third blow struck, he was on his way down.

He was already dead when he hit the floor.

Sunday 7pm

"YES!" came the shout in unison from all eleven visiting players, as the home team's number eleven batsman watched his off stump cartwheeling towards the wicket keeper, the same wicket keeper who had been sledging him mercilessly for the last quarter of an hour.

The game was over with the visiting team gaining a comfortable victory over their old rivals.

There were handshakes all around amongst the visitors, and the keeper was now walking towards the batsman with his now gloveless hand outstretched.

At that precise moment in time, the number eleven felt like shoving his bat somewhere unpleasant where it would do more than just tickle the keeper's prostate gland.

However, the batsman was very much old school and he took off his helmet, tucked his batting gloves and inners inside, and shook the keeper's hand.

Whilst anyone close at hand would have heard him say 'Well done' to his opponent, the batsmen's brain was mentally saying 'Tosser!'

Colin Sharpe, in his early 40s, had been playing for Flitton Green Cricket Club for over 25 years and was a serial number eleven, with a batting average well down in single figures.

Despite being first and foremost a bowler, Sharpe had always taken his batting extremely seriously. Perhaps the one thing that had stopped him doing damage to the opposition wicket keeper was that his bat was new, and today was the first time he'd used it in anger, having spent several hours at home lovingly knocking it in over the previous four or five evenings.

In fact, earlier on, he had managed to annoy three of his own team mates who were getting themselves ready with the game about to restart after the break for tea.

Even the most experienced batsmen have the odd butterfly or two in the stomach when waiting to go out to bat, at least until they've managed to put a few runs on the scoreboard.

Today was no different and the constant 'tap, tap, tap' of bat mallet on willow had got on the nerves of the home side's two openers and number three batsman who were also in the dressing room, with one of them telling him to 'put a sock in it', or words to that effect.

'Sharpey', as he was known by his team mates, had had his usual steady game with the ball, taking three opposition wickets for just 40 runs off his ten overs, with what his teammates laughingly described as 'grenades' or 'pie-chucking'.

Bowling off just a handful of paces, nine times out of ten he gently lobbed the ball high above the batsman's eye line. So high, it was said, that sometimes there was a risk of it landing on a length with snow on it.

The key to his success was no pace on the ball. Teammates joked that you had time to make a cup of tea between the ball leaving Sharpey's hand and reaching the batsman.

With too much time to think about what shot to play, the inexperienced batsman would invariably swing his bat across the line of the ball and miss it completely. Now, completely devoid of pace, the ball would either hit the batsman's pads bang in front of the stumps, or gently dislodge a bail as it just kissed the stumps.

As the disconsolate batsman begins the walk back to the pavilion, he would inevitably hear one of the fielders asking the bowler, "What was that Sharpey, your moon ball, your knuckle ball, or just your usual filth?"

Today was no different.

The two young lads from the visiting Middle Ash Cricket Club, who had helped the fallen umpire back on to his feet, had both perished to the mysteries of Sharpey's pies earlier in the day.

Whilst the match was lost, Sharpey consoled himself by deciding he'd put a coat of linseed oil on his new bat as soon as he got home. He knew he'd bought a good one as today he'd managed to get to double figures for the first time in God knows how long, and had even scored a boundary, his first for two seasons.

Half way back to the pavilion, he passed his skipper who gave him a nod and a "well done, Sharpey".

Midway through his team's innings, when it had become obvious that they were going to fall well short of the score posted by Middle Ash, Andy Hanson, the Flitton Green captain, had decided to have a word with Richard Askell, the League Secretary.

After a brief chat with a couple of the more senior Flitton Green players, it had been agreed that at the end of the match Hanson would tell Askell that, in the team's considered opinion, the performance of the injured umpire had been totally unsatisfactory and unacceptable.

To Hanson though, as the losing captain, it was important that his comments to Askell shouldn't be perceived as a case of sour grapes.

When Askell spotted the home team captain walking purposefully towards him, he guessed that a complaint was coming his way.

"Where did you dig up that old fossil?" asked Hanson.

Having personally selected the umpires to officiate the game, Askell knew he had to accept a degree of responsibility, since both were his choice. He immediately went on the defensive.

"Sorry Andy, what old fossil is that?" replied Askell with a deadpan face.

"Come on, Rich, you know who I mean—the old boy who's probably snoring his head off in the umpire's room at this very moment," stated Hanson.

"Look Andy, I accept that he wasn't on top form today, but Donna knows his stuff," replied Askell. "He was a very decent player in his day; he even played a few games for the county 2nd eleven."

Hanson looked at Askell quizzically. "Who's Donna?"

"Sorry mate, old habits die hard," answered Askell. "That was his nickname ages ago. You see, his real name is Donald Summers. When I first came across him, it was around about the time the singer Donna Summer had several hit songs and so some bright spark started calling him Donna, and it sort of stuck."

"Looking at the size of him, are you sure he isn't called Donna because he stuffs himself with kebabs?" asked Tony Sullivan, the second umpire who had just joined the conversation. "Honestly, he was stuffing himself something silly during tea. He was like a man who hadn't eaten for weeks!"

"How did you find him at tea, Tony? You seemed to be having a bit of chat with him," asked Askell.

"When he came up for air, you mean?" replied Sullivan.

"Well, to be honest, it was just your average chat between two blokes who've never met before. I gather he only moved back to the area a few months ago, and by the sound of it he's kept himself to himself for most of the time since. I don't think he's married, but we didn't really touch too much on personal stuff."

"He did say that he'd been in the building society business for most of his life, and that he'd moved away from here when he got promoted to run a branch somewhere up north. I got the impression that was well over 20 years ago.

"What he did tell me though is that he's going to chuck umpiring in. He said he hadn't done that much lately, but he's begun to get pissed off with all the aggro he's been getting when he does."

"How do you think he did today, Tony? You were out there with him for at least three hours before he retired hurt," asked the Flitton Green skipper, with just a hint of sarcasm.

"If I'm honest with you, Andy, I thought he was just going through the motions. He seemed to be a bit distracted, as if he had something on his mind. It just felt like he wanted to be somewhere else."

"Well, we've all felt like that from time to time though, haven't we?" replied Askell. "But I take your point, Tony, and yours, Andy. I think I need a chat with him. I might see if he wants to stop off for a pint on the way home."

"That sounds like a good idea. Thanks for listening, Rich," said Hanson. "Now I'd better be getting back to the dressing room as I've told the lads we need to have a bit of a post mortem on today's game, and I wouldn't put it past some of them to bugger off to the pub before we have a chin-wag."

With that, Hanson began jogging back to the pavilion.

Askell and Sullivan followed in the Flitton Green skipper's wake, but at a more sedate pace.

And as they walked into the pavilion, the first thing they heard was a volley of bad language from Hanson—evidently some of his team had already done a disappearing act, just like the Flitton Green captain had feared.

When the two men reached the umpire's room, Askell put his left hand on the door handle and pushed down, expecting the door to open.

To his surprise, it didn't move an inch. He pushed harder, it still wouldn't budge. His first thought was that Summers had probably fallen asleep. But why wouldn't the door move? If it was locked, why had he locked himself in?

But if it wasn't locked, something must be stopping the door from opening?

All this flashed through his mind.

Askell and Sullivan exchanged looks.

"Donald! Donald!" shouted Askell, as Sullivan tried the door.

"Come on Donald, open the door," shouted Askell again, knocking on the door at the same time.

The shouting brought several players from both teams out into the corridor.

"What's up? Has the old boy fallen asleep?" asked a voice from the away team dressing room doorway.

"The door won't open," Askell told them.

Running through his mind was the concern that Summers might be ill. Perhaps he'd suffered a stroke or a heart attack. After all, he was no spring chicken, being in his mid to late 60s, was significantly overweight, probably ate all the wrong things, and had just spent a few hours out in the hot sunshine. To cap it all, he had also taken a bit of a tumble. All those factors were against him, and, in hindsight, Askell was beginning to think Donald Summers might be a heart attack waiting to happen.

"He could have collapsed and be lying against the door," said Sullivan, his thoughts mirroring Askell's. "Let me have a go."

As Askell stood aside, Sullivan put all his weight against the door. There was no give in it. He was now pretty certain it was locked from the inside.

"I hope he hasn't locked the door and left the key in the lock," said Andy Hanson, who had by now joined them and was sharing the concerns of the other two. He looked around and saw Flitton Green's young opening bowler Alex Donahue.

"Alex, go over to the village hall and get the spare set of keys from the ladies in the kitchen will you, and be quick about it, lad."

"It doesn't look good, chaps, does it?" said Hanson, quietly.

"We'll know soon enough," replied Askell. "In the meantime, can we have a bit of room please, lads," he said, addressing the half a dozen or so players standing around in the corridor.

"Soon as we know what the score is, we'll let you know." After what seemed an age, but was probably no more than two of three minutes, a slightly breathless Alex Donahue returned with a key ring with seven or eight keys attached. He handed the bunch to his skipper.

"As club captain, I'd better do the honours, chaps, if you don't mind," said Hanson to Askell and Sullivan.

"Go ahead, mate," replied Askell.

The second key he tried was the right one and there was a click as he turned it to the left.

At least there was no key in the lock on the other side.

Hanson pushed open the door and looked in.

"Jesus, Mary and Joseph," he whispered, turning to the others, the colour visibly draining from his face.

Donald Summers was lying on the floor, face down. He hadn't had a stroke or a heart attack. That much was obvious from the bloody and congealed mess that had once been the back of his head.

As the three of them moved into the room, there was complete silence, broken only by the sound of young Alex Donahue vomiting in the doorway.

Sunday 8:15pm

As he pulled into the Flitton Green Village Hall car park, the driver of the black Range Rover looked at the digital clock at the bottom left hand corner of his sat nav screen. It told him that it was 8:15pm on Sunday 24 June—three days after the longest day of the year. From now on, the nights would steadily start to draw in.

For now though, there was still plenty of daylight.

The driver had visited the village hall and cricket ground several times before, both on business and for pleasure.

However, on this occasion, even though he'd parked up and turned the engine off, he stayed in his car for a few minutes taking in the scenery.

Directly opposite him was the cricket pavilion, nowhere near as grand as the name would suggest. There was a lot of activity outside it, far more than you would normally expect to see at this time of the evening.

Getting on for three years ago, very early on a Sunday morning, the old single storey pavilion had gone up in flames. By the time the fire crews had arrived, there was very little they could do other than to dampen the fire down as best they could.

The building and everything inside was completely destroyed, including all of the groundsman's equipment.

Whilst items such as mowers and rollers remained identifiable, they would never be used again due to the intense heat generated by the fire.

Once the area affected by the fire been declared safe, the Fire Investigation Team had been allowed on site. It hadn't taken them long to confirm that the cause of the fire was arson. The windows either side of the front door had been broken, and petrol had been poured into both dressing rooms, and then set alight.

Whilst the cricket club enjoyed a keen rivalry with the other clubs in the area, the players and members were at a complete loss to suggest anyone who might harbour a grievance serious enough for them to want to burn down their pavilion.

However, the general feeling of the police investigating the fire was that there had to be a connection between the cricket club and the arsonist.

If he, or she for that matter, was just interested in the thrill of setting a building alight and then getting their kicks watching it burn, the much larger village hall, just 50 or so yards away, would have been a far better target.

Frustratingly, nobody had ever been arrested for what happened that night, despite the hard work of the police. Within a month of the fire happening, the general feeling was that the culprit would never be found.

Whilst the old pavilion had been much loved by those that had used it, the best word to describe its replacement was 'functional'.

The windows either side of the entrance had metal shutters which were pulled down and locked at the end of each game. These were the pavilion's only windows, the absence of any others an inevitable consequence of the fire, and the restrictions imposed on the cricket club by its insurers.

As with the old pavilion, the new one didn't have any toilets or showers. Those needing to answer a call of nature had to use the toilets in the nearby village hall.

However, with the rear of the pavilion backing onto woodland, anyone needing to answer an urgent call of nature, or those who just couldn't be bothered to walk to the village hall, found it far more convenient simply to go round the back of the building to have a pee.

The only problem was that the narrow public footpath which ran around the cricket ground was no more than three or four yards from the back of the pavilion.

Anyone using the path on a match day would have a ringside view of someone taking a comfort break.

The only other rooms, apart from the two dressing rooms, were a meeting room which doubled up as an umpire's room on a match day, and a slightly larger one that was home to a couple of dozen fold-up chairs, the various items of cricket equipment used for practice purposes and the usual groundsman's tools and equipment, which included a small tractor, two rollers, two mowers and spare boundary ropes. The only access to this room was via a locked roller shutter on the outside of the building.

To the right of the pavilion, at one o'clock when viewed from the car park, was a small scorebox come scoreboard which, as one wag put it, had seen better days like most of the scorers that used it.

At three o'clock, a couple of yards outside the boundary rope, stood a fairly large sightscreen which was repaired and repainted white at the start of every new season. Its twin could be found directly opposite on the other side of the ground, at nine o'clock.

To the immediate rear of the right-hand sightscreen were three football pitches—one full size pitch and two smaller ones. The smaller pitches were used either for practice, or by the Flitton Green Colts football teams.

The decent sized car park with room for at least 60 cars was at six o'clock, directly opposite the cricket pavilion, with the village hall to the immediate left at seven o'clock.

Like most rural village halls, Flitton Green's was one of the focal points of day to day village life.

Used Monday to Friday during school term time by the Little Sparklers Pre-school, at weekends it doubled up as a sports pavilion and changing rooms for the football teams.

The cricket pavilion was locked up and put into hibernation during the winter months, with the spare keys removed from the village hall kitchen to make sure that only the groundsman and the cricket club captain had access to it.

So it had always been, and so it would always be.

On match days throughout the year, the village hall kitchen was in use not only for the benefit of the players, but also for any spectators that would come along to watch the cricket or the football.

Soup, tea, coffee and light refreshments were on offer during the winter, and during the summer, hot and cold drinks accompanied by a large selection of sandwiches and pastries were always readily available.

Run by the Little Sparklers Committee, the profits were ploughed straight back into the pre-school. The children's new play area to the back of the village hall had been bought and paid for from those profits.

On a decent summer's afternoon, the numbers would be swollen by families coming down for afternoon tea, and not necessarily just to watch the cricket, with parents hoping that their offspring would let off steam and wear themselves out on the play equipment.

Past the second sightscreen on the left, at eleven o'clock, were two practice cricket nets which, like the scorebox, were also looking a little bit sorry for themselves.

Unlike the pre-school committee, the cricket team committee invariably found themselves short of money, just managing to get through the season by the seat of their pants thanks to their mid-season quiz night, the traditional end of season barbeque and a well-attended race night which was usually held in January.

Just as he was about to get out of his car, the driver's mobile phone rang and he answered it without looking to see who the caller was.

"DI Hardcastle."

"It's me, boss. Where are you?"

"I'm just getting out of the car Phil. I'll be with you in a tick."

The caller, as he had expected, had been Phil Davison, one of his two sergeants.

When Davison had rung him less than an hour earlier, Steve Hardcastle had been at home on the point of cleaning up his barbeque.

He and his wife Jenny had had friends over for lunch to watch England beat Panama 6-1 in a World Cup match after which they enjoyed the England cricket team completing a 5-0 One Day International whitewash of the old enemy, the Australians; a great, but all too rare afternoon of sport.

Once everyone had drifted off home, Steve and Jenny had begun to clear up. It was amazing how much of a mess a small group of adults and children could leave in their wake.

The call from his sergeant had come just at the right time for Hardcastle—he hated clearing up.

Stopping only to have a quick shower, as he didn't want to arrive at a crime scene smelling like a burnt sausage, he was still tying the knot in his tie as he got behind the wheel of his Range Rover.

His conversation with Davison had been brief, but it had ended with the chilling words, "This is a nasty one, boss."

As he walked across the outfield, the 6ft 2in, 13-stone Hardcastle was pleased to see that things were well underway, and that there were already several cars parked around the small pavilion.

There had been no rain in the area for over a fortnight and as the ground was bone dry, the cars that had driven across the outfield hadn't left any tyre marks on the grass. *At least that will keep the groundsman off my back,* he thought to himself.

As it would be dark within 90 minutes or so, he was glad to see that temporary lighting was already being erected around the pavilion, although any detailed search of the surrounding area would now have to wait for daylight.

As he neared the pavilion, Davison, already wearing a pale blue crime scene suit, walked towards his boss, so they could have their initial chat without being overheard.

"Well, what have we got, Phil?"

"The victim is a Donald Summers, a white male in his mid to late 60s. He was umpiring the game, but went off with an injured ankle which he suffered during the early part of the second innings. This was timed by one of the scorers at 5:10pm.

"Two hours later, at 7:10pm, he was found in the umpire's room with the back of his head bashed in. Whoever did it really meant it, boss, there's no doubt whatsoever about that."

"Who found him?" asked Hardcastle.

"There were three people involved. The second umpire, a Tony Sullivan, and Richard Askell, a cricket league official, found the umpire's room locked after the game had finished," replied Davison reading from his notebook.

"The home team captain, Andrew Hanson, got one of his players to get a spare key from the village hall. When they eventually unlocked the door, they found the victim lying on his stomach. He'd been struck several times to the back of the head."

"Where are both teams now? I hope they're not still in the dressing rooms," enquired Hardcastle.

"Thankfully not, boss, and this is where we had a bit of luck. One of the Middle Ash lads is ex-job. He used to be with the Met, but left to become the owner of a pub down here.

"When he heard there had been a fatality, his old training kicked in. On the promise of a free pint at his pub, he got both teams to leave their gear and go across to the village hall. Most of the players are sitting around still wearing their whites."

"Sounds like he's the one who deserves the pint," said Hardcastle. "What's his name?"

"Danny Willard."

"I'll go over and thank him once I've had a look in the pavilion," replied Hardcastle.

"We do have a bit of a problem though boss. Four of the home team players got changed and left as soon as the game was over. We think that three of them could have gone to the pub, so I've got someone checking both The Cricketers and The Shire," replied Davison.

"What about the fourth man? Any idea where he's gone?" asked Hardcastle.

"Our best guess is that he's gone home. I got his home address from the Flitton skipper, and I've got someone knocking on his front door right about now."

"Have we anyone in the frame?"

"Well, the guy who we think has gone home did have a bit of a barney with the deceased. He disagreed with the umpire's decision which is not unusual in cricket these days, or so I'm told."

"Is that all?" asked Hardcastle.

"Well," continued Davison, "apparently this guy is well known in cricketing circles for being on a very short fuse. He's done the rounds and played for a fair few local clubs. As the saying goes, he's had more clubs than Jack Nicklaus."

"What's his name?"

"Neil Panton," replied Davison.

For a few seconds, all was quiet. Then Hardcastle took a deep breath. No matter how many times he'd had to look at the bodies of victims of violence, he'd never quite got used to it.

"OK, let's have a closer look then," he said to Davison as his sergeant handed him the obligatory protective suit, pale blue latex gloves and overshoes.

"Who's our Crime Scene Manager on this one, Phil?"

"Billy Kiernan," replied Davison. "He should be here in about 10 minutes."

"That's a good start; what about pathologist?"

"Kelly Heywood. She arrived ten minutes ago and is already snapping away with her camera," replied Davison.

"Right, so where are we up to at the moment?"

"As you can see, we've got lights and canvas going up front and back. A couple of local press turned up ten minutes ago, a journo and a snapper. But you know what it's like these days boss, I'm willing to bet it's all over Twitter and Facebook already.

"We're also putting in place an inner and an outer perimeter. The inner will cover the pavilion and the immediate surrounds, and initially the outer will include the woods and footpath, starting behind the village hall, and ending where the footpath splits, about 100 yards past the pavilion."

"We'll need to tell the people that run the pre-school that they'll have to stay closed, until further notice," replied Hardcastle. "We'll need a couple of lads in the car park early in the morning. Some of the mums bringing their kids in might be a bit miffed that the pre-school is shut, but they may also have popped in here at some point this afternoon, so it's possible there could be some potential witnesses amongst them.

"And I'm willing to bet that quite a few people came here during the course of the afternoon, so we'll need to get all their names and addresses as soon as possible."

By now, they were almost at the front door of the pavilion. On either side were about twenty fold-up chairs, which players from both sides had used during the afternoon. Standing by the chairs were several Crime Scene Investigators, all in protective clothing, awaiting the arrival of their boss Billy Kiernan.

"Considering it's just over an hour since the triple nine call was made, we've made really good progress Phil. Well done," said Hardcastle.

"Thanks boss, but what Danny Willard did was crucial, so I can't take all the credit. It's a real stroke of luck that someone with his experience was able to take control before I got here," replied Davison.

"Fingers crossed that our good luck doesn't end there then," said Hardcastle.

A couple of steps more and they were inside the pavilion, standing in the doorway of the away dressing room on their left. Directly opposite was the home one.

Having played a fair amount of cricket himself, the chaotic scenes in both dressing rooms didn't come as any surprise to Hardcastle.

The clothes the players had turned up in were hanging neatly from hooks on the walls, the only things that were tidy.

The floors in both dressing rooms were a completely different story—both looked like a bomb had gone off.

To a non-cricketer like Phil Davison, he just couldn't understand how the players managed to go home with their own clothing and equipment, such was the chaos. He didn't envy the CSI's who would have to sift through and search everything, looking for any evidence.

As they moved up the corridor towards the umpire's room on their left, Davison lightly touched Hardcastle's right arm.

"We need to be a bit careful here, boss. One of the young Flitton players looked in and promptly threw up."

At that precise moment, Hardcastle got a strong whiff of vomit.

"I see what you mean."

Stepping over the pool of dried vomit, the two detectives moved in to have a look at the body themselves.

"Good evening, Kelly."

"Good evening, Steve," replied the young pathologist.

"First thoughts, Doc?" asked Hardcastle. "Any idea of time of death, and what sort of weapon we should be looking for?"

"My initial thought is that he's been dead for between two and three hours; probably nearer three than two," replied Heywood. "I arrived at 8:05pm and the last time the victim was seen alive was around 5:15pm, so it's likely he was attacked between 5:20 and 5:30pm. Judging by his injuries, the killer only had one thing on his mind. His victim was not going to get up again.

"From the blood splatter pattern, I would say that Mr Summers was in the process of getting up from the chair when the first blow struck. The killer struck downwards with all his strength. It was like smashing a coconut with a hammer."

"So are we looking for a hammer then, Doc?" asked Davison.

"Possibly, or something very similar; I can't be exact until I've got him on the slab and examined these injuries more closely," she replied.

"The second blow was almost certainly struck when Mr Summers was on his knees, and that one would have finished him off. The third wasn't necessary, but the attacker was leaving nothing to chance. I'll give you chapter and verse after I've done the post mortem in the morning."

"Have you checked to see what's in the pockets?" Hardcastle asked Davison, nodding at the jacket hanging on the back of the door.

"They were all empty, boss," replied the sergeant.

"So we can't rule out this being a robbery that went wrong," said Hardcastle, moving to the door and glancing to his left.

"Do we know if the back door was open during the game?"

"I've been told it was open all the time," replied Davison.

"So, if this was a robbery gone wrong, the killer most likely would have sneaked in by the back door and then made a bee line to the first door he came to, the door to this room," said Hardcastle thinking aloud.

"At best he would expect to find a wallet or two, maybe get away with a bit of cash and a few credit cards. Not exactly the sort of pickings he'd need to get tooled up for. And as soon as he opened the door, he'd have seen the old boy sat in the chair. Ninety nine times out of a hundred, your run of the mill thief would have been away on their toes at that point, unless he had been recognised by the victim.

"Correct me if I'm wrong, but this has all the hallmarks of something personal between victim and killer."

"So it's possible that he took the keys and the wallet to make it look like it was a robbery that went wrong?" added Davison.

"That's my thoughts at this stage," replied Hardcastle. "We can't completely rule out robbery, but let's start on the basis that the killer and the victim knew one another, and that they weren't on the best of terms."

Hardcastle turned back to Dr Heywood. "So we're looking for a hammer, or something similar. Would the killer have been splattered with the victim's blood?"

"Blood and a lot more besides," replied Heywood, "as bits of brain tend to stick to everything."

Sunday 9pm

Hardcastle and Davison left Kelly Heywood to her own devices. They knew she would be keen to get Summers's body back to the path lab. She mentioned starting the post mortem at 11am, but asked if one of them could give her a call before 9am when she would confirm the exact time.

Hardcastle knew that Heywood, who was in her early thirties, was a rising star in her field and destined for bigger things, so it was a case of making full use of her undoubted abilities whilst they could.

By now, Billy Kiernan, the Crime Scene Manager, had arrived and was in the throes of issuing instructions to his team of CSIs. Hardcastle liked Kiernan, a confirmed bachelor in his early forties. He was a happy-go-lucky chap, with a keen and sometimes wicked sense of humour and, as a CSM, was one of the best Hardcastle had ever come across.

When Kiernan had finished briefing the CSIs, he made a beeline for Hardcastle and Davison, so they could bring him up to speed.

Whilst the three of them were chatting, Hardcastle noticed a giant of a man walking towards them, and guessed that this was Danny Willard, the Middle Ash cricketer and ex-Met Police officer turned publican.

"Danny Willard?" asked Hardcastle.

"That's me. Who's asking?"

"I'm DI Steve Hardcastle, and it seems that we owe you a big thank-you," replied Hardcastle, shaking him by the hand, and flinching slightly at the strength of the big man's grip.

"I'm always happy to help out a fellow copper, guv. I'm hoping you can repay the favour."

"Name it," replied Hardcastle.

"Can you get the Middle Ash boys processed as soon as possible? They've been waiting fairly patiently and, to be honest, there isn't much any of us can do to help you nail the bugger you're looking for.

"The whole team was on the pitch from the beginning to the end of the Flitton Green innings. A couple of the lads nipped off to the village hall to take a leak, but they were gone for less than a minute, so there was absolutely no time for either of them to have done anything you'd be interested in."

"What time did they leave the pitch?" asked Hardcastle.

"I can't give you the exact time, but both went off about half way through the Flitton innings, so I guess that would have been around 6pm."

"OK, that rules them out as it's well outside of the time frame we have for the killing," replied Hardcastle. "I will need a list of your team's names and addresses and contact phone numbers though."

"Already done," replied Willard, handing him an A4 sheet of paper.

"And the CSIs will want to make sure your clothes and equipment are all clean," added Hardcastle. "But I'll have a word with the CSM and ask him to get you and your guys processed as soon as possible."

"And the same applies to our scorer. One of the lads is giving him a lift home and both he and the Flitton scorer never left the scorebox all afternoon, apart from going to tea."

"OK, consider it done," responded Hardcastle.

"Thanks guv, I appreciate it."

"Don't thank me, it should be me thanking you," replied Hardcastle, "and the name's Steve, by the way."

"OK, thanks guv—I mean Steve," joked Willard. "Oh, and I nearly forgot. The other umpire, the guy who was on the pitch the whole time, said he needs to speak to the man in charge. He wouldn't say what it's about, but he seemed a bit agitated. Look, it might be that he just wants away a bit sharpish, but I don't think it's just that. My old copper's nose can still sniff out a timewaster, and I don't think this guy is one. His name is Tony Sullivan, by the way."

With a nod, Danny Willard turned on his heels and ambled back to the village hall. Watching him walk away, Hardcastle made a mental note to visit his pub when he next had some free time.

Turning around, Hardcastle saw that Davison and Kiernan were still deep in conversation.

Whilst he'd been talking to Willard, the pair had organised taking statements from those gathered in the village hall, as well as the search of the clothes and equipment that was strewn around the two dressing room floors. Hardcastle

31

passed on and endorsed Willard's request that the CSI team deal with the Middle Ash players and their dressing room first.

Davison also told his boss that the three lads who had left together at the end of the game had all been found in The Shire public house where they'd been watching the evening's World Cup match on the pub's large screen television. They were now back on-site, and their kit bags and clothing were in the hands of the CSIs.

However, Neil Panton, the missing fourth player, had yet to show up at his home. When he eventually surfaced, he would find a copper waiting outside for him in an unmarked police car.

Hardcastle handed Davison the list of names and addresses that Willard had given him and then headed off to the village hall to find Tony Sullivan.

When he arrived at the hall, he was pleasantly surprised to see that the ladies from the pre-school, never ones to miss an opportunity to swell their coffers, had stayed behind and were doing a decent trade in teas and coffees, although everything edible had long since disappeared.

After buying a coffee, Hardcastle sought out Sullivan and was pointed in the direction of a man in his late fifties, who was chatting to the two elderly match scorers.

After introducing himself, Hardcastle and Sullivan found themselves a quiet corner. Willard had been spot on. It soon became clear that Sullivan was no timewaster.

"So what can I do for you, Mr Sullivan?"

"I had never met Donald Summers before today, Mr Hardcastle," began Sullivan. "Umpires usually take tea together, so that they can discuss the state of the game. You must understand that I have nothing concrete to go on Inspector, but Mr Summers seemed a bit distant, as though there was something on his mind which was distracting him. His eyes were constantly on the move, looking around the room as though he was trying to spot someone."

"Do you think he found the person he was looking for?" asked Hardcastle.

"It's difficult to say for sure, but possibly. But at that time, there were forty or fifty people in the hall, and if he did spot whoever he was looking for, there was no way I could tell who it might have been."

"OK, that's interesting, Mr Sullivan," said Hardcastle. "I'll feed that back to my Sergeant and to the Crime Scene Manager. You can never have too much information."

"But that's not all," continued Sullivan.

Hardcastle could see that the umpire was struggling to decide whether or not he should tell the policeman something that had obviously been praying on his mind.

"Look, I'm sure this is nothing at all; things often get said in the heat of the moment, which are regretted afterwards," said Sullivan.

"Whatever you tell me will be in complete confidence, Mr Sullivan," said Hardcastle trying to coax out of him whatever it was he was struggling to get off his chest.

"Well, during the game, Mr Summers exchanged words with one of Flitton's players, who he'd given out leg before."

"Yes, it has been mentioned to me."

"As I said, I'm sure what was said was done in the heat of battle," replied Sullivan, "and the player in question is well known in cricketing circles for being a bit of a hot-head."

"Are you talking about Neil Panton, Mr Sullivan?" asked Hardcastle.

"Well, yes I am," he replied.

"And what did Mr Panton say?"

"I was standing at square leg, and Panton had to walk past me on his way back to the pavilion."

"And what did he say to you?" repeated Hardcastle, patiently.

Sullivan took a very deep breath.

"He said that my mate, meaning Summers, had made a big mistake, and that if he had been thirty years younger, he would have smashed his face in."

Sunday 9:30pm

"After what Tony Sullivan has just told me, we need some very detailed background on this Neil Panton as quickly as we can. And I want the watch doubled on his house. If he is our man, it's quite possible he wouldn't hesitate to kill again."

Hardcastle paused to collect his thoughts. After finishing his conversation with Sullivan, he had headed straight back to the pavilion to share this latest development with Phil Davison.

"I want a watch on Donald Summers's house put in place straight away please, Phil. If the killer has got our victim's door keys and wallet, there's nothing to stop him going round there as soon as it's dark. He'd have plenty of time to give the place a good going over and help himself to anything that takes his fancy."

"I'm on it, boss," replied DS Davison.

"And Phil, let's have a chat with Andy Hanson, the Flitton skipper. He must know Panton pretty well. There's a small manager's office off the main hall, where we can chat to him with a bit of privacy.

"Give it five minutes and I'll meet you there. And can you bring Billy Kiernan up to speed as well please?"

With a nod, Davison was off, already speaking to the Crime Scene Manager on his phone as he was walking along.

The assault on Donald Summers was possibly one of the most violent Hardcastle had ever been called to attend, and as the senior investigating officer, it was down to him and his team to bring such a violent murderer to justice as soon as possible.

The ferocity of the attack on Summers, even at this very early point in the investigation, meant that Hardcastle was already leaning towards the killer being known to his victim, particularly as in almost four of every five homicides, killer and victim are acquainted.

If that were to be the case in this particular instance, the ferocity of the attack suggested there was some seriously bad blood between the pair.

Could this be the reason why Tony Sullivan felt that Summers had been distracted during their tea-time conversation? Were his eyes 'constantly on the move' because he was looking around the room trying to spot someone?

Could the on-field disagreement between Summers and Panton be just the tip of the iceberg?

Even if Neil Panton has got a short fuse, surely it would take a hell of a lot more than a bad decision during a cricket match for him to end up committing such a violent murder?

But then again, Panton did shoot off in his car as soon as the game had ended, and he still hadn't surfaced at home. What was it Tony Sullivan had said? 'Things often get said in the heat of the moment, which are regretted afterwards.' Could it be that Panton had killed in the heat of the moment?

We really needed to find this man as soon as possible, to either charge him with murder, or to eliminate him from the enquiry, Hardcastle thought to himself.

By the time he'd finished mulling things over in his mind, he found himself walking through the front doors of the village hall towards the manager's office, where Andy Hanson, the Flitton Green captain, and Phil Davison were waiting for him.

A cup of coffee was waiting for him on the small desk. The other two had already begun to drink theirs.

After the introductions, Hardcastle explained that in the absence of Neil Panton, they urgently needed some background information on him.

"No problem, fire away," replied Hanson.

"So, Mr Hanson, how long have you known Panton?"

"I've known of him for around 11 or 12 years, and I played against him quite a bit before he came to play for us," replied Hanson. "He joined us at the beginning of last season."

"Did you approach him, or did he ask if he could join the cricket club?" enquired Davison.

"He contacted me. As club captain, my details are in the directory produced by the league every year, and he gave me a call. He certainly seemed keen."

"Did he say why he wanted to join Flitton specifically?"

At this, Andy Hanson gave a little grin. "Probably because we're the only team in the league he hasn't played for."

Noticing that Phil Davison was taking notes, Hanson felt the need to back-track a little.

"That's a bit unfair on the lad, and a bit of an exaggeration."

"In what way?" asked Hardcastle.

"Look, Neil Panton has a bit of a reputation in local cricketing circles. He's played for at least half a dozen different clubs over the last 10 years or so, but then again, so have one or two others. Neil has moved around more than most, but players move clubs for a variety of reasons, the most common reason is they want to join a club that has a better chance of winning games and winning titles. Neil Panton is very competitive, and he always wants to win no matter what. He really hates losing with a vengeance.

"I certainly don't dispute that he's well known around the clubs for having a short fuse," continued Hanson, "but he is also well known for being an exceptionally good cricketer. If he plays 20 games for a club during a summer, you can expect him to pass 50 in at least half of those games.

"Any club that has Neil playing for them knows that he will get under the skin of both the opposition players and his own teammates from time to time. When you have him in your team, you just have to take the rough with the smooth."

"What about today's game then?" asked Hardcastle. "He wasn't happy about getting out, and I'm told he let the umpire know it. Was that justified? Were you happy that one of your team openly questioned an umpire's decision?"

There was a short pause, while Hanson gave thought to constructing a diplomatic reply.

"Look, I was at the non-striker's end as I always open the batting alongside Neil. The ball hit his pad, no doubt about that. But the umpire made a bad decision. The ball hit Neil's front leg way outside the line of the off stump and the laws of the game say that when that happens the player is not out. It was a shocker of a decision, no way was it out."

"You say that you have to take the rough with the smooth where Panton is concerned," said Davison. "I don't know much about cricket, can't stand the game myself," he said with a grin. "But as a player in any sport, surely you have to accept that sometimes an umpire or a referee will make a mistake. Isn't that just human nature, no one is infallible."

"I know, you're quite right," replied Hanson. "But next week he'll probably go out and hit a century. We played absolute garbage today. Middle Ash is our bogey team, so in a way we were half expecting to lose. But we're still top of the table and we will win the title, I'm certain of that, and one of the main reasons we will be champions at the end of the season is that we have Neil Panton in the side.

"At the end of the day, I know I can handle Neil," continued Hanson, "and I know I can get the best out of him. But, hypothetically, if the rest of the team were to come to me and tell me that they couldn't play with him, I would have to let him go, for the good of the team and for the good of the club."

"OK, point taken," responded Hardcastle. "What about his life away from cricket? What does he do for a living?"

"He's a self-employed car mechanic and works from home. He's pretty good at it, as well. I speak from experience."

"What make of car does he drive?"

"Some sort of Subaru. I can't tell you more than that, other that it's red and a bit on the flash side," replied Hanson.

"Does he have a wife or girlfriend?" asked Davison.

There was a pause.

"As I understand it, he and his wife are in the throes of getting a divorce," replied Hanson cagily.

"Do you know why?" asked Hardcastle.

"I'd rather not say. What I have heard is hearsay, and I think it would be wrong of me to repeat dressing room gossip. It's something you need to talk to Neil about.

"What I do know is that he has a new lady friend, but that's as far as it goes."

Before Hardcastle could reply, Davison's mobile phone rang, and he excused himself, shutting the door behind him.

"Look, between you and me Inspector, surely you haven't got Neil in the frame for killing Donald Summers? Neil might be a lot of things, but I just can't see him doing something that extreme because of a bad umpiring decision. Christ, we'd have run out of umpires years ago if that was the case," reflected Hanson.

At that point, Phil Davison opened the door.

"A word please, boss."

As Hardcastle was about to get up, Hanson asked if he could go.

"I've just got one more question to ask you, Mr Hanson, please bear with me sir, I'll only be a tick," replied Hardcastle.

"Have we found Panton?" he asked, shutting the office door behind him.

"Nothing yet, but we may well have a better idea about the murder weapon. That was Billy Kiernan on the phone. He was with Dr Heywood. It seems that the weapon used may have been made of some type of hard wood, perhaps ash, but she won't be able to confirm that until she's done the post mortem in the morning. But she told Billy that from the circular shape of one of the wounds, something like a large auctioneer's gavel could have been used.

"Now that meant absolutely nothing to me, but Billy's into cricket and he told me that he got out his mobile and googled something which he then showed the good doctor. She looked at a couple of pics and told Billy that it was quite possible that something similar could have been used to kill Summers."

"I think I know what you're going to say, Phil," said Hardcastle. "Billy showed Kelly Heywood pictures of a bat mallet."

"Correct boss. Go to the top of the class."

Smiling, Hardcastle reopened the door to the office and sat back down behind the manager's desk. The Flitton Green captain looked at him expectantly.

"Tell me, Mr Hanson, do you happen to know if Neil Panton carries a bat mallet around in his cricket bag?"

"I don't know about Neil, but it's strange you should ask, Inspector. As you may know, bat mallets are used to knock in a new bat. And it just so happens that our opening bowler, Colin Sharpe, has just bought himself a new bat, and he was using a mallet on it in the dressing room during the tea interval whilst three of us were getting padded up."

"Besides you, who were the others?"

"Young Danny Chamberlain, who bats first wicket down, and Neil Panton. In fact, Neil was a bit uptight about going into bat and told Sharpe to pack it in as it was getting on his nerves."

"What did Sharpe say?"

"Colin is an 'anything for a quiet life' man, and he put the mallet back in his bag and went outside to sit with the rest of the lads. Within 30 seconds or so, Colin would have forgotten all about it."

Hardcastle turned to his sergeant.

"Phil, can you call Billy and ask him if one of his CSIs can look through Colin Sharpe's bag for a bat mallet please?"

"I don't think you'll find it, Inspector," interrupted Hanson. "After Sharpey left the dressing room, Neil grabbed the mallet out of his bag, said something like 'I'll shove this somewhere where he won't find it in a hurry' and went out of the dressing room.

"He was back within a minute or so. I asked him what he had done with the mallet but all he did was to tap the side of his nose. I thought it was a pretty childish thing to do, but young Danny thought it was funny, so I let it go."

There was silence in the room. After 10 seconds or so, Hardcastle made to get up again.

"Was that the question you said you needed to ask me?" enquired Hanson.

"No, I was just going to ask you what team Panton was playing for before he joined Flitton."

"Until he joined us, he had been playing for today's opposition—he used to open the batting for Middle Ash," replied Hanson.

Monday 6:30am

At the time of the 2011 census, Flitton Green had a population of 3,467, of which 93.7% were white, 80.2% were Christians and 1.9% were unemployed. 247 of the 3,467 were aged between 4 and 11 and the vast majority of these children attended the Flitton Green Primary School.

Those numbers had almost certainly increased since the census, as in the last three years or so a number of two, three and four bedroom houses had been built and sold on two fairly large plots at either end of the village.

As well as the two public houses, The Cricketers and The Shire, the little high street was home to a small supermarket, a newsagent with a post office attached, a chemist, an estate agent, two takeaways, a hair dresser, a butcher, a baker (but no candlestick maker), and a fish and chip shop called 'The House of Cod' which, rather aptly, visitors would find situated directly opposite the local parish church.

There was a fairly decent bus service to Dorminster (population 21,892 in 2011), which was just over 5 miles away by road, and at either end of the village were two very tired looking signs informing residents and anyone just passing through that Flitton Green was twinned with some rather obscure village in Belgium.

Steve and Jenny Hardcastle had moved to Flitton Green three years earlier after Steve's promotion to Detective Inspector. Their youngest son, Thomas, now 9 years old, attended the primary school, whilst their eldest, 14-year-old Ethan, travelled to his Grammar school in Dorminster by bus.

Whenever she could, Jenny would pick up Ethan after collecting Thomas.

Being a copper's wife had made Jenny far more protective of her sons than she might otherwise have been.

The house they had bought, thanks to a fairly large helping hand from the County and Country Building Society, was a much extended four bed semi, with a decent sized garden—absolutely essential with two very energetic and sport mad boys in the family. Already though, they were seriously considering extending the house further.

As Hardcastle considered he was fairly handy where DIY was concerned, he had told Jenny that he would do a lot of the work himself.

But from past experience, Jenny had learnt that it would often take her husband two days to do something a local builder could do in two hours, and her concern was that the project could take far longer than necessary, particularly given the long and unsociable hours his job required him to work from time to time.

The murder of Donald Summers was just one such example. By the time he had got home, it was in the small hours of Monday morning.

As he always did when he was late home, he looked in on the two sleeping boys before quietly climbing into bed, doing his best not to disturb his wife. With a team briefing set for 8am prompt, he would be lucky to get more than just a couple hours sleep. As it turned out, he didn't even manage that.

As tired as he was, there was so much going on in his mind that he knew sleep was not going to come easy.

However, it wasn't just the murder of Donald Summers that was preoccupying him. As often happened at that time of the morning, it was his very first case as a detective inspector, some three years earlier, which had returned to haunt him once more.

This was a case that had probably been long forgotten by those that had worked alongside him, but it was a case that at the time he had been desperate to solve to show any doubters, and there had been one or two, that his promotion to detective inspector had been both earned and deserved.

The case was an unsolved arson attack on the cricket pavilion at Flitton Green. Being at the ground just a few hours earlier had stirred up some unwanted memories.

They had never come even remotely close to discovering the culprit, and after three years he knew he really should accept that this was one cold case that should be consigned to history.

Yet, there was something gnawing away in the back of his mind. Something that might just connect the arson with yesterday's murder—but perhaps that was just wishful thinking on his part.

However, he decided that if he had any spare time later on in the day, and he knew that that was highly unlikely, he would try to go through the file one last time.

He looked at his watch. It was a minute past five o'clock and the dawn chorus was in full swing outside the bedroom window. It looked like another hot day in the making.

He decided to get up and have his shower and shave. After that, with a briefing to prepare, he would grab a couple of pieces of toast, and set off for the police station in Dorminster.

Today, like many days, was going to be a busy one.

Try as he might, as he gently rolled off the bed, he couldn't prevent Jenny from waking up.

"Hi," she said, with her eyes half shut.

"Hi," he replied. "Sorry, I tried not to wake you up."

"What time did you get in?" she asked.

"About 1:30am," he replied.

"Fibber! It was nearer three," she said, grinning.

They had an agreement. She would never ask him directly about his work; however, he knew that she was a good and willing listener should he ever want to unburden himself, even though that was something he rarely did.

"Do you have to go yet?"

"Yeah, sorry, but I've got lots to do today. I'll try and get home at a reasonable time this afternoon," he said. "I promise."

"Don't you mean a reasonable time this evening?" she countered.

"You know me too well."

"Don't I just," she replied.

He got out of bed. As he reached the bedroom door, he turned. "Look, it's the school holidays soon. Why don't you book a week away in August for the four of us?"

"Do you really mean that?" she asked, now fully awake.

"Of course I do," he replied with his fingers crossed behind his back. He blew her a kiss, before shutting the bedroom door quietly behind him.

There was very little traffic on the roads when he set off for the police station, and he found himself walking up the stairs to his second floor office just a couple of minutes after 6am.

Yet, even at that time in the morning, someone had already beaten him to it. Sat at his desk, in the open plan part of the CID offices, was Phil Davison.

"Didn't you go home last night?" Hardcastle asked his sergeant.

"You've seen my wife," Davison replied with a grin.

"On many occasions, and as I've said to you before, she's far too good for you," responded Hardcastle, also with a grin on his face.

It was well known in the office that Phil Davison and his wife Sarah were devoted to one another. The fact that she had also been a copper helped.

"What's the latest then, Phil? Any sign of Panton?"

"Nothing yet, boss, he didn't go home last night. Do you think he's scarpered?"

"No, that would be an admission of guilt, and from what we learnt last night, he doesn't strike me as that sort of person," replied Hardcastle.

"I've got the registration number of his Subaru, and I've told uniform, and I'll put it on the board for the briefing," added Davison.

"And our Mr Panton has form. Nothing too serious, but he's been arrested twice for punch ups in pubs. Both of those were over 10 years ago. Five years ago he was arrested for driving without insurance and tax, and more recently cops were called to his home address after neighbours reported shouting and a woman screaming. Things had quietened down by the time our guys arrived, and it was logged as a domestic."

"No surprises there then based on our conversation with Andy Hanson. We may need to speak to his wife, so see if you can get an address for her when you have a minute," replied Hardcastle.

Over the next half an hour or so, other members of the Dorminster CID team arrived, including Detective Sergeant Kath Pearson, who occupied the desk directly opposite Phil Davison.

DS Pearson, who some likened in appearance to singer-songwriter Kate Bush in her prime, was known within the department as the 'inside' sergeant, with Phil Davison the 'outside' one, since she was more desk-bound and admin orientated than Davison, who was some 15 years older than her.

After putting her jacket on the back of her chair, Pearson poked her head round the door of Hardcastle's office.

"Morning sir."

"Good morning, Kath," replied Hardcastle. "Have you heard about the goings on at the cricket club?"

"Yes sir, Phil rang me a couple of times last night and I think I have a fairly good handle on things."

Hardcastle smiled at Pearson. He knew that Phil Davison would have been keeping in touch with her on the phone. Their rapport made his life as their boss that much easier.

He was not looking forward to the day when she moved on, as inevitably she would at some stage in the not too distant future. She was an extremely able and ambitious lady, and very keen to move on up the ladder.

Some sergeants would have been uncomfortable working with a colleague on the same rank, who was as keen as mustard to progress their career.

But it didn't bother Phil Davison a single jot.

Davison no longer harboured such aspirations; in fact he actively encouraged her as much as he could. He was one of those lucky people who thought they had one of the best jobs in the world, and his enthusiasm invariably rubbed off on those that worked alongside him. Some of the team jokingly referred to Davison and Pearson as Cagney and Lacey and, in their different ways, they were the perfect foils to Hardcastle.

"You'll know then that there's a briefing at 8am?" asked Hardcastle.

"Yes sir," she replied, ambling back to her desk.

By this time, there was a steaming cup of coffee waiting for her.

"What, no biscuits, Phil?" she asked in mock horror.

As she spoke, a packet of chocolate hob-nobs appeared in Davison's hand, as if by magic.

"Pinched 'em from home," he replied. "Don't tell the wife, she'll want me nicked."

Hardcastle smiled at the exchange. Sometimes they sounded like an old married couple.

However, the smile vanished from his face as he returned to the open file on his desk and looked at the newspaper report he had read countless times over the last three years. He hadn't been able to resist the temptation to look once again at the file on the Flitton pavilion fire.

It was the last paragraph that really stuck in his throat.

It is five weeks since the Flitton Green Cricket Club pavilion was completely destroyed by an arson attack. Yet the local police, under the control of newly promoted Detective Inspector Steven Hardcastle, are no further forward in their efforts to discover the identity of the culprit.

There are concerns within other local cricket clubs that this may encourage the arsonist to strike again.'

As it turned out, there hadn't been any further attacks, but this had been of little consolation to Hardcastle. His failure to solve the case, his first as a DI, was something that had continued to rankle, even though his boss, Detective Chief Inspector Mark Cryer, had told him a few weeks after the fire that he should try and forget it. That it was just one of those things that happened from time to time. That it was part and parcel of being a senior police officer. That it went with the territory.

While he appreciated those words, they did little to console him.

But now there had been a second, far more serious crime at the same location, and Hardcastle couldn't help thinking of the consequences to his career if this investigation should also end in failure.

And he knew that the press would have a field day the longer it went without them making an arrest.

He could imagine the headlines: *Police Stumped by Umpire Killing* or *Killer Bowls Police a Googly*.

It would be a sub-editor's dream.

His phone rang and pulled him back to the here and now. It was Kelly Heywood.

"I've just got a couple of things, Steve. The post mortem will definitely be at 11am and, secondly, I've sent you an email with some photos for your briefing. You've got three of the back of the head and a couple of the face front on. I hope they're OK and not too gruesome for some of your younger detectives."

"Thanks Kelly, I'm sure they'll be fine. I'll see you later."

With that, Hardcastle put the phone down and pulled up his email on his desktop PC.

Top of the unopened messages was the one from the pathologist, and Hardcastle opened each of the attachments.

He selected two of the five photos and saved and pasted them onto a new email which he would send to Paul Taylor, one of those younger DCs the pathologist had referred to.

"Paul," he shouted.

"Yes sir?"

"I'm just sending you an email with two photos attached. Can you print them out and let me have them before the briefing please?"

"I'm on it, sir."

Hardcastle looked at his watch. It was 7:40am. Already, over 12 hours had passed since the body of Donald Summers had been discovered. He knew that the next 12 hours would be absolutely crucial—crucial for the case, and crucial for him.

Monday 8am

At precisely 8am Steve Hardcastle strolled into the middle of the room and began pinning various items on a large board.

Around him were a dozen or so desks, which were all occupied. A three-line whip issued by Phil Davison ten hours earlier had made sure that every member of the team was there.

Amongst those waiting for the briefing to start were Billy Kiernan, the Crime Scene Manager and two of his more senior Crime Scene Investigators.

No introductions were necessary as everyone had worked together before, including DC Paul Taylor, the youngest and most recent recruit to the CID team.

"Good morning everybody," began Hardcastle. "I hope you all had a good weekend, because we all need to be on top of our game today. I use the word 'game' advisedly, because, as you all know, what happened yesterday at Flitton Green was most definitely not cricket.

"Not for this man, it wasn't," he continued, pointing at the first two photographs on the board.

"His name was Donald Summers and he was the victim of a savage attack during a cricket match between Flitton Green and Middle Ash cricket clubs.

"At the time of the assault, which we believe took place around 5:30pm, Mr Summers, a 66-year-old man, was alone in the umpire's room in the cricket pavilion having left the field of play fifteen minutes earlier with an ankle injury he had sustained whilst umpiring.

"Mr Kiernan and his team have confirmed that the assailant entered and left the pavilion via the back door which traditionally is kept unlocked on match days," continued Hardcastle pointing at a plan of the pavilion that had been pinned on the board.

"It is just three paces from that back door to the door of the umpire's room.

"According to the pathologist, Dr Heywood, Mr Summers was in the throes of getting out of an armchair when he was struck three times on the back of the head.

"Death was virtually instantaneous." Hardcastle paused for effect and to look around at his audience. Not a sound could be heard apart from a telephone ringing somewhere in the distance.

"There were no defence wounds on the body."

He paused again, this time to take a sip of water.

"It appears that the assailant went through the pockets of the victim's jacket which was hanging from the back of the door, as no keys, no wallet or mobile phone were found either in his jacket or on Mr Summers himself.

"As the assailant left the umpire's room, he locked the door behind him and also took the key with him, no doubt to delay discovery of the body.

"The match ended at 7pm. When Tony Sullivan, the second umpire, and Richard Askell, who had replaced Mr Summers, tried the door to the umpire's room, they found it was locked. Initially, they assumed that Summers had locked it himself, so he wouldn't be disturbed whilst he was having a nap. When he didn't reply when they knocked on the door and shouted out to him, they became concerned, fearing he might have had a stroke or a heart attack.

"A second key to the room was fetched from the village hall. Once they had opened the door, they unfortunately found Mr Summers on the floor, face down. It was now 7:09pm and a triple nine call was logged at 7:11pm. I'll now hand over to DS Davison."

As Davison got up from his chair and made his way to the board, Hardcastle perched himself on the edge of the nearest desk.

"The call from the cricket ground was passed through to me, and I was on the scene just before 7:30pm. Uniform were already there.

"We had a stroke of good fortune as one of the Middle Ash players, a Mr Danny Willard, who used to serve in the Metropolitan Police, had ushered everyone still in the pavilion into the village hall, making sure they left all their kit and clothes in the dressing rooms.

"I did a quick head count when I got to the hall and this came to 39, made up of 18 players, two scorers and two umpires, included the guy who had replaced Mr Summers, three ladies who did the player's teas and sold refreshments, seven player's relatives and seven members of the public.

"With only 18 players in the hall, even I, a cricketing Philistine, managed to work out that we were missing four, all from the Flitton Green team. Three of these we found fairly easily as they had got changed quickly so they could go and watch the evening's World Cup football match on the big screen in The Shire—the pub that is, not the place where Bilbo Baggins lives."

There was a smattering of laughter.

"They were immediately brought back to the hall in a squad car while two of Mr Kiernan's CSIs searched their car and their kit which was stuffed in the boot. Do you want to take it up from here, Billy?" asked Davison, turning towards the CSM.

Kiernan nodded and stood up.

"The search of the car and its contents drew a blank as expected. Back at the cricket ground, thanks to the prompt action of Mr Willard, we were able to preserve the crime scene with minimal contamination and also cordon off the immediate area around the pavilion. We were able to confirm that the killer had left the scene by the back door."

"What about the missing player?" asked Alan Rutherford, another of Hardcastle's young detective constables.

"We'll come to that shortly, Alan," answered Hardcastle, who nodded to Kiernan to continue.

"At the same time, pathologist Dr Heywood was completing her initial inspection of the body. Her first thought was that the weapon used to kill Mr Summers was some type of hammer," continued Kiernan.

"However, on closer examination, Dr Heywood was able to be a little bit more specific and told us that the weapon was made of a hard wood, possibly ash, and that it resembled an auctioneer's gavel."

"Could it have been a bat mallet?"

"Go to the top of the class, DC Taylor," replied Kiernan. "Dr Heywood will hopefully confirm it after she's finished the post mortem later this morning, but everything now points to the murder weapon being a bat mallet."

At this point, Kiernan noticed a few blank looks amongst his audience.

"For those of you who don't know what a bat mallet is, or what it looks like, this is a photograph I downloaded from the Internet," continued Kiernan, pointing to the third picture on the board. "For the uninitiated, you use a bat mallet when you've just bought a new cricket bat. If you strike the face of the bat for a couple of hours with a mallet, it strengthens and compresses the face and the edges of the bat, hopefully making it last longer. This process is called 'knocking in' and at £250 quid a time for a decent bat, you'd be a bit daft not to do it.

"Now, since first light, members of my team have been searching the footpaths and woods behind the pavilion, working their way outwards. We are particularly looking for the bat mallet, the key to the umpire's room, and anything belonging to Mr Summers, particularly his wallet and his house keys.

"There's always the chance that the killer might have panicked and tossed these into the woods as he made his getaway."

"Thanks for that, Billy," said Hardcastle. "Phil, perhaps you can update us with regard to the people who were waiting in the village hall while all this was going on?"

"We were able to process the Middle Ash chaps fairly quickly," began Davison, "as they were fielding from 4:30pm to 7pm, and the only players who left the field during that time were a couple of lads who had nipped in to use the toilets in the village hall. We took statements from all eleven Middle Ash players, but to be honest, as you'd expect, they all said virtually the same, that they were concentrating on the game, and not what might have been happening off the pitch.

"We were also able to process the two umpires, including Mr Summers's replacement, and the two scorers who didn't budge from the scorebox during the second innings.

"The ladies who were doing the refreshments in the village hall were also very helpful. They gave us the names of those people they knew who had bought food and drink from them during the afternoon, and in a couple of instances were also able to give us addresses.

"However, between them, they reckon that there were at least another dozen or so people who they know only by sight, but don't know their names or addresses, and at least half a dozen people they had never seen before.

"For those of you who have never been down to watch the cricket, if the weather is good you always get a fair number of people turning up during the course of the afternoon. Apart from the game, there is also the added attraction of a large children's play area behind the village hall.

"So, a priority today will be to fill in the gaps and complete the missing information on everyone who popped into the village hall, as well as those that just came along to watch the cricket or those that came down so their kids could use the play equipment. We will need statements from all of them.

"Now, as for the Flitton Green players, processing them took a lot longer due to the examination of their kit and clothing. We have statements from each of them but we will be going through these again this morning and cross-referencing everything, particularly the statement made by Colin Sharpe.

"It is quite likely that the bat mallet used to murder Mr Summers belonged to Mr Sharpe, who had recently bought both a new cricket bat and a new mallet from Nicholson's, the sports shop in the High Street. When the CSIs went through Sharpe's equipment and clothing, the bat was there, but there was no sign of the mallet.

"I think you might want to take over from this point, boss," said Davison, knowing that Hardcastle would want to be the one to wind things up.

"Thank you, Phil. At this stage, we do not regard Mr Sharpe as a suspect, but we do have two witnesses who saw a bat mallet being taken from his equipment bag by another Flitton Green player.

"That player was Neil Panton. Mr Panton also happens to be the one Flitton Green player who we've been unable to locate. We have had a car waiting outside his house all night, but there has been no sign of him so far.

"I stress at this point, that we are not suggesting Mr Panton is the killer. But until we have had a chance to interview him, locating him has to be our priority. We need to eliminate him as a suspect.

"What we do know of Panton is that he is 32 years old, and has a police record, all for minor offences, although on two occasions minor violence was involved, but mainly handbag stuff so I'm told. We also know that he has a fairly short fuse, is not the most popular player within the dressing room, and that he has moved around most of the local cricket clubs over the last ten years.

"He has been playing for Flitton since the beginning of last season. Before that, he played for Middle Ash, Flitton's opponents yesterday. Panton is a self-employed car mechanic who works from home, and according to his captain, he is good at what he does. He is married, but is apparently in the process of getting a divorce. Uniform were called out to attend a domestic at his house earlier this year.

"He may also have started a new relationship recently, but he has kept this fairly quiet. None of the Flitton players know who the lady is. There is always the possibility that he spent last night with her, which could explain his no-show at his house.

"However, there is one particular reason why we are keen to interview Mr Panton. Having been given out by Mr Summers at the beginning of the Flitton innings, Panton questioned the decision and exchanged words him. And then, on his way back to the pavilion, Panton apparently told the second umpire that 'had Mr Summers been 30 years younger, he would have smashed his face in'."

There was a general murmur and Hardcastle paused until the room was quiet again.

"So, are there any questions so far?"

"Are there any thoughts on a possible motive, sir?" enquired DC Rutherford.

"Personally, I don't see this as an opportunistic robbery gone wrong. It is possible, of course, that our killer just happened to be walking along the public footpath, saw the back door was open and decided to chance his luck," replied Hardcastle.

"But even if Summers had recognised him when he opened the door to the umpire's room, the killer would have to have been really desperate to do what he did, for just a few quid. I think we could be looking at something that goes deeper, but don't ask me what at this stage. In the meantime, all possibilities remain in play.

"So, one of our main priorities this morning is to build up a picture of the victim. If his door keys don't come to light, we'll need to force entry to his house. Paul," said Hardcastle, looking at DC Taylor, "when we are finished here, could you ask the guys waiting outside Mr Summers's house, if they could speak to his neighbours to see if any of them hold a spare front door key to his house.

"We also need to find Neil Panton as soon as possible. When we do, Mr Kiernan's team will need to be let loose on his house, his car and wherever he spent last night. We will also need to interview anyone he stayed the night with and that might include his estranged wife. We will need to speak to her anyway.

"And, as well as those actually involved in the match itself, we will need statements from absolutely everyone who popped in at any time yesterday, not just around the time when the murder was carried out. Anyone who was there at any time is a potential witness, and a potential suspect.

"It might be necessary to make an appeal on television and radio later today, but I'll see what progress we make over the next few hours before I take a decision on that. As usual, DS Pearson will be allocating who does what, where and when. Any questions?"

There were none.

"OK, let's get going, people, and good luck."

Monday 9am

Hardcastle hung up his suit jacket on the hook behind the door and was just about to sit down at his desk when DC Taylor appeared in the doorway to tell him that the lady in the bungalow next door to Mr Summers had a key to his front door.

"She had a similar arrangement with the previous owner who also had a key to her place. Apparently, she's a bit forgetful and a little bit hard of hearing. PC Moffatt particularly wanted you to be aware of this, should you decide to go and have a word with her," explained Taylor.

Hardcastle immediately put on his jacket, patted the right-hand pocket to make sure his car keys were there and walked briskly to the desks occupied by Phil Davison and Kath Pearson.

"It seems we have a key to Summers's place. Fancy having a look inside?" he asked Davison.

"You bet, boss," came the reply.

Hardcastle turned to DS Pearson.

"I'll be at 18 Wildwood Drive, Kath. After that, you'll find me with Dr Heywood. She's doing the post mortem at 11am."

The journey to Wildwood Drive took just over a quarter of an hour, and as they got out of Hardcastle's Range Rover they stopped to give the outside of the property a quick once-over.

Their first impression was that the bungalow appeared to be a bit run down, and that the windows in particular needed a lick of paint fairly urgently.

Calling on his knowledge of similar properties in and around Dorminster, Hardcastle guessed that it had probably been built post war, either in the late 1940s or very early 50s.

After collecting the key from PC Moffatt, Davison and Hardcastle walked up the short path to the front door. The small rectangles of grass either side of the path were overgrown and fairly parched, due to the lack of rain. So far it had been a very warm and dry start to summer with the forecasters unable to foresee any significant rainfall for the area for at least the next seven to ten days.

The newspapers were even suggesting a hosepipe ban later on in the summer if the drought were to continue, despite the winter having been one of the wettest since records began.

To the right of the front door was a well-worn grab handle suggesting that the previous occupants of the bungalow had been fairly elderly.

There were three keys on the key fob in Davison's right hand—a Yale for the front door, a Mortice for the back door and a smaller key that was probably for the garage.

As Davison put the key in the lock, Hardcastle noticed the curtains move in the bungalow to his left, and he caught a glimpse of someone peeking through them.

Once inside, they found the bungalow was a decent size, with two bedrooms, a double and a single, a good sized lounge, a kitchen, a separate dining room and a bathroom with a walk in bath. Placed strategically around the walls, and by the various doors, were several more grab handles, another indication of the likely age of the previous owners.

Hardcastle couldn't help feeling a sense of irony, in that Summers had been living in a bungalow with numerous aids to help prevent him from having a fall, when it had been a fall during a cricket match that had started the chain of events that had led to his death.

Looking through the dining room windows, they could see an average sized square back garden, which was mainly laid to lawn. Peppered with daisies and dandelions, the lawn was in desperate need of a cut. Quite possibly, it hadn't seen a mower since the previous autumn.

In the middle of the lawn was a rotary clothes line with a couple of shirts and some underwear hanging on it. There was also a peg bag hooked over one of the lines. There was no shed.

Amongst the furniture in the dining room were a mahogany bureau and a matching Regency style table and six chairs, making the room seem quite dark despite the full length window. The dark red wallpaper didn't help the overall ambience and Hardcastle's first impression of the interior was it was rather depressing.

On the top of the bureau was a solitary framed photograph of a very young child sitting in a push chair. Having children himself, Hardcastle guessed that the child had been no more than six months old when the photo had been taken.

"I'll go through the bureau, you have a poke around the bedrooms," said Hardcastle to Davison as he picked up the photograph.

There was nothing to indicate who the child in the picture was—it could easily have been a boy or a girl—and as the background was just a wooden fence, there were no clues to suggest when and where the photograph had been taken.

Remembering that his wife Jenny religiously put the date on the back of all the photographs they took of their own children, he removed the back of the picture frame hoping to find something written on the reverse of the photo, but there was nothing there. He put the photo back where he had found it.

In the top drawer of the bureau Hardcastle found a new address book which still had a price tag on the back. There was nothing written inside apart from a single entry under the letter A, where the name of cricket league secretary Richard Askell appeared alongside a local telephone number.

There was also six months' worth of bank statements on a small bulldog clip, the most recent one showing a healthy balance of £24,017.16.

In the debit column were a few monthly direct debits, mainly to utility companies, and two items in the credit column showing incoming payments, one for his state pension, and a more substantial receipt which he guessed could be a pension payment from the County and Country Building Society.

Attached to a larger clip were around 50 or so general receipts, mainly from the local Tesco supermarket.

He would give these to Kath Pearson to analyse.

In the middle drawer, Hardcastle found the deeds to 18 Wildwood Drive which gave the name of the previous owner as Amelia Jane Hilton, as well as Donald James Summers as the new occupant.

There were no charges registered against the property, so Summers must have bought the bungalow outright, without the help of a mortgage. Hardcastle guessed that it was probably bought using the proceeds from the sale of his previous house. Hopefully, Kath would be able to confirm this later.

In the bottom drawer were a couple of tablecloths and a set of plain table mats and coasters which looked like they had never been used.

Moving from the dining room to the kitchen, Hardcastle passed a telephone on a small telephone table. The only thing in the drawer was an out of date local telephone directory.

He picked up the phone and dialled 1471 to see who the last caller had been. The number given was Richard Askell's.

As he put the phone down, Phil Davison came out of the smaller of the two bedrooms.

"Any luck, boss?" he asked Hardcastle.

"Nothing," he replied. "How about you?"

"The single bedroom hasn't got a bed in it, there's just an ironing board and a laundry basket. They both look new," said Davison. There's a double bed in the other room, a couple of bedside tables, a chest of drawers and a single wardrobe. There aren't that many clothes in the wardrobes, less than you'd expect, even for a guy living on his own.

"There were a couple of cricket biographies on one of the bedside tables, and that's about it, apart from this," continued Davison showing his boss a 10" x 8" head and shoulders photograph of a slightly younger Summers with his arm around a vivacious woman about the same age as him.

"I'd guess that was taken about 10 years ago," said Hardcastle. "I wonder who she is?"

"She must have been someone pretty special for him to have it by his bed," replied Davison.

"Possibly," said Hardcastle. "Keep hold of it for now, Phil. See what's in the bathroom and I'll have a quick look in the kitchen. We can finish off in the lounge."

When he opened the door to the kitchen, Hardcastle's first thought was that an estate agent would probably have described it as being 'in need of modernisation'.

The cooker was made by a company called Parkinson Cowan and must have been at least 30 years old, whilst the washing machine looked even older.

At least the fridge freezer was a little more up to date. There wasn't much in it apart from an unopened 2-litre carton of milk, three eggs and half a dozen ready meals. Summers would probably have cooked these in the nearly new microwave oven that was sat on the worktop next to the back door.

In a tall freestanding cupboard next to the fridge freezer were a variety of tins, mainly soups, baked beans and canned fruit, whilst on another work top was an open loaf of white bread, a kettle, a box of tea bags and a half full large jar of mild blend Maxwell House coffee.

Shutting the kitchen door quietly behind him, he walked a couple of paces across the hall and into the lounge where he found Phil Davison already having a rummage through the drawers of a sideboard.

"I've found his birth certificate, boss. It turns out that Summers was born in Woolwich, South East London on 7 October 1951 to an Ernest Summers, described as a painter and decorator, and an Eileen Winifred Summers, described as a comptometer operator, whatever that might be."

Hardcastle took out his phone and out of curiosity, googled the word 'comptometer'.

"Apparently, it was an early type of adding machine," Hardcastle informed his colleague.

"Learn something new every day," replied Davison.

"Find anything interesting in the bathroom?" asked Hardcastle.

"Nothing out of the ordinary, boss; no pills or prescription medication apart from an unopened packet of paracetamol, an open packet of Rennies and an over the counter nasal spray for hay fever sufferers."

Hardcastle looked around the lounge.

In one corner was a small television, probably four or five years old and an old video recorder—but no DVD player, nor any sign of DVDs or video cassettes.

There was a brown leather two-seater settee and two non-matching armchairs. Next to one of these, on a small occasional table, was a hardback book lying face down.

Hardcastle picked it up. According to the text on the back of the dust jacket, it was a biography about Sir Alec Jeffreys, described as;

a British geneticist who in 1984 developed techniques for genetic fingerprinting and DNA profiling, techniques which would be used by forensic science to assist police detective work worldwide and enable them to bring untold thousands of criminals to justice, as well as solving countless immigration and paternity issues.

The name vaguely rang a bell with the DI and he made a mental note of the title and the author. It was the sort of book he would enjoy reading and with his birthday coming up, he would mention it to Jenny in the hope she would take the hint and buy it for him.

Summers was evidently a keen reader and in a fairly large alcove were four shelves full of books, many of these sport-related, predominantly cricket and rugby, but also a smattering of biographies, true crime and murder/mysteries, including a dozen or so Agatha Christie's.

"Anything else of use?" asked Hardcastle. "Have you come across a passport or a will?"

"No, but it looks like he has a car," said Davison, holding up a set of keys attached to a Jaguar-branded key fob.

"Let's have a look in the garage in a tick," replied Hardcastle. "What do you think of this place generally?"

"A bit depressing, if I'm honest, boss. It seems so impersonal," answered the sergeant. "It feels like a house rather than a home, desperately in need of a woman's touch."

"Likewise," replied Hardcastle. "According to the deeds, Summers completed the purchase in January. Having lived here for six months or so, you'd expect to see more personal bits and pieces around the place by now. It feels more like a place he was renting than one he owned outright. The only personal things are the books and the photo of the woman in his bedroom, and the one of the baby in the dining room.

"Maybe he didn't sell his old place and has been renting it out fully or part furnished, so he could always go back to it if he didn't settle down here. That would account for this place being so sparse.

"Or perhaps he did sell it and decided to have a completely fresh start, and only brought the basics with him and sold off the rest of his stuff. Or maybe he'd left most of his stuff is in storage until he'd made up his mind whether or not he was definitely going to settle here. We'll probably never know what his intentions were, now that he's dead.

"I feel we're missing something here, Phil. Let's get Kath on it. We can give her have the picture of him and the woman, the bank statements, the birth certificate and the deeds to this place, and see what she can come up with."

"What about the picture of the baby?" asked Davison.

"That's a fairly old picture," replied Hardcastle, "and I think what we need to look for is something that happened in his life far more recently. We know where it is; we can always come back and get it if we need it. Let's go and have a quick look in the garage. Once we've done that, tell the uniform boys outside that they can stand down, and get them to give you a lift back to the station.

"I'll have a quick chat with the old lady next door and then I'll go on to see Kelly Heywood. She should be starting the post mortem in around 20 minutes," said Hardcastle looking at his watch.

After shutting the front door with a slam, Hardcastle took the key fob from Davison and inserted the smallest key into the lock on the garage door. He turned the key, then the handle and pulled the door upwards.

"Wow," said Davison clearly impressed. "It's a Jag Mk2, an old E reg. plate, made in 1967. Isn't she a beauty? I wonder how long he'd had it for."

Hardcastle couldn't help admiring it even though he wasn't particularly interested in cars.

"This is the car favoured by the villains of the 60s. They used Jags when they needed a fast getaway," Hardcastle reminded Davison. "I have to say though that it's the last car I expected our man to have in his garage. I was thinking more on the lines of a Citroen CV6, a Volvo or a Skoda. It seems so at odds with what we know about him so far. Perhaps there was more to this man than meets the eye."

"Perhaps he was one of the Great Train Robbers who never got caught," joked Davison.

"Unlikely. He would have been twelve years old at the time," replied Hardcastle with a smile.

"It's in brilliant condition though, boss. He's certainly gone up in my estimation. I'd love to have this in my garage," replied Davison.

Having been informed by PC Moffatt that the next door neighbour's name was Mrs Joy Lee, Hardcastle walked up the short driveway as the squad car pulled away with Phil Davison in one of the back seats.

Mrs Lee had obviously been watching through her net curtains as the door opened before Hardcastle had had a chance to ring the front doorbell.

"Are you Mr Harriman, the man in charge?" she asked.

"It's Hardcastle, Mrs Lee, and yes, I am in the man in charge," he replied.

"I'm so upset to hear about poor Mr Summers, he was such a nice man, Mr Hardiman."

Realising she was a little deaf, Hardcastle decided to up the volume a tad.

"Did you see very much of him, Mrs Lee?"

"Come again?" she replied.

He decided to turn up the volume a little further.

"Did you see much of Mr Summers?"

"No need to shout, I'm not deaf, you know, Mr Horniman. No, I didn't see him that often, but when I did he was very helpful. He used to put my dustbin out every week for me, you know."

"Did he have any visitors?"

"I don't think he had any visitors during the time he was living next door."

Seeing how quick she had been to open her front door, Hardcastle was willing to bet that Mrs Lee probably spent a lot of her day looking out from behind her curtains, so if she said she hadn't seen any visitors it was more than likely he hadn't had any, unless they had turned up long after dark.

"What about his car, Mrs Lee. Did he use it much?"

"Oh yes, he used it every Sunday."

"Do you know where he went?"

"Oh yes. He drove it out of the garage, then he cleaned it and then he drove it back into his garage."

Hardcastle, in desperation, looked at his watch and saw that it was almost 11am. Kelly Heywood would already have started the post mortem by the time he arrived at the mortuary.

"Thank you, Mrs Lee, you have been very helpful," he told her.

"Does that mean I can tell my friends that I am helping the police with their enquiries?" she asked him.

"Yes, you certainly can, and thank you again."

The old lady beamed back at Hardcastle and he made his way back down her path. As he reached the pavement, he turned around to see Mrs Lee waving goodbye to him. He smiled returned her wave, and got behind the wheel of his Range Rover.

Next stop: Dorminster Mortuary.

Monday 11am

Having delegated various tasks to the other members of the team, Detective Sergeant Kath Pearson made herself a strong cup of coffee, pinched a couple of chocolate hob-nobs from the top drawer of Phil Davison's desk, settled back in her black leather swivel chair and inadvertently let out a big sigh.

Thankfully, the four DCs left in the room were so engrossed in what they were doing that none of them had heard a thing.

Not that it was any of their business, as the reason for the sigh wasn't work related. No-one, not even Jason, her husband, knew the cause and that was how she wanted it to stay, at least for the time being.

Jason had left for work before she had used the test, so certain had she been that it would just be a false alarm.

So when she saw the result was positive, she was totally and utterly stunned and didn't know quite what to do next, or who to turn to; certainly not to her husband. He would have been dancing around the room turning cartwheels if she had told him that she was expecting their first child.

But the truth was that she had serious doubts about their marriage, so how could she tell him she was pregnant and then say that she wasn't sure if she wanted to become a mother at this particular stage of her life? If only she had a sister to confide in—if only her sister had survived the car crash that had killed her almost twenty years ago now. If only...

"By the look of it, you could use a penny for your thoughts, Kath."

The sound of Phil Davison's voice interrupted her train of thought and snapped her back to the here and now.

"Back already, Phil?" she replied. "How did it go—did you and the DI find anything worthwhile?"

"First things first; are you OK?"

"Of course I am. You know nothing ever bothers me. So what have you got for me?"

Knowing that he wouldn't get anything further out of her, Davison handed over everything that he had brought back from Donald Summers's bungalow. Pearson had a quick look at all the various items, and, as she usually did, decided to start with the bank statements.

With internet banking becoming more and more popular, paper based statements were becoming rarer. And whilst a lot of older people had successfully embraced modern technology, it appeared that Donald Summers was not amongst them. Davison had confirmed that there was no sign of a computer, laptop or iPad at 18 Wildwood Drive.

This was a disappointment to her since a lot of information could be gleaned from a computer's hard drive, particularly personal info.

However, Pearson was more than happy to do things the old way. She enjoyed the challenge.

Apart from monthly direct debits for council tax, water, gas and electricity, there were quarterly debits for a television licence, a biannual debit for car tax and an annual membership renewal to the Jaguar Enthusiasts' Club. Phil Davison had told her about the Jag in the garage. From the way he had eulogised about the car, Pearson could tell that Davison was more than just a little bit envious.

On his way to the mortuary, DI Hardcastle had phoned Davison to let him know about his conversation with the next door neighbour, and also to tell him that the Jaguar only saw the light of the day once a week when he cleaned it. No wonder it seemed in such good condition. It was more than likely that Summers used his bus pass most of the time as there was a bus stop virtually outside the front door of his bungalow in Wildwood Drive, saving him the cost and hassle of finding somewhere to park whenever he went into Dorminster.

Pearson also gleaned from the bank statements that Thursday was Summers's favourite day for going out as there were cash withdrawals of £100 made from his bank account most weeks on that day.

The balance on his bank account had been steadily rising over the period covered by the statements thanks to two payments he received each month.

Every four weeks Summers had been receiving just over £700 in respect of his state pension, and on top of that, there were monthly payments of £1,527.40 being paid in from the County and Country Building Society.

A reference number was quoted on each payment, so her next step was to speak to the payroll department of the building society, whose head office she discovered was in Sheffield.

Once she had navigated the automated messaging system which offered her a choice of six options, she found herself waiting for someone from the HR department to answer.

After hanging on for ten minutes or so, listening to a piece of classical music she recognised but couldn't name, she finally got to speak to a living person, when a young girl's voice chimed, "Good morning, sorry for the delay. This is Sharon speaking, how may I help you today?"

"Good morning Sharon. This is Detective Sergeant Kath Pearson from Dorminster police in Dorset. I need to speak to someone about one of your customers, a Mr Donald James Summers," replied Pearson, who then read out the reference number quoted on the bank statements.

"I'll put you through to my supervisor," answered Sharon, and before Pearson had a chance to reply she was put on hold again. Thankfully, this time, she had to wait for less than a minute.

"Hello there, my name is Angela Hudson. I gather you'd like to speak to someone about Donald Summers."

"That's right," replied Pearson.

"Can you give me an idea what it's concerning," came the reply.

"Firstly, I need to let you know that sadly Mr Summers has passed away," said Pearson.

There was a gasp, followed by silence.

"Hello, are you still there?" asked Pearson, wondering if she had been cut off.

"Yes, I'm very sorry about that. That's just come as a bit of a shock to me. You see, Mr Summers worked for the County and Country for many years, and he was such a nice man. I've known him for more than 10 years myself. Can you tell me how he died?"

"I'm sorry," replied Pearson, "but I can't go into too much detail at this stage, but I can tell you that we are treating his death as suspicious."

"Yes, I appreciate that. But you really need to speak to Martin Baldwin who is Head of HR. I know he's in a meeting at the moment, but I will interrupt him. Can I have your contact number?"

Kath Pearson gave Angela Hudson her direct line and reluctantly put the telephone down having first been assured that Martin Baldwin would ring her back without delay.

She was as good as her word, and within three minutes, Pearson was put through to Baldwin.

"How did Don die?" were his first words.

"I can't go into the full details, but suffice to say we are treating the circumstances of his death as suspicious," replied Pearson.

"Are you sure you can't tell me a little bit more than that?" asked the Head of HR. "I am not exaggerating when I tell you the Don and I are, sorry, Don and I were the best of friends, and in Don's case, since his wife passed away, I was probably his only real friend."

Pearson quickly realised that she had struck gold with Martin Baldwin, and that almost certainly he would be able to fill in a lot of the gaps in their knowledge of Summers—gaps which they needed to fill in a hurry.

"What I can say," began Pearson, "is that one of the lines of enquiry we are exploring is that he may have been the victim of a robbery that went wrong."

"You have to understand that this has come as a real bolt out of the blue," replied Baldwin. "Can you give me an idea where or what Don was doing when this happened?" asked Baldwin.

"He was in the pavilion at a local cricket club. He'd twisted an ankle while he was umpiring, so he was resting up whilst someone else took over from him," confirmed Pearson.

"That does actually give me a small crumb of comfort," said Baldwin. "You see, Don and I shared two passions. One was a love for Jaguar cars and the other was for cricket. It was cricket that brought us together as friends. We used to joke that when it was our time to go, I hoped I would be watching Yorkshire playing cricket at Headingly, and Don said that he'd like to be watching a Test match at Lord's. At least I know that he was doing something he enjoyed when his time came, even if the manner of his passing doesn't sound particularly peaceful.

"So tell me what you need to know, Detective Sergeant Pearson," continued Baldwin with a slight tremor in his voice, "and I'll do my very best to help you. It's the least I can do. And, can you promise to let me know where and when his funeral will be?"

Pearson promised him that she would give him a call as soon as she knew the funeral arrangements, even though, she warned him, it might be some time before the coroner could release the body.

"I appreciate that this is hard for you Mr Baldwin, but can you start by giving me his employment history, going back as far as you can," asked Pearson. "We need to build a detailed picture of Donald as quickly as we can."

"I grabbed his old paper file before ringing you back, sergeant," replied Baldwin, "so I can tell you from his original job application form that he went to Dorminster Grammar School from 1963 to 1970, leaving with a clutch of GCE 'O' levels and 'A' levels.

"His first job was in an accountant's office, from 1970 to 1975, and then he worked as finance manager at a large hotel from 1975 to 1984. He was obviously very good with figures.

"He joined his local branch of the County and Country in 1984 and was promoted to area manager responsible for six branches in 1989. At that time he was based at our Regional Headquarters in Dorminster.

"He was promoted to regional manager in overall charge of 32 branches in the north east in 1993. He would have been 41 years old at the time. It also meant that he had to up sticks and move up here to Sheffield.

"He then moved around internally a couple of times until he retired in October 2016 aged 65."

"You mentioned his wife passing away, Mr Baldwin. We weren't aware that Mr Summers had been married," said Pearson. "Can you give me some details?"

"Yes, of course. He married Dawn Phillips in 2005 and they were the proverbial match made in heaven," said Baldwin. "Dawn worked here at head office, that's how they met.

"She'd had a really rough time with her first husband—he was a drinker and a gambler, a real waste of space by the sound of it, and by the time they split up and divorced, he had spent all of their savings and a lot more besides. She had no choice but to sell their house to pay off all the debts.

"She ended up moving into rented accommodation with her two daughters and had to start again literally from scratch. Everyone liked Dawn and we were all delighted when she and Don got together. I was best man at their wedding.

"Don owned a little cottage at that time, but he wanted to do things properly, so they went house-hunting shortly after the wedding and ended up moving into a nice, fairly new, four bedroom house. That was in 2006.

"They sold off most of the furniture from the cottage, so that everything they had in the new place was their choice, and not just Don's old stuff."

"How did Mr Summers get on with Dawn's two daughters?" asked Pearson. "It can be difficult for children to accept the new man in their mother's life."

"Dawn was five years older than Don, although you'd never think it to look at her, so the girls were in their early 30s with families of their own. They were over the moon for their mum when she began seeing him, and they both liked and got on well with him," answered Baldwin.

"You mentioned that his wife passed away. When did this happen?" asked Pearson.

"It was the middle of last year. She hadn't been feeling too well for a couple of weeks so Don took her to see her doctor. The doctor referred her for scans and they were totally devastated when she was diagnosed with pancreatic cancer. Just three weeks later, Dawn was dead. She was just 71 years old.

"The cancer had spread to her brain. It was so tragic. Don was utterly devastated."

"Was this the reason Donald decided to move back to Dorminster?" enquired Pearson.

"Yes, there were just too many memories for him in the house they'd bought, furnished and decorated together. They did everything together. They had been inseparable, and within the space of a few weeks, it was all taken away from Don. He was heartbroken, and I wasn't convinced that he would ever be able to get over her death.

"So he put the house up for sale, and as soon as he had exchanged contracts, he sold all the furniture. He had more than enough cash to buy the place in Dorminster outright, and what was leftover he split between Dawn's two daughters. That, more than anything, showed what a decent sort of guy Don was.

"He certainly didn't need to give the girls anything, nor were they expecting it, but he said that's what Dawn would have wanted him to do. They also shared all of their mum's jewellery. Don just kept the rings he had bought her, a wedding ring and an eternity ring."

"Did he say why he had decided to return to Dorminster after all those years living away?" asked Pearson.

"I don't think there was any specific reason as far as I'm aware," replied Baldwin. "He needed to get away from Sheffield, and I don't think he wanted to go somewhere he'd never been before.

"He told me that his parents had moved the family to Dorminster when he was only four years old, so he'd spent almost 40 years of his life there before he moved up to Yorkshire. It seemed the logical choice to him. And he'd always spoken fondly about the area. And I got the impression that someone special to him still lived there—but it was only an impression, nothing more than that."

"Do you know if Mr Summers had any brothers or sisters we need to get in touch with?" enquired Pearson.

"I know for a fact that he had an older brother, Jeremy, who he fell out with a few years ago. He lives in Thetford in Norfolk."

"Do you happen to know why they fell out?" asked Pearson.

"Yes. It was over their mother who died in 2015. She spent the last three years of her life in a residential care home in Northampton and Don visited her as often as he could. The brother never made the effort to go and see her all the time she was in care and this really angered Don, which was most out of character for him. He was such an amiable guy.

"And when the old lady died, the brother couldn't even be bothered to go to the funeral. Don told me that he and his brother had never been that close, but that this was the straw that broke the camel's back. He told me that it wouldn't bother him if he never saw his brother again."

While Baldwin had been talking, Pearson made a note to contact the police in Thetford to ask them if they could track down Jeremy Summers, and let him know that his brother had died. She would also ask them to make sure he had an alibi for Sunday afternoon.

"Thank you, Mr Baldwin, you have been really helpful," replied Pearson. "Can you let me have your email address? I have a picture of Donald Summers with a lady who I assume is Dawn. I'll scan and email it to you, and it would be helpful if you could confirm it is her."

"Yes, of course. And please feel free to contact me any time you want. I will miss Don, and people here that knew him will be really upset."

When she put the telephone down, Kath Pearson began to write up her notes of the conversation. She knew there would be other things she would need to speak to Martin Baldwin about, but this was a really good start.

She sent off the email to Baldwin, and a couple of minutes later received his confirmation that it was Dawn in the photograph.

In reply, she asked Baldwin if he had any idea of the names and addresses of Dawn's two daughters.

Again he replied promptly and said he would see what he could do.

"How are you getting on, Kath?" asked Phil Davison, who had just returned to his desk after a quick cup of tea and a sandwich in the canteen.

"I've done OK, thanks Phil. I've almost finished writing up my notes and I'll give you a copy as soon as I'm done."

"Terrific, and I've just had some good news which will cheer the boss up," replied Davison. "It seems that our missing cricketer has just turned up at his house."

Monday 12pm

Steve Hardcastle, relieved that he had finished at the mortuary, was now on his way back to the office.

Despite having attended numerous post mortems in the past, he had never quite got used to the unique smell of the mortuary, and knew that the smell would probably stay with him for the rest of the day.

He could easily have delegated the task to Phil Davison, but felt it was his responsibility to attend since he was the senior investigating officer, and that delegating was the easy way out. He prided himself that he would never ask any of his staff to do something he wouldn't do himself.

This latest visit to the mortuary had proven worthwhile on two counts.

Firstly, Kelly Heywood had been able to confirm that the weapon that killed Donald Summers had definitely been a bat mallet.

She had contacted Nicholson's, the sports shop that had sold the mallet to Flitton Green's Colin Sharpe, as soon as it had opened at 9am. The shop owner had been more than happy to help and had wasted no time in sending up an identical one so that she could compare it with the small slivers of wood she'd found in the head wounds suffered by Donald Summers.

Not only were the slivers identical, but the curved head of the mallet had also exactly matched the shape of the impressions the blows had made to the victims skull. This came as no surprise to Hardcastle.

However, he had been surprised when the pathologist told him that Summers had been suffering from a fairly rare condition which could have killed him at any time.

During the post mortem, Heywood had discovered that Summers had been suffering from an abdominal aortic aneurysm which, she explained, is a swelling to the main blood vessel which carries blood away from the heart down through the abdomen to the rest of the body.

In this instance the swelling had been almost 6 centimetres wide, three times the normal width of the aorta and there was every chance that it could have ruptured without warning causing massive internal bleeding. More often than not, when this happens it proves to be fatal.

According to Heywood, Summers had probably been totally unaware that he was suffering from the condition as it is fairly common that an aneurysm causes no noticeable symptoms. In this instance, as the aneurysm was so large, Summers might have felt some pain, or could have noticed a pulsating feeling in his abdomen, or perhaps had just felt generally out of sorts. These symptoms would have worsened rapidly had the aneurysm burst.

Heywood had also told Hardcastle that Summers had been a prime candidate for an abdominal aortic aneurysm. Whilst those at risk are generally over 65, that risk increases exponentially if they smoke, are overweight, have high blood pressure and a high cholesterol level.

"So what you are saying is that if he hadn't been killed yesterday, he could have dropped down dead at any time because of this aneurysm?"

"Because of the abnormal size of the aneurysm, that's exactly what I'm saying," the pathologist had replied.

As he was mulling this over in his car, his mobile phone rang. It was Phil Davison.

"Hi boss, how did the post mortem go?"

"It went well, Phil. Kelly confirmed that the murder weapon was definitely a bat mallet. But I've got some surprising news. She also found that Summers had been suffering from a massive swelling in his aorta, the artery which pumps the blood around the body. It could have ruptured and killed him at any time, completely without warning.

"Can you ask Kath to find out who his GP was, and then perhaps she could ring him and find out when Summers last paid the surgery a visit. If it was fairly recent, get her to ask him if Summers was aware that he had an aortic aneurysm?"

"Will do, boss. Purpose of my call is that we've got some good news from this end. We've found Panton. He turned up at his house about a quarter of an hour ago and he's being brought to the station as we speak. Billy Kiernan and his lads are already on their way to his house to go through everything."

"Terrific. I'll be back at the station in ten minutes or so," replied Hardcastle. "Let's have a quick catch up before we tackle Panton."

Hardcastle pressed the button to end the call.

Things were moving along just as he had hoped.

Monday 12:30pm

Hardcastle was relieved that they had finally found Neil Panton, and for the rest of his journey back to the police station he was thinking about how he and Davison would handle the upcoming interview with Panton.

If he was the killer, he had had almost18 hours to perfect an alibi and the two detectives would need to go through it very carefully trying to pick holes in it.

But before seeing Panton, Hardcastle wanted to catch up with Phil Davison and Kath Pearson and, if possible, Billy Kiernan. He wasn't concerned about making Panton wait; after all, he had kept them waiting long enough.

After parking his car in the station's underground car park, Hardcastle was bounding up the stairs two at a time when he met Davison on the first floor landing.

"How's Panton doing, Phil. Did he come quietly?" asked Hardcastle.

"I wouldn't say he came quietly, boss. He told the two cops waiting outside his house to piss off. He's in Interview Room Two and is on his own," replied Davison. "He's just told me he doesn't need a solicitor as he's got nothing to hide. My first impression is that he's a right cocky so and so."

"So he didn't put his hands up and say 'it's a fair cop, it was me that did it'?" asked Hardcastle with a wry grin on his face.

"Afraid not," replied Davison, also grinning. "Actually, I live in hope that someone will say that to me one day, before they pension me off."

Once back in the CID offices, their first port of call was Kath Pearson to make sure that she was up to speed with the result of the post mortem. As usual, Phil Davison had told her pretty much everything she needed to know, and she was already in the process of funnelling that information down the line to the DCs that were in the office.

Having completed her notes on her conversation with Martin Baldwin at the County and Country Building Society, Pearson gave copies to both Hardcastle and Davison. She had a dozen or so extra copies on her desk which she would also pass on to the other team members once the DI had finished reading his copy.

"That's good, Kath, really good," said Hardcastle when he had finished reading.

"Until now, I'd had the feeling that our victim had been a confirmed bachelor and I must admit to feeling a bit sorry for him. It's nice to know that he had been married and that the marriage had been a happy one," continued Hardcastle, "even though it ended in tragic circumstances."

He looked at his watch, and turned to Davison.

"Time for a quick cup of coffee and a digestive, and then let's see what Panton has to say for himself."

Back in his own office, Hardcastle rang Billy Kiernan, but after a couple of rings, the phone diverted to voice mail, and so he left a message asking Kiernan to return his call as soon as he could.

Ten minutes later, and still no reply from Kiernan, Hardcastle decided that it was time to interview Panton.

Collecting Davison on his way, the pair made their way down the one flight of stairs to Interview Room Two.

"And about bloody time too. I've got things to do today you know, even if you two haven't," said Panton as the pair walked into the room.

Nice to meet you too, Mr Panton, thought Hardcastle. Even though he'd been a copper for almost 20 years and had met some right nasty bits of work during that time, Hardcastle could count on the fingers of one hand the number of times he had taken an instant dislike to someone. Panton was right up there with the worst.

The 33-year-old Neil Panton was dressed like a walking advert for Nike, wearing the brand's tracksuit, baseball cap, and trainers, which were on feet that were perched on top of the table that was in the middle of the windowless room.

An uneasy silence was broken by Hardcastle.

"I would appreciate it if you would take your feet off the table please, Mr Panton."

With an obvious show of resentment, Panton slowly removed his feet from the table top.

"My name is Detective Inspector Steven Hardcastle and this is Detective Sergeant Philip Davison. I believe you know why you are here."

"As far as I'm aware," began Panton, "it's about the old boy who was umpiring yesterday. I've been told that someone bumped him off."

Hardcastle's dislike of Panton was growing by the second.

72

"It is about the murder of Donald Summers, and you are correct that Mr Summers was one of the umpires officiating at yesterday's match between Flitton Green and Middle Ash cricket clubs.

"We were able to interview the rest of your team last night, including three players who left the ground around about the same time as you did," continued Hardcastle.

"I hope you're not suggesting I had anything to do with it?" asked Panton.

"Not at all, Mr Panton, but like everyone else who was at the ground yesterday afternoon, we will a need a written statement from you. You might have some relevant information for us—for all we know you might have seen something out of the ordinary or someone acting suspiciously during the afternoon.

"As I'm sure you will appreciate, we need to eliminate you from our enquiries," replied Hardcastle.

"Well, that's OK then," answered Panton. "As I told your buddy here, I've got nothing to hide. If I had, I would have made sure I had a solicitor with me before talking to you."

"Our understanding is that Mr Summers returned to the area just a few months ago, having lived in these parts until he moved up north around 25 years ago. Did you know him, or had you met him prior to yesterday's game?" asked Hardcastle.

"Not as far as I'm aware," came the reply.

"We understand that you were the first Flitton Green batsman to be given out yesterday. That would have been just after 5pm," said Phil Davison. "We also understand that you left the ground shortly after 7pm. Can you tell us what you did for the two hours in between? Several of your teammates in their statements said they don't remember seeing you during that time."

"Well, they wouldn't have," was the reply. "I was ticking a bit after being given out, so after I'd taken off my pads, my gloves and my box, I put them with my bat on top of my kit bag, and then I went for a bit of a walk to help me calm down."

"Where did you go?" asked Hardcastle. "Did you leave the ground at all?"

"No, I did what I usually do after getting out and went for a stroll around the ground. I found a nice quiet spot where no one would bother me and I watched the rest of the game from there."

"And would anyone have seen you?" enquired Davison.

"I doubt it. I was tucked away amongst some trees, between the sightscreen and the car park. I couldn't see the pavilion from there, so I assume that they couldn't see me."

"That's convenient," responded Davison.

"Actually, I'd say it was pretty inconvenient," replied Panton. "If I'd chosen a more public spot, then you wouldn't be asking me so many damn fool questions."

He looked at Hardcastle and then Davison, with a little smirk on his face.

"Tell you what though. If you get one of your flatfoots to walk over there, they'll find an empty can of coke and some fag ends—all mine. Feel free to nick me for dropping litter on the ground."

"Oh, we'll take a look Mr Panton," said Davison. "You can rely on that."

"When did you hear about the murder Mr Panton, as you appear to have left the ground before the body was discovered?" asked Hardcastle.

"That would be about 10:30am this morning. We were out of milk, so my girlfriend went down the shops to get a couple of pints. When she got there, apparently everyone was talking about what had happened, so she told me as soon as she got back. You could have knocked me down with a feather when I heard. He was a crap umpire, there's no denying that. But nobody deserves to die like that."

"Die like what?" interrupted Davison.

"Having his head smashed in. That's what my girlfriend heard."

He looked at the two detectives expecting a reply.

"Please continue, Mr Panton," answered Hardcastle.

"Anyway, as soon as I heard what happened, I got dressed, had a quick spot of breakfast and headed home. I was going to come and see you chaps once I'd freshened up, but the two goons who were waiting outside my house grabbed me and hauled me down here before I had a chance to say anything. So, have you guys got any idea who might have done it?"

"Why did you leave the cricket ground when you did, Mr Panton, as you seem to have left in a bit of a hurry?" asked Davison, ignoring Panton's question.

"A couple of reasons actually," replied Panton. "I had arranged to meet up with my girlfriend and I'd told her I would be around as soon as the game finished.

"And on top of that, I used to play for Middle Ash, so I know quite a few of their team. I don't particularly like a couple of their guys and just didn't feel like

74

shaking hands with them at the end, so I thought I would clear off before I had to. I'm no hypocrite, you see."

"What is your girlfriend's name?" asked Davison.

"Debra. Debra Patterson."

"Have you known her long?" asked Hardcastle.

"I've known her for a year or so, but we've only been going out together for about a month," answered Panton.

Handing Panton a sheet of paper and a biro, Davison asked him to write down her address and telephone number. When he'd finished, Panton handed the pen and paper back.

"Is that Miss, or Mrs Patterson?" asked Davison.

"Mrs," came the reply. "She's a widow."

"I see she lives in Brewer Street. That's only a mile or so from the cricket ground. What time did you get to her place then?" asked Davison.

"It must have been after seven, but no later than a quarter past," answered Panton.

"What did you do for the rest of the evening?" asked Hardcastle.

"We had a bite to eat, watched a film on the telly, finished off a bottle of wine and then we had an early night," he replied with a sly grin on his face.

"What does Mrs Patterson do for a living?" asked Hardcastle.

"She's a nurse."

"We will need to check your story with her. Is she likely to be at home now?" asked Davison.

"Yes. She's working nights this week, so she'll be home until late afternoon. You might need to wake her up though as she was pretty tired when I left," replied Panton, smirking at both the coppers once again.

"What did you do with the bat mallet you took out of Colin Sharpe's bag?" asked Hardcastle, deciding that it was time to go on the offensive. Panton seemed far too comfortable for his liking.

It had the desired effect and for the first time, Panton seemed to be rattled. The smug look disappeared quickly from his face.

"Who said I took his bat mallet?"

"Answer the question please, Mr Panton. What did you do with the bat mallet you took out of Colin Sharpe's bag?"

"I put it behind the large waste bin at the back of the pavilion. Look, Sharpe had been getting on my nerves banging away on his bat with that bloody mallet, so I thought I would hide it. I was going to tell him where it was at the end of the game. But I forgot and left before I could tell him."

"Did anyone see exactly where you put it?" continued Hardcastle.

"I don't know. Possibly, possibly not," replied Panton.

"Would it surprise you to know that there was no sign of a bat mallet when the area behind the pavilion was searched last night? Are you sure you didn't take it with you when you left the ground?"

Hardcastle was looking directly into Panton's eyes, and was sure that Panton was weighing up his reply very carefully.

"Why are you so bothered about a poxy bat mallet?" he asked.

"Because the weapon used to batter Mr Summers to death happens to have been a bat mallet, and as far as we are aware, the only bat mallet at the ground yesterday was the one you took from Colin Sharpe's bag."

There was no reply from Panton. Hardcastle decided to press home his advantage.

"After you were given out by Mr Summers yesterday, do you remember what you said to the square leg umpire as you walked off?"

Panton replied with a shrug of the shoulders, "Sorry, I don't remember."

"I'll jog your memory then. You told him that, and I quote, 'if your mate had been thirty years younger, I would have smashed his face in'."

Hardcastle felt he was nearly there. He was certain that Panton was on the verge of breaking.

But at that precise moment, his mobile phone rang. He swore under his breath, but then looked at the phone and saw the caller was Billy Kiernan. Could this be a nail in Panton's coffin? Had they found some evidence? Was it decent enough to allow them to charge him?

Hardcastle got up, excused himself and left the room before taking the call.

"Billy. Please tell me you've got something for me."

"I'm afraid nothing at the moment, Steve. His car seems fairly clean and so is his kit bag. One thing is missing though. There's no sign of any of his whites— no shirt, jumper, trousers or spikes or trainers.

"We've still got most of the house and the garage to do, but if he is our man, we need to get hold of what he was wearing yesterday, and we need it as quick as possible. How's it going at your end? Have you started interviewing him yet, Steve?" asked the CSM.

"Yeah, and he's such a delightful chap. You would really like him," was Hardcastle's sarcastic reply. "Bear with me for five minutes or so please, Billy. I'll give you a call back. According to Panton, he spent last night with a girlfriend, so it's more than likely that he left what he'd been wearing at her house. Have you got enough guys to start a search of the girlfriend's place, without compromising the search at Panton's?"

"That won't be a problem," replied Billy. "I've got three lads spare who could be on the road as soon as I give them the go ahead."

"One last thing, Billy," asked Hardcastle. "Can you also get someone back to the cricket ground? Panton said he spent the last couple of hours of the match from a spot between one of the sightscreens and the car park. It's the area where there is a large clump of trees. You should find an empty coke can and some cigarette butts. Can you let me know if your guy doesn't find anything?"

Hardcastle ended the call, and walked back into the interview room.

"I've just spoken to the team that are searching your house and your car, Mr Panton. They've been through the bag in your boot, and have told me that they can't find the clothing you wore during yesterday's game, and neither can they find your spikes, or whatever footwear you were using. Can you tell me what you've done with it?" asked Hardcastle.

"Debra took it out of the bag and bunged it in her washing machine. Anyone who plays cricket will tell you that it's a bugger of a job to get grass stains out of your trousers, especially the ones on the knees," replied Panton.

"Look mate, are you trying to fit me up or something? I tell you now that I did not kill that umpire. Anyway, what proof have you got?

"Yes, I took the bat mallet, I don't deny that. But I've told you why, and I've told you that I put it behind the bin where Sharpe couldn't see it, especially if he just looked out of the back door that is. He would have found it if he'd looked round the other side of the waste bin. It's not my fault that he didn't. And anyone walking behind the pavilion, or walking on the footpath would have seen it.

"It's pretty obvious to me that whoever killed the umpire must have picked up the bat mallet as he walked round the back of the pavilion. And as for what I said to the other umpire, well, that was said in the heat of the moment. I didn't mean a word of it. I'd never do anything to harm someone twice my age."

"All right, Mr Panton, your response is noted," replied Hardcastle. "But we're going to have to suspend this interview whilst we ask Mrs Patterson to verify your movements from the time you arrived at her house yesterday evening until you left her this morning. Hopefully, that shouldn't take too long."

"Alright, but hurry it up. I've got to see a man about a car this afternoon. Sitting here all day isn't going to pay my mortgage," replied Panton, knowing from past experience that the police could hold him for up to 24 hours without charge, even longer if they thought they had a decent case to put before the Crown Prosecution Service.

The two policemen got up and left the interview room.

"What do you think, Phil?" asked Hardcastle.

"He's hiding something, there's no doubt about that, boss. But whether he's our killer, it's too early to say."

"I agree. We've just got to see how this pans out. Can you go and talk to Mrs Patterson—take Paul Taylor with you; the experience will be good for the lad. There are a few bits and pieces I need to catch up on. We'll compare notes when you get back, and decide if we've got any grounds to hold him overnight."

On his way back to his office, Hardcastle rang Billy Kiernan as he'd promised, gave him the girlfriend's address and asked him to get his three CSIs over there as soon as possible, but ask them to wait for Phil Davison to arrive.

His gut feeling now was that this was going to be another long day.

Monday 1:45pm

Phil Davison and Paul Taylor arrived at Debra Patterson's house at exactly the same time as the crime scene investigators despatched by Billy Kiernan.

Whilst en route, Davison had built a picture of Mrs Patterson in his mind. He was amazed to see that he was completely wrong.

Given that Panton had come across as a crude loudmouth know-it-all, it was a pleasant surprise that Debra Patterson was the complete opposite. She was certainly not the archetypal Essex girl Davison was expecting her to be.

She was tall, blonde and very attractive, the sort of woman who would look good no matter what she was wearing. She reminded Davison of a young Susan Hampshire, and when she spoke, she sounded more Eton than Epping.

Appearances, of course, can be deceptive, and he was fully expecting Mrs Patterson to be seriously put out when two detectives and three crime scene investigators suddenly turn up unannounced and uninvited on her doorstep.

Once again, Phil Davison was in for a surprise.

Instead of being annoyed, she warmly welcomed all five into her home, invited the three CSIs to do whatever they needed to do, go wherever they needed to go, and even offered to make tea or coffee for her visitors.

Her house was as impeccable as her manners, tastefully furnished, spotlessly clean and smelling of cinnamon—they had descended on her whilst she was in the middle of baking some cakes which, she told them, she would be taking into the hospital when her shift began later that evening. "Something to keep us going during the night shift when we begin to flag a little," she had told them.

As she put two cups of coffee on place mats on the coffee table in front of the policemen, she handed DC Taylor a small plate on which were half a dozen assorted chocolate biscuits.

Looking around the lounge, Davison could see why Neil Panton was keen to get his feet under her table. But he couldn't help thinking that they made an odd pair; she wouldn't look out of place at a Buckingham Palace garden party, whilst he would look far more at home at a football match between Millwall and West Ham.

Davison felt almost reluctant to start the conversation that was the reason for their visit, but with time not exactly on their side, he knew he would have to get the ball rolling soon.

To his surprise, it was their host who got the discussion under way.

"Can I assume gentlemen that you are here because of what happened at the cricket ground yesterday?"

"Yes, we are, Mrs Patterson," replied Davison. "As a matter of routine, Mr Neil Panton is currently being interviewed at Dorminster police station as he was one of the cricketers playing in yesterday's match during which one of the umpires was murdered. Mr Panton is the last of the twenty two players to be interviewed. We already have statements from the others, which we took last night.

"Mr Panton has provided details of his whereabouts from 5pm yesterday afternoon to the time he arrived back at his house this morning. He has told us that he spent yesterday evening and much of this morning with you at this address. Can you confirm that that is correct please?"

"I can," replied Mrs Patterson.

"And can you confirm what time he arrived?"

"It was around about 7:45pm, certainly no earlier than that."

DC Taylor glanced at Davison. According to Panton, he had arrived at his girlfriend's house 'no later than a quarter past seven'. That left at least half an hour unaccounted for.

"And what time did he leave?" asked Davison.

"That would have been somewhere between 11am and 11:15am this morning," came the reply.

"Where were you when you first heard about the incident at the cricket ground?"

"I was at the little supermarket down the road. I'd popped out to buy some milk as I'd run out. I suspect that Neil must have raided the refrigerator during the night. The ladies in the shop were full of it," continued Mrs Patterson. "As far as I know, nothing like this has ever happened in the village before. I was so surprised when I heard them talking that I almost forgot to buy the milk."

"About what time would that have been?" asked Davison.

"It was 10:15am on the dot. They had the radio on in the shop, and I remember hearing a time check as I opened the shop door."

"When you told Neil that someone had been murdered during the cricket match, what was his reaction?" continued Davison.

"He was mildly surprised; at least that's how I would define his reaction. He certainly wasn't as stunned as I had been when I heard the news. After a few seconds he asked me if I was joking, which, of course, I wasn't.

"He said that the police would probably want to interview everyone that had been at the ground, so I quickly did him some breakfast, nothing fancy, just egg and bacon. He finished off his cup of coffee, got his things together, and left."

"Did he leave anything behind?" asked Davison.

"Some of his cricket clothing is hanging on the wash line, and there is a pair of trainers at the back door."

"I suspect they will already have been inspected and bagged up by our colleagues. Standard procedure," said Davison.

"Whose idea was it to wash the clothing?" asked DC Taylor.

"Not mine," replied Mrs Patterson. "The first I knew about it was when I heard the washing machine going."

"Is that normal?" enquired Davison.

"What do you mean by normal?" asked Mrs Patterson.

"Well, what usually happens with his kit?" enquired Davison, a bit intrigued by her question, and the old-fashioned look that had appeared on her face.

"I think I should set the record straight here, as there may have been a bit of a misunderstanding," she replied. "I've known Neil for a year or so. He's serviced my car on a couple of occasions.

"Normally, my husband would have dealt with things like that, but he passed away 15 months ago. Fifteen months and eleven days to be precise."

"I'm very sorry to hear that, Mrs Patterson," said Davison gently.

"Thank you. As I'm sure you will appreciate, I am still coming to terms with it, but life has to go on, as the saying goes. Anyway, a few weeks ago, when I went to collect my car from his house, Neil asked if I fancied having a drink one evening. I thought about it hard and long. He isn't my type for one thing, and it's still far too early for me to even think about beginning any new relationship. But, I haven't been out socially since my husband died, and I saw no harm in having a quiet drink.

"I told the girls at work about it, and they said I should go, so I rang Neil up and I said I'd be happy to meet up with him. A couple of nights later, we went to a pub in the town. It was a pleasant evening. A week or so later, he rang and asked if I'd like to go out for a meal. Again, I accepted. It would have been churlish of me not to. But I stressed that we would go Dutch. I did not want him getting the wrong idea.

"During the meal, I told him that I enjoyed his company, but that was as far as things could go at this time in my life. I said I was quite happy to be considered a friend, if he still wanted, but no more than that. He was obviously disappointed, but he seemed to take it on the chin.

"That was around a fortnight ago, and I thought he had decided to leave it at that. To my surprise, he rang me yesterday around about 6:45pm. He said he'd been playing cricket, had had a hard game and that he could do with a chat.

"A little reluctantly, I told him he could come around after he had finished and an hour or so later he was knocking on my door."

"Can I ask how you spent the evening?" asked Davison.

"Of course, you can. I've nothing to hide. We had a bite to eat; I made a salad as it was another warm evening. Then we watched a film on the television—*Evil under the Sun*, the one based on the Agatha Christie book. Peter Ustinov plays Hercule Poirot.

"Neil fell asleep during the film; I don't think it was his cup of tea. Anyway, he'd finished off a bottle of white wine, and as he had also downed a couple of cans of lager when he got here, he asked if he could stay over as he knew he was over the limit. I wasn't overly keen on the idea and suggested he got a cab instead. But that would have meant he'd have to come back in the morning to collect his car, so I relented.

"The film ended just after 11pm and we went to bed—separately. I made up the bed in the spare room for him and that was that.

"My alarm went off at 7:30am, but I didn't disturb Neil until it was after 9am, when I knocked on his door and suggested it was time for him to get up. He said he wasn't in too much of a hurry as he was going to a second-hand car auction later, and that it didn't start until 2pm."

"Thank you for being so candid, Mrs Patterson," said Davison. "You have been really helpful."

"Could I ask a favour in return, Mr Davison?"

"Ask away," replied Davison.

"As you say, I have been quite candid about my friendship with Neil. I hope you can offer me the same courtesy."

"I shall try."

"Is Neil a suspect?"

"That, unfortunately, I can't answer, because at this stage we are simply gathering information from anyone who was at the cricket ground between 1pm and 7pm yesterday, so our enquiries are at a very early stage. There's a lot of legwork still to be done."

"I understand that; it was wrong of me to ask. However, I have the feeling that you came here thinking that Neil and I are having a relationship of some sort. Did Neil give you that impression?" persisted Mrs Patterson.

"Let's just say some of his comments to us were open to misinterpretation."

"Thank you, Mr Davison. That comes as no surprise," she replied with a smile. "Let's just say that I will be looking for someone else to service my car in the future."

Monday 2:30pm

Steve Hardcastle looked at his watch and realised he hadn't had anything to eat since leaving home just after 5:30am that morning. It was little wonder that his stomach was rumbling.

He thought about asking Paul Taylor to pop out and get him a sandwich, but then remembered that the young DC was out interviewing Debra Patterson with Phil Davison.

So instead he decided to walk to the local bakers. A breath of fresh air would do him good and hopefully blow away some of the cobwebs.

After buying himself a BLT and a Diet Coke, he decided to walk the couple of hundred yards to the park. He soon found himself a vacant bench, opened the sandwich and removed the ring pull from the can of Coke.

It was yet another warm day and the park was fairly busy, and he was glad that he had left his jacket back in his office.

He looked at his watch again and saw that he still had half an hour before the catch-up meeting with Phil Davison and Kath Pearson. He also hoped that Billy Kiernan would be able to join them, although he had told the CSM not to worry if he couldn't make it. The pair of them could catch up later in the day.

Some of his early optimism about the case had already begun to dissipate. As much as he disliked Neil Panton, he already had some doubt that he was the man they were looking for. And if Billy Kiernan's team couldn't find any forensic evidence to link him to the murder, and if Debra Patterson confirmed his alibi, they would have to let Panton go, and the investigation, which had started fairly optimistically, would be back to square one.

His gut feeling was still that there had to be a very strong motive behind the murder, and, as it stood, he couldn't see any motive to tie Panton to the victim. Nor could he see a bad umpiring decision being the trigger for such a savage attack, even by someone like Neil Panton who was well known for having a short fuse.

He looked at his watch once more and realised it was time to make his way back to the police station.

Phil Davison had already returned by the time Hardcastle arrived at the office, and he was also pleased to see that Billy Kiernan had made it after all.

After getting themselves something to drink, the four of them sat around the conference table in Hardcastle's office.

"Shall we have some updates then?" began Hardcastle. "Can you kick off, please Billy? How have your CSIs got on? Have they had any joy with their various searches?"

Kiernan took a sip of his coffee before beginning his report. He hated being the bearer of bad news.

"Unfortunately Steve, I've got nothing positive for you as things stand at the moment. There was no sign of the bat mallet, the key to the Umpire's Room, Mr Summers's house keys or his wallet when we searched the footpath and the woods.

"We also thoroughly searched the village hall but found nothing there either. I suspect the killer took anything incriminating away with him when he left the cricket ground.

"Panton's cricket clothing was clean having gone through Mrs Patterson's washing machine, and his trainers had been given a proper scrubbing. We've taken away all the items so we can have a more detailed look, but I'm not that hopeful of finding anything incriminating.

"The search of his house and garage is ongoing, but we've found nothing so far. The garage is full of tools as you'd expect for a car mechanic who works from home, including a large range of hammers, spanners, screwdrivers and so forth—but again no sign of the bat mallet or anything else remotely suspicious.

"I'm just sorry that I haven't got anything more encouraging to tell you at the moment."

"That's how it goes," replied Hardcastle. "How did your visit to Debra Patterson go, Phil?"

"Well boss, she is one very classy lady," replied Davison. "And contrary to the impression that Panton gave us, he and Mrs Patterson are just friends, and no more than that. I suspect it's more a case of wishful thinking on his part, and I can't really blame him for that.

"She lost her husband fifteen months ago, and told us that she's not ready to start a new relationship. But when she is, she'll have them queuing at her front door and Panton won't stand a cat in hell's chance of making it to the top of the queue.

"But the good news, boss, is that there are a couple of anomalies from what he told us when we interviewed him. It was Panton who put the cricket clothing in the washing machine, and not Mrs Patterson. The first she knew about it was when she heard her washing machine going."

"Why lie about that?" asked Pearson.

"God knows. We'll ask him that when we re-interview him," replied Hardcastle. "What about the second anomaly, Phil?"

"Panton told us that he got to Mrs Patterson's house no later than a quarter past seven. However, Mrs Patterson said that he didn't arrive until 7:45pm, so we have at least half an hour unaccounted for; plenty of time to dispose of a bat mallet, wallet and keys. Something else we can quiz him on."

"Anything else come out of the conversation?"

"Nothing, other than I don't think Panton will be seeing much more of Mrs Patterson," replied Davison. "By the way, young Paul Taylor did well logging everything, and even threw in the odd question. He's one for the future."

"You'd better watch your back then, Phil. Don't forget, you're not getting any younger," joked Pearson.

"Your turn now, Kath; anything further from your chat to the guy at the building society?" asked Hardcastle.

"I've managed to speak to Jeremy Summers, Donald's brother," replied Pearson.

"Thetford police had already given him the bad news about Donald, and despite having fallen out with him, he was still pretty cut up about it. He and his wife were out with friends yesterday afternoon at the time his brother was murdered, so he has a cast iron alibi.

"I asked him if he knew anyone who might have had it in for his brother, but he said he couldn't think of anyone off the top of his head, particularly as he hadn't seen much of him during the last few years. I asked him to get in touch if anyone springs to mind, but I don't think we'll hear from him again.

"I've also got the names and addresses of Mr Summers's two stepdaughters. One lives in Dewsbury, the other in Rotherham. I'll speak to them both as soon as I've got their phone numbers."

"When you do, Kath, there was a photograph of a young baby in Donald's house. Can you ask them both whether they know anything about it, who it might be?" asked Hardcastle. "Perhaps it's of one of their children."

"I'll do that, sir. I'll also ring the brother again and ask him," replied Pearson. "There's a possibility it could be a niece or a nephew, particularly as he had no children of his own.

"I also managed to track down Mr Summers's GP and spoke to the practice administrator. She confirmed that he had visited the surgery in January to register with them, but that was the only time they had seen him.

"She also gave me the details of his previous GP in Yorkshire and he's on my list to call. I'll let you know if this throws up anything.

"We've also been going through the various statements taken at the cricket ground last night. There are one or two minor anomalies, but nothing serious, and we're sorting those out as we go along.

"We've also been taking statements from some of the non-cricketers who spent time at the ground yesterday and several people have rung up unsolicited to say they were also there at some stage during the afternoon, so we're asking them either to come in here, or go to the village hall where one of our team will take a statement from them."

"Are we asking why they were there yesterday?" interrupted Hardcastle.

"We are," replied Pearson. "So far, we've had the wives and children of two of the Flitton Green players, the father of another and several from families that had just gone there so their kids could spend time on the play equipment.

"However, we know we are still missing at least a dozen people who were there at some point, and I think we may need to make that appeal on local radio and regional television to speed things up."

"I agree. I'll get on to the Press and PR department at HQ and ask them to deal with that, and I'll also ask them to send a press release to the local hacks. I'll get them to liaise with you, Kath. Anything else?" asked Hardcastle.

"No, that's all from me, sir," she replied. "Apart from the pre-school asking when they can reopen."

"No reason why they can't reopen tomorrow as long as they realise some areas will still be cordoned off. We'll continue to have a presence there for at least the next couple of days, particularly if we get a decent response from the appeal.

"Now, unless there is anything else we need to discuss, Phil and I will talk to Panton again. The way things are going, I think we're going to have to let him go."

Monday 3:15pm

"I hope we gave you a spot of lunch while you were waiting?" enquired Hardcastle, as he took his place alongside Phil Davison, opposite a very sullen-looking Neil Panton.

"If you call lunch a meal deal from Tesco, followed by a cup of weak lukewarm tea, then yes I have," replied Panton, obviously wound up by having had to wait so long for them to continue the interview.

"Strangely enough, that's more or less what I had," said Hardcastle amiably, "without the tea."

"And that's more than I had," added Davison. "But then again, I was enjoying the company of your Mrs Patterson. What a delightful and attractive lady she is."

"Well, now you've met her, I assume I can go," said Panton, beginning to get up from his chair.

"I'm sorry, but not yet, Mr Panton. Please sit back down. There are a couple of points we need to double check with you," said Davison.

"Like what?" came the surly reply.

Davison looked at Hardcastle, a look that asked 'are we about to see the famous Panton temper?'

Hardcastle nodded back at his sergeant. A nod that said 'hit him with both barrels'.

"Mrs Patterson was very helpful. We had a nice long chat. And you'll be pleased to know that as my DC and I were leaving, she was putting the sheets from your bed into the washing machine. The sheets from the single bed in the spare room that is, the one you slept in last night. On your own."

Hardcastle could sense that Panton was close to boiling point, but at the very last moment, common sense seemed to prevail as he remembered where he was.

He was obviously desperate to get out of the police station as soon as he could, and he realised the only way to do that was to get the questioning over and done with.

"So what?" he replied.

"And whilst on the subject of washing machines," continued Davison, "do you want to reconsider what you told us about who put your cricket whites into the wash? Mrs Patterson told us that you put them in, and not her."

"It might have been me, come to think of it. If that's what Debra said, then I'll go along with it," replied Panton.

"Do you normally wash your kit the same day you use it?" asked Hardcastle.

"Depends how dirty it is," answered Panton, with a smirk.

"Well, we've brought back your whites and your trainers, and they will be given a very thorough forensic examination. You'd be surprised how many people think they can get rid of bloodstains on a shirt by just putting it into a washing machine set for a normal wash."

"How long are you going to keep them for?" asked Panton. "I'll need them for next Sunday's game."

"We'll let you know," replied Davison. "Now, this morning you told us that you arrived at Mrs Patterson's house no later than 7:15pm yesterday evening. However, according to Mrs Patterson, you didn't arrive until 7:45pm. So where were you during those thirty minutes?"

"Does it matter if we don't agree on the time I got to her place? Anyway, why take her word against mine?"

"For a start, it's amazing how many different things you can get up to in half an hour," replied Davison.

"Like what?" asked Panton.

"Let's see. You could find a nice quite field somewhere. A field where no one would see you bury a bat mallet, a wallet and a set of keys, for example," replied Davison.

"Yeah, well, I didn't. If you must know, I had a little drive around for half an hour or so. I'd had a crap game, and I've already told you that I didn't want to socialise with my team or any of the Middle Ash players because I was still a bit wound up, and the last thing I wanted to do was to arrive at Debra's place in a bad mood.

"Look, I really like her and I enjoy her company, and I was hoping that something would come of it. For once in my life, I was prepared to be patient; but by the sound of it, you lot have already queered the pitch for me."

"Well, you shouldn't tell lies, should you?" replied Davison forcefully. "You've only got yourself to blame."

"Can I go now?" asked Panton.

Hardcastle and Davison looked at each other. Hardcastle gave a nod to his sergeant.

"Yes, you can go," replied Davison, "at least for the time being. But don't go too far, Mr Panton. I'm sure we'll need to talk to you again."

Whilst Davison saw Panton off the premises, Hardcastle reluctantly returned to the CID offices.

"How did it go, sir?" asked Kath Pearson, as he passed her desk.

"We've had to let him go, Kath. We've got nothing to hold him on at the moment. It would be nice if Forensic could find something on his kit, but I just don't think that's going to happen."

"So you don't think he's our man?" asked Pearson.

"On balance, I don't think so, Kath," he replied, and wandered back into his office.

As Hardcastle looked out of his window, Phil Davison walked into the office and stood by his boss's side, and also looked out of the window.

"Did he have anything else to say for himself before he left?" enquired Hardcastle.

"Not a word. I was half expecting him to ask for a lift back to his house, but he just kept his mouth shut."

At that moment, Panton came into view as he crossed the road, walking towards the shopping precinct.

"I know we've had to let him go, Phil," said Hardcastle, "but somehow, I don't think it will be the last we see of him."

Monday 4pm

Neil Panton was in a foul mood.

In a way, he was relieved that the police sergeant hadn't offered to give him a lift home. If he had, he probably would have told him to stick his lift where the sun doesn't shine.

Right now though, he needed some thinking time and decided to go for a cup of coffee at the local Costa in the town's shopping precinct.

Having a very sweet tooth, Panton ordered a large latte with a couple of shots of caramel syrup, and after looking around to make sure there was nobody he knew in the coffee shop, he made his way to a table for two in the corner where he hoped no one would notice him.

It also meant he could watch the people walking past the shop. He wouldn't put it past the Old Bill to have someone following him.

If what the two coppers had told him was true, it sounded like it might be the end of his relationship with Debra Patterson before it had really got off the ground. Even though she'd told him that he wasn't her type, and that she wasn't ready to begin dating again following the death of her husband, Panton, who was incredibly thick skinned, had still harboured a hope that he would grow on her the more that they saw of each other.

Now it sounded like those hopes may have sunk without a trace, just like the Titanic.

However, he decided he would ring Debra on his mobile once he'd finished his coffee. Hopefully, there was still time to catch her before she left for work and try and salvage something.

There was also the matter of the second phone call he needed to make; a call that would solve many of his problems if he played his cards carefully.

Sitting there alone in the corner, Panton couldn't stop himself brooding on the hand that life in general had dealt him.

As a child he had been very close to his mother and sister as the three of them had one thing in common—a husband and a father who was an alcoholic, and who was physically and mentally abusive to both his wife and his children, but more so to him than his sister.

No matter how hard Panton tried to make his father love him and be proud of him, all he ever received was a cold shoulder.

The friction between father and son remained a constant throughout Panton's childhood and adolescence.

His father's chosen means of disciplining his son was a thick leather belt with a large buckle that carried the inscription 'Born to be Wild'.

Whether his father hit him with the belt, or with the more painful buckle, depended on how much alcohol the old man had poured down his throat that day.

Yet the young boy never stopped trying to make his father love him. But on the rare occasion the pair went out together, more often than not the boy still had to contend with his father's verbal abuse and persistent belittlement. Thankfully the one thing his father never did was to hit him in public.

Often in front of the few friends he had, the boy would be called dumb, stupid, ignorant, or worst of all, a sissy by his father.

Unable to put up with this abuse any longer, Panton had left home when he was just 17 and had not spoken to his father since.

Even when his beloved mother passed away after suffering a massive stroke, he couldn't bring himself to go to her funeral, knowing his father would be there, assuming the old man wasn't too drunk to attend.

His only family now was his sister Christine who lived an hour's car journey from Dorminster, and who he tried to meet up with at least once a month. Christine, happily married with two young children, had promised her brother that she would never let their father know where he was living.

Whilst she was still in fairly regular contact with her father, she had told Panton that after he had left home the old man had never spoken about him, nor ever mentioned his name again.

But even though Panton had told Christine that as far as he was concerned their father was as dead to him as their mother, deep down he knew that if he ever came into any money, by fair means or foul, he would go running back to the family home where the old man now lived on his own, waving a wad of cash and shouting out at the top of his voice 'Look dad, I told you I'd make something of my life'.

And in his dream, his father would take his hand, shake it and then hug him, saying, 'well done, welcome home, son.'

The sound of someone scraping a chair across the tiled floor brought him back to reality, and he grabbed a paper serviette to wipe the tears away from his eyes, before anyone might notice.

Still sat in the corner, he picked up his mobile phone and pressed a couple of buttons. After four rings, his call was answered.

"Hello Neil. I wondered if you might ring me. Have the police released you, or are you calling me from Wormwood Scrubs?"

One of the many things he liked about Debra Patterson was her keen sense of humour. Attractive and funny, what more could you ask for in a woman?

"Actually, I'm calling from the Tower of London where they've chained me up. I'm being guarded by a couple of Beefeaters at the moment," he replied.

"Seriously though, I'm glad they let you out," she replied. "It couldn't have been much fun."

"It wasn't. I can think of better ways to spend a few hours. Look Debra, can I come around and see you?" he asked.

There was silence on the other end of the phone and he was beginning to think she had ended the call.

"I'm sorry, Neil, but I'm off to work shortly. And I've already told you that it's far too soon for me to even think about going out with anybody. So let's leave it for six months or so. Call me up in the New Year and let's just see where I'm at with my life then. Who knows, you might have met someone else by then."

This time, it was Panton's turn to be silent as he thought how best to reply.

"OK," he said finally. "But you'll be sorry."

He pressed the end call button.

He immediately regretted finishing the call like that. It had come out all wrong. It must have sounded like a threat to her, when what he really meant to say was "You'll be sorry as you won't meet anyone else as nice as me."

But the damage was done.

In the back of his mind was the thought that the police, and Detective Sergeant Davison in particular, must have told Debra about his previous run-ins with the law.

Did they tell her about the couple of pub fights he'd been caught up in which had both led to court appearances, or the time when he had been nicked for driving without tax and insurance, a time when he was out of work and didn't have two halfpennies to rub together?

And what about the domestic with his wife earlier in the year which had ended when a neighbour dialled 999? No charge had been brought against him and he'd been let off with a warning.

And, of course, they knew nothing about the other half a dozen times when he had broken the law, the last time being just over three years ago.

He looked at his watch and decided it was time to make the second phone call, a follow-up to the one he had made yesterday evening at precisely 7:30 pm.

He'd told Hardcastle and Davison that at that time he'd been driving around trying to calm himself after losing the match against Middle Ash.

He had certainly been driving around—that wasn't a lie.

However, he had been driving around trying to find a telephone box that was still in working order. For what he wanted to say, he needed to find a telephone box that was not in busy area, nor somewhere he might be recognised or interrupted.

And he didn't want to use his mobile since calls made from it could be traced.

As he left Costa, he turned left and walked out of the shopping precinct towards the park, on his way to the railway station where he knew there were two telephones boxes. At least one of those should be working.

When he got there, he was surprised to find that both phones were working and, after looking carefully around him, he dialled the number he had rung less than 24 hours earlier. The person he was ringing was expecting another call from him.

The first time he rang there was no answer, even though he let it ring at least a dozen times. Swearing under his breath, he rang the number for a second time.

This time, after five rings, the phone was picked up.

"Hello."

"It's me," replied Panton.

"Go on," came the reply.

"I've just spent the last few hours with the police."

"And?"

"They had it in their mind that I might have killed Summers."

"What did you tell them?"

"Enough for them to realise that it wasn't me," answered Panton.

"So where do we go from here?" came the reply.

"Well, either I tell them that I know who did it, and then show them the photo on my mobile of you walking away from the back door of the pavilion, or you pay me what I need to keep me quiet. The choice is yours—but after today, the price has doubled."

"You have got to be joking."

"It's not a joke. That's the amount it will cost me to pay off my wife. I need to keep the house out of her hands," replied Panton.

"You need to give me time," was the reply. "I can't just go down to the bank and ask to borrow £50,000 just like that. I'll need at least a week to get that sort of sum together. Use some common sense, man."

"How much can you let me have straight away?" asked Panton.

"I might be able to let you have £5,000 within 48 hours. The rest will take a bit of time."

"I'll ring you again tomorrow. I'll let you have a time and a place where you can hand over the £5,000. If I don't get the rest within a few days, I'll go to the police and that's you sent down for life."

Panton put the receiver down and began the walk home. He was satisfied with how the conversation had gone.

Today was Monday, and he'd made good progress since yesterday evening. With any luck he would have five grand in his back pocket come Wednesday.

With another £45,000 to follow, he could pay off his wife and still have £25,000 to do whatever he wanted.

Top of the list was a decent holiday in the sun somewhere, and then a new car perhaps. It was time to ditch the Subaru.

It's just a shame that things had gone a bit pear-shaped with Debra Patterson.

He even thought about ringing her later in the week and inviting her on a no strings attached holiday in the Caribbean.

But at that precise moment, what was giving him almost as much pleasure as the money, was the fact that he was giving the police a bit of a run-around. After all, he knew far more than they did about who had killed Donald Summers.

"That'll teach them to mess me around," he muttered to himself.

He was convinced he had thought everything through and that he had his victim dangling just where he wanted him.

He was certain that nothing could go wrong.

Monday 6:15pm

Steve Hardcastle resisted the temptation to throw the phone across the office.

He'd just heard from Billy Kiernan that all the tests done on Neil Panton's cricket equipment, clothing and training shoes had come back negative.

If nothing else, it justified Hardcastle's decision to let Panton go, rather than keep him under lock and key overnight.

Now, for the time being at least, he and the team would have to turn their attentions elsewhere. The trouble with this, unfortunately, was that the list of alternative suspects was very small; in fact the number was a big fat zero.

Just as he let out a long, doleful sigh, Kath Pearson knocked on the open door and walked into Hardcastle's office.

"Like that is it, sir?"

"I'm afraid so, Kath," he replied, motioning her to sit down. "I've just heard that the tests on Panton's kit, clothing and trainers have all came back negative. I was expecting it, but even so, it's disappointing when it's finally confirmed. Deep down, I still harboured the hope that they would find a tiny speck of Summers's blood somewhere, just enough so we could charge him, and wipe that smug look off his face."

"I'm sure it's only a matter of time before we make a breakthrough," replied Pearson, "and it'll probably happen when we least expect it."

"I'm sure you're right, Kath. Anyway, how have you been getting on?" asked Hardcastle.

"Well, I've managed to speak to Jeremy Summers again. From what he told me, any baby pictures his brother might have had are very unlikely to be of Jeremy's kids as the brothers had never been particularly close, and he'd certainly never thought of asking Donald to be a godfather to any of them.

"He did say he would have a look at the photo if we could scan it and email him a copy."

"OK, I'll deal with that," replied Hardcastle. "I want to go back to Summers's place anyway, so I'll bring it back with me tomorrow morning. What else have you got?"

"I've spoken to Charlotte Thompson, one of Mr Summers's stepdaughters. The other one, Emily Farthing, is on holiday in the USA at the moment. Charlotte was extremely upset about her stepfather's murder. She said that whilst Donald had been a very private man, who rarely talked about his past, both she and her sister had absolutely adored him. He had been like a proper dad to them.

"She also asked if I could e mail a copy of the baby photo to her. She was certain she'd never seen it on show at the house where her mum and stepdad lived.

"And I've spoken to the doctor's surgery in Sheffield where Mr Summers was registered as a patient. The only visit he had made in recent times was to ask his GP for some sleeping pills. This was shortly after his wife passed away. He never went back for a repeat prescription, and that was the last they heard of him until they received a request for his records to be sent to the GP here in Dorminster."

"So, I think we can safely say that Mr Summers didn't know that he was walking around with a ticking time bomb inside him," said Hardcastle.

"It's such an irony," he continued, "that if he hadn't been murdered, his aorta could have ruptured and killed him at any time. If the killer had just waited for another week or two, Mother Nature might well have done the job for him."

"So you still think the killing could have been pre-planned?" asked Pearson.

"I do, even though there's no evidence one way or the other, I just don't see it as being spontaneous. The fact that there is so little for us to go on at the moment, suggests a fair bit of planning went in to it."

"But how would the killer have known that Summers was going to come off injured when he did?" asked Pearson. "Surely it wasn't prearranged?"

"That is one possibility," replied Hardcastle, "But it might just have been coincidence. Perhaps the killer had spent some time planning to murder Summers. Then, just by chance, he happened to be watching the cricket at Flitton yesterday and suddenly realised that Summers was one of the umpires. Then, when he went off midway during the game, the killer couldn't believe his luck, and took his chance.

"That's just one possibility, and I know it's a long shot. But there's absolutely nothing else specific to go on."

At that moment, Phil Davison appeared in the doorway.

"The local news is on the telly in a moment, boss."

"I'll put it on in here," said Hardcastle, pointing a remote control at the television in the corner of his office.

Davison and Pearson sat down to watch with the DI.

Within a couple of minutes, some archive footage of the Flitton Green Village Hall and cricket ground appeared on the screen with one of the regular presenters doing the voiceover.

'Dorminster Police are appealing for witnesses and information following the death under suspicious circumstances of a 66 year old man during a cricket match at Flitton Green Cricket Club yesterday afternoon.'

The picture then changed to the exterior of the regional police headquarters with the head of PR standing outside the main entrance. The name Alex Till appeared at the bottom of the screen. Speaking to camera, Till said:

'Dorminster Police were yesterday informed of a serious incident at Flitton Green Cricket Club shortly after 7pm.

Officers were on the scene within minutes. However, a short time after their arrival a 66 year old local man was pronounced dead at the scene from injuries received.

The death is considered to be suspicious and a murder investigation has been launched by the Dorminster Major Crimes Unit.

This is a fast-moving investigation with a number of lines of enquiry currently being pursued. We would appeal to anyone who was in the vicinity of the Flitton Green Village Hall and Cricket Club between 1pm and 7pm yesterday to contact Dorminster Police as a matter of urgency.'

The picture on the television screen then changed to a live studio shot with the presenter sat behind a desk who proceeded to give the telephone number of DI Hardcastle's unit, with the number repeated at the bottom of the screen. There was a short silence whilst the phone number remained on screen, before the presenter began his next story line.

"All we need to do now is to sit and wait for the telephone to start ringing," said Hardcastle, switching the television off.

On cue, two telephones began to ring simultaneously in the outer office.

"Have we got enough bodies manning the phones, Kath?"

"Yes sir, I've got that all arranged."

"Well done. That appeal was just what we needed. Is the same info going out on the radio?"

"Yes sir, on the hour, every hour. And press releases have been e mailed to all relevant local media," replied Pearson. "So if you'll excuse me, I'll go and lend a hand with the phones."

As Pearson left the office, Phil Davison moved into the chair she had vacated.

"I'll be here for a while yet boss, why don't you go home. It's been a long old 24 hours. You must be knackered."

"No more than you, Phil," replied Hardcastle. "Have you heard that Panton's kit and trainers were all clean?"

"Yes, I was just talking to Billy. It was no real surprise though was it. Let's hope the appeal brings in more than just a couple of phone calls," said Davison pointedly, as the phones had stopped ringing as quickly as they'd started.

Hardcastle smiled and nodded.

They sat in silence for a couple of minutes, both deep in thought.

"You know, Phil," said Hardcastle eventually, "I just think we are missing something. The more I think about things, the more I feel that the answer lies in our victim's past.

"We know the killer had the means and the opportunity, but we've no idea whatsoever of his motive. We need to concentrate our resources in pulling together the various strands of Donald Summers's life.

"Sometime in his past he must have done something pretty serious, serious enough for someone to hold a real grudge against him. Who knows, it could even date back to when he first lived around these parts. And when he returned decades later, perhaps that past came back to haunt him and ended up with him being battered to death yesterday afternoon."

"That certainly sounds feasible, boss."

"We'll get moving on this first thing in the morning," said Hardcastle. "I'm going to go back to Summers's bungalow on my way in to the office in the morning and have another rummage around. There's always the chance that we might have missed something."

A telephone started ringing somewhere.

"Let's give it an hour or so, Phil, and then call it a night. There's not much else we can do this evening. Tomorrow's another day."

Monday 8:35pm

On his way home, Steve Hardcastle suddenly remembered the promise he'd made that morning to his wife Jenny that he would do his level best to get home at a reasonable time that afternoon.

As he pulled into the driveway and looked at the clock on the dashboard, he knew that, not for the first time during their marriage, he was going to be in the doghouse.

"Now the face is familiar, I just can't remember the name," said Jenny as he walked into their kitchen. "Your dinner is in the dog by the way," she added.

"We don't have a dog," replied Hardcastle after a couple of seconds.

"Well, it would have been if we'd had one," she said with a grin on her face.

"I'm so sorry, love," said Hardcastle apologetically, "I really did try to get away early, but we've been up against it for most of the day."

"I know. I saw the appeal on the news. I guessed you'd be late. Frankly, by your normal standards, you're really quite early," replied Jenny. "Want to talk about it?"

"I'll see how I feel after I've eaten dinner. Any chance you can get it out of our imaginary dog?"

"I'll do a deal with you. I'll get your dinner organised if you go up and help Ethan with his maths homework. He seemed a bit stuck when I looked in on him earlier."

"Maths. Me?" was her husband's reply.

"Well, go and lend him some moral support. You know Ethan, he'll figure it out some way or another," replied Jenny.

He gave his wife a peck on the cheek and took the stairs two at a time. There was no sign of their younger son Thomas in his bedroom, and Hardcastle found both boys watching a Marvel Super Heroes film on the television in Ethan's room.

"Hi boys."

"Hi dad," replied the pair in unison, without looking at him.

"Mum said you needed some help with your homework, Ethan."

"I finished that ages ago," replied his eldest son. "Anyway, it was algebra, and it was way out of your league, dad," replied Ethan.

"Shush," said Thomas, "I'm trying to follow the film."

"OK," said Hardcastle in an exaggerated whisper. "I'll pretend to mum that I sorted your algebra out, so I can have my dinner."

"Get real, dad. Mum knows you're rubbish at maths. You struggle with your two times table!" said Ethan, cheekily.

"That's true," replied Hardcastle. "But I'll still try it on and see if I can get away with it. Back me up, if she asks."

He had a big grin on his face as he walked back down the stairs to the kitchen.

"What are you grinning at?" asked his wife.

"I was just thinking. I might be the boss at work, but I'm a distant fourth in this household."

"Fifth, you mean," replied Jenny. "The imaginary dog comes before you."

"What's for dinner then?"

"Spag Bol. Is that OK?" replied Jenny, knowing that it was one of his favourites.

"Sure is."

An hour or so later, he and Jenny were relaxing in their lounge watching an early James Bond film with Sean Connery playing Bond. They had both seen the film a couple of times before and were able to chat away to each other without losing the plot of the film.

As usual, Jenny had quietly encouraged her husband to talk about the case he was working on. She was a good listener and confined her responses to the occasional nod here and there until he got to the point where he was speculating on the killer's motive.

"That's obvious, isn't it?" she said. "It has to be money, or a woman, or both."

"Probably, but whoever the killer is, he—"

"Or she," interrupted Jenny.

"OK. Whoever the killer is, if he or she is the person who Summers upset in the first place, they would probably be in their sixties now. Alternatively, he or she could be a relative or very close friend of Summers's victim, in which case they could be any age from teenager to pensioner.

"We've got nothing concrete to go on at the moment, but I'm convinced the key to solving this case is buried somewhere in the dead man's past. Whichever it is, we are going to have to dig deep into the years he spent in the Dorminster area, up until he moved to Yorkshire in 1993. If we can discover his secret, there's a good chance it will lead us to his killer."

"You make it sound pretty straightforward. But is it going to be that easy?" asked Jenny.

"I wish it was," replied her husband. "The problem is it seems that the dead guy was a very private man. If he shared his secret with anyone, it would have been his wife, and unfortunately she passed away just over a year ago.

"And we've also spoken to the man in Yorkshire who was Summers's best friend, but he knew nothing that could shed any light on the matter.

"So, in the morning, we will start delving deep into the first four decades of our victim's life, stripping it bare layer by layer," said Hardcastle, struggling to stifle a yawn.

Just a couple of hours sleep in the last thirty-six was suddenly catching up on him.

"Why don't you go up to bed?" said Jenny.

"We've got to tidy up the kitchen first."

"Don't worry, I'll do that. You go on up. I won't be long."

"If you're sure you don't mind?" asked Hardcastle, this time unable to stifle the yawn. "You know, I don't deserve you."

"Of course you don't," said Jenny. "But as I'm going into town tomorrow to book that week away you promised, I'm in a fairly generous mood at the moment."

This time Hardcastle took the stairs a lot slower than when he'd first got home. And this time, when he looked into Thomas's room, he found his youngest son fast asleep. He then looked around the door of Ethan's room and found the fourteen-year-old tapping away on his mobile phone.

"Another 10 minutes, then turn your light off please Ethan."

"OK," replied Ethan, without taking his eyes off the screen of his iPhone. "Goodnight dad."

"Goodnight boy."

Hardcastle opened the door to his and Jenny's bedroom. He sat down on the bed, trying to summon up the energy to undress himself.

Ten minutes later, Jenny came up the stairs. She too looked in on the sleeping Thomas, and then tapped on the door of Ethan's room, where she found her eldest boy still texting away on his phone.

"Another 10 minutes, then turn your light off please Ethan," she said.

"OK," replied Ethan, again without taking his eyes off the screen of his iPhone. "Goodnight mum."

"Goodnight sweetheart."

Jenny opened the door to the large double bedroom, and found her husband fast asleep on top of the duvet.

He was still fully clothed.

Monday 8:45pm

As Phil Davison pulled into the driveway of the bungalow he shared with his wife Sarah, he had a quick glance at his watch which he wore on his right wrist. It was a quarter to nine. Once again, he was late home.

He knew, however, that his wife would be waiting to greet him with a beaming smile. He put the key in the lock and opened the front door, calling out "I'm home sweetheart," as usual.

"It's a good job that the milkman just left by the back door then," came the reply.

He walked into the lounge just as his wife was struggling to get out of the armchair.

"Stay there love, there's no need for you to move. Been watching anything good on the telly?"

"Yes," replied Sarah, "I've just finished watching *The Blue Lamp*. Do you remember it? They made it in the 1950s in black and white with Jack Warner playing PC George Dixon."

"Isn't that the one where they kill off Dixon midway through the film?" asked her husband.

"That's the one. And then the BBC brought him back to life in *Dixon of Dock Green*. Did you know that the series ran for over 20 years?" replied Sarah. "I checked that on my iPad."

Both Phil and Sarah enjoyed police dramas, one of the many things they had in common. Sarah had also been in the police force, which is how the pair had first met. Despite Phil being ten years older than her, they had got on famously from day one, and had married within the year.

He had been a detective constable in the CID at the time, and was promoted to detective sergeant just six months later. Things were going really well for them, and they had been discussing starting a family when Sarah had her accident.

They called it 'the accident', but in reality it was no accident. She had been the victim of a hit and run whilst on duty, trying to stop two young hooligans who had just robbed a newsagent's at knifepoint.

The robbers, who got away with just £108, were eventually caught and both received eight year sentences. They were out of prison within five. But it was a different story for Sarah.

She had spent 17 days in intensive care, with the life-changing injuries she had suffered that day, injuries that put an end to her career in the police force.

But if that wasn't bad enough, the day she was told that she would never be able to have children left her and her husband utterly devastated. A child would have made their marriage complete, and one moment of sheer madness by two petty thieves had robbed them of that dream.

Despite several operations and hundreds of hours of physiotherapy, Sarah was eventually told that, at best, she would only ever be able to walk a few paces without the aid of a walking stick.

The years that followed the accident were very difficult for husband and wife as they struggled to adapt to their new circumstances. They had discussed the possibility of adopting a child, but this was as far as they got. It soon became obvious that physically Sarah would never be able to cope.

When they had first married, they talked about Phil taking his inspector's exams, and Sarah possibly taking the sergeant's.

However, shortly after the accident, it became obvious to Phil that any spare time he had would have to be spent caring for his wife, so taking exams was completely out of the question.

And as the years went on, he also realised that he was not really inspector material anyway. He enjoyed being a number two, rather than being the 'boss'.

Well, that was what he would tell friends and family.

However, as the saying goes, *sometimes good can come out of bad situations.*

Sarah was one of those people that had always felt there was a book inside of her just waiting to be written.

At first she found it therapeutic to simply commit to paper the details of her accident and the physical and mental pain that followed over the years. By the time she had finished writing this, she realised that she had finally accepted that how she was now, was how she was going to be for the rest of her life.

And out of what she had written sprang her very first novel, a story that was semi-autobiographical, as the hero of the story was a young WPC who had suffered serious injuries whilst answering a 999 call. However, Sarah's fictitious WPC recovered and would later move up the ranks until she became a detective inspector. To date, Sarah had written five novels about the character using a pseudonym, and only very close family and friends knew that Sarah was in fact the author.

The extra money that her books brought in enabled them to buy and adapt the bungalow they were now living in. Situated in a semi-rural area, the tranquillity that the property afforded meant that they couldn't see themselves ever wishing to move away.

Having made sure Sarah had eaten well during the day; Phil went into the kitchen, took out an M&S ready meal from the freezer and put it in the microwave.

Once he had eaten, he would then sit in the armchair next to his wife and tell her all about his day—a sort of debriefing session. It was good for Phil to get anything he needed off his chest, and good for Sarah, as whatever her husband told her, might eventually find its way into one of her books—with the names changed to protect the innocent, as the saying goes.

And, just occasionally, she would spot something, or come up with an angle that her husband and his colleagues at work hadn't yet thought about.

On those occasions, Phil would think to himself that Sarah would have made one hell of a detective.

Monday 8:55pm

As Kath Pearson pulled up outside the two-bedroom semi she shared with her husband Jason, she could tell he wasn't home as his white Renault van was nowhere to be seen.

With no driveway, parking close to the house was never easy and occasionally one or both of them would find themselves parked up a fair distance away, since many of the neighbouring properties had dropped kerbs outside, reducing even further the available parking for those that hadn't.

As a self-employed plumber specialising in installing and repairing boilers, Jason, like Kath, often worked long and irregular hours, something that both of them had had to get used to.

The couple had originally met when they both attended the same secondary school, although they were never in the same class as Jason was two years older.

Once Jason had left school, they lost touch with one another with both following different career paths.

Kath went to university where she completed a law degree, and subsequently joined the police force. Jason managed to get an apprenticeship with a large central heating manufacturer and then went to work for his father in the family plumbing business, before going it alone.

After two fairly long-term unsuccessful relationships, Kath was on a 'girl's night out' when she bumped into Jason who was out having a drink with his older brother.

The pair exchanged telephone numbers, and within two months they were living together and were married within the year. That had been five years ago, and it was fair to say that there were times when being married hadn't lived up to her expectations.

She was certain that Jason felt the same way.

They had discussed starting a family as Jason in particular thought that this might bring them closer together, but Kath hadn't been exactly enthusiastic with the idea, which caused more friction between them.

As she opened the front door, Kath turned on the outside light, assuming it would be dark by the time Jason finished work for the day.

She walked into the kitchen, put her handbag on the worktop, and took out her mobile phone with the intention of sending her husband a text to ask if he knew what time he would be home. However, she decided against it, and instead went to a cupboard, took out a Genoa cake and cut herself a very generous slice.

This she took into the lounge, together with a glass of white wine, and sat down on the sofa in total darkness, before kicking off her shoes. She quickly polished off the cake and was just contemplating a second slice, when she heard the sound of an incoming text on her mobile phone which she had left in the kitchen.

Taking her plate with her she returned to the kitchen, cutting off another slice of Genoa cake before picking up her phone.

The message was from Jason: *Just popping into The Cricketers for a quick pint. I'll get myself a kebab on the way home.*

OK. I've an early start tomorrow so try not to wake me up when you get home was her reply.

From past experience, a quick pint meant she probably wouldn't see him this side of midnight. And by that time, she hoped she would definitely be fast asleep. If not, she would pretend to be when Jason finally came up to bed.

Not that he would have been drinking, as he knew he couldn't afford to lose his driving licence if he was caught driving over the legal limit. Because of that, Jason would make the pint last the evening whilst he played pool with his friends from the pub's pool team, because he was there for the game and not the beer.

Some women were golf widows, and others cricketing widows. Kath Pearson was a pool widow as her husband filled every minute of his leisure time shooting pool, a game which he had only become serious about some 10 months earlier, when he had first played a couple of frames with his brother.

To his amazement (and to his brother's, since Jason had shown no aptitude whatsoever for ball games throughout his life), he discovered that he was a natural. Would that change if they were to have a baby? Would Jason really be able to cut back drastically on the amount of pool he played?

Kath doubted it, so obsessed with the game had he become.

At least she didn't have to make an immediate decision about the baby, as she was still in the early weeks of her pregnancy. It would be some time before she showed any visible signs.

But she desperately felt the need to discuss her dilemma with someone. Someone close, who could look objectively at her predicament. Unfortunately, for the first time she could remember, she knew she couldn't talk to the one person she would normally turn to whenever she felt the need to discuss a problem.

Her friendship with Phil Davison was very precious to her; increasingly of late she felt that that friendship meant more to her than her marriage to her husband.

Phil was so level-headed and such a good listener that he invariably came up with sound and practical advice whenever she felt the need to use him as a sounding board. This included discussing both work related issues and personal problems.

Phil knew about the difficulties Kath had been having with her marriage, as she had confided in him a few months back. His advice then had been to have a heart to heart discussion with Jason.

She knew Phil's advice was sound, but she just hadn't been able to bring the subject up with her husband. But on this occasion she knew it would be totally wrong and utterly selfish of her to ask Phil for his advice.

How could she talk to him about whether or not she should keep the baby that she was expecting when he and Sarah had been so cruelly denied the opportunity to have one of their own?

She was adamant that she would not risk losing or damaging the friendship she shared with Phil. It was that important to her.

And if it meant not talking to Jason, then so be it.

Kath and Jason Pearson had become like ships that pass in the night, and the distance between those ships was growing by the day.

If she wasn't careful, they would soon be too far out of sight.

Monday 9pm

About the same time as Kath Pearson arrived home, the telephone rang in the hall of Neil Panton's house. At the time, he was laying on his sofa watching a film called *World War Z* on his DVD player. Starring Brad Pitt, it was a film he had watched several times before, with the storyline about a plague that was quickly turning the earth's population into zombies. It was right up his street.

He picked up the DVD remote control and put the film on pause before answering the call, expecting it to be someone trying to sell him double glazing, or asking if he'd made a claim against any lender who might have mis-sold him PPI cover.

Those types of calls got right up his nose.

Panton snatched at the phone. His normal response to nuisance calls was to tell the person on the other end of the phone to 'bugger off and get a proper job'.

"Yes," he snapped down the phone.

"I see you are being your normal pleasant self," was the sarcastic reply.

It was, to his surprise, his estranged wife Tanya, who he hadn't spoken to for over three months. They had parted a couple of months before that; just a week or so after the police had been called out by neighbours when an argument between the pair seemed to be getting out of hand. Panton had been let off with a warning after a good talking to from the two cops who had attended the scene.

His attempts at reconciliation had been met with a stubborn refusal from his wife, and communication between them had quickly become increasingly strained and vitriolic, so much so that, almost inevitably, Tanya had felt she was left with no option other than to seek legal advice.

The first letter from her solicitor was completely ignored by Panton, as were the second, third and fourth.

However, the fifth was the one he really couldn't afford to ignore, as it advised him that Tanya was seeking a divorce on the grounds of his unreasonable behaviour, and cited several instances where he had been violent towards her during the course of their marriage. The letter also gave several examples of when Panton had verbally abused and threatened her, including the instance when the police were called at the beginning of the year.

However, as the marriage had been childless, continued the letter, Mrs Panton would be reasonable with regard to any financial settlement, if Panton accepted that the marriage had irretrievably broken down and if he agreed not to contest his wife's application for a divorce.

The letter further stated that should Panton accept those terms, Mrs Panton would accept a payment of £20,000 in respect of her 50% share of the equity in the matrimonial home, and a further payment of £4,500 in respect of her share of the contents of the home, and a payment of £500 being his contribution towards her legal costs.

After reading this letter, his first instinct was to drive the 40 miles or so to Tanya's parents' house, where he assumed she was now living, and have it out with her face to face.

However, realising that this might be playing into her hands, Panton decided to go to the local Citizen's Advice Bureau first and see what they had to say. If he didn't like the advice the CAB gave him, then he would still go to her parent's house, have it out with her, and sod the consequences.

As it happened, the CAB solicitor turned out to be someone who he could relate to and who didn't beat about the bush, and who let him have it straight from the hip. He left Panton in no doubt that what his wife was asking for was the very best that he could expect.

If he decided to contest either the divorce, or the suggested financial arrangement, he would almost certainly find himself on the losing side and would end up far worse off. He would also rack up some pretty hefty legal costs.

After a few drinks in the pub around the corner from the CAB office, Panton had decided that he had no choice other than to go along with what Tanya was asking for. He consoled himself with the thought that one day, long after the divorce had gone through, he would get revenge on her one way or another. Panton was a man who held a grudge against anyone who dared to cross him.

"Are you still there?" asked Tanya, as there had been several seconds of silence from his end of the phone.

"I'm here. What do you want? Hurry up, I'm busy at the moment," he replied.

"What are you up to then? Watching some crap zombie film on the telly?"

Panton slammed down the phone. He knew that if whatever she was calling about was that important to her, she would soon ring back.

Sure enough, 10 seconds later, the phone rang again.

"Yes."

"Look Neil. Can't we for once have a civilised conversation?" she asked. "It's pointless arguing. The sooner we get things sorted out, the sooner we can both move on."

"OK. I'm listening," replied Panton.

"You've had my solicitor's latest letter for over a week now. Are you going to ignore this one like you've ignored the other four? My solicitor said that I'm being uncommonly reasonable. In fact, she wanted me to go for more money."

"Typical, another bloody woman trying to screw me," he replied; but this time, some of the harshness had left his voice, something that Tanya instantly recognised.

"Well, she is a bit of an old dragon," said Tanya. "Actually, she scares the life out of me."

There was another pause from Panton.

"Look Neil, I'm ringing you to try and get things moving. I have a little proposition for you."

"Go on, I'm listening," replied Panton, now just a little bit interested.

"I'm willing to reduce what I'm asking for overall by £2,000 to £23,000," said Tanya, "on one condition. You let me have £3,000 cash by Wednesday at the latest. You can let me have the remaining £20,000 when the divorce is finalised."

"Why do you need £3,000 so quickly?"

"I could tell you it's none of your business, but this time I won't," replied Tanya. "As it happens, I've seen a little flat which would really suit me. It's only a 10-minute walk from my mum and dad's house, and they're giving me £3,000 towards the deposit of £6,000. That's why I'm asking you for the other £3,000."

"It's all working out nicely for you, isn't it?" replied Panton, experiencing a pang or two of jealousy.

"Come on Neil, you know that things hadn't been good between us for ages. We've both got an opportunity now for fresh starts."

"Yeah, but unlike you I don't have any parents to help me out," replied Panton, with a mixture of bitterness and sarcasm.

Tanya knew she shouldn't rise to the bait. From past experience she had learnt how quickly her husband's attitude could change from being affable to being abusive.

She had in fact only told Panton half the story. She hadn't mentioned that she'd been seeing someone for several months and that a pregnancy test done three days earlier had been positive. Had she done so, he would have gone into total meltdown, and she would have feared not only for her own safety, but also for her boyfriend's, particularly as he was someone who Panton knew fairly well.

She knew it was only a matter of time before her husband found out the truth, but she and her boyfriend would have to deal with that as and when it happened.

"So, what do you say?" she asked. "Can you do it? Can you let me have £3,000 by Wednesday?"

Panton needed time to think about Tanya's offer. At that precise moment he had the grand sum of £89.43 in his bank account and a further £2.74 in his building society easy access account.

Moreover, his credit rating was just about as low as it could get, so that left him with just the one option. He would need to make a phone call.

"I'll do what I can—but no promises," he replied finally.

"Thank you. When do you think you might be able to let me know?" asked Tanya.

"I'll call you when I can. Should I ring you at your parents' house, or are you going to give me your new mobile number?" asked Panton.

"I'd prefer it if you rang me at mum and dad's," replied Tanya.

"OK. As I said, I'll do what I can."

Panton put the phone down. It was a no-brainer really. Giving Tanya £3,000 now would save him £2,000, and the money saved would pay for the holiday he'd promised himself.

He decided to strike whilst the iron was hot and switched off the DVD player and the television.

Within ten minutes he had parked up some three hundred yards away from a telephone box. Blackmailing someone was a completely new experience for him and he was taking no chance that someone might see him and remember the make and registration number of his car. Unlikely as that was, Panton had told himself better to be safe than sorry.

He dialled the number from memory and waited for the call to be answered. He sensed his heart was beating faster than normal and he was feeling slightly nauseous, as increased levels of adrenaline were pumping around his body.

"Hello."

"It's me again."

"What now?"

"Have you got the £5,000?"

"I thought you said you'd ring me tomorrow?"

"Things have changed. Have you got the money?" repeated Panton.

"Not yet."

"I must have the five grand tomorrow in cash. I'll ring you tomorrow evening and tell you where and when you can hand it over to me."

"What if I can't get that much cash together by then?"

"Then you'll have the police knocking on your front door, and it'll be goodbye Dorminster, hello Parkhurst. It's your choice, my old mate."

"I'll see what I can do. Ring me after 6pm. I won't have anything to tell you until then."

Panton didn't like to be told what to do at the best of times, certainly not by someone he'd got just where he wanted. He was getting considerable pleasure from dangling his victim on a piece of string.

"I'll ring you when I want, not when you say," replied Panton, who slammed the phone down with such force that he was lucky it didn't smash into little pieces.

As he opened the door of the telephone box, and sauntered leisurely back to his car, he began to whistle the old ABBA song, *Money, Money, Money*, happy now with how well things seemed to be going for him at long last.

Tuesday 5:35am

When Steve Hardcastle woke up at 5:35am, he realised he was still fully clothed and lying on top of the duvet. He turned his head to the left and saw that Jenny was fast asleep, tucked underneath the duvet. A light sleeper, her husband's sudden movement woke her up.

"Hiya," she said sleepily. "Sleep OK?"

"Like a log. You?" he asked.

"Yeah, good thanks."

"Why didn't you wake me up when you came to bed?"

"I was worried that if I did, you wouldn't be able to go back to sleep. I know you've got a lot on your mind at the moment."

"Thanks," he replied, rubbing his eyes. "Sorry, but I need to get up now. I've told the team that I'm going to have another look around Donald Summers's bungalow on my way to work. No need for you to get up though. Have a lay in."

"Don't be daft. Knowing you, you won't have anything to eat if I don't get up. You go and have a quick shower and I'll do you some eggs and bacon."

He leant across, kissed her gently on the lips and rolled off the bed.

A quarter of an hour later, now dressed in his favourite dark blue suit, he walked into a kitchen smelling of bacon and strong filtered coffee. The bacon was cooked just as he liked it—very crisp and one step short of being cremated.

"I don't suppose there's any point in me asking what time we'll see you this evening, but please try and get home before the boys go to bed, if you can," asked Jenny as her husband polished off the remains of his breakfast.

"I promise I'll do my best," he said finishing off his coffee and grabbing a slice of buttered toast. He kissed Jenny on her left cheek, grabbed his car keys off the worktop and was gone.

As the door shut behind him, Jenny found herself wiping away a small tear from the corner of her right eye.

With little traffic on the road at that time of the morning, Hardcastle was soon walking up the path to the front door of Donald Summers's bungalow.

He guessed that it was too early even for Mrs Lee, the next door neighbour, as her curtains remained firmly closed.

Putting on a pair of blue latex gloves, he decided to start his search with the garage. Apart from the Jaguar, there was little room for anything else, and all seemed as it had been yesterday.

Once inside the bungalow, he decided to start with the dining room. As soon as he walked through the door his eyes went to top of the bureau. He took a sharp intake of breathe.

The small photograph of the young child in a pushchair was no longer there. "Bloody hell," he said out loud.

He pulled a dining room chair to one side and was about to sit down to gather his thoughts, when he realised he needed to speak to Billy Kiernan and ask him to get some CSIs to the bungalow as soon as possible.

The only person who could have taken away the photo had to be the killer using the keys he had taken from Donald Summers's jacket as he left the umpire's room on Sunday afternoon.

If the killer had been roaming around the bungalow during the night, he needed the CSIs on site to see if he had left any trace evidence behind him, although he thought that was highly unlikely.

He pressed Kiernan's number on his mobile. After a couple of rings, the CSM's voice mail kicked in and Hardcastle left a brief message which he hoped Kiernan would pick up sooner rather than later.

He cautiously continued his search, but as far as he could tell, nothing else had been taken.

As he was finishing off his search in the lounge, his mobile phone rang. It was Billy Kiernan telling him that two of his chaps were already on their way over to the bungalow.

Just as he was putting his phone back into his jacket pocket there was a gentle tap on the front door. The CSIs had arrived.

He explained why he had called them in, gave them the keys to the bungalow and asked that they return them to Kath Pearson at the nick when they had finished.

Closing the door quietly behind him, Hardcastle walked down the bungalow's front path and decided to see if Mrs Lee was up yet. Tapping lightly on her front door in case she was still in bed, he was taken by surprise when it was opened straight away. Already dressed and looking immaculate, it was obvious she was an early riser, and had been waiting for him to knock on her door.

As expected though, she told him that she hadn't heard a sound from the bungalow during the night.

Turning down her offer of a cup of tea, Hardcastle got into his Range Rover and made his way to the office, where he found Phil Davison, Kath Pearson, Alan Rutherford, Paul Taylor and Isha Hussein, another of his young DCs, already hard at work.

"Morning everybody."

"Morning boss," said Davison. "How did it go at Summers's bungalow?"

"Nothing much to report, other than the photograph of the young kiddy has gone."

"You're joking," replied Phil Davison, clearly shocked at this revelation.

"I wish I was, Phil. The killer obviously paid the bungalow a visit during the night."

The office had gone quiet, as everyone had turned their attention to the DI. This was a development no-one had expected.

"Let me just get rid of my jacket and briefcase and I'll fill you all in," said Hardcastle walking towards his office. He also wanted to see if there were any messages on his desk or on his office phone. There were none. He wasn't that surprised given how late he had left yesterday evening.

A minute or so later, he was back in the outer office.

"OK, as I said, the first thing I noticed after I let myself in was that the photo on top of the bureau had gone. It stumped me for a second or two, but the only possibility is that the killer had also been in the bungalow and must have taken it away with him.

"I checked with the next door neighbour, but she hadn't seen or heard a thing.

"I called Billy Kiernan and left a message on his phone and two of his CSIs turned up just as I was leaving.

"I think the chances of them finding anything are pretty slim. By the way Kath, they're going to drop in the keys to the bungalow, so perhaps you can look after them. And I think we ought to change all the locks, including the garage door. I don't think the killer will chance it for a second time, but you can never say never, so perhaps you can get someone to organise that ASAP please, Kath."

"Of course I will sir," replied the DS.

"So, what does this tell us about our man?" asked Hardcastle.

"I'd say he must be a pretty cool customer," ventured DC Rutherford.

"And at least we now know for certain that he's got Mr Summers's keys," chimed in DC Hussein, "and most probably his wallet. So we don't need to search for them anymore."

"The photo he took away with him must be the link between him and Summers. Why else would he take it? Find the link and we find the killer," said DC Taylor.

"Exactly," replied Hardcastle. "Another point that occurred to me is the killer might have been in the bungalow before, when Summers was alive and seen the photo then. He might even have been someone Summers had considered a friend."

"Or maybe he just went to the house last night to make sure there wasn't anything there that could link him to the killing," chipped in Davison. "He saw the photo and took it away with him. He's either still got it or by now he's torn it up and ditched the frame."

"Either way, it did make him break cover," said Pearson. "This could be a big mistake."

"But leaving the photo there might have been an even bigger mistake," suggested Hardcastle. "One way or another, he must have considered going to the bungalow was a risk worth taking. So let's see if the CSIs come up with anything. In the meantime, Kath, how did last night's appeal go? How many people did it flush out?"

"We received 17 calls, sir. Of those, 2 were a waste of time, but we have 15 to follow up. We have 7 people going to the village hall to make their statements, 6 are coming in here and we'll see the other two in their homes. We should have them all completed by lunchtime, or early afternoon at the latest.

"We can then cross-reference these with the statements we already have, and see if there is any commonality between them. Paul and Isha will be working on that."

"Thanks Kath," replied Hardcastle. "In the meantime, I want us to delve as deep as possible into Summers's past from when his parents moved to Dorminster, when he would have been four or five, right up to the time when he moved to Sheffield in 1993.

"Ideally, we want to find someone he went to school with. I know that that was over 50 years ago, but there must be someone out there who will remember him from their schooldays. We also know that Summers worked in an accountant's office from 1970 to 1975, and then joined a hotel as finance manager where he stayed until 1984. By that time he was in his early thirties.

"I know that there is every chance that neither the accountant's nor the hotel is still in business, but they might have changed hands or just changed their names in the meantime. In the case of the hotel, we might find that it is now part of a big chain.

"From 1984 until 1993 when he moved to Sheffield, Summers worked locally for the County and Country Building Society. Now we know that the County and Country still exists, so there is a strong chance that we can track down someone who also worked for the C&C. Anyone joining them straight from school, around about the same time as Summers joined, would only be in their early fifties now.

"Kath, your man Martin Baldwin in Sheffield should be able to help there," continued Hardcastle. "And it's worth talking to Richard Askell, the cricket league secretary. He might be a useful source of background information.

"In the meantime, I'll speak to Alex Till at HQ and ask him to issue another media release, this time releasing the victim's name. It's always possible that this will generate a response from those who may have known Summers in the past. OK, let's have a catch-up at midday, unless something urgent crops up in the meantime."

Back in his office, Hardcastle was feeling angry with himself. If only he had brought back the photo yesterday when he had had the chance to. The only saving grace was the probability that the photo, like Paul Taylor had said, was the link between Summers and his killer.

At least it was something to go on, but discovering the nature of that link was not going to be easy.

Tuesday 11:30am

Neil Panton looked at his watch and saw that the dial was almost completely obscured; it was covered by a large blob of grease. He reached for the cleanest rag he could see on the workbench, wiped the dial and saw that it was now 11:30am.

Normally, he would have taken off his watch whilst he was working, but today was different. He needed to keep a check on the time.

As the old saying goes, *a watched kettle never boils* and time seemed to be dragging, even though he had had an early start and had a fairly busy day still ahead of him. Normally, busy days just flew by. But today was different.

Prompt at 8:30am, one of his regulars had dropped off his 2009 Mazda MX-5 for a routine service. He had virtually finished this when his second job of the day arrived, half an hour early. The car, a thirteen-year-old Ford Focus with a power steering problem, was brought in by a lad of 19 who Panton knew through cricket. He expected to finish this around mid-afternoon, and had managed to squeeze in a third job, a 2006 Peugeot 207 with an electrical fault. With any luck though, he should still be finished by 6pm.

Despite having his hands full work-wise, he was having difficulty in concentrating on the jobs in hand. His mind kept returning to the two telephone calls he was due to make later in the day.

The one to his wife would be the more straightforward of the two, and he would make that after he'd made the first call. Tanya would be well pleased when he told her that he'd managed to get the £3,000 she needed, and he would arrange to meet her lunchtime tomorrow to hand over the cash.

The other call was far more problematic.

Panton had no qualms about blackmailing the man who had brutally murdered Donald Summers. Nor did he have any qualms about hiding the identity of the killer from the police.

He considered that a fair pay back. After all they had buggered up his relationship with Debra Patterson.

His biggest concern was dealing with a man who was capable of launching such a savage attack on an old age pensioner, killing him in the process.

He had no idea why this man had killed Summers, and, as it happened, he wasn't really that interested in the motive; all he was interested in was the money.

To most people, £50,000 was a heck of a lot of money. But he knew the guy he was blackmailing could well afford it. Sure, it might take him a while to get that much cash together, but it wouldn't break the bank.

No, what was niggling away at the back of his mind was that having killed once, there was always the possibility that the man might try to do it again.

Panton looked at his watch again. He had plenty of thinking time ahead of him whilst he was working on his customer's cars, and he resolved to take every precaution to make sure he didn't become the killer's second victim.

I'm a bit too clever for that to happen, he told himself.

Tuesday 1pm

Hardcastle spent much of the morning on the telephone, and trying to clear the mountain of paper work that had been accumulating on his desk, much of which was internal memos and updates to various procedural manuals. Because of the volume of work he had decided to put back the planned midday meeting by an hour. As it happened everyone else in his team was grateful for the extra 60 minutes.

The first phone call Hardcastle made had been to Alex Till, Head of PR, to ask him if he could now arrange to go public with the identity of the victim.

"And can you add that we particularly want to hear from anyone who might have come into contact with Donald Summers since the beginning of the year, and from anyone who might have known him prior to 1993. That was when he went to work in Sheffield, by the way."

Always anxious to oblige, Till had told Hardcastle that he would have a media release ready in time for the lunchtime news on both television and radio.

One of the many calls Hardcastle had taken had been from Billy Kiernan who had confirmed, as expected, that his chaps had found nothing new at the bungalow.

"I think we are dealing with one tricky customer here, Steve," Kiernan had told Hardcastle. "I'm sorry we haven't been able to come up with anything remotely resembling a lead. It hasn't been for want of trying."

When Hardcastle started the meeting on the stroke of 1pm, he noticed that some of Billy Kiernan's colleagues had taken the trouble to come to the meeting. He began by thanking them for attending and then telling those assembled what Kiernan had told him.

"I can only endorse what Mr Kiernan said. Our man appears to be a very cool customer.

"Now, the next question we have to ask ourselves is why was the killer at the cricket ground on Sunday? Was he there to watch the game? If he was, does that mean he's connected to either of the two teams, or is he just a cricket lover in general? Either way, in my opinion, it suggests that this wasn't the first time he'd been to the ground.

"If he wasn't at the ground to watch the cricket, what other reasons would explain why he was there? Was he there with his family so his children could use the play equipment, or was he there to have something to eat and drink?

"I think it is highly unlikely that he had company. I cannot see anyone committing such a violent crime, and then going back to family or friends and acting like nothing had happened. For a start, it's pretty certain that he would have evidence of the attack on his clothing. As our esteemed pathologist told me at the time, 'bits of brain tend to stick to everything'.

"My opinion is that he'd have wanted to put as much distance as possible between himself and the scene of the crime, and he would have wanted to do this as quickly as possible, to minimise the risk of coming into contact with anyone.

"So, that begs the question was he there for afternoon tea? We know the ladies who provide the refreshments in the village hall have an excellent reputation, so that is a distinct possibility. That leads on to my next question. Did the killer see Summers and recognise him, or did the opposite happen; did Summers recognise the killer?

"Now, according to the statement made by the other umpire, who was sat with Summers during the tea interval, Summers seemed a bit distant, as though there was something on his mind which was distracting him; his eyes were constantly on the move, looking around the room as though he was trying to spot someone. So, did he spot that someone? Did Summers see and recognise his killer?

"For argument's sake, let's say they had seen each other. It's unlikely that Summers would have felt too threatened as there were plenty of people around. The killer probably would have thought the same—there were just too many people around for him to confront Summers.

"But once the tea interval was over, the game restarted, and as we know, shortly after the restart, Mr Summers had a fall and had to go off injured. Everyone watching the game would have seen him make his way back to the pavilion. Could this have been the moment when the killer saw his opportunity? Could this have been the moment that all the resentment he felt towards Summers suddenly reached boiling point? Was it at that moment that he decided it was now or never?

"Now, maybe the killer had been making plans to murder Summers for some time—perhaps months or even years. Even if that is the case, those plans could have gone out the window as soon as he clapped his eyes on Summers. Did he think that this was the time and opportunity for him to have his revenge?

"Now, the only way to get into the pavilion unseen was through the back door—there were far too many Flitton Green players standing or sitting around the front door. We know that it is only three paces from the back door to the door of the umpire's room door. It's possible the killer knew this, especially if he was a regular at the cricket ground. If he didn't know it, it was obviously a risk he was prepared to take.

"Once in the umpire's room, he struck Mr Summers three times on the back of the head, and then went through the victim's jacket pockets as he was leaving. We now know that he definitely took Mr Summers's door keys and almost certainly his wallet. On his way out he stopped long enough to lock the door to the umpire's room from the outside which give him plenty of time to get well away from the ground before his victim's body was found. He was probably in and out in less than a minute. So, my view is that the actual murder was not pre-meditated.

"As I've already suggested, he may have been thinking about killing Summers for some time, but suddenly, out of the blue, a chance came his way, and he decided it to grab it with both hands."

Hardcastle paused to let the team take all this in.

"Now, as experience tells us, anyone committing a crime on impulse, will, more often than not, leave behind some evidence, evidence which will eventually convict them.

"However, at the moment, it seems that this man has left us absolutely nothing to work on. No DNA, no fingerprints, no footprints and no mistakes. That suggests that the killer didn't panic at any stage and kept his cool throughout.

"As you all know by now, last night the killer used Mr Summers's own keys to search his bungalow, and as far as we can tell the only thing he took away with him was a photograph of a very young child. I have no doubt that this is very significant and I believe he took it away with him because it links him to the victim.

"There is one last thought that I would like to throw into the mix at this point. We are dealing with someone who committed a violent crime within yards of at least 15 people. He was able to get well away from the scene of his crime without anyone noticing anything suspicious about him, and without leaving any evidence that he was ever there.

"Because of this, I think we have to consider the possibility that this man has killed before."

At this point, Hardcastle paused again to let his suggestion sink in.

"OK, any questions at this point?"

There were none.

"So ladies and gentlemen, that brings us back to where we are at this moment in time. Kath, how are things going with the witness statements?"

"We've received 12 out of the 15 that were outstanding, sir," replied the detective sergeant.

"The other three should be completed by mid-afternoon. Unfortunately none of them saw anything suspicious or anyone acting out of the ordinary. At least we can tick them off our list," continued Pearson. "However, Isha has spotted something from the statements we took on Sunday."

"Let's hear it then, Isha. Brighten up our day for us," asked Hardcastle, smiling in encouragement.

"I'm not sure I can do that, sir," she replied, a little nervously. "It's just that two people mentioned that they'd seen a figure dressed all in black walking around the back of the village hall towards the pavilion about 20 minutes after Mr Summers went off injured.

"Both said that it was definitely a man, and that he was wearing a black baseball cap. One of the statements said that the guy was walking along with his head down, which could suggest that he might have been trying to hide his face.

"I thought it could be important, sir. You see the two people who said they saw this chap are regulars at the cricket, so they are more likely to notice these things than someone who just happened to be there with their kids. I mean, from what I've seen, cricket is really boring, with not much happening, so you'd have more time to look around and notice something out of the ordinary," continued DC Hussein.

There was a smattering of laughter, and Isha's comments even managed to bring a smile to Hardcastle's face.

"I quite agree with you, Isha; to the uninitiated, cricket might appear extremely boring. So who were these two people?"

"One was a Mrs Ellie Compton, who is the wife of David Compton, a bowler in the Flitton side, and the other is a Mr Brian Tregunno, whose son is a batsman and also plays for Flitton."

"Tregunno," said Hardcastle. "That's a good old Cornish name. What do you suggest we do, Isha?"

"Speak to them both and see if they can add anything to their statements?"

"Perhaps you can do that, and then let DS Pearson know how you get on. This could be important," replied Hardcastle.

"I will sir."

"Paul, have you had any joy with the accountants and the hotel where Summers worked before he joined the building society?"

"I'm afraid both turned out to be dead ends sir," replied DC Taylor. "The accountants ceased trading when the owner, a Mr Edwards, died in 1978. And as for the hotel, it shut down in 1987 and was converted into flats a year or so later."

"OK, thanks Paul. I suppose it was a bit of a long shot. But let's continue to delve back into the victim's past.

"With that in mind, I spoke to Alex Till this morning and gave him the go ahead to release the victim's name to the press. At the same time he will be appealing for anyone who knew Summers before 1993 to contact us as a matter of urgency, along with anyone who might have been in contact with him since the beginning of this year."

"What do you think the chances are of anyone coming out the woodwork sir?" asked DC Alan Rutherford.

"I learnt many years ago not to be too optimistic when asking the general public for help or information Alan," replied Hardcastle. "Of those that knew him prior to 1993, some will have passed away, some would have left the area, and others will have forgotten that they'd ever met him. Of the rest, most will either think they've got nothing useful to tell us, or they just won't want to get involved.

"As for the relatively short time that he's lived back in the area, I don't hold up that much hope as, from what we've learnt about him so far, he wasn't much of a socialiser and kept himself to himself most of the time.

"I hope I'm not being overly pessimistic, but we'll know soon enough as the appeal should be on the radio and television news around about now."

As if on cue, a telephone rang in the office. Rutherford picked it up, gave his name, and then turned to his colleagues shaking his head.

"Did anything new come out of your chat with Richard Askell?" asked Hardcastle, turning to Kathy Pearson.

"Nothing new, I'm afraid. Even back then, it seems that Mr Summers was a very private individual."

"Have you spoken again to the guy from the building society? There's always a chance that Summers might have been having a fling with someone he worked with back then, maybe someone in the same office. It's a long shot, I know, but it's a question worth asking," suggested Hardcastle.

"Martin Baldwin was out of the office when I rang, so I asked if they could get him to call me as soon as he gets back. They said he should be back sometime this afternoon," replied Pearson.

"OK Kath, thanks for that," replied Hardcastle looking at his watch.

"Well thank you everybody—good work. Let's get our heads together later on this afternoon before we call it a day."

As he walked back to his office, he remembered that he had promised his wife that he would do his best to get home at a reasonable time. As things stood at the moment, keeping that promise was in the balance.

Tuesday 6pm

Neil Panton's day continued to drag, and the more it dragged, the more uptight he was becoming.

By the time he began working on the last job of the day, he was beginning to think that perhaps he should have gone to the police on Sunday afternoon after all. Telling them that he knew who had murdered Donald Summers would have been the right thing to do. However, for most of his life, Neil Panton had rarely done the right thing.

Doing the right thing for once would certainly have put him in the spotlight for a day or two, something he wouldn't have been that adverse to. And it might have made some people see him in a completely different light.

By some people, he really meant Debra Patterson.

But there was no money to be had in doing the right thing. It wouldn't solve his financial problems. It also meant that he wouldn't have the money to buy out his wife's share of the house, and that would mean putting it up for sale.

And by the time he had settled all his outstanding debts, and there were quite a lot of them, what remained out of his share of the equity probably meant he'd have to move into rented accommodation.

And, very likely, he wouldn't be able to continue his car repair business from his new home since most landlords were funny about things like that.

So, in Neil Panton's mind, this completely justified not going to the police. Besides, he knew the man he was blackmailing was fairly loaded, and could easily afford the £50,000. But, as far as Panton was concerned, £50,000 was no more than the starting point.

He looked at his watch for the umpteenth time, and decided it was now time to make the first of the two calls. After a very quick freshen up, he got into his car and drove the short distance to the telephone box he had used the previous evening. He took a couple of deep breaths and dialled the number.

After seven rings, he was just about to put the receiver down when a voice answered.

"Hello."

"Guess who?"

"What do you want now?"

"You know why I'm ringing. Have you got my five grand?"

There was silence at the other end of the phone.

"Well, have you got it?" repeated Panton.

"Yes, I've got it."

"In cash?"

"Yes."

"There you go. I knew you could do it. Just goes to show what you can do when you put your mind to it," replied Panton.

"Get on with it."

"We are a bit touchy today, aren't we? I'm doing you a big favour here and don't you forget it. Better to pay me than spend the rest of your life in prison."

There was another silence, before the reply came.

"Tell me where you want to meet."

Panton had given this a lot of thought during the afternoon. It had to be somewhere secluded. He couldn't risk being seen.

"I'll see you in the graveyard behind the church in the High Street tonight at midnight on the dot, and no funny business. If you're a minute late, expect the Old Bill to come knocking at your door."

Panton slammed the phone down. He didn't want any further discussion on the matter; after all he had the upper hand, and wanted to keep it that way.

He walked slowly back to his car, taking more deep breaths. At least the second call he had to make would be done on his mobile and from the comfort of the sofa in his lounge.

Five minutes later, he was sat there with a large scotch by his side and his mobile phone in his hand.

"Hello."

"Hi Tanya, it's me."

"Hi, Neil, have you got any news for me?"

"Sure have. If you can make it to the house at midday tomorrow, you can collect your £3,000."

"Oh that's brilliant, Neil. Thank you ever so much. Mum and dad will be ever so pleased."

"Well, I'll see you tomorrow then," replied Panton as he pressed the end call button on his mobile.

For once, it looked like everything was going his way.

However, as insurance, he decided to take some sort of weapon along with him for his nocturnal trip to the graveyard behind the church. He had plenty to choose from in his garage. After all, it was better to be safe than sorry.

Tuesday 6:30pm

With the clock on his wall showing it was 6:30pm, Hardcastle decided it was time to wrap things up and call it a day. Perhaps he would actually get home before the boys went to bed for once.

"Meeting in five minutes everybody," he called out from his office. "Just enough time to get yourselves a drink first; milk and two sugars in mine, please, thank you!"

As the team reassembled a few minutes later, Hardcastle realised that he wasn't the only one who needed a decent night's sleep, noticing DC Paul Taylor doing his best to stifle a yawn.

"I'll try and make this as brief as possible so we can all clear off home," began the DI. "Can I start with you, Kath? How are we getting on with the witness statements?"

"We're now up to date, sir. The remaining three were done this afternoon. Unfortunately, there's nothing new to report."

"And what of the relatives of the two Flitton Green players, Mr Tregunno and Mrs…what's her name?" asked Hardcastle turning to Isha Hussein.

"Compton, sir, Mrs Ellie Compton," replied the young DC. "I've only just finished speaking to her, but she had nothing more to add to her original statement."

"And our Cornishman?" asked Hardcastle.

"When I spoke to him after lunch, he was actually on the point of leaving to come into town to do some shopping," replied Hussein, "and he offered to come in and see me once he'd done whatever it was he was going to do.

"He got here just after 3pm. Nice old chap, in his late sixties. He reminded me of my grandad."

"And did he have anything to add to his statement?"

"Well, he told me that he watches his son play cricket every weekend, home and away, and has missed only a handful of his games since he first started playing for Flitton over nine years ago, even though his son no longer lives at home."

"So, was he able to give us any sort of description of the mystery man?" enquired Hardcastle patiently.

"Well, rather than just sitting in one place, Mr Tregunno likes to wander around the ground. Apparently he gets really nervous when his son is batting.

"Anyway, he told me that he'd decided to pop into the hall to get a cup of tea when he saw this fellow walking towards him, about thirty yards away. He thinks the chap may have seen him looking in his direction, and thought that the man deliberately turned his head away, and gave him a bit of a wide berth. The man carried on to the footpath that runs behind the hall, whilst Mr Tregunno carried on into the hall itself."

"And what about a description?" asked Hardcastle, outwardly seemingly his normal patient self, but in truth beginning to get a little irritated.

"Mr Tregunno thought that the man was in his mid to late twenties, certainly no older than that because apparently he didn't walk like an older person. And he either had a beard, or hadn't shaved for a few days, he couldn't tell which."

"What about his height and build?"

"Mr Tregunno said that the man was average height and average build. He did say that when he first saw him, he remembered thinking to himself that the man looked shifty."

"Did he say why he thought he looked shifty?" enquired Hardcastle.

"I did ask, sir," replied Hussein looking through the notes of her interview with Mr Tregunno. "Here it is. His exact words were 'well, he looked a bit shifty, as if he was up to no good'."

Hardcastle smiled at her.

"I'm sorry I can't be more exact, sir."

"Don't apologise, Isha. You've done very well," replied Hardcastle. "Is there any chance of Mr Tregunno doing an e-fit?"

"I did suggest it, but he really didn't think he had seen enough of the man's face, particularly as he was wearing a baseball cap, and had turned his head away. Mr Tregunno said that if the man was to pass him in the street today he wasn't sure if he would recognise him."

"Ok, shame—but at least we have something to go on—even if it doesn't add up to much at this stage," replied Hardcastle.

"Anyway, moving on, let me tell you about a conversation I had this afternoon with Andrew Hanson, the Flitton Green skipper.

"As it happens, Flitton were due to be playing at home again this Sunday coming, but out of respect for Mr Summers, the club have decided to postpone the game.

"I ran past him the possibility of us doing a reconstruction of Sunday's events and he was more than happy to go along with the idea, if that's what we decide to do. He's certain that everyone connected to the cricket club would be very supportive.

"Hopefully, between now and next Sunday we will have caught our killer. But if not I think we may well need to organise a reconstruction. What do we think?" asked Hardcastle throwing the question out to the team.

"I'm with you, boss," said Phil Davison. "A reconstruction might well jog a few memories."

The other members of the team nodded in agreement.

"What's the response been to the latest appeal?" asked Hardcastle, changing the subject.

"Well, the first call we received was from a Mrs Lee who said that she knew Mr Summers," responded DC Alan Rutherford. "However, she turned out to be his next door neighbour, the elderly lady you've spoken to a few times sir."

"Did she have her hearing aid in?" asked Hardcastle with a smile.

"Unfortunately not sir, but as she'd had the decency to ring in, I said I'd pop in to see her early tomorrow morning, on my way in to work."

"That's a very nice idea, Alan, well done," replied Hardcastle, "Anyone else call in, apart from Mrs Lee?"

"A few others who we will visit to take statements, but none of them remember Mr Summers particularly well," said Kath Pearson. "But who knows what we may tease out of them once we're sitting face to face."

"OK," replied Hardcastle. "The appeal will continue to go out on all of this evening's news programmes, so let's hope we have a better response. Have we got cover on the phones, Kath?"

"Yes sir. I've got a couple of volunteers lined up," replied Pearson. "We're not going to need any more than that, and they've been told to ring me straight away if anything important crops up. I'll ring you and Phil if I do get a call.

"And as promised, Martin Baldwin from the County and Country building society in Sheffield rang me back during the afternoon," continued Pearson.

"Unfortunately, there wasn't anything else he could add to our original discussion. He did say that if Donald had been having an affair with someone in one of the local offices back in 1993, he would have been amazed as that would have been so out of character for Mr Summers.

"He also said that if there had been anything going on, and it became common knowledge, the C&C would have split the pair up. Due to Donald's seniority, he probably would have been moved to another office, and the C&C definitely wouldn't have offered him the regional manager's job in Sheffield. An affair with a colleague would have been considered a serious error of judgement on his part."

"Well, that's probably put an end to that particular line of enquiry, but it doesn't rule out the possibility of an affair with someone outside of work," said Hardcastle, winding up the meeting.

"But I think that that's as far as we can go this evening. Well done for all your efforts today. Go home and get a good night's sleep. We go again tomorrow."

Back in the office, Hardcastle thought about ringing Jenny to let her know he was on his way home, but decided against it. It would be nice to surprise her and the boys when he walked through the front door on the right side of 7:30pm for once.

Although he had urged his team to get a good night's sleep, he knew that wouldn't apply to him. He knew from past experience that the lack of any breakthrough would mean a restless night as he churned things over in his mind.

He'd slept well the previous night, but tonight he'd be lucky to get more than a couple of hours.

Tuesday 11pm

After finishing the phone call to his wife, Neil Panton decided to kill time by watching a DVD, and eventually chose the police comedy *Hot Fuzz* as the best way to kill time.

Starring Simon Pegg, Nick Frost, Jim Broadbent and Timothy Dalton, *Hot Fuzz* was another one of Panton's favourite films and it helped him to relax, as did the three large glasses of whisky he downed whilst he was watching it.

Having convinced himself that he was doing the right thing, his main concern was what he would do if the rendezvous with the killer turned nasty. After all, the man he was blackmailing had already killed once. What were the odds that he might try to do it a second time?

His victim, Donald Summers, had been in his mid-sixties, obese and certainly not quick on his toes. Mixing it with someone half of Summers's age would be a completely different proposition.

Panton had always considered himself handy with his fists, but if things took a turn for the worse he wouldn't want to get too close to the man. Better that he took something along with him, like a monkey wrench or a jemmy.

However, despite having a garage full of tools to choose from, he eventually, rather aptly, decided to go with a cricket stump.

At twenty-eight inches long and one end tapering to a point, a blow from a stump would do considerable damage to an opponent, and it had the added advantage of being fairly easy to conceal.

Time continued to drag, but once *Hot Fuzz* had ended, he turned off the television.

Whilst he would never admit it, in case it ruined his 'hard man' reputation, Panton was apprehensive, bordering on being scared. He would be stupid not to be, he told himself. But the flow of adrenaline going through his veins would keep him on his toes.

He looked at his watch. It was just after 11pm, and it was time to get going.

He had decided to take his car, but would park up around half a mile from the church, and then walk the rest of the way.

By the time he got to the church, the clock was showing 11:35pm. Rather than go straight to the graveyard, he decided to wait in the shadows of a shop doorway and chose 'The House of Cod', the local chippie, which was directly opposite the church.

It was yet another warm night, and after a while Panton could feel drips of perspiration running down the back of his neck and nestling at the base of his spine. He desperately wanted to take off his jacket, but decided not to since the cricket stump was up the left sleeve—handily placed in case he needed it in a hurry.

As midnight approached, the number of cars passing the chip shop got fewer and far between and Panton began to get concerned that there had been no sign of the man he was waiting to meet.

Whilst Donald Summers's killer could have got into the graveyard by climbing over the six foot high wall that ran along the back, Panton had expected him to walk down the side of the church, and enter through a wooden gate that traditionally was always kept unlocked.

With his watch now showing it was just a minute to midnight, Panton decided it was time to break cover.

He crossed the road as quickly as he could and said a silent prayer that the old gate wouldn't make any noise when he opened it. His prayer was granted—the vicar or the verger must have recently sprayed some WD40 on the hinges.

By now he was standing at the foot of the path that ran through the graves and crypts. With a clear sky, and an almost full moon, Panton was relieved that he would have no trouble spotting the man when he finally appeared. With his back to the wall of the church, and his right hand around the left hand cuff of his jacket, he was ready for anything.

When his watch showed that it was 12:15pm, Panton began to think that the man was playing games, keeping him waiting so as to increase the tension he knew he would be feeling.

But all it was doing was making him more and more angry. By 12:25pm, Panton's temper was beginning to get the better of him, and had the man appeared at that particular moment, Lord knows what might have happened.

But the man didn't appear, and nor had he appeared by 12:45pm, when Panton finally decided to call it a night.

Walking back to his car, Panton no longer felt that he had the upper hand over the man. What were his options now? He could hardly go to the police and explain that the man he was trying to blackmail hadn't turned up with the £5,000 in cash he promised he would hand over.

At the end of the day, he still needed the other £45,000 so he could buy out his wife's share of their house, and do the other things he had planned to do.

And heaven knows what Tanya would say if she turned up at the house at midday expecting the £3,000, only to be told that he hadn't got it.

With this running through his mind, he suddenly realised that he had arrived outside his house, without actually remembering how he'd got there.

As he got out of the car, he chucked the stump onto the back seat; this was quickly followed by the jacket. He took a deep breath and decided to have another large whisky when he got in, before going to bed.

As he walked up the path to the front door, he realised that he hadn't left the hall light on, which he normally did whenever he went out for the evening. It was understandable, considering all the other things that had been spinning through his mind when he'd left home a couple of hours earlier.

Either that or the light bulb had blown.

He put the key in the lock, let himself in and put the keys on the hall table.

He went to switch on the light, but nothing happened. He opened the lounge door, felt for the switch—and again, nothing happened.

"Bugger it," he said out loud.

Panton looked out of the lounge window and saw that the house directly opposite had lights showing both upstairs and downstairs which meant that the problem was most likely to be an internal one. Probably a fuse had gone somewhere in the house which would have tripped out all the electrics.

The fuse box was in a cupboard underneath the stairs and fortunately he always kept a torch in there for this very eventuality. With his eyes now accustomed to the dark, he made his way to the cupboard and bent down to open the door.

But as his hand grasped the doorknob, he suddenly felt an excruciating pain on the back of his neck. And at that precise moment, like his house, all the lights went out for Neil Panton.

Wednesday 1:30am

Slowly but surely, Neil Panton began to regain consciousness.

He had no idea how long he'd been out. It could have been five minutes or five hours for all he knew. His first thought was that he'd been electrified when he touched the door knob on the cupboard under the stairs. However, he quickly dismissed this. He was no electrician, but even he knew there was no way the door knob could have been live.

Despite being totally disorientated, he realised that he was lying on his back, since he was looking directly up at a light fitting. After staring at it for a few seconds, he worked out that the fitting was the one which hung from the hall ceiling. He tried to move his head, but had to stop immediately as a searing pain went through his neck and travelled down to his feet.

This time his first thought was that he had broken his back, but was quickly able to put that out of his mind as he could wiggle the toes on both feet.

It was then that he heard someone moving about the house and he noticed a small circle of light dancing across the ceiling.

Panton began to panic. He was not alone.

He knew he had to get to his feet.

It was then that he realised his hands were tied behind his back. That and the pain from his neck made it virtually impossible for him to move, let alone get back onto his feet. He wanted to shout out for help, but couldn't because something had been stretched tightly over his mouth.

He was helpless and at the mercy of whoever was coming towards him. He realised the light he had seen bouncing across the ceiling was from a very small but powerful torch.

"My, my, my, what have we here?" came a whisper from just a few feet away. It was a voice he instantly recognised.

All the time Panton had been waiting at the church, the man he was trying to blackmail had been in his house, waiting for him to return.

"So, you thought you would try your hand at a little bit of blackmail, did you? Naughty boy Panton, you could get yourself into a lot of trouble doing that."

As the man spoke, he was slapping him across the left cheek.

Panton desperately wanted to reply.

"You should have kept your mouth shut. Unfortunately you didn't, so I've had to shut it for you. Believe me, you're just a little boy, trying to play a man's game."

All Panton could do in response was to make a muffled squealing sound which he forced from the back of his throat—a sound which no one but the two of them could hear.

"Did you really think I was going to pay hush money to a pond life like you?"

The man stood over Panton, the light from the torch distorting his features, making his face appear like a hideous gargoyle.

Panton wanted to scream out in terror, but the pain from his neck made him wince and he closed his eyes, fearing he was about to lose consciousness again.

"Look at me," hissed the man, giving Panton a vicious kick in the kidneys.

"Look at me," he repeated. "I want you to look into my eyes and know that they are the very last thing you'll ever see. And you know what, Panton? Nobody on this earth is going to miss you one little bit."

The man and the light moved away. For the next couple of minutes, all was quiet, and for a moment, Panton thought that the man had gone away; but those hopes were soon dashed as he saw the light from the torch bouncing across the ceiling again.

And then Panton felt more excruciating pain as the man put a knee on his chest.

"Goodbye, Panton," were the last words Neil Panton would ever hear.

With the knee forcing down even harder on his chest, Panton felt a hand on his face.

Two gloved fingers grasped his nose and squeezed both nostrils together. With the tape covering his mouth, Panton realised he couldn't breathe. He was being suffocated to death. With his head feeling that it was about to explode, mercifully Panton lost consciousness.

At that point, the man released his fingers from his victim's nose. Turning around, he picked up a small bowl he had brought in from the kitchen and slowly began pushing its contents up both of Panton's nostrils, ramming it up as far as he could.

The man got up to stretch his legs, continuing to stare down at the body at his feet. The torch was firmly fixed on his victim's face, watching without any emotion.

Slowly but surely, the life force was ebbing away from the man he had come to despise.

Revenge was oh so sweet.

Wednesday 5:45am

As Steve Hardcastle had expected, Jenny and the boys were delighted to see him walk through the front door of the family home just a few minutes after 7pm. It was good to spend some time as a family, and the four of them watched a couple of episodes of the Simpsons whilst he ate his dinner off a tray in the lounge.

Unfortunately, as he had anticipated, he found it really difficult to get to sleep, and in the end, worried that his tossing and turning might wake up his wife, he quietly got out of bed and decamped to the spare bedroom.

Jenny kept the bed in that room permanently made up as she was used to her husband's tendency to suffer from insomnia whenever he was in the middle of a difficult case.

He'd finally got off to sleep just after 2:30am, and when his alarm went off at 5:45am, it brought him out of a very deep sleep.

Having heard her husband's alarm go off, Jenny got out of bed at the same time, and the two came face to face on the landing.

"Restless night?" she enquired.

"Fairly," he replied.

"Have your shower and I'll make you some breakfast. Egg and bacon do you?"

"I need to consider my waistline as well as my cholesterol level," he said with a grimace. "Don't forget, it was right on the upper limit at my last medical."

"Then how about a couple of pieces of toast?" asked Jenny.

"With marmalade please," was the reply. "And make it three pieces. Sod the cholesterol!"

"You'll be on the statins if you're not careful. Just like your dad," she warned him, semi-seriously.

Twenty-five minutes later, and he was on his way to work, hoping against hope that there had been a breakthrough overnight, although the absence of a phone call from Kath Pearson suggested otherwise.

As he pulled into the station car park, Phil Davison was just getting out of his car, a six-year-old Renault Espace that had been especially adapted to accommodate his wife's needs, not that she went out much these days, unfortunately.

Hardcastle noticed that Kath Pearson's car was already parked up.

Pearson's husband Jason had eventually arrived home just before midnight, and she had been woken up by the sound of the front door shutting. A couple of minutes later, the bedroom door had opened and she had heard her husband whisper, "Are you awake?"

She pretended to be asleep.

When she'd left home just before 5:30am, she had deliberately made as little noise as possible. She couldn't face having to talk to him, no matter how brief the conversation might have been.

Hardcastle and Davison met at the police station's back door.

"Good morning, Phil."

"Good morning, boss."

"Sleep OK?" asked Hardcastle.

"So-so," was the reply. "How about you?"

"So-so," replied Hardcastle. They smiled at each other, knowing that neither of them would have had a good night.

They walked up the stairs to the second floor, and Hardcastle opened the door to the main office allowing his sergeant to go in first. The first thing Davison noticed was Kath Pearson beavering away at her desk.

"Morning, Kath," he said. "Sleep OK?"

"So-so," answered Pearson, also with a smile on her face.

The three of them had been there many times before.

"Morning, Kath," said Hardcastle, "I've been thinking about the two people who Isha interviewed yesterday. I'm sure Isha did a really good job, but I'd like someone with a bit more experience to speak to the pair of them.

"It might be a good idea if you ask them to come in for a chat at the same time—who knows, it might just jog a memory or two if they compare notes on what they saw, or what they think they saw.

"I'd also like our e-fit guy to be there to see if there is anything we can tease out of them, like the way he walked, his height, his weight and so on. You know the form. Maybe we might just get something we can work with, particularly as the more I think about it, the more I feel we'll need to do the reconstruction on

144

Sunday. We'll need the person who plays this mystery man to look as accurate as possible."

"I'll sort that out, sir," replied Pearson.

"And include Isha of course. I wouldn't want her thinking that we weren't happy with what she got out of them yesterday," added Hardcastle. "Explain to her that we are now going to come at this from a different direction, and that direction is going to be dictated by the reconstruction."

"What about Sunday's reconstruction, sir?" asked Pearson.

"Perhaps you can get the ball rolling on that as well please, Kath. You'll need to liaise with Andy Hanson, the Flitton captain, by the way."

"How did we get on with the appeal?" continued Hardcastle. "Did it generate any more phone calls after we left last night?"

"The guys rang me last night to say they'd taken 6 more calls," replied Pearson. "That was just after 10:30pm. We've now got 10 people to take statements from so we'll get cracking on those this morning. But from what the lads said last night, I wouldn't hold your breath though sir. That's why I didn't give you a call."

"Fair enough," he replied. "Just to keep you both in the picture, I'm going to give Danny Willard a call this morning, and try to arrange to meet him at his pub at lunchtime. I'm sure his regulars will have been having a proper gossip about what happened on Sunday, and I'd like to know what people are generally saying about it."

"I'm told he does a decent lunch, boss," chimed in Davison.

"That never entered my mind, Phil," replied Hardcastle with a grin. "Let's catch up with each other after lunch unless anything crops up in the meantime."

Wednesday 10am

Olivia MacDonald sat back in the two seater leather settee and rested her feet on the pouffe one of her grandchildren had thoughtfully placed in front of her.

She had arrived at her daughter's house in Edinburgh two days earlier, and was enjoying herself, although she couldn't quite shrug off the guilt she felt on having left her husband Roderick behind.

Roderick, at 78 years old, was eleven years older than his wife, and was suffering from middle-stage Alzheimer's.

Although Olivia had promised her husband that she would do her level best to keep him at home in the cottage they had shared in Forgandenny, just outside of Perth, for over thirty years, she had recently had to admit to herself that she could no longer provide him with the constant care and attention his illness demanded of her.

Consequently, just over a month ago, Roderick had become a full-time resident at the Sunrise Care Home, a five minute drive from their cottage. Olivia had been warned that the rate of progress of her husband's Alzheimer's would ultimately see him having to move to full time nursing care, although they couldn't give her any idea of when it might become necessary. It could be six weeks, six months or six years.

However, with Roderick seemingly settled at Sunrise, she had decided to accept the open invitation to spend some time with her eldest daughter Helen, her son-in-law David, and their three young children, Alex, Andrew and Emily.

Even though Helen had told her mum that she could stay as long as she liked, Olivia had already decided to return home on Friday. Four days was as long as she could bear to be parted from Roderick, even though lately there had been signs that her husband had not immediately recognised her as she walked through the door of his room at the care home.

Despite the fact that she was mentally exhausted having constantly cared for Roderick for almost three years since the Alzheimer's had been diagnosed, physically Olivia was in good shape, and was looking forward to joining Helen

146

in taking the family dog, a Gordon Setter the children had named Loki, for a long walk after lunch.

In the meantime, she had agreed to help ten year old Andrew with his school project, which involved her answering questions about her childhood, so he could write an essay about how things have changed since his grandma went to school, sixty or so years earlier.

Andrew had woken up several times during the night with earache, and as he was due to have grommets inserted in both ears in a couple of weeks' time, his mum and dad had agreed that he could stay off school, as long as he spent time working on his project.

Watching Andrew tapping away on his iPad took Olivia back to the end of the 1950s when she was at primary school.

There, she was provided with a nib pen which she had to dip in the inkwell set into her desk, before she could start writing. Even though the school provided plenty of blotting paper, most days the young Olivia still went home with the tips of the fingers of her writing hand covered in dry ink.

How times have changed, she thought to herself. *Andrew will think I went to school in the Dark Ages.*

"Come on then, young Andrew. Let's get started. I'm all ready for your questions."

"OK, grandma," replied Andrew. "First question is where did you go to school?"

"That's an easy one. When I was your age, I was going to Dorminster Primary School."

"Where's Dorminster?"

"If you show me a map of Great Britain, I'll show you exactly where it is. Where's your atlas?"

"I don't need an atlas," replied Andrew, who had already begun tapping away on his iPad.

"There you are," he said to his grandma, handing her the tablet.

"You do it please, Andrew," she replied, handing the iPad back to her grandson, and then searching in her handbag for her reading glasses. "You'll be far quicker at that than me. Now, you'll find Dorminster is in the South of England."

Andrew quickly googled 'Dorminster' and he soon had the right part of the UK on the screen.

"Did you actually live in Dorminster?" asked Andrew.

"For some of the time we did," replied Olivia. "But we also lived in a little village called Flitton Green. It was such a lovely place in those days."

"I could get some pictures on my screen of Flitton Green, if you'd like?"

"Well, that would be nice, Andrew. But I'm sure it will have changed a lot since I lived there."

"How about the latest news then?" asked her grandson, who had already googled 'Flitton Green latest news' while they were talking.

"Nothing much used to happen when we lived there, apart from the odd pint of milk being stolen off the doorstep by someone on their way to work early in the morning," replied Olivia, smiling at Andrew. "I bet you don't have your milk delivered by a milkman anymore?"

"We certainly don't," chimed in Olivia's daughter Helen, who had just walked into the lounge. "We get all our shopping delivered by Tesco's once a week, every Friday evening between 6 and 7 o'clock. It saves so much time and hassle."

Olivia was on the verge of replying when Andrew suddenly let out a loud 'Wow'.

"What's up, Andy Pandy?" asked Helen.

"Mum, you know I hate it when you call me that," complained her son.

"Sorry, Andrew," replied Helen more formally. "Anyway, what have you found?"

"You'll never believe this grandma, but someone's been murdered in Flitton Green."

This took Olivia completely by surprise. "That's not possible. Nothing like that ever happened in my day," she said almost indignantly. "It used to be such a nice quiet little village."

Helen took the iPad from Andrew to see for herself.

"Hey mum, the person killed was nearly the same age as you, he was just a year or so younger."

"Do they give his name?" asked Olivia, now sitting on the edge of the settee.

"Let's see," replied Helen. "Yep, here it is—his name was Donald Summers. It seems he was killed during a game of cricket. That would be really funny, if it wasn't so sad."

Helen looked up from the screen of the iPad as her mother hadn't replied.

"Mum, are you OK? You look like you've just seen a ghost. You look ever so pale. Did you know the chap?"

"Can I see, please Helen? I'd like to read it for myself," replied Olivia softly and with a slight tremor in her voice.

Her daughter handed her the iPad, and showed her how to scroll down the page, as the news item was fairly long.

She noticed that her mum's hands were trembling as she held the tablet.

The room was silent for several minutes as Olivia read the news story twice, each time very slowly.

"Did you know him, mum?" asked Helen, quite concerned that her mother might be on the verge of a stroke or heart attack—she looked that ill.

"Yes and no," replied Olivia.

"What do you mean by that? You either knew him or you didn't."

"I met him a couple of times, but I can't say that I knew him that well."

"But mum, you seem really upset. Surely there's more to it than that?"

"There is, but many years ago I made a promise to someone that I would never repeat what they had told me, as they said it was in the strictest confidence." Olivia took a deep breath before continuing. "But if I don't break that confidence, the man who I think may have murdered Donald Summers might well go free."

"Look mum, you know you can tell me—I promise I won't tell another soul, not even David if you don't want me to."

"OK dear. But let's go into the kitchen first. What I have to tell you is not for the ears of a ten-year-old boy."

Wednesday 10:30am

"That's some story, mum," said Helen once her mother had finished. "But it all sounds a bit too far-fetched to me."

"Do you think I made it up then?" replied Olivia, somewhat indignantly.

"Of course I don't. But perhaps your friend did."

"Helen, this lady was a very special person. I would have known if she had made it up. We never ever lied to one another."

"OK, perhaps made up isn't the right choice of word," replied her daughter, now searching her brain for the right word. "Maybe she embellished it a little bit."

Her mother was silent and Helen was worried she had upset her.

"No Helen, I'm sure she didn't," replied Olivia eventually. "She had no reason to."

"OK mum. Let's say this lady told you the truth. What sort of man was this Donald Summers?"

"Why do you ask?"

"Well, was he the type of man who might have gone through life making enemies? Was he a bit of a Jack the Lad?"

"Not that I was aware of. Why do you ask?"

"Well, if he had several enemies, any one of them could have been responsible for killing him."

Again, there was silence in the room whilst Olivia considered that as a possibility.

"No, he wouldn't have been that sort of person. My friend would not have been interested in him had he been. And the way she spoke about him, he must have been a decent man."

It was Helen's turn to be silent.

"Helen, what do you think I should do?" prompted her mother, almost pleading to her daughter.

"Well mum, as I see it, you have three choices."

150

"And what are they?"

"Firstly, you do nothing at all. Just let things run their course," replied Helen, holding up one finger. "For all you know, the police might already have made an arrest. Don't forget that the story on Andy's iPad is dated yesterday. A lot can happen in twenty four hours."

Helen could see that her mother was weighing up that option.

"The second option," said Helen now holding up two fingers, "is to ring the police and tell them what you've just told me. If you do that, they might want you to go down to Dorminster and make a statement, or at the very least they'll get the local police to come here to see you.

"And ask yourself mum, what would dad want you to do in this type of situation? Do you remember one of his favourite sayings?"

"*Let sleeping dogs lie*," replied Olivia.

"Exactly, *let sleeping dogs lie*," repeated Helen.

"What about the third option?" asked Olivia.

"Well, we can keep an eye on the news coming out of Dorminster. I'll have the web page as one of the favourites on my iPad, and I'll check for updates every few hours or so. The chances are that sooner or later the story will be updated and I'm willing to bet that the police will say that they've arrested someone and that'll be the end of it."

"But what if they don't?" asked Olivia.

"Well, let's give it a couple of days or so. If they still haven't arrested anybody by Friday, then we can call the police."

"I suppose you're right, Helen. Another couple of days won't do any harm, will it?"

"No it won't. And don't fret over it in the meantime, mum," replied Helen. "Now, let's have a nice cup of tea."

As her daughter busied herself in the kitchen making tea the proper way (using tea leaves instead of tea bags, and pouring the hot tea into china cups which already had the milk in), Olivia mulled over the three options her daughter had given her.

Helen was right; one of Roderick's favourite sayings was *let sleeping dogs lie*. However, her husband also believed in always doing the right thing. He was a stickler for that.

Olivia's quandary though was deciding just what the right thing was.

Wednesday 11:55am

After speaking to her estranged husband on Monday evening, Tanya Panton was so confident he would manage to rustle up the £3,000 she had asked for, that she decided to take Wednesday as a day's leave. She knew that Neil would find the opportunity to save himself £2,000 far too irresistible to ignore.

And so it had turned out, when he rang yesterday evening to say that he had the cash.

What she hadn't told Neil was that on top of his £3,000 and the £3,000 coming from her parent's, her boyfriend, Glen Finnemore, was adding an additional £4,000 towards the deposit they needed for the two-bedroom ground-floor flat they had fallen in love with and were so desperate to buy.

With a baby on the way, Tanya and Glen wanted the purchase to go through as quickly as possible so they could get the flat decorated and furnished in time for the baby's arrival.

The only dark cloud on their horizon was the inevitable fallout there would be when Neil eventually found out that not only had Tanya been dating someone he knew very well from his playing days with Middle Ash, but also that she was expecting his child. As far as Tanya was concerned, Glen was everything Neil wasn't.

During his time playing for Middle Ash, Neil Panton was, by some distance, the most unpopular cricketer his team mates had ever come across. By complete contrast, Glen Finnemore was probably one of the most popular players ever to don a Middle Ash shirt and he and Panton had shared numerous rows both on and off the pitch. Predictably, the other members of the team were all firmly on Glen's side, which simply fuelled the antipathy Panton felt towards the other man.

Tanya's marriage to Neil had been on the rocks long before she and Glen had become involved.

The early months of their marriage had been relatively OK, but gradually the good times had been interspersed with some very bad ones. In the months leading up to the day they eventually parted, the bad times had become very much the norm, and the constant threat of physical violence towards her had finally snuffed out any lingering affection she may have once felt towards her husband.

When she finally summoned up the courage to leave the house she had shared with Neil for over 6 years, Tanya felt a tremendous sense of relief, an emotion shared by her parents, who during the last few months had seriously feared for her safety.

Glen Finnemore had been in a long term relationship with someone he had met in his first year at university. That relationship endured far beyond their uni days, but eventually just seemed to peter out for no specific reason.

When the pair eventually parted, it was as good friends, and when he learnt that his erstwhile partner had met and moved in with someone else, Glen was genuinely really pleased for her.

Tanya had first met Glen a couple of years earlier when she made one of her rare visits to the cricket club to watch Neil play. Their conversation was necessarily brief as Tanya was used to her husband giving her the third degree whenever he saw her speaking to another man for more than five seconds.

However, a couple of months before last Christmas, she had bumped into Glen whilst shopping in Dorminster and the pair had enjoyed a coffee together in the local Costa coffee shop.

The conversation flowed so easily, that they both were disappointed when the time came for them to go their separate ways, but not before they exchanged mobile phone numbers.

As he was fully aware of how possessive Panton was of his wife, the couple agreed that Glen would only ring Tanya if and when he knew for certain that Neil was not in the offing, and the most common time for them to chat was either when Tanya was at work or when Neil was off watching football somewhere.

Otherwise, Tanya would call Glen whenever the coast was clear.

As an extra precaution, Tanya saved Glen's details in her mobile as 'Helen T', just in case Neil broke the password she had set on her phone. She also changed her password on a regular basis.

By Christmas, Tanya and Glen knew that they wanted to spend the rest of their lives together, and they once joked about getting someone to 'bump' Neil off, because Tanya truly believed that he would never willingly let her leave him for another man—least of all for Glen Finnemore, a man he had come to hate with a vengeance.

The pair found it so difficult to be apart over the festive period that they made a New Year's resolution that they would finally be together come what may, at the earliest possible opportunity.

It was early in the New Year that Tanya finally plucked up the courage to suggest to Neil that they should call time on their marriage. Inevitably things got quickly out of hand, and the resultant screaming and shouting caused their next door neighbours to call the police.

Rather than arrest Neil, the police officers attending the scene had given him a damn good talking to, and left him in no doubt that should he ever again behave in such an aggressive way towards his wife, he would be arrested for breach of the peace.

Shortly afterwards, when Neil was away from home watching Bournemouth play a Premier League football match in Manchester, Tanya, assisted by her parents, got all her belongings together and left the marital home once and for all, leaving a front door key and a carefully drafted note on the dining room table, telling her husband that should he try to contact her, she would immediately call the police.

For the first six weeks after she'd left Neil, Tanya and Glen continued to keep their relationship a secret. However, the time eventually came when they thought it would be appropriate to introduce Glen to her parents, and Tanya was so relieved when her mum and dad took an instant liking to him.

The pair soon got into a comfortable routine whereby she would stay over at Glen's rented flat at weekends, and then spend Monday to Thursday at her parent's house, although she and Glen would still meet up at least a couple of times during the week.

When, a few days earlier, Tanya had found out that she was pregnant, she was really worried how her parents would react, given that they were more than just a little bit 'old school'.

However, to her great surprise and relief, her mum and dad were overjoyed at the news that they were to become grandparents. As her dad had put it, their biggest fear over the last few years had been that their first grandchild would have Neil Panton as a father.

As Tanya and Glen celebrated with Tanya's parents, the four of them discussed the possibility of the couple buying a house or flat in time for baby's arrival, and that was when Tanya's dad offered to give them £3,000 towards a deposit.

That weekend, Tanya and Glen had gone house hunting, and on the Sunday, after Glen had told the Middle Ash skipper that he was unavailable to play in the fateful game away to Flitton Green, they found and fell in love with just the third property they viewed.

And here she was now, three days later, standing outside the house she had lived in for six years waiting to collect the £3,000 Neil had told her last night she could get from him at midday.

Glen was not with her and was waiting for Tanya to call him to say that all had gone as planned. He was naturally concerned as to how Neil would react on seeing her for the first time since they'd parted. As a precaution, he had decided to park up just a few streets away ready to come to her help if needed.

Once Tanya had collected the money, the pair had arranged to go immediately to the estate agent and complete the necessary paperwork to secure the purchase of the flat.

Whilst she wouldn't admit it, Tanya was more than just a little bit nervous. She knew how nasty and sarcastic Neil could be, and there was no way he could have mellowed since she last saw him.

But with the hands on her watch now showing it was noon; she took a very deep breath and walked up the path to the front door.

She knew he was at home as his beloved Subaru was parked in front of the garage.

She rang the doorbell and waited. No answer.

She rang it for a second time. Again there was no answer.

For God's sake, surely he wasn't playing silly-buggers, she asked herself. What was the point of making her wait on the doorstep?

She walked back down the path.

What Neil wasn't aware of was that when she had left the house with her belongings back in January, the front door key she had left with the note saying she was leaving him, had been a copy, and she still had the original, just in case there was ever a need to go back there.

But she hesitated to use the key as she was worried what his reaction would be if she opened the front door. Uncertain what to do next, she rang Glen from her mobile.

"Hiya love, all done and dusted?" he answered.

"No, not yet. Typical of him, he won't answer the front door, Glen. I know he's in there because his car's outside. He never goes anywhere without it."

"OK," replied Glen, "I'm driving around now. No time like the present. We might as well come clean. We'd have to tell him sometime that we've got together, so let's get it over and done with now."

"I suppose you're right," replied Tanya. "But just park fifty yards up the road, so you can still see the house from the car. I'll open the front door but won't go in. There's no reason why I should go inside. I can just take the money from him on the doorstep, say thanks very much and then that's that."

"OK, but don't do anything until you see my car. I'll be there in two minutes."

Within 90 seconds, he had arrived. Tanya felt so much better knowing that he was there to watch her back.

She gave Glen a little wave as she walked back up the path, and he gave her a reassuring smile and a wave back. She knocked on the door. Again, there was no reply, so she got out the key and turned it in the lock, as she had done hundreds of times before. This time, though, it was different. It was very different.

As the door opened, she pushed it aside and looked into the hall.

She stopped in her tracks.

A few seconds later, she screamed like she had never screamed before.

Wednesday 12:15pm

Danny Willard had been delighted to hear from Steve Hardcastle and readily agreed to meet up and have a chat over lunch at his pub, The Waterman's Arms, at Long Ash.

Hardcastle decided to have a quick catch up with Kath Pearson before leaving. Pearson, as always, had lost no time in actioning the matters that she and her boss had discussed earlier that morning.

"I've got Mrs Compton and Mr Tregunno coming in at 2:30pm to see me, Isha and Max Dawson from the Techies," she told Hardcastle. "Hopefully, it won't be a waste of time and we'll end up with an e-fit of sorts which we can use. I've also got the ball rolling for the reconstruction. Andy Hanson was very helpful. What happened on Sunday has obviously hit him and the rest of the team very hard."

"Any more responses to yesterday's appeal?" asked Hardcastle.

"We've had two more this morning which brings the total up to a dozen. Hopefully, we'll have all the statements available for you to have a look through later on today."

"That's good work, Kath, thank you. I'm off now; you know where to find me if you need me."

Hardcastle picked up his car keys from his desk, put his jacket on and began to walk down the stairs to the car park.

He'd gone down one flight when he heard a shout from above.

"Boss, you need to come back, and quick." It was Phil Davison.

"What's the problem, Phil?" replied Hardcastle going back up the stairs two at a time.

"You're never going to believe this, but we've got another body."

"Jesus, where?"

"It's not so much where, it's more a case of who," replied Davison. "It's Neil Panton, and it sounds like he's been murdered."

"You're kidding me."

"I wish I was, boss," replied his sergeant.

By now they were back in the main office where there was a stunned silence amongst the rest of the team.

"First things first: Paul, can you do me a favour and ring Danny Willard and pass on my apologies and tell him I've had to cancel our lunch," instructed Hardcastle. "Just tell him something has come up out of the blue. Don't go into any detail at this stage, and tell him I'll be in touch later."

"On it now, sir," replied Paul Taylor.

"And Kath, can you put the DCI in the picture?"

"Will do, sir."

"Right Phil, tell me what you know as we go," said Hardcastle as he and Davison began running down the stairs towards the car park.

"I'm told that someone rang treble nine at 12:05pm. Uniform arrived at 12:09pm where they found a hysterical woman and a man who apparently is her boyfriend. One of the cops recognised the woman as Mrs Tanya Panton, wife of Neil. At this stage we have no idea who the boyfriend is."

"Are we certain the body is Panton?" asked Hardcastle.

"Yes boss, the cop who recognised Mrs Panton also attended a domestic at that address a few months ago. He was able to confirm the deceased man is definitely Neil Panton."

"Good God. And we know for a fact that he was murdered? It wasn't an accident?" asked Hardcastle.

"Yes, according to the two cops at the scene it is definitely murder, but we don't know how. That's about it at the moment, you know as much as I do."

"Has Billy Kiernan been notified yet?" asked Hardcastle.

"Probably, but I'll call him now to make sure," said Davison, holding his mobile phone to his ear. His call went to Kiernan's voice mail, and Davison left him a brief message, asking him to ring back if he wasn't already on his way to Panton's house.

"It's a bit early, I know, but any gut feeling on this one?" asked Hardcastle.

"You mean, do I think it's linked to Sunday's killing?"

"That has to be the most likely scenario. What do you think?"

"My gut instinct is it has to be. It would be too much of a coincidence otherwise," replied Davison.

"Yep, I think that too," replied Hardcastle.

They continued the rest of the journey in silence, both men wrapped up in their thoughts, trying to make some sense of this second murder in less than three days.

Wednesday 12:30pm

By the time Steve Hardcastle turned his Range Rover into Wallace Drive, the scene around number 114, home to Neil Panton, was a hive of activity.

There were three police cars, a small police van and an ambulance already parked up, with three other cars looking for somewhere to park as close to number 114 as possible.

Hardcastle was relieved to see that one of the cars trying to park belonged to Billy Kiernan.

Most of the properties in Wallace Drive had been built in the 1950s and were mainly three bed semi-detached houses originally owned by the local council. There was still a handful which remained in council ownership, but the vast majority had fallen into private ownership following the introduction of Margaret Thatcher's Right to Buy scheme in the 1980s.

Sold by the council to sitting tenants at a discount ranging anywhere between 33 and 50% of market value, many of the houses had been significantly improved, by installing new windows and doors, and by adding conservatories and loft conversions.

However, despite this, Wallace Drive still retained the overall feel of a council estate, and whenever a for sale board appeared in a front garden, prospective purchasers were drawn to the area knowing that the sale price would be around 10% lower than for similar properties on the market elsewhere in Dorminster.

As Hardcastle's Range Rover coasted towards number 114, it was recognised by one of the uniformed officers, who immediately removed a couple of bollards, and gestured to the Detective Inspector that he could park where the bollards had been.

"Rank still has its privileges, I see," commented Phil Davison.

"And where parking a car is concerned, long may it continue," replied Hardcastle with a smile.

As they got out of the car, Hardcastle looked towards the ambulance and noticed a fairly young woman with a blanket across her shoulders talking to a paramedic. He guessed that the young woman was Tanya Panton.

As he and Davison walked towards number 114, Hardcastle recognised the uniformed constable who had shown him where to park his car. The same officer had been on duty outside Donald Summers's bungalow on Monday morning, and he'd obviously remembered Hardcastle's car from then.

"Good morning, Constable Moffatt. How are you doing today?"

"Fine thank you, sir," replied Moffatt, flattered that the DI should even have recognised him, let alone have remembered his name.

"I'd like to speak to the two officers who were the first ones on the scene. Can you point me in their direction please?"

"That would be PCs Anderson and Henry sir. That's them over there talking to the deceased's next door neighbours," said Moffatt.

"Thank you," replied Hardcastle. "Phil, can you catch up with Billy Kiernan whilst I have a chat to Anderson and Henry?" said the DI, turning to Davison. "I shouldn't be more than five minutes or so."

The two constables had evidently seen Hardcastle coming in their direction and knowing that he would want to speak to them, they quickly finished their conversation with the neighbours.

"I understand you two were the first ones to arrive on the scene. Can you give me a quick run through on what you found when you got here?" asked Hardcastle.

"Yes sir," replied Anderson, evidently the senior of the two PCs. "The first person we saw was Mrs Panton who was being comforted by her partner, whose name is Mr Glen Finnemore," he said looking at his notebook.

"Apparently, Mrs Panton had arranged to meet her husband here at the house at 12 noon sharp. When he failed to answer the front door, she let herself in. Even though the Pantons had separated several months ago, she'd kept a door key which the victim didn't know she had," continued Anderson, still referring to the notebook.

"Unfortunately, the first thing she saw when she opened the door was Mr Panton's body. It was obvious that he was dead."

"Obvious?" enquired Hardcastle.

"I'm no expert, sir, but from experience, I'd say he'd been dead for several hours," replied Anderson.

161

Hardcastle couldn't help smiling to himself. Obviously, PC Anderson had been round the block many times during his time in the force.

"We didn't go into the hall, as we could see what we needed to see from the doorway," continued Anderson, "and I was concerned about contaminating the crime scene. PC Henry here called it in and also called for an ambulance for Mrs Panton as she was quite hysterical although she seems to have quietened down a bit now. Whilst PC Henry was doing that I got some barrier tape from the car, and began to cordon off the scene."

"Excellent. Well done both of you. I'll let you get on," replied Hardcastle, nodding to the pair.

Although he was keen to look inside the house, Hardcastle decided first to have a word with Tanya Panton and her boyfriend.

While he'd been talking to Anderson, he'd noticed that reinforcements had arrived in the shape of DC's Paul Taylor and Alan Rutherford, and he motioned to the two of them to join him. He quickly brought them up to speed.

"Let's have a few words with Mrs Panton and Mr Finnemore now, and then perhaps you can take them back to the station and take full statements from them—assuming the lady has recovered sufficiently."

They walked towards the ambulance, making a beeline for the paramedic who was sitting on a garden wall filling in some forms whilst his colleague was attending to their patient.

"How is Mrs Panton?" asked Hardcastle.

"She'll be OK. She's obviously had a very nasty shock, but she and her boyfriend are more concerned that she might lose the baby she's expecting. I've reassured them that that is very unlikely."

"So it's OK for us to have a word with her?"

"Be my guest, we've done everything we need to do. My mate's just finishing off."

The three policemen walked the remaining few yards to the ambulance and Hardcastle introduced himself and the two DCs to Mrs Panton and Mr Finnemore.

"I'll be brief, as these officers," he said pointing to Taylor and Rutherford, "will be taking you back to the station to take statements from both of you. But before you go, I need to ask you a few questions. Do you both feel up to it?"

They nodded in agreement.

"Mrs Panton, I've been told that you had arranged to meet your husband here at midday. Can you tell me why that was as I understand that you and Mr Panton have been separated for some time?"

Hardcastle noticed Finnemore take hold of her left hand and give it a squeeze.

"Well," she replied, "it's really very simple. Neil and I split up early in the New Year and we've been going through the process of getting a divorce. My solicitor had written to Neil and told him that I would sign over my share of the house for £25,000. I was happy for that to take its course.

"But then, a few days ago, I found out I was pregnant. When I told my mum and dad, they suggested that Glen and I find somewhere to buy which would be suitable for bringing up a young baby. We went out house hunting at the weekend and more by luck than judgement found the perfect place, which had only just come on the market. My parents had already told us that they would give us £3,000 towards the deposit.

"With what Glen has got saved and other bits and pieces, we were £3,000 short. So I rang Neil and said if he could let me have £3,000 as soon as possible, preferably in cash, I would reduce the divorce settlement by £5,000, saving him £2,000. I knew that would be an offer he just couldn't refuse."

"Why did you ask for the money in cash?" enquired Hardcastle.

"To be honest, I'd never take a cheque from Neil as I know it would bounce," replied Tanya.

Hardcastle nodded to her to continue.

"Anyway," she continued, "Neil said he would think about it, and then yesterday evening, he rang me to say that he'd got the £3,000 and that I could collect it from him here at the house today at midday. That's about it, really."

"Did Neil say where he'd got the cash from?" asked Hardcastle.

"He didn't say and I didn't ask him," she replied. "I really didn't want to have that sort of conversation with him. That's his business now and not mine and I didn't want him to get the idea I was still interested in whatever he was doing. Those days are long gone."

"From your knowledge of Neil, what was the likelihood that he already had the money tucked away somewhere?"

"What, Neil? No chance. He rarely had the price of a pint on him, let alone £3,000. Money has always burnt a hole in his pocket."

"OK. Now, when you both arrived at the house, did everything seem normal?"

"Yes, everything looked fine," replied Mrs Panton. "But, Glen wasn't with me at that time."

"Why was that?" asked Hardcastle, curiously.

"For a start, Neil didn't know I have been seeing Glen. Had he known, he'd have gone totally ballistic and would have slammed the front door in my face."

"Why would he have reacted like that? After all, you've been apart for several months and surely he would have known that everyone moves on eventually," asked Hardcastle.

"Well, yes, but Neil is, I'm sorry, was, a very jealous man. He'd always get really angry if he saw me talking to another man. But finding out that Glen was my new partner would have been the straw that broke the camel's back. Trust me, if I'd have turned up at his front door with Glen, he'd have gone right off his trolley, and the last thing I wanted was for him to change his mind about the money."

"Why was that?" chimed in Paul Taylor. "Why would he have been that bothered?"

"Neil and I used to play cricket together for Middle Ash," replied Finnemore. "To say we didn't get on is something of an understatement. So I decided to keep out of sight, and I parked the car a couple of streets away."

"OK," replied Hardcastle. "Can you continue please, Mrs Panton?"

"I knocked on the door a couple of times, but there was no answer. I didn't think too much of it, as keeping me waiting on the doorstep is just the sort of thing that Neil would do. He'd think it was hilarious. That's just the sort of person he was. But I still have a front door key you see, which Neil didn't know about, and I thought he'd kick up a real fuss if I suddenly opened the door.

"So I rang Glen and told him, and he drove down here straight away to keep an eye on me, in case Neil blew a fuse. Then I opened the front door, and that's when I saw him lying on his back in the hallway."

At that point, Tanya Panton burst into tears again.

"Perhaps you can take up the story at that point please, Mr Finnemore?" asked Hardcastle.

"Yes, of course, Inspector. It was obvious that something was wrong because Tanya was screaming and shouting for me," replied Finnemore.

"I ran over, looked in the doorway and saw Neil on his back on the floor, so I rang 999 on my mobile. And that's about it."

There was a brief pause while Hardcastle took stock of the situation.

"OK, thanks Mr Finnemore," he replied after a few seconds. "I've just got a couple more questions for you both before my colleagues take you down the station.

"Firstly, Mrs Panton, do you have any idea who might have wanted to kill your husband?"

"No, I don't. He wasn't exactly the most popular man on the planet, and he didn't really have any friends because of the way he was. But he didn't deserve to die. Not like that," she replied, with tears flowing down both cheeks.

"Last question; where were you both last night?"

"I was at my mum and dad's house," replied Tanya, dabbing her eyes with a tissue. "I cooked a meal for the three of us, and then I had an early night."

"And you, Mr Finnemore?"

"I was at home on my own. I had to make do with a Marks and Sparks ready meal," he replied smiling gently at his girlfriend. "Then I watched the football on the television."

Hardcastle nodded, had a quick word with his two detective constables and then left them to it as he headed back across the road to number 114.

"Find out anything useful, boss?" asked Phil Davison, who by now was wearing the obligatory protective clothing.

"Could be," replied Hardcastle. "It seems Panton had somehow managed to rustle up £3,000 in cash, yet according to Mrs Panton, he never had two halfpennies to rub together, so he must have got it from somewhere or from someone."

"Well, the obvious places would be his bank, or a building society. But if his credit rating was poor, he'd have to go to a pawnbroker or one of those short term money lenders, like those that advertise on the television. The one's that charge extortionate rates of interest," replied Davison. "I would have included friends for most people, but Panton didn't seem the sort of guy to have many of those."

"Of course, you're right there, Phil. But it's worth speaking to Debra Patterson. You never know, she might have been feeling a bit guilty at dumping Panton and lent him the money to make up for it."

Davison nodded, and made a note to speak to her.

"I'd also add blackmail or he got it by threatening someone. We need to keep all options on the table, but that's something we can talk about a bit later. It sounds like a job for Kath," said Hardcastle. "Anyway, what have I missed?" he added, nodding towards the house.

"Billy and his team of CSIs are inside with Kelly Heywood. I've had a quick look boss, but thought I'd wait for you before having a good look around the place."

"Do we know the cause of death yet?" asked Hardcastle.

"I think you ought to have a look first, boss," replied Davison, handing Hardcastle a set of protective clothing.

"OK," replied Hardcastle, giving his sergeant a slightly bemused look as he donned a white boiler suit, latex gloves and overshoes.

As they walked through the open front door, Panton's body was partially obscured by two figures in white, who turned around to face Hardcastle when they heard movement behind them.

"Hi guys," said Hardcastle, nodding to the pair. "What can you tell me?"

As Kiernan and Heywood stood back, Hardcastle got his first look at the body of Neil Panton.

"God Almighty!" he exclaimed.

"That's exactly what I said when I saw him," said Davison.

Moving closer, Hardcastle could see that Panton was laying face upwards, with his eyes closed and his hands behind his back, probably restrained in some way. Whilst a large piece of silver duct tape was covering Panton's mouth, it was to the man's nose that the policeman's eyes were drawn.

"What in heaven's name has this bastard done to him?"

"I won't know for certain until I get him back to the lab, but it's obvious that some type of filler has been rammed up both nostrils," responded Kelly Heywood.

"Was that done before or after death?"

"At this stage, Steve, my best guess would be after, but it could have been at the point of death."

"So the cause of death was suffocation?"

"Yes, I think I can confirm that," replied the pathologist. "But there is also severe bruising from a blow to the side of the neck, and depending on how hard he was hit, there's a good chance that he would have been unconscious when he hit the ground. The killer then tied the man's hands behind his back using black nylon cable ties, and tied his legs together the same way. And, as you can see, he covered the victim's mouth with a heavy duty duct tape, so the only way he could breathe at that point was through his nostrils.

"He probably then waited for Mr Panton to regain consciousness, and then pinned him down, possibly by kneeling on his chest. To finish the job, all he had to do was to pinch both nostrils together and wait."

"Would he have struggled?" asked Davison.

"The blow to the neck would have weakened and disorientated him, so the best he could probably do was to try and move his head from side to side. But there are strands of hair on the carpet, so I'd say the killer was forcing his head backwards by grabbing his hair. Thankfully, he would have lost consciousness fairly quickly and death would have followed soon after."

"That's something to be grateful for," said Hardcastle.

"I gather Mr Panton was a self-employed car mechanic," said Billy Kiernan. "I'd bet a pound to a penny that the killer got the tape and the filler from the garage. I've asked a couple of my CSIs to start searching there first," said Billy Kiernan.

"This killing has to be linked to Sunday's," added the Crime Scene Manager.

"Too much of a coincidence for it not to be," said Hardcastle. "But let's keep all options open for the time being.

"I know that it's far too early to deal in specifics," continued Hardcastle, looking towards Kelly Heywood, "but is there anything you've seen to link the two killings together?"

"Apart from the fact that both men were involved in the same game of cricket on Sunday, I have to say that forensically, nothing links the two at this stage," replied Heywood. "Sunday's killing had an element of spontaneity about it. The killer saw an opportunity, picked up the bat mallet, opened the door and then wallop. He was probably in and out within a minute, if not less.

"However, what we have here has all the hallmarks of having been carefully planned in advance. And there's something about the method he's used that rings a bell with me. Somewhere and sometime in the past I've come across it before, but don't ask me where at the moment; it was probably in a medical journal, or a reference book. It might take me some time, but I'll find it."

"I've no doubt you will, Kelly," replied Hardcastle. "In the meantime, I don't suppose either of you have found £3,000 in cash lying around the place?" he added, looking at Kiernan and Heywood.

"Why's that?" asked Kiernan.

"Well, the reason his wife was the one who found the body was that she was due to collect £3,000 in cash from Panton at midday."

"You think that robbery was the motive behind the murder then?" asked Heywood.

"Possibly," replied Hardcastle. "Or the killer might want us to think that."

"You mentioned blackmail earlier, boss," interrupted Davison. "You still think that's a possibility?"

"I think it could be more than a possibility, Phil. As I said earlier, we have to keep all options open at this stage, but if Panton had somehow got hold of proof to link the killer to Sunday's murder, then for someone like him, who was lacking in both scruples and money, blackmail is a fairly easy step to make, particularly as he was in the middle of a divorce, and needed some cash urgently.

"And, then look at it from the killer's point of view. The only thing stopping him from getting away with the murder of Summers is Panton who has this hold over him. From what we already know about Panton I'm willing to bet that his silence wouldn't have come cheaply. For the killer, committing a second murder could have been an easy decision to make."

"And that means we have a double killer on our hands," said Davison rhetorically.

"And someone who is ruthless enough not to stop at two," added Billy Kiernan. "One more and we've got a serial killer on our hands."

Wednesday 12:55pm

The idea of a potential serial killer on the loose in their own backyard was enough to send shivers down the spine of all those standing around the body of Neil Panton.

Steve Hardcastle knew that once the word got out that a second murder had been committed on his patch, less than 72 hours after the first, there would be an instant media rush, and he would be under far more pressure to make an arrest than at any time in his career as a copper. Pressure from the media, both local and national, pressure from the general public concerned that a double murderer might be on the loose amongst them and pressure internally from the powers that be at regional headquarters. The likelihood of a more senior officer taking charge of his investigation could quickly turn into a distinct possibility. As far as his career was concerned, this could well be a defining moment.

The silence was broken by Hardcastle himself.

"There is an alternate scenario, however."

The DI had everyone's attention.

"There are others who will benefit from Neil Panton being out of the way, Panton's wife and her boyfriend, for instance."

"I really can't see his wife having anything to do with it," responded Phil Davison. "Those weren't crocodile tears she was shedding, boss. We've all seen people suffering from shock and Tanya Panton had all the classic signs. And I'm sure the paramedics would have said something to us if they thought she was shamming it."

"As it happens, I completely agree with you, Phil, and that's why we need to concentrate on Glen Finnemore, the boyfriend, rather than her," replied Hardcastle.

"What makes you think he could be a suspect, Steve?" asked Billy Kiernan.

"I do have the advantage over you," replied Hardcastle, "as I've already spoken to him. What you don't know is that Panton and Finnemore used to play cricket together for Middle Ash, and by the sound of it, they didn't get on at all, so much so, that Tanya Panton said that her husband 'would go totally ballistic' if he found out that she and Finnemore were now an item.

"We also know that Panton's marriage to Tanya was a stormy one, and you can bet your bottom dollar that she has told her new partner how badly Panton treated her, and especially how bad things got towards the end of their relationship. Finnemore's dislike of Panton could easily have turned to hatred.

"And Finnemore hasn't got an alibi for last night. He told me that he was at home alone watching the football with only a tv dinner for company. What's to say that Finnemore didn't pay Panton a visit sometime during the night? We also know that Tanya Panton still has a front door key to this house. Finnemore could easily have borrowed it, got a spare one cut, and then put the original back where he'd got it from without Tanya ever knowing."

"What about a motive, boss?" asked Davison. "Fair enough Panton and Finnemore didn't like each other, but from what we already know, no-one seemed to like Panton. I don't see that leading to murder—a punch up, maybe, but certainly not murder."

"Who benefits from Panton being out of the way?" asked Hardcastle rhetorically. "It'll save Tanya Panton a small fortune in solicitor's fees with no divorce to pay for. And if the house was in joint names, which I'm willing to bet it was, it now legally becomes hers. She can sell it if she wants, and whatever is left after the mortgage has been paid off, will be more than enough to cover the deposit on the new place she and Finnemore intend to buy together. It might even mean that they can look for somewhere bigger to live."

"So we pull Finnemore in?" asked Kiernan, thinking ahead to the possibility that he and his CSIs might need to search Finnemore's car and home for evidence.

"That's not necessary," replied Hardcastle. "At this very moment, Finnemore and Tanya Panton are on their way to the nick so that Paul Taylor and Alan Rutherford can take statements from them.

"I'd like you to nip back to the nick please, Phil. Let Alan take Mrs Panton's statement on his own, but I'd rather you and Paul dealt with Mr Finnemore. He's got some questions that need answering.

"In the meantime, I'll speak to Danny Willard. As a Middle Ash player, he's known Finnemore since he moved here from the Met, and being a publican as well as a player he'll probably be in the know about any gossip that's been doing the rounds in the dressing room. And it will be helpful to have Danny's view on

170

what sort of bloke Finnemore is and whether or not he thinks he's capable of murder. I'll let you have his opinions before you and Paul sit down to interview him."

As Davison went outside to cadge a lift back to the nick, Hardcastle followed him out and went to his Range Rover, wanting some privacy before calling Willard.

He took out his mobile phone, and pressed the dial button. After three rings Willard answered.

After the usual pleasantries Hardcastle lost no time in explaining why he had had to cancel their lunch date. Willard was stunned on hearing the news that Panton had been murdered.

"I assume you think that the same guy is responsible for both killings?"

"Yes and no," answered Hardcastle. "Keep this under your hat for the moment, but Phil Davison is on his way back to the nick to interview Glen Finnemore, who we think is a potential suspect for the Panton murder."

"You're joking," replied Willard, much to Hardcastle's surprise. "I can assure you that you're way off the mark there, Steve. Of everyone I know, Glen is the least likely person to have done anything like that. Are you able to tell me what you've got on him and why you think he might have killed Panton?"

Hardcastle quickly ran through the questions that Davison and Paul Taylor would soon be putting to Finnemore. When he had finished, Willard took a few seconds to collect his thoughts.

"OK, I can see where you are coming from Steve, and I can't argue that Glen won't be shedding any tears over Panton's death. But I know a hell of a lot of others who will feel exactly the same way, and that includes anyone who has played cricket with or against him. Trust me on this, Steve, the guy was absolute poison, and of all those that hated him, you know as well as I do that a fair number of them won't have an alibi for last night.

"And now her husband is out of the way, I agree that this will ease the financial burden on Mrs Panton, and on her and Glen as a couple. But what you don't know is that Glen is not actually hard up for cash. In fact, it's quite the opposite.

"He got a decent law degree at University, and has been working for a firm of local solicitors for several years now. He's very much his own man, and I know from chatting to him that he's determined to stand on his own two feet and not take any handouts from his parents.

"And believe me, the Finnemore family is loaded. His father is a London barrister with his own chambers and his mother runs her own PR firm. They are a very respectable and successful family."

"He sounds too good to be true," replied Hardcastle.

"Believe me, Steve; what you see is what you get with Glen. Christ mate I should be higher up your list of suspects than Glen Finnemore.

"And one other thing, if Glen had murdered Panton, you can bet your bottom dollar that he would have made sure he had a cast iron alibi. He's a very, very bright lad."

"OK, I believe you, Danny. By the way, where were you last night?" joked Hardcastle. "Look, thanks for the info. I need to speak to Phil Davison and give him the heads up on Finnemore before he begins to interview him.

"And I really do appreciate your help, Danny. There are other things I need to talk to you about. As soon as I get a bit of spare time I'll get back to you, hopefully within the next day or so."

"No problems Steve. By the way, there's one other thing I think you should know," replied Willard. "I'm told that the Flitton Green pavilion got torched three years or so ago."

"Yep, that's correct. In fact, we never found out who the arsonist was. It's still a bit of a sore point with me. It was my very first case as a DI, and I was desperate to hit the ground running, but we never even got close to finding out who did it. I still have nightmares about it. Why do you ask?"

"For what it's worth, the guys at Middle Ash all thought that Neil Panton was responsible. He was playing for us at that time, and he'd had a run in with several of the Flitton lads during a match. A month or so later, the Flitton pavilion was toast."

Wednesday 1:30pm

Steve Hardcastle put his mobile phone back into his pocket.

Could it be possible? Was Neil Panton really responsible for the arson attack on the Flitton Green pavilion? Surely he hadn't missed something that obvious during the investigation? For a brief moment, he had a strong urge to go back to the station and read through the Flitton Green pavilion fire file one more time. But that urge lasted just a few seconds as he realised he had to get his priorities right.

The job in hand demanded his immediate and undivided attention, and for the time being, having yet another look at the pavilion fire file would have to wait. He couldn't afford any distractions. After all, his career could be on the line.

He took his mobile phone back out of his pocket and called Phil Davison's number. Davison was in the front passenger seat of a squad car on his way back to the police station and answered the call on the second ring.

Hardcastle quickly ran through the conversation he had had with Danny Willard and they agreed that there were still some questions that Glen Finnemore needed to answer.

However, what had seemed to be a fairly strong lead half an hour ago now seemed to be no more than a routine conversation to exclude Finnemore from their enquiries. Once again it seemed that they were indebted to Danny Willard.

And given Finnemore's legal background, Davison knew that he would have to tread very carefully during the interview, and make sure that everything was done by the book. After finishing the call, Hardcastle went back into the house, and told Kiernan and Heywood about his phone conversations with Danny Willard and Phil Davison.

"So, assuming Phil finds the saintly Mr Finnemore is as clean as Danny Willard suggests, we're back to square one—looking for just the one person," summed up Kiernan.

"It looks that way," replied Hardcastle. "Anyway, Finnemore has a cast iron alibi for Sunday since he and Mrs Panton were out house hunting, so he couldn't have had anything to do with the murder of Donald Summers. As you say Billy, things still point towards both killings being the work of one person, even if there are no similarities in the way he despatched both victims."

There was a brief pause whilst Hardcastle rubbed his eyes. The pollen count had been very high for several days now, and the policeman could feel the impending onset of hay fever, something he had suffered from since childhood. That was the last thing he needed at this moment in time.

"Any idea when you'll be able to do the post mortem, Kelly?" asked the DI, turning towards the pathologist. "Is there any chance you can rush this one through?"

"You're in luck," she replied. "I've called in a couple of favours and managed to rearrange the rest of my day so everything will be set up for 4pm. I know you're under pressure with this one, so the sooner I can get you some answers, the more chance we've got to nail this bastard before he kills again. And I do think he is more than capable of killing again. He has no respect for life."

"Thanks Kelly, I really appreciate it. I'll make sure that either Phil or I are at the mortuary in time for when you start. It would be great if you were to find something that links both murders, otherwise at this precise moment we have sod all else to go on."

"No pressure there then," answered the pathologist with a smile.

Leaving them to get on with their jobs, Hardcastle decided to have a quick look around the house and wandered into the lounge. The room was very untidy and he ran the index finger of his gloved right hand across a layer of dust that covered a coffee table.

The house probably hadn't seen a duster or a vacuum cleaner since Panton's wife had left him, thought Hardcastle. Housekeeping was obviously pretty low down on his priorities.

In a small upstairs bedroom, he found a ring binder with the best part of a year's bank statements inside which showed a balance that had spent most of its time hovering perilously close to zero. What was it Tanya Panton had said about her husband? Oh yes—'He rarely had the price of a pint in his pocket.'

There was no sign of a mobile phone in the house, and as nothing had been found in the clothes Panton had been wearing when he died, the murderer had almost certainly taken it away with him; the second mobile he'd acquired in three days. No doubt he'd have turned it off straight away so that its whereabouts couldn't be traced, and by now it was probably in at least a dozen pieces.

There was also no sign of a computer or a laptop in the house, although there was a printer plugged into the mains. Another thing he must have taken away with him. *If it's ever found, pound to a penny it will be in bits and missing its hard drive*, he thought to himself.

Before he left Panton's house, the killer would have spent time searching for anything that might point a finger in his direction, as no doubt he also did when he was ferreting around Donald Summer's bungalow on Monday evening.

In the unlikely event that he'd left behind any evidence linking him to the murders, Hardcastle was confident that the CSIs would find it.

He looked at his watch, and decided to call it a day and go back to the office.

As he made his way back downstairs, he almost bumped into Billy Kiernan who was coming the other way.

"Are you off then, Steve?" asked the CSM.

"Yeah, I thought I would leave you and your lads to it," replied Hardcastle, "Just a couple of things before I go though."

"Fire away."

"Have you found an address book?" asked Hardcastle.

"No, not yet we haven't. These days a lot of people use their mobiles instead. You often find that it's the wife that keeps an address book up to date so there's a good chance that Mrs Panton took it with her when she moved out."

"Good point, I'll ask her about that when I get back to the nick," replied Hardcastle. "Have you come across any paper work for Panton's car business? I couldn't find a thing."

"Same here," responded Kiernan. "Maybe he kept everything on a computer?"

"Unfortunately the killer seems to have taken that away with him as well," said Hardcastle. "Even so, I would have expected him to have some hard copies of receipts for the bits and bobs he bought, like spare parts, oil and so on—all the usual stuff he'd need to give his accountant, assuming he had one that is."

"Are you wondering if Panton might have done some work on the killer's car?"

"That's what I was thinking," replied Hardcastle. "Last thing, Billy, and then I'll leave you alone; have you found any signs of a forced entry?"

"No, no signs at all. Perhaps he just knocked on the front door."

"Perhaps," said Hardcastle, "but I doubt it. I don't see this guy taking any chance of being seen. That would mean he must have come in by the back door or through the garage. And I reckon he's good enough to do this without leaving a trace—and he probably locked the door behind him when he left, just like he did on Sunday."

"We are dealing with one clever and resourceful man."

"Or woman," chimed in Kelly Heywood, who suddenly appeared at the bottom of the stairs.

"Or woman," repeated Hardcastle. "Once he was inside this house, Panton had no chance. I'm afraid that at that point, he was a dead man walking."

Wednesday 2:30pm

Having had to cancel his lunch appointment with Danny Willard, Hardcastle suddenly realised that he was really hungry having had nothing to eat since 6am that morning. No wonder his stomach was grumbling.

On his way back to the police station, he called into a petrol station and bought himself a diet coke, some crisps and a chicken salad sandwich which he intended to eat at his desk when he got back to his office.

His arrival back at the station coincided with the departure of Tanya Panton and Glen Finnemore and he was able to check with Mrs Panton as to whether or not she and her husband had kept an address book during their marriage.

"We did, but it was more of a record of Neil's regular customers, so I left it with him when I moved out. Glen and I have our own one now. Why do you ask?"

"There was no sign of one at the house," replied Hardcastle. "We think the killer must have taken it away with him. And do you know if Neil had a desktop PC or a laptop?"

"He had a laptop. Why, has that gone too?"

"I'm afraid so," replied Hardcastle, holding the door open for the couple.

He watched them as they left, hand in hand, making their way to the waiting police car that was going to take them back to Wallace Drive where Finnemore's car was still parked up.

After watching the car pull away, Hardcastle took the stairs to the second floor in double quick time.

"How did the interview with Finnemore go?" asked Hardcastle as he passed Phil Davison sat at his desk.

"I've no doubt that he's straight as the proverbial dye, boss," replied the detective, "He's the sort of bloke you take an instant liking to, and I'm 100 per cent certain that he wouldn't do anything to risk his relationship with Mrs Panton. And I know it sounds schmaltzy, but they seem pretty besotted with one another.

"And whilst he hasn't got an alibi for last night, your theory about him getting a copy made of the key to Panton's house doesn't hold up. He told me that he didn't even know that Tanya had kept a key; it had never come up in any conversation until today. She confirmed this."

"Fair enough, Phil," replied Hardcastle, "If you're happy, then I'm happy too. Where's Kath, by the way?"

"She's downstairs with Isha and Max Dawson. They're trying to put together a usable e-fit of the mystery man with Mrs Compton and Mr Tregunno," replied Davison.

"Oh that's right, I remember now," said Hardcastle. "I ought to go down and show my face and introduce myself to them both."

Pausing only to put his unopened crisps, sandwich and drink on his desk, the DI hurried downstairs, tapped lightly on the door and went in.

"Hello there, I'm Detective Inspector Steve Hardcastle. You must be Mrs Compton," he said, offering his hand to a stunningly beautiful woman in her mid-thirties, who reminded him of the actress Scarlett Johansson.

Mrs Compton, who was wearing a white tee shirt and an extremely tight pair of jeans, took hold of Hardcastle's hand and looked him straight in the eye for a couple of seconds, before replying, "I suppose I must be."

For the first time in years, Hardcastle could feel he was beginning to blush, so he quickly turned away and smiled at a slightly built man who he guessed was in his late sixties or early seventies.

"And you must be Mr Tregunno."

Once again, Hardcastle held out his hand.

However, this time, the offer of a handshake was declined.

"I'm sorry, Inspector," replied Tregunno. "My arthritis is playing me up a bit today, and my hands are particularly tender."

"No problem. You have my sympathy, Mr Tregunno. My father also suffers from arthritis and I know how painful it can be at times. I just wanted to say how grateful we are to you both for taking the time and trouble to come in today."

"It's no trouble, Inspector. I'm sure Ellie feels the same as me. It's the least we can do after what happened on Sunday. Who'd have thought that something like this could happen in Flitton?" said Tregunno.

"I agree with Brian," said Mrs Compton. "I'm just afraid that I won't be much help to you. I'm sure Brian got a far better look at the guy than I did."

"I'm sure you will do your best, Mrs Compton. We can ask no more than that," replied Hardcastle.

"How is your investigation going, inspector?" asked Tregunno.

Hardcastle hated having to be evasive. But he could hardly say that they hadn't a clue who had killed Summers; that they were now investigating a second murder; and that the latest victim was a teammate of his son and Mrs Compton's husband.

"We're following several lines of enquiry at the moment, and trying to identify the man you both caught a glimpse of is extremely important to us. It may turn out to be a just a case of eliminating him from our enquiries, but we are keeping an open mind at this stage."

With that said, Hardcastle excused himself. The lure of the sandwich on his desk was getting stronger by the minute, and he was beginning to regret just buying the one.

He hurried back upstairs and was just a few yards from his office when Phil Davison called out to him.

"Have you got a sec, boss?"

The sandwich would have to wait just a little while longer.

"Of course, Phil, fire away."

"I've just got off the phone from speaking to Debra Patterson. She was genuinely stunned. Panton might not have been her type, but she quite enjoyed going out with him. She hasn't a clue who might have killed him and he certainly hadn't tried to borrow any money off her.

"She did suggest that we speak to his sister, a Mrs Christine Williams. Mrs Patterson doesn't have her address or telephone number, but I'll try Tanya Panton and see if she knows where Mrs Williams lives."

"OK Phil, that's good. I'd be surprised if Tanya doesn't have contact details for Mrs Williams. They are still sisters-in-law after all."

Hardcastle left Davison to it, and made his way fairly rapidly to his office and the long-awaited sandwich. He was just about to pick it up, when his phone rang. He looked from the phone to his sandwich, carefully weighing both up. Which should he pick up first?

As always, the phone won.

It was DCI Cryer, Hardcastle's boss.

He wanted to see Hardcastle in his office on the third floor as soon as possible.

Hardcastle put the phone down, took one last look at the sandwich and then walked out of his office. *Bloody thing will be stale by the time I get to eat it*, he thought to himself.

Wednesday 2:45pm

It took Hardcastle less than 60 seconds to make the short journey to the third floor.

The door to Detective Chief Inspector Mark Cryer's office was open as usual and although he was obviously in the middle of an important telephone conversation, as soon as he saw Hardcastle approaching, he motioned for him to come in and sit down in one of the three expensive looking chairs that were positioned around a well-used coffee table.

That gesture indicated that his meeting with the DCI would be a fairly informal one. Those officers that were told to sit in one of the two straight-backed chairs immediately in front of Cryer's desk knew that, more often than not, they were in for a rollicking. Luckily, Hardcastle had never had that experience.

Mark Cryer had joined the police force direct from university over thirty years ago and whilst he hadn't said anything specific, the general consensus was that he would be looking to retire in around 18 months' time when he turned fifty five.

Even if this was the case, there were certainly no signs that he was beginning to wind down. In fact the reverse was true, as he continued to put in the hours as he had done when he joined the force all those years ago.

When the vacancy for a DI in Cryer's team had been advertised three years earlier, Steve Hardcastle had been an outside bet, and if the criteria for the appointment had been based on age and length of service alone, Hardcastle would have been considered a non-starter.

However, at the interview, Cryer had obviously seen something different in the young man, and he was so impressed that he put forward a very convincing argument to his fellow members of the promotion's board, as to why Hardcastle should be appointed ahead of the other candidates. Since he would be working directly for Cryer, the others on the panel were happy to agree, and Hardcastle got the job.

The news quickly circulated that Detective Sergeant Hardcastle had been promoted to the rank of Detective Inspector, against all expectations.

It soon became apparent to observers that Cryer looked upon his new DI as his protégé, and almost inevitably, particularly amongst those that had been overlooked for promotion, there were some who hoped that Hardcastle would be completely out of his depth in his new role, and fall at the first hurdle.

And when the new DI failed to solve his very first case, the arson of the Flitton Green cricket pavilion, those with obvious antipathy towards Hardcastle believed that his future as a detective inspector could be measured in weeks rather than months.

However, against all the odds, and with Cryer's backing and encouragement, Hardcastle, on the surface at least, put that unsuccessful investigation behind him, and slowly but surely proved to his detractors that he was there to stay.

"What an absolute idiot," said the DI as he hung up the phone.

"Who's that, sir, the Chief Constable?" asked Hardcastle.

"Simon Osborne at the Echo," replied Cryer, with a smile.

"What did he want?"

"He's just sniffing around as usual. Anyway, it sounds like you've got a lot on your plate at the moment, Steve."

"That's a bit of an understatement, sir. I take it that DS Pearson put you in the picture. I would have done it myself, but I needed to get to the murder scene as soon as I could."

"Yes, she did. She's certainly a bright one. You'll need to keep an eye on her, or she'll be after your job."

"Is that the way the wind is blowing up here?" asked Hardcastle. "Where I'm concerned, that is?"

"Of course not, but I will be questioned on progress by the ACC Ops later today, particularly now we've got a second murder on our hands. So, tell me, what is your current thinking? I assume you are looking for just one man."

"I'm not totally ruling out two but I'm 99% certain that the same man was responsible for both murders sir," replied Hardcastle. "I believe that the murder of the umpire was to be a one-off, but my theory is that on Sunday the killer was seen by someone as he made his getaway, but instead of reporting it to the police as most right minded people would have done, he decided to play a little game of blackmail."

"And you think that today's victim, this guy Neil Panton, was the blackmailer?" asked Cryer.

"Yes, I do, sir. Everything points to that."

"But at the moment, we have no idea who the killer might be," said Cryer, more by way of a statement than a question.

"I'm afraid not," replied Hardcastle. "But I believe our best chance of discovering his identity is still by concentrating most of our efforts on trying to find a link between the killer and his first victim."

"That sounds fair enough," replied the DCI. "But I wouldn't rule out two killers, myself.

"Consider this scenario, Steve. Killer number one murders the umpire. Now killer number two has for some time been thinking of a way to commit a murder himself. As chance would have it, his proposed victim just happens to be associated with Sunday's cricket match.

"When the first murder takes place, killer number two brings forward his plans to bump off his victim as he's been presented with a heaven sent opportunity. He knows that the cops would almost certainly think that killer number one committed both murders.

"So, having done the dirty deed, killer number two walks off into the sunset, and killer number one is arrested, tried and convicted of both murders."

There was silence as Hardcastle gave thought to the DCI's suggestion which he thought was pretty far-fetched. At least he knew his boss wouldn't take offence if he told him politely that he was talking out the top of his head.

"It is possible sir, but, in my view, highly unlikely. I mean, what are the odds of there being two people connected with Sunday's game that would have the balls to commit a murder.

"Let's say that there were around 60 or 70 people who were in some way connected with Sunday's game—this includes players, officials, and player's families. Two killers and two victims out of such a small sample really is stretching it a bit."

"I don't disagree with you, Steve," answered Cryer, "and I thought that way too until I looked through the witness statements that your team have collected so far. One name stood out to me."

The DCI handed him a small brown A4 file.

"I think you should have a look at this."

It was obvious to Hardcastle that the contents were scans of original documents. He then looked at the heading of the first document and looked at Cryer in astonishment.

"I don't believe it."

"I know. But do you see what I mean, Steve? Once you've read the file you may want to reconsider the direction your investigation should now take. And remember what Al Pacino's character in *The Godfather* said: '*Keep your friends close and your enemies closer*'."

Wednesday 3:30pm

Hardcastle sat back in his office chair and took another look at the file that DCI Cryer had given him.

The sandwich remained unopened on his desk, his appetite having all but disappeared. He picked it up and tossed it into the waste paper bin.

He looked at his watch. It was just past 3:30pm. He would need to leave the office fairly soon as he was due at the mortuary at 4pm for the post mortem on Neil Panton's body. Whilst he wanted to share the contents of the file with both Phil Davison and Kath Pearson, he knew he didn't have enough time at the moment.

He grabbed his car keys and walked out into the main office, stopping at Davison's desk.

"I'm off to the mortuary, Phil. Any luck with Tanya Panton?"

"No, she's not answering her phone, but I'll keep trying."

"When you speak to her, can you ask her to jot down the names of any of her husband's regular customers that she can remember? I know it's a long shot, but you never know she might come up with something interesting.

"And we need to have a catch-up when I get back. Perhaps you can mention it to Kath when you see her. I assume she's still working on the e-fit."

"Yeah," replied Davison. "I put my head round the door 10 minutes ago, and they were still hard at it, although Kath did roll her eyes at me. I suspect she's finding Mr Tregunno and Mrs Compton hard going. Mind you, I wouldn't mind spending an hour or so looking at Mrs Compton!"

Unfortunately for Hardcastle, he got stuck in a queue due to some temporary traffic lights, and he was 10 minutes late getting to the mortuary. The post mortem had already begun.

While he was watching and listening to Kelly Heywood as she went about her business, he found that for much of the time his mind was elsewhere, and his meeting with DCI Cryer was still uppermost in his thoughts.

"Are you still with me, Steve?" asked Heywood.

The sound of the pathologist's voice brought him back to the present.

"Sorry Kelly, what were you saying?"

"I said that the blow to the side of the neck probably didn't cause Panton to black out. As he fell, he must have hit the back of his head on the wall with some force, and that almost certainly concussed him. However, the killer knew exactly what he was doing. Looking at the bruising to the neck, I'd say he hit Panton with a knife-hand strike, also known as a karate chop, which he used to cause maximum damage without actually killing him. The force of the blow damaged the carotid artery and the vagus nerve.

"If Panton had survived, he would have needed surgery to the carotid artery. But the compression of the vagus nerve had a more immediate effect."

"Which was?" asked Hardcastle.

"He wouldn't have been able to talk. So the duct tape over the mouth wasn't really necessary."

"Belt and braces," replied Hardcastle. "Jesus, the man really knew what he was doing. He made sure Panton was helpless and unable to cry out."

"Yep," answered Heywood. "That's just about it."

"Tell me, Kelly, in your view, are there any similarities in the cause of death of both Summers and Panton?"

"If you are asking me if two different men could each have committed one murder, I would be able to say that so far my findings could support that hypothesis.

"However, if you asking me categorically to say that it was two different killers, and not just the one, I would have to say that it's equally possible that one person killed both victims.

"It is also possible that someone deliberately chose a completely different way to kill both men, to make us think that we are looking for two people and not the one. I'm sorry I can't be more helpful."

"That's OK. It just means that all options remain in play," replied Hardcastle.

"However, there is one mystery I have been able to clear up. Have a look at this," said Heywood, handing him a large book she'd taken off one of the shelves in her office.

"While I was on the way back from Panton's house, I was wracking my brain because I was pretty certain I had come across something similar to the method used to kill him. I knew I had never done a post mortem on anyone killed that way, and the more I thought about, the more certain I was that I'd read about it when I was studying to become a pathologist. I've marked the relevant passage."

Hardcastle read:

During the early 19th century, 'resurrectionists' Burke and Hare excavated graveyard bodies to sell to medical schools. They decided that preying upon live alcoholics would make their job easier. Burke sat on the victim's chest, used one hand to cover the victim's nose and mouth, and the other to close the victim's jaws, resulting in traumatic asphyxia, thereby providing a body without digging.

This is an example of homicidal traumatic asphyxia in combination with smothering, now called 'Burking'. There have been reports of police custody deaths attributed to this mechanism.

For a few seconds, Hardcastle was quiet as he took stock of what he had just read.

"Do you think there is a connection between this and Neil Panton's death? Could the killer have studied forensic science, or have a medical background?" asked Hardcastle.

"I wouldn't totally rule it out," replied Kelly Heywood. "But realistically, anyone could come across this sort of thing on the internet."

"Out of interest, what happened to Burke and Hare?" asked Hardcastle.

"They were arrested for the last murder they committed, and Hare turned King's evidence in return for immunity from prosecution," said Heywood. "Burke was found guilty and executed. His body was publicly dissected."

"No honour amongst thieves," replied Hardcastle. "What happened to Hare?"

"He was released and was never heard from again," answered Heywood.

"So in this instance, justice wasn't served," said Hardcastle. "Let's hope we have better luck."

Wednesday 5:30pm

When Hardcastle eventually left the mortuary, he didn't immediately return to the station. Instead he sat in his car mulling over the outcome of the post mortem.

He was also debating whether or not to talk to Phil Davison and Kath Pearson about his meeting with the DCI when he got back to the nick, or whether to leave it until the morning's briefing.

By the time he arrived back, he had made up his mind to leave it until the morning, especially as he had now decided to pay Danny Willard a belated visit at his pub on the way home.

As he was walking through the main office he saw that Kath Pearson was back at her desk.

"All go OK with the e-fit Kath?"

"I wish I'd gone with you to the mortuary instead. I'd have enjoyed myself a hell of a lot more if I had," she replied.

Hardcastle noticed that Phil Davison was struggling to keep a straight face.

"Why's that?"

"Well, for a start, Mrs Compton wasn't that much help as she never really got that close to the mystery man. And as for Mr Tregunno, he just couldn't make his mind up. He changed the man's hairstyle and colour at least ten times. One minute the e-fit looked like Donald Trump, the next it looked like Donald Duck.

"Don't get me wrong, he's a nice enough chap but he is one hell of a ditherer."

"I'm afraid it goes with age, Kath," said Hardcastle. "It'll come to us all. You should try spending ten minutes with my old dad."

"Anyway, I've left a copy of the finished article on your desk," replied Pearson, "but to be perfectly frank, I wouldn't attach too much accuracy to it sir, but it's better than nothing I suppose."

"Any luck in contacting Tanya Panton, Phil?" asked Hardcastle turning to his other sergeant.

"She eventually called me about an hour or so ago, and gave me the contact details for Christine Williams, Panton's sister. I got the local cops onto this and they've just rung to confirm that they've delivered the bad news. They did say that she was very distraught.

"They also gave her my phone number and she told them she would give me a call tomorrow morning if she feels up to it.

"And I asked Mrs Panton if she could let me have a list of her husband's regular customers and she said she would e mail me tomorrow morning, although she did say that she only knew a few of them by name."

"OK, it will be better than nothing. Now I've just got to make a quick phone call and then I'll fill you two in on the post mortem," replied Hardcastle.

Back in his office, Hardcastle picked up the e-fit and immediately understood where Kath had been coming from. There was nothing that really stood out, but at least it was a starting point. Whether it was an accurate likeness of the killer was another matter. He would speak to Alex Till about releasing copies of the e-fit to the media after he had had his chat with Pearson and Davison.

His next job was to ring Danny Willard to see whether or not he could spare ten minutes for a quick chat. Willard was more than happy to do this and suggested they meet up at 7pm, before his pub got too busy.

He had also invited Hardcastle to have a meal at the pub on the house, but the DI declined, telling Willard that Mrs Hardcastle would be pleasantly surprised by her husband getting home early for once. That was part of the reason he had turned down the offer, the other being that he had always felt uncomfortable accepting anything for free from a member of the general public, even though in this instance, the member of the public was a former copper. Tempting though Willard's offer had been, he had decided to stick to his principles.

As he was putting the phone down, he called out to Davison and Pearson to say that he was now free to update them on the post mortem.

Ten minutes later Hardcastle had finished giving his colleagues a précis of his time at the mortuary, including Kelly Heywood's brief history lesson on the body snatchers Burke and Hare.

"I know that there's a small chance that we have two killers on our hands and not just the one, boss," said Davison. "But it really is highly unlikely."

"What do you think, Kath?" asked Hardcastle.

"I agree with Phil, I just don't see it, sir."

"For what it's worth, I agree with you, but we can't ignore the possibility that we might have two murderers at large, irrespective of the odds against it," replied Hardcastle, looking at his watch which showed that it was just past 6pm.

"Anyway, it's getting late and we've all clocked up at least twelve hours today, so let's call it a day," continued the DI.

"One last question, sir; what are you going to do with the e-fit?" asked Pearson.

"I know you aren't too impressed with the end result, Kath, but I've really no choice other than to get it out into the public domain as quickly as I can. Pardon the pun, but we have to take it at face value.

"If I don't do it, and sometime later we catch the killer and his face is a dead ringer for the e-fit, I'll end up spending the rest of my career pounding the beat. So I'll speak to Alex Till about it. By the way, I'm popping in to see Danny Willard on my way home. I'll let you know in the morning if he comes up with anything worth sharing. Now, bugger off, the pair of you," he said with a grin. "And well done for a good day's work, by the way."

As his two sergeants were returning to their desks, Hardcastle rang Alex Till on his mobile.

Whist they were chatting, Hardcastle scanned the e-fit and sent it to Till's email address.

"I'll send the likeness to all the usual suspects straight away," said Till. "And are you happy if I say something on the lines of

'Dorminster Police have issued an e-fit image of a man believed to be in his mid to late twenties who they want to speak to as part of their ongoing investigation into the death of Donald Summers. This man was seen in the vicinity of the Flitton Green cricket pavilion around 5pm on Sunday afternoon, and anyone recognising him should immediately ring the number below.'?"

"Perfect Alex," replied Hardcastle. "I couldn't have put it better myself. Thanks for your help as always."

Hardcastle put his phone down. As he did, he noticed the sandwich he'd thrown into the bin a few hours earlier. All of a sudden, he began feeling really hungry again.

He decided he would ring Jenny from his car whilst he was on his way to see Danny Willard and ask her to rustle up some dinner for him. Something tasty and plenty of it would be the instruction.

Wednesday 7pm

Steve Hardcastle pulled into the car park of The Waterman's Arms, bang on 7pm. There were at least 20 other vehicles parked up, evidence of the growing popularity of the establishment now under the ownership of former Metropolitan Police officer Danny Willard.

As he walked through the front door, Hardcastle was immediately greeted by Willard who had obviously been keeping an eye out for him.

"Welcome to The Waterman's Arms, Steve," said Willard as the pair shook hands. "Now are you sure I can't tempt you to have something to eat? Tonight's special is Seared Sea Bass Fillets, served on ribbons of courgettes marinated in lemon, with asparagus, baby potatoes, tender stem broccoli and a vermouth velouté. And if that doesn't take your fancy, my chef does a mean steak and kidney pudding and chips."

"Tempting as the steak and kidney pudding is, my wife is expecting me home for dinner soon," replied Hardcastle.

"Well, why don't you ring your good lady, tell her to drop everything and get over here for a meal she won't forget in a hurry," replied Willard.

"Steady on Danny, I can't have you spoiling her," said Hardcastle with a smile. "I've got low standards to keep, you know."

"Well, if I can't persuade you to have something to eat, what would you like to drink?" asked Willard.

"I'd love a nice hot strong cup of coffee if I could, please."

Willard signalled to one of his bar staff to do two coffees and led Hardcastle to a table tucked away in the far corner of the bar.

"Well, how are things going? Did you get anywhere with Glen Finnemore?" asked Willard.

"I didn't talk to him myself, but I'm told by my sergeant that he seems a decent young man. And if he was in any way involved with the murder of Neil Panton, my sergeant would have soon sniffed him out. We took his statement and that was all," said Hardcastle. "We won't need to call him back."

"So you're back to looking for just the one person?"

"Not exactly," replied Hardcastle. "We're keeping an open mind, and my guvnor came up with a suggestion this afternoon that I'm going to follow through tomorrow."

"And what's that?" asked Willard.

"You know I can't tell you that, Danny. More than my job's worth," replied Hardcastle.

"You're right of course, I shouldn't have asked," said the contrite publican. "Let's call it force of habit, or old habits die hard."

"Have you heard any chatter about Neil Panton since we last spoke?" asked Hardcastle quickly changing the subject.

"I've had a few phone calls from members of the cricket team asking me if I'd heard that he'd been killed, and Glen rang to tell me what had happened when he and Tanya turned up at Neil's house. I don't think he has any idea that for a couple of hours or so, he'd been a suspect. So, full credit goes to your sergeant."

"And what was the general feeling from those who called you?" asked Hardcastle.

"Well, for starters, it's fair to say no one was shedding any tears for Neil. As you know, he had this unerring ability to rub everybody up the wrong way," replied Willard. "But there was also deep concern."

"In what way?" asked Hardcastle.

"Well, let's face it; two people who were involved in the same game of cricket have been killed within 72 hours of each other. People are concerned that whoever did it, might not stop at two. It sounds like an Agatha Christie novel to me."

"Would they still be concerned if, hypothetically, they found out that the murders were carried out by two different people?" asked Hardcastle.

Just as Willard was about to answer, Hardcastle's mobile phone began to ring. Excusing himself, Hardcastle got up and walked outside to the car park for a bit of privacy.

Less than a minute later, he was back inside. Willard, who was still sat at the table, looked up expectantly.

"Sorry about that, Danny. Emergency at home, so I'm afraid I'm going to have to love you and leave you," said Hardcastle.

"Nothing serious I hope?"

"No, but the missus is a bit upset. You know how it is."

"Not these days, I don't," replied Willard. "The wife and I split up a couple of years back. She's got sole custody of the kids."

"I'm really sorry to hear that, Danny."

"Thanks Steve, I appreciate it. Look, you need to get off home."

"Yeah, you're right. I'll be in touch," replied Hardcastle as the two men shook hands again.

Within a minute, Hardcastle was back in his car. Within a quarter of an hour, he was walking through his front door.

"Hiya love, I'm home," called Hardcastle.

"Hi Mr Mysterious," replied Jenny. "So, tell me. Why did you ask me to call you on the dot of 7:15pm?"

Thursday 6:30am

Contrary to his expectations, for once during a major investigation Steve Hardcastle had enjoyed a decent night's sleep, and he was feeling on good form when he arrived at the police station, despite the fact that he was about to deliver a bombshell to his two sergeants.

As usual, Phil Davison and Kath Pearson had beaten him to it, as had Paul Taylor and Isha Hussein. It was good to see the commitment being made by two of the younger members of his team.

"Just give me five minutes to check my email and voice mail messages and then I'll fill you in with regard to my visit to Danny Willard's pub last night," said Hardcastle, addressing his two sergeants.

Finding nothing important on either his phone or his computer, the DI opened the file that DCI Cryer had handed him yesterday afternoon. He was looking through it as Davison and Pearson appeared in the doorway, the latter holding two cups of coffee.

"Hot and strong as you like it, sir," said Pearson.

"You're a lifesaver, Kath," replied Hardcastle.

"Anything interesting come out of your meeting with Mr Willard then?" enquired Davison.

Hardcastle paused. He knew he needed to choose his words carefully.

"As from this moment, we have two separate murder investigations on the go, and Danny Willard is now a suspect for the murder of Neil Panton."

Having been completely taken by surprise, both sergeants spoke simultaneously.

"Wow, I didn't see that coming," said Davison.

"Where in heavens name has that come from?" asked Pearson.

"It began yesterday afternoon when I was called up to see the DCI. During our conversation, he mentioned that he'd been looking through the witness statements for the Donald Summers murder, and that one in particular had jumped out at him. This was the statement given by Danny Willard.

"He then contacted a Detective Chief Inspector Graham Cook, a long standing friend in the Met, who confirmed his suspicions. DCI Cook then emailed Mr Cryer copies of certain documents taken from Willard's old personnel file.

"Just over two years ago Danny Willard, along with two other officers, was suspended following the death in custody of a 27-year-old white man who had been arrested on suspicion of being a drug dealer. It seems they had been trying to nick this guy for some time, but he was a fairly slippery customer, and they could never quite get enough on him to charge him. All three officers were accused of excessive use of restraint and the matter was referred to the Independent Police Complaints Commission, as it was known at that time.

"The IPCC served a notice of misconduct on all three officers. However, after interviewing all witnesses and reviewing the video evidence, they subsequently determined that there was no case to answer, although it did recommend that all three officers involved should undertake some additional training.

"The Met accepted this recommendation in respect of two of the officers involved in the incident, but the third was issued with a final written warning, as he had been given a written warning a couple of months earlier, just nine months after he had been given a verbal warning. That officer was Daniel Anthony Willard."

"Do we know why the Met decided to punish Willard, and not the other two?" asked Phil Davison.

"From what the DCI told me, they couldn't wait to get rid of him, and this was seen as a heaven-sent opportunity," replied Hardcastle. "Shortly after receiving his final written warning, Willard told his boss that it was obvious he had no future in the Met and that he would immediately resign from the force on two conditions: that he would retain all his pension rights, and that, as far as everyone else was concerned, it was his decision to retire after having completed 25 years' service.

"That was quickly agreed, and as far as most of his colleagues were concerned, PC Danny Willard had decided to retire to concentrate on other opportunities. Apparently, he had often talked to his colleagues about owning a pub one day."

"So, backtracking a bit," said Kath Pearson, "what happened with this suspected drug dealer in the custody suite that started the ball rolling?"

"It seemed the dealer, a man named Darren Groom, lost the plot whilst he was being processed," replied Hardcastle. "He head-butted one of the cops who went down for a count of ten. It was all over by the time he woke up, so he was never under investigation.

"There was a general melee with arms and legs everywhere and someone, and it wasn't clear from the CCTV who it was, took Groom's legs away, and he whacked the back of his head on the wall on the way down.

"With him sprawled out on the floor, Danny Willard can be seen placing his knee on Groom's chest. According to Willard, the guy had started spitting at him, so he put his hand over the man's mouth while the two other cops helped pin him down. After thirty seconds or so, Darren Groom started convulsing violently which the three cops took as an attempt to free himself, so they continued to hold him down until he stopped struggling.

"Whilst they were getting their breath back, Groom started convulsing again, and by now they realised that he was having some sort of fit, and needed urgent medical assistance. As it happened, there was a doctor on site who was able to examine him, and he immediately called for an ambulance. Unfortunately, Groom never regained consciousness and he died a couple of days later. The post mortem revealed that he had died from an intracranial haemorrhage caused by hitting his head against the wall."

"So, basically, it was an accident," said Phil Davison. "The guy brought it on himself when he decided to take on all-comers in the custody suite. But I don't see how that puts Danny Willard in the frame for killing Neil Panton."

"I wouldn't disagree with you, Phil, were it not for one thing," answered Hardcastle.

"And what is that, boss?"

"Before he gave his formal statement, PC Alan Goodrich, one of those involved in restraining Darren Groom, told the custody sergeant that he thought Groom's seizures were caused by Danny Willard.

"It couldn't be seen on the CCTV, but Goodrich said that when Willard pinned Groom to the floor with his knee, not only did he put a hand over the man's mouth, he also pinched his nostrils together for at least 30 seconds. Does that sound familiar?"

Davison and Pearson looked at each other.

"Just a bit," replied Davison.

"And that's not all," continued Hardcastle. "Remember yesterday when I briefed you about the post mortem on Neil Panton? I also mentioned that Kelly Heywood likened the cause of death to the way the mass murderers Burke and Hare went about their business during the 1820s."

Davison and Pearson both nodded.

"Well, Kelly showed me a page from one of her reference books, and I took a couple of photocopies of it before I left the mortuary," said Hardcastle, handing a copy to both of them. "It's the last paragraph that I have highlighted, which I was most interested in."

They both read:

During the early 19th century, 'resurrectionists' Burke and Hare excavated graveyard bodies to sell to medical schools. They decided that preying upon live alcoholics would make their job easier. Burke sat on the victim's chest, used one hand to cover the victim's nose and mouth, and the other to close the victim's jaws, resulting in traumatic asphyxia, thereby providing a body without digging.

This is an example of homicidal traumatic asphyxia in combination with smothering, now called 'Burking'. There have been reports of police custody deaths attributed to this mechanism.

"Blimey," said Phil Davison. "I see what you mean. It certainly puts Willard in the frame. So what do we do now, boss?"

"Well, the first thing I'm going to do is to speak to DCI Cook at the Met. It's important that we get more background info on Willard. I'm particularly keen to find out why he received verbal and written warnings in the months leading up to the Darren Groom incident.

"After I've done that, we can have another chat, and then I think we're going to have to get him in to answer a few questions."

They looked at each other—none of them particularly relishing the idea.

"What about motive, sir?" asked Kath Pearson. "From what Tanya Panton told us, we know that her husband expected to come into some money."

"I think the motive remains the same," replied Hardcastle. "Perhaps Panton had found out about Danny Willard's past and was threatening to tell everybody if he didn't cough up some cash.

"Anyway, I'll speak to DCI Cook as soon as I can, and then let's have another chat after that. One way or another, we need to know if we are looking for one or two murderers. For what it is worth, my view is that we are still hunting for just the one, but of course, I may be wrong."

Thursday 9:55am

It was almost 10am before Hardcastle was able to speak to DCI Cook. Over three hours had elapsed since his meeting with Phil Davison and Kath Pearson, and by the time he was eventually put through to the DCI, he was feeling a little frustrated.

"Good morning, DI Hardcastle. I was expecting you to call me at some stage. I assume this is about Daniel Willard?"

"That's correct sir."

"Well, I'm afraid that I have another meeting starting shortly, so you'll need to be brief."

"I'll do my best, sir," replied Hardcastle, biting his tongue. "I understand that PC Willard received a verbal warning and a written warning in the months leading up to the death in custody of Darren Groom. Are you able to give me some background to those warnings?"

"To put them into some sort of context, both were considered to be misconduct rather than gross misconduct," replied Cook.

"His first transgression was for swearing at a member of the public, who subsequently made a complaint against him. On investigation, it became evident that there was a degree of provocation from the complainant, and it was decided to administer a verbal rebuke to Willard for allowing himself to be deliberately goaded into an argument with this individual."

"And the second, sir?" asked Hardcastle.

"That came about when officers were called to a disturbance at a public house and found that PC Willard, who was off duty at the time, had been involved in an altercation with a man who suffered a severely bruised cheekbone. The man, however, was at great pains to stress that he didn't want to press charges. Even though he was off duty at the time, Willard received a written warning."

"Were there any extenuating circumstances to the second incident sir?" asked Hardcastle.

There was silence at the other end of the phone.

"Are you still there, sir?"

"The person who Willard assaulted was, allegedly, having an affair with his wife—hence the reason the man did not want to press charges," replied DCI Cook.

"I believe that Willard and his wife are separated and that she has sole custody of their children," said Hardcastle. "Did this impact on his work?"

"I'm afraid it did," replied Cook. "Before that happened, his work and conduct was satisfactory. He certainly didn't possess the desire or ability to progress beyond the level of constable, but he was reliable, and his disciplinary record was clean.

"However, his domestic difficulties became apparent when there was a significant deterioration in all aspects of his work, and, to be honest with you DI Hardcastle, he would have and should have been dismissed from the force several months before the Darren Groom incident, had it not been for his colleagues covering up for him."

"The fact that they did cover for him, must say something about his popularity amongst his colleagues," said Hardcastle.

"To a certain extent, yes," replied Cook. "However, even their patience eventually ran out, and when the opportunity presented itself to remove Willard from the force, it was to everybody's advantage, especially PC Willard's.

"That's why we agreed to accept his resignation, and why we went along with the pretence that it was a retirement and not a dismissal."

"I'm sure sir that you are aware that Willard became the owner of The Waterman's Arms public house in Long Ash, and he seems to be doing fairly well at it," said Hardcastle.

"Yes, Mr Cryer told me that when we spoke yesterday afternoon. I was most surprised to hear that he was the owner and not the tenant. I could suggest that you make enquiries as to where the money came from to buy the establishment, but that's for you to decide. It's none of my business now," replied Cook. "Look, I'm sorry DI Hardcastle, but I'm going to have to dash as I have a senior staff meeting to chair."

"One last question before you go sir," interjected Hardcastle. "Do you feel that Willard is capable of committing murder?"

There was a brief pause at the other end of the phone.

"I believe that given a certain set of circumstances, most of us are capable of murder; when family members are under threat, for example," replied Cook.

"But in this instance," cut in Hardcastle, "the victim was an acquaintance and the method used was fairly gruesome."

"That certainly had me scratching my head. If it had been a violent death, such as the victim receiving a severe beating with fists, I would say that Willard could be capable of despatching someone in that way. But from what I knew of him, it would be completely out of character to kill someone in the manner described to me by DCI Cryer.

"To put it bluntly, I don't think Willard has the malevolence in him to impose a lingering death on someone, no matter what the circumstances are. He's far more likely to act impulsively. *Act in haste, repent at leisure* as the old saying goes.

"Look, I'm really sorry to rush you, DI Hardcastle, but when you're a stickler for punctuality like I am, the last thing you should do is to keep your staff waiting. I would be interested to hear how your investigation proceeds though, it sounds like you've got a lot on your plate. If there is anything I can do to help, and Mr Cryer is ok about it, do feel free to call me again. Cheerio."

And with that, the line went dead.

At least his last impression of DCI Cook was better than his first.

While he was mulling over his conversation with DCI Cook, Phil Davison tapped lightly on the door.

"Ready for us yet, boss?"

"Yes, just about. Can you give Kath a shout please, Phil."

With the three of them ensconced in his office, Hardcastle decided to have his door closed for once.

"First things first," he began, "has Tanya Panton remembered the names of any of her husband's customers?"

"I received her email about half an hour ago. She came up with a dozen names, and said she'll let me know if she thinks of any others," replied Davison. "There are a few names we know, including one Danny Willard."

"So Willard had his car serviced by Neil Panton," replied Hardcastle. "In the few conversations I've had with him, he always gave me the impression that he knew Panton by reputation only. That'll be one question he will have to answer. Who are the other names I'd recognise?"

"Three Flitton Green players, Colin Sharpe, David Compton and Jethro Tregunno," replied Davison.

"I thought his name was Brian?" asked Hardcastle.

"Jethro is Brian Tregunno's son," said Davison.

"Ah, got it. What about the other names on her list?"

"I've got Paul Taylor working on these," replied Pearson.

"OK. And have you spoken to Panton's sister today Phil?"

"Yes, I have," answered Davison. "Understandably, she was still very emotional, and wanted to know when we would be able to release the body. She did say that she had spoken to her brother on Tuesday evening and that he was in a really good mood, although he didn't say why, just that things seemed to be going his way for once in his life. I told her that I'd get someone to visit her and take a statement."

After nodding his thanks to Davison, Hardcastle proceeded to run through his conversation with DCI Cook.

"So what do you think sir?" enquired Kath Pearson when he'd finished. "Is Willard really in the frame for killing Neil Panton?"

"Well, it appears he's not the person he has led us to believe he is. We can't deny that he has been very helpful, but perhaps there are reasons for that. Maybe he has his own agenda. Maybe it suits him to have us thinking that he's a good all-round chap," answered Hardcastle. "At the very least, he has some questions to answer."

"So when do we go and get him, boss?" asked Davison.

"Let's get him picked up, but let's do it quietly," replied Hardcastle. "No need to make a song and dance about it. Let's not give him any idea that we have him in the frame for Panton's murder until he's in the interview room.

"Now, I'd like you to do me a favour please, Kath," he said, looking at Pearson.

"Fire away, sir," replied Pearson.

"I'd like you and Phil to do the interview."

"I'm more than happy to do it," she replied with a degree of curiosity; normally he and Davison carried out suspect interviews. "Is there any particular reason why you want me in on it, sir?"

"I just think he would feel a little bit too comfortable talking to me and as he doesn't know you, he may feel that he's at a little bit of a disadvantage."

"Well, I'll certainly make sure he doesn't feel comfortable with me," she replied.

Thursday 10:55am

To say that Danny Willard was annoyed would have been a gross understatement. He was fuming.

The last thing he had needed that particular morning was two plain-clothed police officers knocking on the door of his pub just minutes before it was due to open. He had recognised the older of the two coppers standing on his doorstep as DS Phil Davison, but the second, who introduced himself as DC Alan Rutherford was a new face to him.

He had assumed that they were there as a routine follow up visit in connection with the statement he'd made on Sunday evening, and as he was really busy trying to sort out some problems, he had politely asked them to come back a little later on when he would have more time.

He had been completely taken aback when Davison had told him that someone else would have to sort out those problems, as they were there to take him back to the police station to answer some questions in connection with their ongoing investigations into the deaths of Donald Summers and Neil Panton.

Struggling to keep his temper, Willard had replied that he had already told them all he knew about the murder of Donald Summers, and that he knew absolutely nothing about the death of Neil Panton, other than what he had been told by DI Hardcastle the previous evening.

Willard's less than subtle mention of Hardcastle's name had cut no ice whatsoever with DS Davison who had told him that if he didn't go with them willingly, there were two uniformed cops in a marked police car parked a few hundred yards up the lane and that being collected from his pub by two police cars would get tongues wagging and might not be particularly good for business.

Realising that he didn't have a choice, Willard got into the back seat of the unmarked car after calling out to whoever was in the bar that he shouldn't be too long.

By the time the car driven by Rutherford had been parked up in the station car park, Willard was really ticking, despite repeatedly telling himself that he needed to calm down. He knew only too well what the ramifications might be were he to lose his temper.

"I assume you're taking me to see Steve Hardcastle?" asked Willard as the three men made their way to one of the station's interview rooms.

"Unfortunately, Mr Hardcastle is tied up this morning, so DS Kath Pearson and I will be having a chat with you as soon as I let Sergeant Pearson know that we've arrived," replied Davison as he opened the door to Interview Room Three.

"Make yourself at home, Mr Willard," said Davison gesturing to one of the chairs behind a small desk. "I'm sure you've seen the insides of enough interview rooms to last you a lifetime. Can I get you anything; how about a nice cup of tea or coffee?"

"Water will be fine, thanks," replied Willard. "There's no such thing as a nice cup of tea or coffee in the average nick!"

"Water it is then," replied Davison. "I'll be back in a couple of minutes with DS Pearson."

Leaving Willard on his own, but with a uniformed officer standing outside the interview room, Davison and Rutherford made their way back to their second floor offices where they found Hardcastle sat on the edge of a desk talking to Kath Pearson.

"He came quietly then?" asked Hardcastle.

"More or less," replied Davison, "but I'm pretty certain that he's really simmering under the surface."

"OK, leave him to stew for ten minutes or so, and then see what you can get out of him."

Davison and Pearson used those ten minutes to run through the questions they were going to put to Willard, and then took a slow walk down to Interview Room Three, stopping off to get themselves cups of coffee and a glass of cold water for their reluctant guest.

"That was a long couple of minutes," said Willard sarcastically as the two police officers entered the room.

"Apologies for that, Mr Willard," answered Davison. "These things happen, you know how it is. By the way, this is Detective Sergeant Pearson."

Willard gave her a nod.

"I assume that this is a voluntary interview or are you going to caution me?" enquired Willard.

"Purely voluntary, Mr Willard," replied Pearson. "You can leave any time you want and, as you know, you are also entitled to have a solicitor present during this meeting."

"That would take too long to arrange, and I need to get back to the pub as soon as possible. The two bar staff I left in charge are both fairly inexperienced, so can we please get on with things? I've got nothing to hide."

"Of course," said Pearson. "Where were you on Tuesday night between 11pm and 7am?"

"Why do you ask?" enquired Willard.

"Just answer the question please, Mr Willard," replied Pearson.

"Let me see now. I worked in the bar until 1am. After that I went upstairs and watched some television until I was ready to go to bed. That would have been around 1:45am."

"Were there any witnesses?" asked Davison.

"Well, the last customers didn't leave until 11:45pm, which left just me and two barmen. They helped me to clean the bar and wash up the glasses and they left just before 1am. I can give you their names and addresses if you like."

"That will be helpful, thank you," replied Davison. "After your barmen left, were you alone, or did you have any company?"

"Unfortunately, I was alone. That seems to be the story of my life these days."

"How well did you know Neil Panton?" asked Pearson.

That question came out of the blue and took Willard by surprise. His eyes narrowed noticeably.

"I knew him by reputation only. I don't think I ever met the man apart from on the cricket pitch," he replied somewhat cautiously.

"Now that is a surprise. We've been informed that Mr Panton serviced your car on at least one occasion. Would you like to reconsider your answer, Mr Willard?" asked Pearson.

It was a few seconds before the former policeman replied.

"Now I come to think about it, he did do some work on my car. I'd clean forgotten about that. It must have been over a year ago now. Someone, I can't remember who, had recommended him to me. However, I wasn't particularly satisfied with the work he did, and so I never went back to him."

"What do you know about Burke and Hare?" asked Pearson completely changing the subject and again taking Willard by surprise.

"I'm sorry, what the hell do you mean by that," replied Willard, seemingly genuinely stumped by the question.

"The grave robbers Burke and Hare—surely you've heard of them."

"Heard of them, yes. But, pardon my French, I know bugger all about them. What is this, a history lesson?"

"I'm sure we can refresh your memory, just like we did when you said you didn't know Neil Panton," added Kath Pearson. "But we'll come back to that later.

"Now can you tell us about the verbal warning you received when working for the Metropolitan Police when a member of the public made a complaint against you."

"You have been doing your homework, haven't you," replied Willard. "That was something about nothing. The guy was a toerag, well known to everybody. I nicked him for receiving and he got really mouthy, calling me all the names under the sun.

"I wasn't having the best of times at home as I suspected my missus was having an affair, and I let my temper get the better of me and I grabbed him by the throat. It was all over before it began really, and I calmed down a lot quicker than he did.

"He thought that by threatening to make a complaint, I would let him off with just a warning. When I didn't, he made his complaint, and that was that. As I said, it was a small storm in a very small tea-cup. By the way, the lad got 18 months, so justice was done."

"OK," replied Pearson, "Now, what about the written warning you received a few months later for fighting in a pub? You were off duty at the time, I believe?"

Willard sighed, and gently shook his head.

"I was convinced that my wife had been having an affair, so I paid a local private eye to follow her for a week. It didn't take him that long to get to the bottom of things. It turned out the guy she was seeing was a long-standing mate of mine. He'd actually been best man at our wedding, so I was totally gutted when I found out what the pair of them had been getting up to behind my back.

"I knew where he drank, so after reading the report the private eye had given me, I decided to pay my so-called mate a visit. I admit that I was well wound up, but who wouldn't have been given the circumstances? I went there with the intention of embarrassing him in front of his mates, so they would know what a real low-life he was.

"You should have seen the look on his face when he saw me walk into the bar. I was the last person he expected to see. He thought he had been so clever covering his tracks, and that I didn't have a clue what had been going on between him and my missus. He forgot I had a copper's nose.

"I know I shouldn't have done it, but I whacked him once, and he went down. Even though I was ready for it, none of his mates reacted, and as I looked down at him, whimpering on the floor, I realised what I had done. And you know what? I felt absolutely nothing—no satisfaction, no regret.

"The landlord had been quick to ring the cops, and I knew there was no point in me leaving. So I ordered a pint, sat down in the corner on my own, and waited for the Old Bill to arrive. As it turned out, I knew the two cops well, and as the guy who was seeing my wife didn't want to press charges, I thought that I'd got away with it.

"However, it was my wife who made the complaint against me, saying that even though I had been off duty I had let the force down by assaulting her new partner, the man she said she was going to marry once the divorce came through. She even had the cheek to say that she feared for her own safety, knowing that I had never ever laid a hand on her.

"Inevitably, I received a dressing down and a written warning. Twenty years or so with a clean sheet, and then bang, bang—I get two warnings within a few months of each other. Who'd have believed it?

"And you know what? A couple of months later, my so-called mate told my missus that it was all over between them. It was too late to save our marriage though; too much water had passed under the bridge."

"And what about the death in custody of Darren Groom?" asked Phil Davison.

Willard once again shook his head. Davison noticed that the colour had drained from his face, and he was looking decidedly tired.

Once again, it was several seconds before he replied.

"I just happened to be in the custody suite when a couple of lads from CID brought Groom in for processing. Apparently, they had been after him for some time, and were pretty geed up at nicking him at long last, so they were giving him a fair bit of verbal. Totally out of the blue, Groom lost it and began to lash out. He knocked out one of my mates with a head butt, and then everyone piled in. There were fists and feet flying everywhere. Someone managed to get him on the floor, and that's when I jumped in and pinned him down."

"By planting a knee on his chest?" asked Pearson.

"Well, yes. We didn't want to give him the chance to get back up on his feet," replied Willard. "At this point the two CID boys decided to leave us to it. I don't think they wanted to get their suits dirty. You know what these CID types are like," he said with a degree of sarcasm, looking at Pearson and then Davison.

"According to one of your uniformed colleagues, apart from your knee on his chest, you also had one hand over his mouth and the other one over his nose. You had effectively stopped him from breathing," butted in Phil Davison.

"The man started spitting at me, so I put my left hand over his mouth. What else could I do? He also had a really heavy nosebleed, so my medical training kicked in, and without thinking I pinched both of his nostrils shut with the thumb and forefinger of my right hand. I was the only one who had the rubber gloves on, so it was down to me.

"It seemed to have worked as he calmed down, so I took my hand away from his mouth, but kept the pressure up on his nose as I hadn't been able to stop the bleeding. He then started flailing away with his arms and legs, so we had to make sure that we kept him pinned down, until he stopped.

"We thought that he had calmed down and were just about to get him back up on his feet, when it happened again, only this time it seemed to be more like a convulsion. It was at that point that we all realised that it might be something more serious. Luckily, there was a police doctor in the station, and after a quick look at Groom, he told us to call for an ambulance immediately.

"It turned out that Groom had hit the back of his head against the custody suite wall during the scrum and a couple of days later he died in hospital of a brain haemorrhage. His death was completely accidental, and the IPCC decided that there should be no action taken against either me or the other officers.

"Unfortunately, the Met had other ideas, and decided to issue me with a final warning notice. It was then that I realised my days as a copper were numbered, and, after a lot of thought, I decided to hand in my notice on one condition—that it would show on my record that I had taken early retirement. The Met agreed, and that was the end of my career in the Metropolitan Police Service after nigh on twenty-five years."

"You sound quite bitter about the way things ended, Mr Willard," said Kath Pearson. "But from the Met's perspective, there was a clear pattern emerging; a pattern of violence in situations where you could, and should have been able to keep your temper in check. To be frank, you had become a liability and the Met could no longer allow this to continue. I'd say you have no one else to blame but yourself."

"Well you would say that, wouldn't you Sergeant Pearson, sat safely behind your desk letting everyone else do all the dirty work," said Willard angrily, and he stood up and pushed his chair away with such force that it slammed into the interview room wall.

"I've had enough of all this," he said. "I'll leave you to play your silly games with some other poor mug."

"Sit down please, Mr Willard," said Phil Davison softly, "otherwise, we will have to continue this interview under caution, and if we do that, there's every chance that you won't get back to your pub until way after closing time tonight."

Reluctantly, Willard picked up the chair and sat back down at the desk. He took a couple of deep breaths.

"Thank you, Mr Willard," said Davison. "Now earlier, DS Pearson asked you what you knew about Burke and Hare."

"And I said I hadn't got a clue what she was on about," replied Willard. "And I still haven't."

"Well, let me enlighten you then," said Kath Pearson. "Burke and Hare committed sixteen killings over a 10-month period in Edinburgh in 1828. Burke would sit on the victim's chest and use a hand to cover his mouth and his nose. This method, which became known as burking, resulted in death by combining smothering and traumatic asphyxia.

"According to our pathologist, there have been instances of police custody deaths attributed to this method, and you admitted to using something virtually identical to burking when subduing Darren Groom."

"Maybe, but you should remember that Groom died of a brain haemorrhage, and the IPCC absolved us from any responsibility for his death," countered Willard. "But please tell me, what has all this got to do with me and your investigation into Neil Panton's death?"

"Because, Mr Willard, Neil Panton was struck on the side of the neck by his killer and as he fell he hit the back of his head on a wall. His assailant then pinned him to the ground by placing a knee on his chest, having already covered his mouth with tape, and then prevented him from breathing by stopping the air flowing through his nostrils. Neil Panton died from a combination of smothering and traumatic asphyxia. He was a victim of burking."

Willard looked at Kath Pearson in total disbelief.

"I can see where you are going with this," said Willard. "I therefore refuse to answer any more of your damn fool questions until my solicitor is present."

And with that, he turned his back on DS Davison and DS Pearson.

Thursday 12:45pm

"And at that point, Willard said he was refusing to answer any more questions until his solicitor was present. He then turned his back on us and got out his mobile phone, so Kath and I decided to let him stew for a while," said Phil Davison.

"Well, I wanted to see if you could get a reaction out of him, and you certainly got it by the sound of it," replied Hardcastle.

"That was mainly Kath's doing, boss. You know how persistent she is when she gets her teeth stuck in to something," said Davison, smiling at his fellow detective sergeant.

"That's exactly why I wanted the pair of you in there. Tell me, what do you think of him, Kath?"

"Well, for starters, he desperately needs some anger management therapy. He's got a very short fuse. But he also seems to calm down fairly quickly and I think that I would agree with what DCI Cook told you about him. If he had decided to kill Neil Panton, then I think it would probably have been over and done with pretty quickly. I don't think he's got the patience to take his time over killing someone."

"What about you, Phil?" asked Hardcastle.

"I agree with Kath," replied Davison. "The irony of it is that if he didn't have such a cast iron alibi, I would have had him in the frame for killing Donald Summers because of his quick temper. But I don't think he killed Panton."

"So what do you want us to do with him, sir?" asked Pearson. "I know he hasn't got an alibi for Tuesday night, but then again he doesn't seem to have any reason to kill Panton. He's got no motive, and we've got nothing that places him at Panton's house either. All we've got is a similarity between the way Panton was killed, and the technique Willard used to subdue a violent criminal, a man who had already assaulted and knocked out a fellow police officer."

"You're both right, of course," replied Hardcastle. "His temper doesn't do him any favours, and you can see why DCI Cryer and DCI Cook both thought he was worth interviewing.

"But based on your interview and the fact that his own DCI didn't think Willard was capable of killing someone the way Panton was killed, I don't think we have any option other than to release him without charge.

"I'll see Mr Cryer this afternoon and tell him why we've let him go, but I'll also tell him that we'll keep an eye on him."

"Do you want me to go and give Willard the good news, boss?" asked Davison.

"No thanks, Phil. I think I should do that myself."

On his way down to Interview Room Three, Hardcastle stopped off to get two cups of coffee. With a file in one hand and the cups in the other, he found himself having to back into the room.

"For God's sake, give me some more time, will you?" growled Willard, with his back to the door. "I haven't been able to get hold of my solicitor, and I need to speak to DI Hardcastle urgently."

"Your wish is my command," replied Hardcastle. "And I bring a peace offering, a decent cup of coffee which I made myself."

Willard spun around immediately. "It'll take more than a cup of coffee to calm me down."

"And that might well be the crux of your problem, Danny, and why you ended up here today," replied Hardcastle.

"What the hell do you mean by that?"

"From what my officers have told me, and the information we've had from your old boss, it seems like your temper keeps getting you into trouble."

"Cobblers," replied Willard, although Hardcastle could detect a softening in his voice. "Oh well, maybe you're right. In hindsight, the verbal and the written warnings were both avoidable."

"And if you hadn't already got those warnings on your record, at worst, you'd probably have got away with just a verbal warning over the Darren Groom incident," said Hardcastle. "And who knows, you might still have been working at the Met."

"Maybe, but unlikely," replied Willard. "It wouldn't have changed what's been the root cause of all my problems. My wife would still have had an affair with my best friend, and once I found out about it, I wouldn't have been able to leave it at that."

"I gather that your wife and her lover split up not long after you stuck one on him. You must have scared him off. I don't suppose there's any chance of the two of you ever getting back together again, even if it's only for the children's sake?" asked Hardcastle.

"No chance whatsoever," replied Willard. "Even though she's also on her own as far as I know, too much water has passed under the bridge for that to happen. I think that once the trust has gone from a marriage, the marriage itself has gone. We remain civil to each other, but that's just for the children's sake."

"I'm sorry to hear that, Danny. It can't have been easy for you."

Willard nodded in acknowledgement.

"Why did you tell my two sergeants that you had never met Neil Panton?" asked Hardcastle softly.

"That was wrong, and I regretted saying it straight away. I should have known better. But please believe me that when he did some work on my car, it was the one and only time I spoke to him. I'd played against him, of course, but never had cause to speak to him," continued Willard. "So, what happens now? I assume I'm going to be cautioned?"

"Not exactly," answered Hardcastle. "In fact, you are free to leave, Mr Willard."

Willard let out a long sigh of relief.

"Thank you, Steve. I do appreciate it, I really do. Is there anything I can do for you in return?"

"Well, you can keep out of trouble for a start. I'm not sure how my DCI will react when I tell him that I've let you go."

"OK, I promise to keep my nose clean," replied Willard.

"I'll see if we've got someone who's free to drop you back at the pub," offered Hardcastle as he walked Willard to the back door of the police station.

"Don't worry about that, I'll get a cab," replied Willard. "God knows what a mess I'll find when I get back."

He smiled, opened the door and was gone. There had been no handshake.

As he walked back to his office, Hardcastle couldn't help feeling that that would not be the last he saw of the publican.

Something was bothering him, but he couldn't quite put his finger on it.

Thursday 1:05pm

Instead of going back to his office, Hardcastle decided to carry on up the stairs to the third floor and have a quick word with DCI Cryer.

His luck was in. His boss agreed with the way he had dealt with Willard and he also agreed that it was unlikely that the publican had played any part in the murder of Neil Panton.

However, DCI Cryer had some bad news to pass on and he waited until Hardcastle had finished and was about to get up out of his chair to return to his own office.

"Actually, I'm glad you came up to see me, Steve. You'll remember I told you yesterday that I had a meeting scheduled with the ACC Ops?"

Hardcastle nodded.

"Now, he has asked me to assure you that this is no reflection on you whatsoever, but he asked me to assume overall operational control of this enquiry."

Hardcastle was about to butt in, but was stopped in his tracks when DCI Cryer held up his right hand.

"Hang on, Steve, hear me out—and then you can have your say. The ACC suggested that I take immediate control, but I declined. I was able to convince him that your investigation has a degree of momentum working in its favour, and he has agreed that you will retain total responsibility until after Sunday afternoon's reconstruction when he will again take stock of the overall situation."

"So basically, I have three days to find the killer," said Hardcastle.

"Putting it that way, then yes, you have three days," replied Cryer. "But we both know that in this business a lot can happen in three days."

"In that case, I'd better find the killer in two."

Out of respect for his boss, Hardcastle managed to get the words out without any hint of sarcasm, but there was no doubt he was very disappointed with the ACC's decision.

"Actually, I think his decision was inevitable once we had the second murder on our hands," said Cryer. "Most forces would have had at least a DCI in charge by now, and I think you should consider it a compliment that the ACC is prepared to give you another 72 hours before deciding whether or not I take overall command.

"And, if that happens, it won't be like having a complete stranger walk in and take over. You and I have worked well together in the past, and I'm sure we would do the same this time if it becomes necessary. And, for what it's worth, I really hope that we track down this monster before Sunday."

On his way back down to his own office, Hardcastle decided it wasn't the right time to tell his team about the ACC's intervention. He didn't want to put more pressure on them as they were already working their tails off, so he would choose the right moment to break the news. Now wasn't that moment.

"Did Mr Willard get off OK?" asked Davison, as he saw Hardcastle returning to his office.

"Eventually, but not until he had had a bit of a whinge," replied Hardcastle.

"That's no surprise. So, we're back to hunting for just the one killer?"

"Yes, but it's not quite the end of our investigation into Willard."

Davison and Kath Pearson looked at each other, and then at their boss expectantly.

"I know that this will only add to our workload, but something that his old boss said to me this morning has been gnawing away and I think that it could be very important, even if it isn't relevant to our current investigation."

"What was that boss?" asked Davison.

"DCI Cook told me that he was surprised that Willard was the owner of The Waterman's Arms and not the tenant, and that perhaps we should try and find out where the money to buy it had come from. Now we could park this until after we've found our killer, but the fact DCI Cook mentioned it to me suggests he thinks it important that we delve into Willard's finances sooner rather than later. So I'd like you to start making some discreet enquiries please, Kath," asked Hardcastle, knowing that this was just the sort of task she revelled in.

"That's fine, sir," she replied. "Have you any idea how much he might have paid for the pub?"

"At least three quarters of a million I'd guess, perhaps even more," replied Hardcastle. "Whichever way you look at it, it will have cost him a small fortune, and don't forget he's probably paying a fair amount in child maintenance for his two children," added Hardcastle.

"So we could be trying to find how he got access to over a million pounds," replied Pearson. "That's a lot more than a humble police constable could save up, even one who had put in his 25 years' service. I'll certainly do what I can to find out, sir."

"Thanks Kath," replied Hardcastle. "By the way, have we had any response to the e-fit? I saw it was in this morning's Echo."

"It's been a bit disappointing so far, sir. Just four calls which we are following up." answered Pearson. "At least one of them sounds like a wind-up."

"OK," replied Hardcastle. "Look, it's been a tough few days, and I'd like you to make sure that everyone gets away on time tonight—and that includes you two!"

"My wife will think I've been up to something if I'm home a lot earlier than normal," joked Davison. "But, much appreciated boss."

"Likewise," said Pearson, "unless, of course, something else turns up in the meantime."

Thursday 2pm

With Olivia MacDonald in a deep sleep on the sofa, her daughter Helen decided it would be a good time to go onto her iPad to see if there was more news regarding the murder of Donald Summers. Having added the Dorminster Echo website as one of the favourites on her iPad, their home page appeared almost immediately on the screen.

What she saw took her breath away, and inadvertently she let out a loud 'bloody hell!'

'CRICKET CLUB MURDERER CLAIMS SECOND VICTIM' read the headline.

Helen looked across the lounge at her mother, to make sure she was still asleep before reading the article:

Whilst police have yet to confirm a connection between Sunday's death of local umpire Donald Summers, and yesterday's discovery of the body of Flitton Green cricketer Neil Panton, late last night a source close to the investigation informed this newspaper that police enquiries are proceeding on the premise that the same person is responsible for both killings, this despite the fact that, to the best of their knowledge, Mr Summers and Mr Panton had never met prior to Sunday's match between Flitton Green and Middle Ash cricket clubs.

Dorminster Police have today issued an e-fit image (left) of a man they want to speak to as part of their ongoing investigation into the death of Mr Summers.

This man, believed to be in his mid-twenties, was seen in the vicinity of the Flitton Green cricket pavilion around 5pm on Sunday afternoon, and anyone recognising him should immediately ring the number below.

Helen's immediate thought was how to put this latest development into context for her mother. What she was desperately trying to avoid was Olivia becoming embroiled in something that was happening some 450 miles away.

After all, her mother had more than enough on her plate, looking after herself, and visiting her husband every day in his care home.

Looking at the e-fit, the face staring back at Helen was obviously that of a man in his mid-twenties, as the website news item had suggested. If that person had murdered Donald Summers, that should be the end the matter, as the e-fit was definitely not the face of a person who, according to her mother, would have been much older than that.

So the task facing Helen was to make sure that her mother was suitably convinced that her speculation as to who might have killed Mr Summers had been proven to be no more than a wild guess and that the police were hunting for a man in his mid-twenties who they believed was responsible for both murders.

And that, hopefully, would be the end of the story.

With her mother planning to return home to her cottage in Forgandenny the following day, Helen didn't want the last day of her visit to be soured by her fretting that she might have some vital information that should be passed onto the police in Dorminster.

So, she decided that after dinner that evening she would put her mother's concerns to bed once and for all.

And if that didn't do the trick, she would show her the e-fit image of the person the police believed to be responsible for the two killings. If that didn't work, nothing would.

Just at that moment, there was the sound of her mother stirring.

"You OK, mum?" asked Helen.

"Yes, I'm fine thanks, dear," replied Olivia.

"Fancy a cuppa?"

"Yes please."

"Look mum, you know you don't have to go home tomorrow. Why not stay for the weekend. Dad will be OK in the care home."

"You know I don't like being away from him for too long, dear, so I'll probably still go back tomorrow morning."

"Well, we'll have a nice meal tonight, and we'll see if David and the children can persuade you to stay a little longer. I'll just go and put the kettle on."

As Helen walked from the lounge to kitchen, she couldn't help thinking how stubborn her mum could be at times. So stubborn that she might still want to have her say to the police about the death of Mr Summers.

Thursday 5:30pm

Detective Inspector Steve Hardcastle was feeling downcast after his earlier conversation with DCI Cryer.

He actually felt sorry for his boss who was merely passing on the instructions he had received from the ACC. The fact that Cryer had gone out on a limb to get him a three day stay of execution was something he should have shown more gratitude for.

But by telling the ACC that the investigation had built up a 'degree of momentum', Cryer had actually added to the pressure on Hardcastle who was now beginning to worry that the investigation was on the verge of stalling.

He had spent the afternoon going through the various witness statements, hoping against hope that he might find something that nobody else had picked up on, something that could open up another line of enquiry.

But deep down he knew that was unlikely. His team had gone about things with their customary thoroughness and the chance of any of them missing a vital piece of information diminished with every page he turned.

If only I'd brought back the photograph of the child when I first visited Summers's bungalow, we might have had the enquiry wrapped up by now, he kept reminding himself.

At that moment, there was a gentle tap at his door.

"Come in, Kath. What can I do for you?"

"I thought I ought to update you regarding Sunday's reconstruction."

"Fire away."

"I've just been speaking to Andy Hanson. I wanted to see if Panton's death yesterday had made him and the team change their minds about going ahead with it."

"What did he say?"

"He'd spent the afternoon ringing around the other members of the team, and virtually all of them are keen to go ahead as planned. The general consensus was that they should forget that Panton wasn't that popular; he was still one of the team, and they are as keen as anyone that we should find his killer.

"And, as Hanson said, if the reconstruction jogs a few memories, and helps to find the man who killed Mr Summers, then they've also helped to find whoever killed Panton."

"You said virtually all of them were keen?"

"The one exception is Alex Donahue. He was the young lad who was there when they found the body. According to his GP, he's suffering from mild Post-Traumatic Stress Disorder, and he needs some time away from cricket."

"Understandable," replied Hardcastle. "Can you do me a favour and speak to Alex Till and ask him to send out a press release publicising the reconstruction.

"Can you also get someone to ring everyone that has made a statement, apart from the players? We want as many people as possible who were there last Sunday to be there this coming Sunday."

"I've already got that in hand, sir."

"And have we got someone who will double for the mystery man yet?" asked Hardcastle.

"Yes sir; uniform is letting us have one of their PCs. He's the right age and build, and he's a cricketer, so he's really keen to help out."

"OK Kath. Anything else?"

"Nothing really, sir, other than to let you know that I have made a few discrete calls regarding Mr Willard's purchase of The Waterman's Arms, so at least I've got the ball rolling there."

After she had left, Hardcastle got out of his chair and went to the window to look at what was happening in the world outside the police station. Life seemed to be going on as normal.

He shook his head and sat back down behind his desk.

"Fancy a cup of coffee, boss? I thought you might need cheering up," said Phil Davison who had appeared with a large steaming mug in his right hand.

"You are a lifesaver, Phil."

"You know me, always happy to oblige."

"Do you know, Phil, as it stands at the moment, I'm pinning all my hopes on Sunday's reconstruction. We really need a major stroke of luck, and as things stand I just don't have a clue where it is going to come from."

Thursday 8:30pm

The family dinner had gone really well, and Olivia MacDonald had been in her element, surrounded by her daughter Helen, her son-in-law David, and her three grandchildren.

The only person missing was her husband Roderick, but at least she knew that he was being well cared for back at the Sunrise Care Home.

With the children now in their rooms getting ready for bed, Helen felt the time was right to try and persuade her mother to stay with them in Edinburgh for a few more days before returning home to Forgandenny. She also wanted to give her the latest news from Dorminster.

She looked at her husband who gave her the slightest of nods to signify that he too thought it was time to start the conversation rolling.

"The children have really loved having you here, mum, and they were quite upset when I told them that you had to go home tomorrow."

"And I've loved being here too, Helen," replied her mother, "but I just think I should go back home for your dad's sake. I will have been away for four days by the time I get to see him, and I worry that he will be missing me and maybe even thinking that I have abandoned him. I can't remember the last time we were apart for so long."

"But the care home has our number here," said Helen "and I'm sure if dad was upset or unwell, they would have given us a call by now. So what do you think, mum? I think the respite has done you the world of good, and I'm sure dad would never begrudge you having an extra couple of days here with us."

Helen could see her mother was beginning to waver, and decided to press home the advantage.

"I'll tell you what I'll do, why don't I ring the care home in the morning and ask them how dad is. If they say he's fretting or asking for you, I'll drive you back home after lunch.

"But if they say he's fine, as I'm sure they will, why don't you stay here for another couple of days and either David or I will take you back on Sunday. Well, what do you think? The children will be so pleased to have you here a little while longer."

"And while you're thinking about it, would you like another glass of Baileys, Olivia, or even a wee dram?" added David.

That did the trick.

"OK. If the care home says that your dad is well, I'll stay with you until Sunday. And I'll have another Baileys, thank you, David."

"While David is pouring us both a Baileys," said Helen handing her empty glass to her husband, "why don't I give you the latest news from Flitton Green, mum?"

"I was hoping you would, dear," replied Olivia. "I'd be lying if I said that it hasn't been on my mind."

Helen took a deep breath.

"The bad news is that there has been a second murder. This happened yesterday."

Helen could see that her mother was taken aback by this latest revelation.

"The victim was named Neil Panton and he was one of the Flitton Green cricket team, the same cricket team that Mr Summers was umpiring for just before he was killed on Sunday."

"We must do something now, Helen, before this monster kills again," implored Olivia, now distraught and with the colour visibly draining from her face. "The killings must be linked. It would be too much of a coincidence to have two separate killers on the loose in a little place like Flitton Green."

"Hold your horses, mum," countered Helen. "The police agree with you. They think that the same man committed both murders."

"If we had contacted the police yesterday, we might have been able to save this poor man's life," said Olivia, taking out her handkerchief, which had been up the sleeve of her cardigan, and wiping away the tears that had started to flow freely.

"Why don't you tell your mum the good news, Helen?" said David.

"Well firstly mum, this man was already dead when we saw the news item on the iPad. According to the police, Mr Panton died in the early hours of yesterday morning. And secondly, the police have a suspect for both murders, and it says on the newspaper's website that he is in his mid-twenties. So that rules out the man you suspected of killing Mr Summers."

Helen could see that her mother was already beginning to calm down, having taken the news on board.

"Are you sure, Helen? Are you sure that I was wrong?"

"I am absolutely sure, mum. It's there in black and white, if you want to read it on my iPad?"

Olivia was feeling almost back to normal, the colour having returned to her face.

"No, of course I believe you, Helen. It is such a relief," she replied. "It really is a load off my mind."

"In that case," said David, handing the two women their Baileys, and now holding a large glass of Scotch whisky in his hand, "Slàinte mhath, and your very good health."

"Do dheagh shlainte," replied mother and daughter in unison.

Friday 6am

Even though he'd made sure that most of the team had gone home by 6:30pm, Hardcastle hadn't left the office until almost 10pm.

After quietly closing the front door, he went straight upstairs to check on the boys, who were both fast asleep. The light was on in the main bedroom where he found Jenny still awake, reading her book.

"Hiya, have you eaten?" she asked her husband.

"I've been snacking all day, so I'm OK, thanks."

"How was your day?"

"I've had better," he replied. "How was yours?"

"OK thanks. Do you want to talk about yours?"

"I'll pass thanks," he said, starting to get undressed. "I'll need to leave early in the morning, so I'll try not to wake you when I go."

Jenny recognised the signs. He must have had a bad day, and whenever that happened, she knew it was best to keep the conversation as brief as possible.

"Ok. Night-night," she replied, and turned off her bedside light.

After a predictably restless night, he left home at 5:30am, without having any breakfast; Jenny and the boys were still asleep.

By 6am he was walking up the stairs to his office.

It came as no surprise to him that both Phil Davison and Kath Pearson had beaten him to it once again.

"Good morning to you both; any new developments overnight?"

"Nothing from me, sir," replied Pearson.

"Nor from me either, boss," chimed in Davison. "Just to let you know that I'll be popping out this morning to visit Christine Williams, Neil Panton's sister. She wasn't up to seeing anyone again yesterday, so I thought the best thing was for me to go and see her, as I've been her only contact so far. I'll take Isha with me; it'll be more good experience for her."

"Good luck with that then, Phil," replied Hardcastle, looking around to make sure the three of them were the only ones in the office. "Before anyone else arrives, I thought I should let you two know that if we haven't made significant progress by the time Sunday's reconstruction is over, I'm to be replaced as Senior Investigating Officer by DCI Cryer. And before you say anything, this was the ACC's decision and not Mr Cryer's."

"How do you feel about that, boss?" asked Davison.

"To be frank, I was really miffed when he told me yesterday, but I've had time to think it over. I can see the logic in it from the ACC's point of view. He's got two murders on his patch and he has to be seen to be doing something to reassure the general public that he's on top of things, and the easiest way to do this is to replace the hapless DI and put a more experienced man in charge. It's a no-brainer as far as he's concerned."

"You shouldn't be so hard on yourself sir," said Pearson.

"You've done everything possible, boss," added Davison, "and I'm sure that it is only a matter of time before we get a break. We just need a little bit of luck to fall our way."

"Trouble is, Phil, we'll need that bit of luck to land on our plates within the next 60 hours."

And with that, Hardcastle turned and made his way to his office.

Friday 9:30am

Having completed the daily school run, Helen was now back in her kitchen drinking a strong cup of coffee and nibbling on a milk chocolate Hobnob biscuit.

As yet, there was no sign of her mother, which was hardly surprising since the old lady had knocked back several more generous glasses of Baileys before finally retiring for the night, albeit a trifle unsteadily.

Beside Helen at the kitchen table was a cordless telephone and the family address book which she needed to consult for the phone number of her father's care home. Helen managed to get through at the first attempt and was quickly put through to the senior person in charge of those residents suffering from Alzheimer's and other related conditions.

"You can tell your mother that Mr MacDonald is absolutely fine. He's eating well and sleeping well, and as far as I am aware, he has shown no signs of missing his wife. And to put your mind at rest, I can honestly say that your father is no trouble whatsoever, and he has settled in to daily life at Sunrise extremely well."

I should bloody well hope so, thought Helen to herself as she put the phone down, given that the monthly cost of her father's stay at Sunrise was in excess of five thousand pounds. With a good report from Sunrise, at least she now knew that Olivia would be staying with them for an extra couple of days.

After the old lady had gone to bed, David and Helen had agreed that he would look after the children on Sunday whilst she would drive her mother home to Forgandenny, via the care home first.

Helen was particularly pleased with this arrangement as it had been several weeks since she had seen her dad. The only downside was her concern that the time might be fast approaching when her dad didn't recognise her. She dreaded that happening as she had no idea how she would cope with it.

"Good morning, dear," said Olivia as she came into the kitchen. "I thought I could smell coffee."

"Anything else you need, mum," replied Helen. "Would you like a couple of paracetamol to go with your coffee?"

"Cheeky," said Olivia, smiling at her daughter. "I feel as fit as a fiddle, and I had the best night's sleep I've had for ages. The air really suits me here."

"So does the Baileys."

"Well, that might have helped a little," replied Olivia. "Anyway, have you managed to speak to the care home to see how your dad is this morning?"

"I have, and they said that dad is absolutely fine and in good form. So that means you can stay here until Sunday. We'll have Sunday lunch, and then I'll take you home via the care home as I'd like to see dad as well."

"That would be lovely, dear; dad will be so pleased to see you."

The pair continued to chat whilst Helen made her mother breakfast: a glass of fresh orange juice, followed by toast and marmalade and a top up of coffee.

"I've got a few chores to do that will take me an hour or so," said Helen. "So why don't you take today's paper into the lounge. You can put the television on as well. I know how you like to watch *Loose Women*."

"Whatever gave you that idea," replied Olivia. "Anyway, it doesn't come on until 12:30. What I'd really like to do though, is to have a look at your iPad. It seems fairly easy to use, and if I can get the hang of it, I'd be sorely tempted to buy one for myself."

"That would be a great idea, mum. If you were to get one, we could message one another, speak to each other via Skype and send each other photographs."

"Whoa, hold your horses, Helen," interrupted Olivia. "I'll need to walk very slowly before I can learn to run."

"Yeah, sorry mum, I was getting a bit carried away," replied Helen. "But it would help us keep in touch even more than we do now, without having to use the phone. I'm sure it would save us both some money."

The two women walked into the lounge, and Helen gave her mum a brief lesson on how to switch on the iPad, how to open it using the password and then how to open the various apps Helen had downloaded.

Hoping that her mother had taken all of this in, Helen left her to it and went back to the kitchen where she began to load up the dishwasher with all the breakfast crockery and cutlery. She had hardly got halfway through this when there was a shout from the lounge.

"Helen, come here quickly, please."

She was at her mother's side within a matter of seconds.

"What's the matter, mum?"

As she spoke, Helen looked at her iPad in her mother's hands. She saw that Olivia had been looking at the Dorminster Echo website.

"Look at this," said her mother, handing Helen the iPad.

The first thing she noticed was that the news page dealing with the Flitton Green killings had been updated since she had last looked. This latest update gave notice that this coming Sunday the police would be staging a reconstruction of the events that had happened last Sunday, when Donald Summers had been murdered.

"It's quite normal to stage a reconstruction of a serious crime, mum. It happens all the time."

"I know that, girl. I'm not daft," snapped back Olivia.

Immediately, Helen knew something serious was up. Her mother was a very even-tempered person and she knew that snapping back at her mum would achieve absolutely nothing.

"I know that, mum. Please tell me what's bothering you now. I really want to help you."

"I need to go to Flitton, Helen. I need to be there at this reconstruction on Sunday. Please don't ask me why. All I can say at the moment is that it is imperative that I am there. I need to see him, and confront him."

"Who?" asked Helen.

"I have to see the man who has killed both of those poor people. If I don't go, there's every chance that he will kill again. And I don't want that on my conscience."

"You've got to tell me more than that mum."

"I can't, Helen."

"Well, why don't we ring the police and you can tell them what you know?"

"They would probably think that I'm a daft old biddy who's off her rocker. That's why I've got to be there on Sunday. If I confront him, the police have got to take notice."

At that precise moment, Helen wished that David was at home. He would know what to say; he would know what they should do next.

Friday 11am

As Phil Davison and Isha Hussein left the office to go to their meeting with Neil Panton's sister, Kath Pearson stood up, took a very deep breath, and walked purposefully across the room to DI Hardcastle's office.

"Can you spare me a few minutes please sir? I've got something personal I need to discuss with you."

"Of course, Kath, as long as you're not going to hand in your notice," replied Hardcastle jokingly.

As she gently closed the door behind her, Steve Hardcastle realised that Kath must have something really important to discuss with him. Now was not the time for levity.

"Fire away, Kath, I'm all yours for as long as you need."

She took a deep breath.

"I'm pregnant sir, and please, no congratulations."

There was a pause as Hardcastle thought carefully before replying.

"OK. And what was your husband's reaction when you told him?"

"I've not said anything to him yet," she replied.

"Don't you think you should have told him before speaking to me?"

This time it was Kath's turn to think carefully how to phrase her reply.

"And that is part of the problem, sir. I need to decide what I am going to do about the baby first. In fact, if I decided not to keep it, it would be far better in the long term if he never knew."

"That's one hell of a decision you have to make. Have you told anyone else that you're pregnant?"

"There's only really my mum, sir, and I already know what she will say."

"And what will that be?"

"That I would be mad to give up the chance of starting a family of my own. I know she would put pressure on me to tell Jason and to keep the baby."

"And what would be so wrong about that?" asked Hardcastle. "Many women have children and go on to enjoy very successful careers. Some would say that combining both had made them a better, more rounded person."

"I'd be very rounded if I go ahead and keep the baby," joked Kath. "Quite a few people I know have never been able to regain their pre-pregnancy figure."

Hardcastle smiled back at her.

"What about Phil? You two always seem to be as thick as thieves, if you pardon the pun. Have you mentioned anything to him?"

"For once, this is something I just wouldn't have the heart to discuss with him, sir," she replied. "I'm sure you know that Phil and Sarah were told that they would never be able to have children of their own after Sarah's accident."

Hardcastle nodded.

"How can I talk to Phil about whether or not I should keep the baby when he and Sarah have been denied the chance to have one of their own? That would be so selfish of me. And I really don't want to jeopardise my friendship with Phil."

"I've known Phil a lot longer than you have, Kath," replied Hardcastle, "and I think he would be hurt if he knew that you had spoken to me and not to him. And for what it's worth, I believe Phil and Sarah accepted some time ago that they wouldn't be able to have a family of their own, and I'm sure they would both be absolutely delighted for you. And you know that they would make wonderful godparents."

Kath nodded and smiled. Hardcastle paused for a few seconds before continuing.

"But I also think that Phil would fully understand your dilemma. He would give you his advice, there's no doubt about that, and he would give it to you straight. But he would respect that it is your decision to make. And whatever you decide to do, I'm certain it wouldn't affect your friendship which I think is as important to him as it is to you."

"My other concern is my career, sir," said Kath. "I've worked really hard to get where I am, and as you know, I've passed the inspectors' examination. Am I being over optimistic to think that promotion to inspector is a possibility in the not too distant future?"

"That's not something I can answer, Kath. That's a decision others will make. But what I can tell you is if I was asked for my opinion, I would say that you are more than ready to take that step up.

"And I also know that you are very well thought of by those that live on the third floor. As recently as Wednesday, DI Cryer paid you a compliment and told me I should keep an eye on you, or you'll be after my job. So the signs are good, Kath, and you just have to be patient. It will happen, sooner rather than later."

"Thank you sir," replied Kath, as she stood up. "You have been really helpful. I know you've got a lot on your mind at the moment, but I am very grateful for your advice."

"Keep me posted if you can, Kath," replied Hardcastle. "My door is always open to you."

As she returned to her desk, Kath decided she would have a heart to heart with Phil when the opportunity arose. She just felt so very sad that she could talk to him, and to DI Hardcastle, about things which she could no longer discuss with her own husband.

Friday 3:30pm

"Afternoon boss, just to let you know that I'm back, and that Kath and I have a couple of things we think you'll be interested in."

"Of course," replied Hardcastle. "Come on in. How did you and Isha get on with Panton's sister, Phil?" asked Hardcastle once the pair had sat down. "What was her name again?"

"Christine Williams. She is a really nice person, and chalk and cheese compared to her brother. And much of what she told us certainly helped to explain why Neil Panton was the person he was.

"As a child, he was abused physically and mentally by his alcoholic father, as were his mother and Christine herself, although they didn't suffer anywhere near to the same extent as he did. In fact it got so bad that Neil left home not long after he turned seventeen, and he has not seen his father since.

"Even when their mother died, Neil felt he couldn't go to the funeral. By then, according to Christine, her father was only a shadow of his former self as the alcoholism had taken its toll, so Neil knew that his father was no longer a physical threat to him. But he suspected that his father would still have laid into him verbally the minute he saw him, so he decided to stay away, despite the fact that he absolutely adored his mum, and was heartbroken when Christine called him to say that she had passed away.

"However, by the sound of it," continued Davison, "I think Christine was actually quite relieved he didn't go; she was frightened that he might have snapped and taken revenge on the old man for all the years of abuse he had suffered. And that was the last thing she wanted to happen at her mum's funeral."

"Did Christine have any idea who might have killed her brother?" asked Hardcastle.

"Not specifically. But she did say that he mixed with some pretty unsavoury characters from time to time."

"Did she provide us with any names?"

"No, I think she preferred not to know what he had been getting up to, so she never asked him.

"But when he called her on Tuesday evening she said he sounded like a completely different person. He told her that at long last things were looking up in the world, particularly from a financial point of view. She said he sounded like he had suddenly come into some money, but that he sounded as high as a kite."

"As in a drug induced high?" asked Hardcastle.

"I did ask her that, and she said she really couldn't say. He might have been drinking, but she knew that he had dabbled in drugs from time to time over the years, both in a criminal and a recreational sense."

"Anything else, Phil?" asked Hardcastle.

"No, that's about it, boss," replied Davison.

"OK, thanks. Over to you now, Kath," said Hardcastle turning his swivel chair slightly to face her.

"I mentioned to you yesterday, sir, that I'd made some enquiries about Danny Willard. I think that I must have rattled a few cages as out of the blue I received a call from someone at the National Crime Agency regarding Willard who they describe as being a 'person of interest' to them. Apparently, we are not the only ones interested in where the money came from to buy The Waterman's Arms.

"A few months ago they had an anonymous phone call from someone suggesting that Willard couldn't have funded the purchase of the pub as he didn't have the money."

"And did they follow up on this call?" asked Hardcastle.

"Eventually they did. But it seems calls of this nature are not uncommon. And usually the caller is the spouse, or the ex-spouse, who has an axe to grind against their former partner."

"So the call could have been made by Mrs Willard?"

"That was my first thought, but it was actually a male caller, so it may have been the guy who had been having the affair with Willard's wife. It's almost certain that we will never know who made the call."

"So is this still an active investigation?" asked Davison. "If it is, it would have been nice to have known about it."

"I asked the question, Phil, and all I got back was the sort of thing we would have said had the roles been reversed; that it was an ongoing investigation in conjunction with the Metropolitan Police and that we would be informed if the focus of the investigation moves to Dorminster or any of the surrounding villages.

"Apparently, the scale of money laundering in the UK runs into hundreds of billions of pounds every year, so investigating the source of funds used to purchase a medium-sized pub somewhere out in the sticks was never going to be their highest priority.

"The chap also mentioned that when laundered money from drug trafficking is used to buy a property, particularly a going concern like a pub, that property often then becomes another outlet for the sale of drugs. The cash received is then laundered through the till, and the cycle goes on. Eventually, the property is sold, and the proceeds from the sale become legitimised and are no longer considered to be laundered money."

"So what they are really saying is that the best we can do is to keep an eye on The Waterman's Arms for potential drug dealing?" asked Hardcastle.

"That's right sir. And that's how I regarded the matter until I received a second call about a quarter of an hour ago."

"From your new-found best friend at the National Crime Agency?" asked Davison.

"Not quite," replied Pearson. "The call came from a Mrs Stacey Barnes, who is the senior bar person at The Waterman's Arms. She wanted to know if and when Danny Willard was going to be released."

"Eh?"

"She was under the impression that we still had Willard in custody as he hasn't been seen since he was picked up by Phil and Alan Rutherford just before 11am yesterday morning."

"But he left here just before one o'clock," said Hardcastle. "I offered to organise a lift to the pub in a squad car, but he said he would get a cab back."

"That isn't all, sir," continued Pearson. "On Wednesday evening, Willard had told Stacey Barnes that she didn't need to come in yesterday morning until mid-day, instead of her usual start time, which is 10am. The reason he gave was that he was going to interview a couple of guys he knew as potential new bar staff. Stacey said that that in itself was unusual, as she normally does all the hiring and firing, and she was really put out by this.

"However, one of the pub's chefs, a Mr Kevin Prior, happened to arrive a bit early yesterday morning and, as he normally does, entered the pub through the back door which leads straight from the car park into the kitchen. He said that he heard raised voices coming from the bar and decided to take a peep. He saw Willard talking to two guys who definitely didn't look like they were there to be interviewed for bar work. They were both wearing very expensive-looking suits.

"The chef heard a tap on the front door, which must have been Phil and Alan. According to Mr Prior, when Willard went to open the door the two guys disappeared into the toilets. They obviously didn't want to be seen. Mr Prior heard Willard say over his shoulder that he wouldn't be long, and then he closed the door behind him.

"He then went quietly back to the kitchen, saw Willard get into a car, which then pulled away, and noticed that it was being followed by a second car, a marked police car.

"A couple of minutes later, the other two guys must have come out of the toilets, opened the front door and walked around the back to the car park as the chef saw them get into a black BMW. They pulled out of the pub car park in a hurry and went in the opposite direction to the police cars."

"Has Mrs Barnes made an official missing person's report?" asked Hardcastle.

"No, she hasn't. Apparently, Willard has done this before when things were getting a bit on top of him. He was gone for a day and half, and when he eventually returned, he had a mega hangover."

"OK, thanks for that, Kath. It looks like Danny Willard is back on our own 'persons of interest' list," replied Hardcastle.

"Do you think I should make the guy at the NCA aware that Willard has gone missing?" asked Pearson.

"Not at the moment," answered Hardcastle, after a moment's thought. "We can let them know if or when Mrs Barnes makes his disappearance official. But I suggest you keep in touch with her in the meantime. Perhaps get an update before you leave to go home."

"What's your take on all this, Phil?" asked Hardcastle. "I assume you didn't get a good look at the two men when you and Alan picked up Willard?"

"I'll check with Alan, boss, but I definitely didn't see anyone since Willard was standing at the front door. You know what a size he is, so he was blocking the view," replied Davison.

"It's funny how things can change so quickly," said Hardcastle. "At the beginning of the week, we were in his debt for all the help he'd given us. Now at the end of the week, we're trying to work out which side of the law he's on.

"From what the pub's chef said, it's pretty obvious that the two guys he met yesterday morning didn't want anyone else to know they were there."

"Perhaps Willard's the victim of a protection racket," answered Davison. "Those guys could have been there to collect a payment from him."

"That sounds feasible," replied Pearson. "Perhaps Willard borrowed the money to buy the pub from some villain, and he hasn't been making his regular repayments, and the two guys were there to put the frighteners on him."

"Or whatever they were discussing could have been drug related given what the NCA guy told you. That could explain why he's done a runner," said Hardcastle, "and maybe he won't resurface until he's got the money he owes. So he could be missing for a few days."

"And all the time, these guys will be looking for him," chipped in Davison. "So he's going to have to keep a low profile."

"We could be completely barking up the wrong tree," said Hardcastle. "He's probably gone on a bender and won't turn up until he's sobered up.

"But, to be on the safe side, let's get the word out to uniform to keep an eye out for Willard just in case we're right. For his sake, if he is being chased for money he owes, it might be better if we get to him before the other guys do."

Friday 5:30pm

When speaking to his wife shortly after 10am that morning, David Stewart had promised her that he would do his very best to be home as early as possible. It sounded like Helen needed some help with her mother again.

However, as managing director of a fairly large house builder, matters would sometimes crop up completely out of the blue which needed his immediate attention, and by the time he got into his car, a two-month-old BMW X3 SUV, the clock showed that it was almost 4:40pm—not as early as his wife Helen had hoped for, but still almost two hours earlier than he normally left work for home.

As it was a Friday, the traffic was a little lighter than normal, and David pulled into their driveway on the dot of 5:30pm. The first thing that caught his attention was the sight of his three children, Alex, Andrew and Emily, waving furiously at him from the lounge window. This had become something of a daily ritual, but this afternoon their welcome was more animated than normal because it was Friday and they had the weekend to look forward to.

The demands of his job invariably meant that during the week he wasn't able to spend as much time with the children as he would have liked.

However, most weekends, he and Helen did their best to come up with a family activity which involved all five of them, by way of compensation.

Unfortunately, after taking Helen's morning phone call he was really concerned that the children would be disappointed this particular weekend.

The front door opened before he could put his key in the lock.

"Thank God you're home," said Helen. "She's been driving me mad since she got up this morning."

"Where is she now?" asked David.

"She's having a nap in the guest room."

"Good, that gives us a bit of time to decide how we handle her and deal with this daft idea of her going down to Dorminster, and the even dafter idea that we go with her."

"I don't see her changing her mind, Davie; you know how stubborn she can be."

"Like mother, like daughter," replied David, with a smile. "But all we've got to do is tell her that we haven't got the time. Tell her we've already got plans. Tell her anything. It's not like Flitton is just around the corner. It must be over 400 miles by road, and I'm definitely not driving over 800 miles this weekend, just because she's got some ridiculous bee in her bonnet. Not after the week I've had."

"Shush, she might hear you!"

"I hope she does!" replied David, pretending to shout up the stairs.

"Come into the kitchen, Davie, I've done you a G&T, just how you like it."

"Hopefully, it's half a bottle of gin mixed with a finger of tonic," he said with a large grin.

They walked into the kitchen together, hand in hand. Helen knew she was blessed to have married a man with such a keen sense of humour, and a keen sense of fun. And she also knew how much David looked forward to his weekends. But she also knew that her mother had made up her mind to be in Flitton on Sunday afternoon.

Helen Stewart was well and truly stuck between a rock and a hard place. Somehow, she needed to come up with a compromise to satisfy her husband, her mother and, of course, the three children.

"So tell me again why she has changed her mind from last night?" asked David.

"I wish I'd never let her look at my iPad," answered Helen. "As soon as she saw there was a reconstruction being staged on Sunday, she became really agitated and kept repeating that she had to be there."

"But I thought that she had abandoned the idea after you told her the police were looking for a man in his mid-twenties."

"So did I. But then everything changed again when she read about the reconstruction," replied Helen.

"It wasn't just the reconstruction," said a voice from the kitchen doorway.

Helen and David turned around to see Olivia standing just a few feet away from them holding a cup and saucer in her left hand. They wondered how much of their conversation had she heard.

"Let me have your cup and saucer, mum, and I'll make us all a nice pot of tea," said Helen, "and then the three of us can sit down and try and sort things out."

"I'm not going to change my mind, you know," said Olivia. "I'm quite capable of going down to Flitton on my own; I certainly don't want to put you out."

There was an icy silence between the three of them, whilst Helen busied herself making the tea. After warming the empty teapot and cups with some of the boiled water, Helen put four teaspoons of loose tea into the pot and then poured in the piping hot water from the kettle.

"I'll let it draw for a few minutes," said Helen putting milk into the three china cups. "So why don't we all sit down?"

With a glance and a nod to Helen, David decided it was up to him to take the lead.

"First things first, Olivia, last night you seemed quite happy to stay here until Sunday. Then after looking at Helen's iPad you told her that you now needed to go down to Flitton. What in heaven's name has made you change your mind?"

"As I told Helen, I can't tell you why," replied Olivia.

"Can't or won't?" asked David.

There was a pause whilst Olivia thought carefully about how to reply.

"I told Helen earlier in the week that I knew who had killed Donald Summers. Then yesterday, she told me that the police had a suspect and that he was in his mid-twenties. Because of that, I was more than happy to stay with you for an extra couple of days. Then, this morning I looked on the iPad and saw an identikit picture of the man police are looking for. That's what made me change my mind."

"But for God's sake, why? The picture is of a man in his twenties," persisted David.

"I know he is, David, I've got eyes, you know."

"Come on mum, you need to give us more than that," implored Helen.

Olivia gave a huge sigh. "I have to go to Flitton on Sunday because I recognised the man in the picture."

Friday 5:45pm

"I'm sorry, Olivia, but I just don't see how that's possible," said David. "If this man is in his mid-twenties, then he would have been born several years after you left Dorminster to come and live here in Scotland."

"I knew you wouldn't believe me," replied Olivia. "And, I suppose, I can understand that. You probably think that I'm going the same way as your dad, Helen. But I promise you, I know what I am doing, and by hook or by crook, I am going to Flitton. I owe it to my friend, and to the two poor souls who this monster has killed."

And with that, she got up and went out of the kitchen, leaving her cup of tea behind her, untouched. They heard her go up the stairs, followed by the sound of the guest room door closing.

"We won't be able to stop her, Davie. You know how she is. And I've got no choice. I'm going to have to go with her."

"I know that," replied David. "So it's just as well then that I've already worked out how to get you and your mum to Flitton in time for this damn reconstruction on Sunday."

A look of relief spread across Helen's face.

"And I've also got the telephone number for the Dorminster CID, so I can ring them and tell them to expect you and your mum on Sunday."

Helen gave her husband a huge hug, followed by a tender kiss.

"Thank you Davie, I don't deserve you."

"You're right there," he replied smiling.

"But what are you and the children going to do? You know how much they look forward to going out at the weekend."

"Already sorted," replied David. "I'm going to take them to Edinburgh Zoo. We've not been there for ages. Now, here's your itinerary for tomorrow," he said, handing his wife a folded piece of paper. "I'll drop you and your mum at Edinburgh station in time for you to catch the 10am train which gets into London

Kings Cross just before 2:45pm. I'll book you both into the same hotel we stayed at when we went to see *Les Misérables* on your birthday.

"Then, on Sunday, you can catch the 9:30am train from Waterloo to Dorminster which will get you there about 12:45pm. You'll have time for a spot of lunch if you want, and then you can get a taxi to the cricket ground at Flitton. How does that sound?"

"I'm really lost for words, Davie."

"Well, you better get your powers of speech back pretty damn quick, as you need to tell your mum. But before that, I'll leave it to you to explain to the kids why you and granny will be away for the weekend. In the meantime, I'm going to sit down in the lounge and polish off my G&T. I think I've earned it."

Friday 6:30pm

Steve Hardcastle looked at his watch. It was 6:30pm, and time to go home.

Five minutes earlier, Kath Pearson had poked her head around his door to tell him that she had spoken to Stacey Barnes at The Waterman's Arms, who had confirmed that there was still no sign of Danny Willard, and that he wasn't answering his mobile phone either.

Kath had said that she had given Stacey her own mobile number and asked her to call should Willard put in an appearance during the evening. After Saturday, Friday evening was the busiest of the week at the pub and Stacey said it would be very much out of character for Danny not to be around.

"Did you sense she was a bit concerned that they hadn't heard from him?" Hardcastle had asked Pearson.

"More than a bit concerned actually, sir. I got the impression that there might be something going on between them. She sounded like she was more than just a concerned employee."

"That's interesting, Kath. If you get a call from Stacey during the evening, give me a call at home if you can."

"Will do, sir," replied Pearson, "Goodnight."

"Goodnight, Kath."

It had been another very long day. He'd been at the office for just over 12 and a half hours and they had made little progress in the hunt for the double murderer, and now less than 48 hours remained until he would have to hand over control of his investigation to DCI Cryer.

Hardcastle took his jacket off the hook on the back of his office door, patted the right hand pocket to make sure his car keys were still there, and began walking wearily through the main office towards the staircase that would lead him down to the station car park.

He was just on the point of texting Jenny to say that he was on his way home, when the telephone on Phil Davison's desk began to ring. Although he was sorely tempted to ignore it, he picked it up on the off chance that it might be something important.

"Dorminster CID."

"Hello there. Sorry to disturb you. I actually didn't think I would get through to anybody at this time of the day."

"Well, you've got through to me, sir. To whom am I speaking?"

"My name is David Stewart."

"Good evening, Mr Stewart, you are through to Detective Inspector Steve Hardcastle. How can I help you, sir?"

"Well, I am ringing to let you know that my wife, Helen Stewart, and my mother-in-law, Mrs Olivia MacDonald, are coming down from Edinburgh to attend your crime scene reconstruction at Flitton Green Cricket Club on Sunday."

Already, Hardcastle was beginning to regret picking up the phone.

"I will pass that information on to Detective Sergeant Pearson who is co-ordinating the reconstruction. Thank you for letting us know," said Hardcastle, doing his best to be polite, and only just about managing it.

He was about to put the phone down, when David Stewart began speaking again.

"I'm sorry, I haven't explained myself very well, Mr Hardcastle. The reason they are making such a long journey, is that Mrs MacDonald used to live in Flitton, and actually knew the first man who was murdered."

David Stewart now had Hardcastle's undivided attention.

"She knew Donald Summers? How along ago was this?"

"Well over 25 years ago," replied David.

"Can I speak to her?"

"Unfortunately, she doesn't want to talk over the phone, which is why Mrs MacDonald and my wife are making the long trek south this weekend. But it doesn't end there, Mr Hardcastle. Mrs MacDonald says that she knows the identity of the person you are looking for. You see, she recognised the e-fit picture that appears on the Dorminster Echo website."

Hardcastle took a deep breath. Was this the breakthrough they'd been hoping for, or was it another hoax call. At that moment, he wasn't sure which it was.

"Do you happen to know when was the last time Mrs MacDonald was in the Flitton area, Mr Stewart?"

"She had been thinking of coming down earlier this year, but didn't make it because of her husband's ill health. Before that, to the best of my knowledge, she's only been back once, and that was a very long time ago."

"And you're sure that I can't speak to her over the phone?" persisted Hardcastle.

"Believe me when I say that I really wish you could," replied Stewart, "It would save my wife having to spend her weekend traipsing around the country with her mother, and it would save me the cost of two return train tickets and a couple of nights in a decent hotel for the pair of them. But she is a very stubborn old lady, Mr Hardcastle, and she's adamant that she wants to explain everything to you in person."

"Mr Stewart, do you believe that your mother-in-law has information relevant to this investigation? Information which could lead to the arrest of the person responsible for killing both Mr Donald Summers, and the Flitton Green cricketer Neil Panton? We are certain that the same man is responsible for both murders, and whilst I accept that she might have known Mr Summers, the likelihood of her knowing Mr Panton must be virtually nil."

This time it was David Stewart's turn to take a deep breath.

"My honest answer, Mr Hardcastle, is that I just don't know," he replied. "I'm absolutely certain that she thinks she has some vital information for you. There is no doubt about that. But whether or not it turns out to be that important to your investigation, I'd say it was 50/50 at best. But, at the end of the day, what have you got to lose?"

Hardcastle scratched his head with his right hand, whilst holding the phone in his left. He couldn't disagree with Stewart.

"Then let's both hope that it's not a wasted journey," said Hardcastle. "If I give you my mobile phone number, Mr Stewart, could you pass this on to your wife. If she calls me when she and her mother arrive at Dorminster station on Sunday, I'll send a car down to collect them."

Once he had finished talking to David Stewart, Steve Hardcastle sat down at Phil Davison's desk. As things had turned out, he was glad that he hadn't sent a text to Jenny to say he was on his way home.

He would still send her a text, but only when he was ready to. Just for now, he wanted to take stock of his conversation with the Scotsman.

Friday 8pm

Steve Hardcastle finally arrived home just before 8pm having sent Jenny a text as he was leaving the office. As he had hoped, dinner was ready and waiting as he walked through the front door. The dining room table had been set for two as Jenny had decided earlier in the day that she wouldn't eat with Ethan and Thomas at teatime, but would wait until her husband came home, no matter what time that turned out to be.

After he had had a wash and a quick change of clothes, they were soon tucking into a very tasty ham salad, which they washed down with a bottle of Pinot Grigio. Jenny deliberately kept the conversation to domestic matters, knowing that her husband rarely wanted to speak about his work. But as it happened, tonight was one of the exceptions.

When Hardcastle finally got around to telling her that on Sunday he was due to be replaced as the senior investigating officer of the double murder case by his boss, she knew just how much that must have hurt him, and as he spoke, she reached across the table and took hold of his left hand, caressing it gently.

"You've always said that you get on well with Mr Cryer, so you'll still be in the thick of things, won't you?" she asked.

"Yes, he's a really decent bloke, but he's not the problem," he replied.

"So what's the problem?"

"Well, word will get around quite quickly and I suppose part of the problem is that my pride's been hurt. They say that *pride comes before a fall*, so maybe I've got no one to blame but myself."

"Why do you say that?" asked Jenny, slightly perplexed.

"It's fairly common knowledge that DI Cryer will be retiring in around 18 months or so, and I wanted to have a shot at his job when it came up. So being replaced by him on such a high profile case as this one won't look that great on my record."

"What are the chances of solving the case within the next couple of days then?" asked Jenny.

"As it stands at the moment, very slim," he replied.

"And what are the chances of Mr Cryer making a breakthrough when he takes over?"

"As it stands at the moment, even slimmer," replied Steve. "I've done everything by the book so far, so unless Mr Cryer has learnt from a different book to me, he'll be in the same boat as I am—keeping his fingers crossed for a stroke of luck. Whoever the killer is, he seems to be the one with all the luck at the moment, or else he's killed before."

"What makes you say that?" asked Jenny.

"We've had so little to go on. He just hasn't made any mistakes, and it feels like he's been one step ahead of us all the time. And where there is the potential for something to go wrong, he's anticipated it and dealt with it. To me, that's not luck—that's called tradecraft and being professional."

"Surely you don't think he's some sort of hired killer?"

"It's possible; he could be being paid to do someone else's dirty work," said Steve, emptying his wine glass. "Oh, just ignore me, Jen, it's the wine talking. Forget what I just said."

There was silence in the dining room whilst Jenny poured out two cups of strong coffee from the cafetière.

Whilst they sipped their coffee, he also told Jenny about the mysterious disappearance of Danny Willard.

"Could that be connected with Sunday's reconstruction?" she asked.

"I doubt it," replied Hardcastle. "But I think he's gone to ground for a reason. I just hope he turns up on Sunday, that's all."

He looked at his watch. It was just after 9:15pm.

"I need to speak to Kath and Phil, so why don't you fill up the dishwasher, and then we can get to bed at a reasonable time for once?"

He rang Davison first and told him about his conversation with David Stewart. His view was that Olivia MacDonald sounded completely batty and that the only reason to play along with her was the one in a thousand chances that she really might have some useful information.

As he put it, "she might turn out to be our best worst option."

When he rang Pearson's number it was engaged, and he didn't get through to her until his 4th attempt. When she eventually answered, Hardcastle thought that she sounded a little fraught.

"Hi Kath, how are you?"

"I'm fine sir, thank you."

"Is Jason home with you?"

"Actually, I've just been talking to him on the phone," she answered. "I was hoping to have a chat with him this evening when he gets home, but it seems like he's going to be late again. But I'm sure we'll get some time together over the weekend."

"I'll keep my fingers crossed," replied Hardcastle. "I'm sure it's the right thing to do. You never know, he might surprise you when you tell him your news."

Steve was expecting her to reply, but there was silence at the other end of the phone.

"Anyway, is there any update on Danny Willard?"

"Stacey's heard nothing at all, and she's beginning to get a little worried, so I told her that I would call her again in the morning. If he doesn't surface overnight, I think Stacey will want to formally report him as a 'Misper' as he will have been AWOL for almost 48 hours."

"Let's hope he gets in touch with her before then," replied Hardcastle. "Despite what's gone on with him over the last couple of days, I really want him to be there on Sunday, as he played an integral part of what went on after the body was discovered. The other reason for ringing you, Kath, is to put you in the picture regarding a phone call I took before leaving the office this evening and I'd like to hear your take on it."

"I'm all ears in that case, sir," replied Pearson.

Five minutes later, and for the second time in the last 20 minutes, Steve had finished describing the saga of David Stewart's telephone call concerning his wife and her mother.

"So what do you think, Kath?"

"One question before I give you my opinion, sir. What was your impression of Mr Stewart?"

"Good question," replied Hardcastle. "I thought he was honest, well-spoken, probably a business man, and that deep down he thinks his mother-in-law might be on to something. Probably not the identity of the killer, but she might know some scrap of information that will help us to make the link between the victim and the killer."

"I thought that might be the case sir, after all Mr Stewart is a Scotsman, and most Scotsmen are fairly canny about money," said Kath. "And if he felt that his mother-in-law was wasting everybody's time, and several hundred pounds of his own hard earned cash, I think he would have knocked it all on the head by now, no matter how stubborn the old lady may be.

"Excuse me for asking sir," she continued "But what was Phil's view?"

"He agreed that Mrs MacDonald might have some useful information, although he put the odds of that happening at a thousand to one," replied Steve. "At least we won't have to wait too long to find out.

"By the way," he continued, "I'm going to have one last look around Donald Summers's bungalow tomorrow morning, and after that I think I'll pop into The Waterman's Arms and have a word with Stacey Barnes and the chef who overheard some of the conversation Danny Willard had with the two guys in the black BMW. I'll let you know how I get on."

Saturday 10:10am

David Stewart had been as good as his word, depositing his wife and mother-in-law at Edinburgh railway station just before 9:45am, giving them plenty of time to collect their tickets and to find the seats that David had pre-booked for them in the first-class carriage.

The train had left on time, and they had quickly settled themselves down, both with plenty to read for the journey to London Kings Cross which would take just under five hours.

Helen's three children had been disappointed that their mum and grandma wouldn't be going to the zoo with them; but that disappointment disappeared as soon as Olivia gave each of them £10 spending money.

She had thoroughly enjoyed seeing her grandchildren and told them that she would see them again very soon. But even as she said it, she knew how difficult it might be to keep to that promise, given that so much of her time was now taken up with her daily visits to Roderick's care home.

But that was all in the future. For now, Olivia's mind was fully focussed on the present, and her visit to Flitton Green, the village where she had spent much of her time when she was the same age as her grandchildren.

She had often thought about returning there, but had never dreamed that the next time she saw the village would be to fulfil what she considered to be an act of duty, rather than one of pleasure.

Olivia looked across at her daughter who was reading Saturday's Scottish Daily Mail on her iPad. As much as she was pleased that Helen was accompanying her on the trip, she was also worried that she might be leading her into a dangerous situation. It was a shame that David hadn't been able to make the journey with them.

However, she remembered that tomorrow they were being picked up from Dorminster station by a police car, and that should surely guarantee their safety. At least the police were taking her visit seriously, she told herself.

But what if I have made a huge mistake? Everybody would take me for a silly old fool. And what about the police, what would they think? Would they arrest me for wasting their time? she asked herself.

This was not the first time those doubts had surfaced. She had spent much of the night wide awake going over everything in her mind.

Even when she eventually managed to get some sleep, those concerns had still been doing the rounds in her subconscious mind. *That's why I feel so tired*, she told herself.

"Are you OK, mum?" asked Helen.

"I'm fine, why do you ask?"

"You just seem a bit distant."

"Honestly, I'm fine," replied Olivia. "Actually I was just thinking of having a nap to make the journey go quicker."

She closed her eyes. She hated telling lies to Helen, even little white ones. But those doubts were still there.

What if he isn't there tomorrow? What if he is and I don't recognise him? Would he recognise me? If he does, how would he react? Would my life be in danger?

Olivia knew that she was in for a very restless time between now and Sunday afternoon.

Saturday 10:30am

Having spent the first part of the day in his office clearing paperwork, as well as reading through his copy of Kath Pearson's running order for the following day's reconstruction, Steve Hardcastle pulled up outside Donald Summer's bungalow on the dot of 10:30am.

As he looked at the bungalow from the comfort of his Range Rover, he couldn't help thinking about its owner. Despite him and his team working their socks off over the last six days, they were still no closer to finding the murderer and he couldn't help thinking that he had let Summers down.

The way things were going, he would be handing over the mantle to DCI Cryer in just over 30 hours' time. However, he had no intention of throwing in the towel just yet, and was still determined to do his very best to bring the murderer to justice, either as the senior investigating officer, or as his assistant.

In the back of his mind was the nagging thought that he had overlooked something important during his previous two visits to the bungalow. As he got out of his car, he saw Mrs Lee from next door looking out of her window and he gave her a cheery wave as he walked up the short path towards Summers's front door.

Once inside the bungalow, his first port of call was the dining room and his eyes immediately went to the top of the mahogany bureau where the photo of the young child had been. There was no doubt it had been removed by the killer, and that still rankled deeply within him.

Next he looked around the bathroom, followed by the kitchen, the two bedrooms and finally the lounge. He looked around, and noticed the book that was lying face down on the small table next to him. This was the biography of Sir Alec Jeffreys, the scientist who had developed techniques for genetic fingerprinting and DNA profiling.

He sat down in the armchair and picked up the book. As he went to flick through the pages, he noticed that one of them had a corner turned down.

Opening the book at that page, his eyes were drawn to a sentence that had been underlined which read:

Today on a day-to-day basis, DNA evidence is used to settle paternity disputes over who is the biological father of a child.

Hardcastle took a deep breath. Could this be the connection to the missing photograph? Was there a paternity dispute involving the child in the photo?

His brief sense of excitement soon began to wane. How could he find out if Summers had believed he was the child's father when the only person likely to be able to confirm this was either the boy's mother or the dead man himself?

And without the photograph, they couldn't identify the child. And if they couldn't identify the child, they wouldn't be able to trace the mother.

Hardcastle remained in the armchair for another ten minutes before getting up. He looked at his watch and saw it was 11:30am. He had spoken to Kath earlier and she had confirmed that there was still no sign of Danny Willard at the pub, so he had told her that he would aim to get over to The Waterman's Arms at around midday. It was time to leave.

He shut the front door behind him and walked briskly towards his car. However, out of the corner of his eye, he noticed that Mrs Lee was waving at him. Too polite to ignore her, he changed direction and made his way up the path towards her front door.

"Can I interest you in a nice cup of tea and a digestive biscuit, Mr Hardcastle?" she asked.

Surprised that she had gotten his name right for once, he looked at his watch and then replied, "I have time for a very quick cup, thank you, Mrs Lee," and followed her through the front door and into her lounge.

She had obviously been waiting for him to come out from next door as a pot of tea, covered by a knitted cosy, was on her coffee table, alongside china cups, saucers, a milk jug, a sugar bowl and a plate on which she had placed half a dozen digestives.

As she poured, Hardcastle decided to ask her a couple of questions which he very much doubted she would be able to answer. Using Phil Davison's terminology, the odds on getting positive replies were a thousand to one.

"Have you ever been inside Mr Summer's bungalow, Mrs Lee?" he began.

"Yes I have, twice actually, on the day he was moving in," came her reply. "The first time I took him a cup of tea as a way to introduce myself, and then I went back a little later to collect the empty cup."

That's a good start, Hardcastle thought to himself.

"And did you notice a photograph of a very young child on the bureau in his dining room?"

"You mean the photograph of his son?"

Hardcastle was stunned.

"He told you about his son?" he asked.

"Only that it was a picture of his son, and that he hadn't seen him for a very long time. He didn't seem as though he wanted to talk about it, so that was all that was said. I wonder if his son knows that his father has passed away."

"Don't you worry about that, Mrs Lee, we'll deal with it," said Hardcastle reassuringly.

Five minutes later, he was on his way to The Waterman's Arms, and while he was driving he called both Kath Pearson and Phil Davison to let them know what he had learnt from Mrs Lee.

He was rather pleased that he hadn't turned down her offer of a cup of tea and a digestive biscuit.

Saturday 12:15pm

Kath Pearson had been able to unearth the selling agent's marketing leaflet from the last time The Waterman's Arms had been put up for sale. The introduction informed potential purchasers that the property was:

'a well-established traditional country Pub / Restaurant dating from 1849 with a renowned reputation amongst local residents. The Bar offers a choice of real ales straight from the cask and an impressive selection of traditional ciders from local independent breweries and homemade lemonade and orange fruit drinks. The business prides itself on its extensive wine list which includes local wines and spirits and an eclectic range of new and old-world wines. In tandem with this, The Waterman's Arms also offers a varied selection of Whiskies, Armagnac and Brandies along with Ports, Sherries and other aperitifs and digestifs.'

The initial selling price had been £999,995 and Pearson had managed to find out that Willard had paid the full asking price. How he had managed to conjure up a cool million pounds was still a mystery, although Pearson was continuing her discreet enquiries in an effort to track down the source of the money.

Hardcastle had no doubt that she would soon find out where it had originated from.

The DI parked his car in the pub car park at exactly 12:15pm. Had he been any later, he probably would have had to have parked out on the road.

Once inside, he bought himself a lager shandy and was lucky enough to find a seat in the corner where he could observe all the comings and goings.

As well as the restaurant which had a 75 cover capacity, customers had a fairly wide range of sandwiches and bar meals to choose from. Judging from the activity behind the bar and the sounds coming from the kitchen, the demand for food today was very high.

Busy behind the bar was a slim blonde woman who Hardcastle guessed was in her mid to late 30s. Judging from her general demeanour, and the respect she was shown by the other staff, this had to be Stacey Barnes, the woman he had come to see.

Hardcastle waited for a lull at the bar before introducing himself.

"Sergeant Pearson told me that you might be calling in at some stage today. I'm really glad you have, Mr Hardcastle, as I'm getting really worried about Danny. It's so out of character for him to be missing, and it's been over two days now. I'm really worried that something serious might have happened to him."

"Do you know any reason why he might have gone missing?"

"Not really," she replied somewhat cagily.

"Not really?" repeated Hardcastle. "That sounds to me like you're hedging your bets a bit."

"Look, can we go upstairs so we won't be overheard. I'm due a break now anyway," replied Stacey.

After she had given some instructions to a couple of the staff, Hardcastle followed her upstairs to a large and very tastefully decorated lounge.

"This is very nice," said Hardcastle.

"Thank you. Before I came to work here, I was an interior designer and had my own business."

"What made you give it up?" asked Hardcastle.

"I was in partnership with my husband, but when he became my ex-husband I decided it was time for a change. I'd done a fair bit of bar work when I was younger, so I applied for a job here and was lucky enough to get it. That was just over three years ago, when the previous owners were still here. They were thinking of selling, but the living accommodation was pretty basic—very 1950s. They knew my background of course, and so they asked me to help to revitalise everything, which, I think, I managed to achieve."

"You certainly did," replied Hardcastle. "It's all very impressive. So Ms Barnes, do you live here?"

"Please call me Stacey, and yes, I do stay over occasionally. I have my own little cottage which is a 10-minute drive from here and as Danny and I like to have our own space from time to time; the arrangement suits the pair of us."

"Do you know much about Danny's past?" asked Hardcastle.

"Actually, I know very little, but that also suits me," replied Stacey. "I know he's separated from his wife and that their two children live with their mother.

He used to be a copper and he told me he left the force because he wanted to do something completely different, hence the reason he bought this place. That's about all I know."

"And everything was going OK between the two of you?" asked Hardcastle.

"Yes, all was fine, until about a month ago."

"What happened then?"

"He changed."

"In what way did he change?"

"Before then, he'd been real fun to be with. He didn't seem to have a care in the world. It was a Sunday evening and he had just arrived back at the pub after playing cricket. He went straight upstairs, and as it was fairly quiet in the bar, I came up as well. We were having a pleasant chat about his game, and trying to decide what we were going to have to eat, when his mobile phone rang. He looked at it to see who was calling and I swear to you, his face suddenly went as white as a sheet.

"He asked me to leave while he took the call, and at first I said I wouldn't. To be honest with you, I thought it might be another woman, and that he had been cheating on me. He asked me to leave again, and again I said no. But this time he got hold of my wrist and dragged me to the top of the stairs, and then shut the lounge door behind him.

"He really frightened me, Mr Hardcastle. I desperately wanted to listen in to his conversation, but I was too scared to go back into the lounge, so I went downstairs and did my best to act as if nothing had happened. I couldn't let the punters know that I was upset. Five minutes later, Danny came downstairs and without a word, went out through the kitchen to his car and drove off."

"How long was he gone?"

"No more than about twenty minutes."

"And what was he like when he got back?"

"He was very subdued, subdued and contrite. But he still refused to tell me who had called and what it had been about. He said it was just a bit of business. And, for most of the time, that's how he's been ever since—apart from this Sunday, that is."

"This Sunday?" asked Hardcastle. "The day the umpire was killed?"

"Yes," replied Stacey. "I found it difficult to believe at the time, but when he eventually got back to the pub, he was in a really good mood, like something in his life had completely changed, changed for the better. I found it quite bizarre,

258

but I didn't ask him why he was so cheerful as I was just glad that he seemed to be back to his old self.

"But it didn't last long. I had a day off on Wednesday as I had a bit to do at the cottage. Then he rang me in the evening to say that I didn't need to come in Thursday until midday. I usually start at 10am. When I asked why, he said he had a couple of guys coming in who were looking for some bar work, and he was going to interview them.

"I was really surprised at that, and a bit put out to be honest because we've got more than enough bar staff at the moment, and anyway, I'm the one who does all the hiring and firing."

"What was his reply?"

"He was very curt; he told me that it was his pub and he'd do what he damn well liked. Then he put the phone down on me. I felt we were back to square one. I resisted the temptation to call him back, and just hoped that he would be in a better frame of mind when I got in the next day.

"That call on Wednesday evening was the last time I spoke to him. On Thursday morning, just after 11am, I got a call from Kevin, one of our chefs, to say that Danny had been arrested."

"That's not quite correct," interrupted Hardcastle. "We certainly didn't arrest him. There were some inaccuracies in what he had previously told us, and we needed to get them cleared up. Once we'd done that, we were more than happy for him to go, and I even offered to arrange a lift back to the pub, but he said he'd call a cab. I promise you, we parted on good terms."

"So what happens about Danny now?" asked Stacey.

"I'll get somebody to come over this afternoon and take a statement from you, and then we'll get the ball rolling," replied Hardcastle. "I know it's easy for me to say this, but I'm sure he'll turn up soon. The vast majority of people reported missing usually turn up within 24-48 hours of being reported."

Stacey nodded, but Hardcastle could see that he hadn't been able to reassure her.

"Thanks for coming over, Mr Hardcastle. I really appreciate it. Is there anything else I can do for you while you're here?"

"Actually, I'd like to have a quick word with Kevin Prior please," asked Hardcastle. "I gather he saw the two men Danny told you he was going to interview."

"That's right," replied Stacey. "I'll see what he's up to at the moment, and if he's free, I'll send him up."

Stacey Barnes was true to her word and within a couple of minutes, Kevin Prior, a 25-year-old Liverpudlian, was sat in the chair Stacey had vacated.

Unfortunately, Prior had very little to add to what he had already told Stacey. On the two occasions he had caught sight of the men—firstly in the bar and then in the car park—they had had their backs turned towards him.

And whilst he had caught a glimpse of their car, a black BMW, it hadn't occurred to him to take down the registration number.

After saying goodbye to Stacey Barnes, Hardcastle walked back to his car. He couldn't help wondering what had happened to Danny Willard. He still hoped that he would resurface in time for the reconstruction.

If he didn't, it would probably be time to start looking for him properly.

Saturday 2:30pm

As he drove back to the station, rain unexpectedly began to fall and Hardcastle had to turn on his windscreen wipers for the first time in ages. There hadn't been any rain for nigh on three weeks, and no doubt keen gardeners would be looking out of their shed windows delighted that their prayers had been answered at long last.

By the time he pulled into the station car park, the rain, mixed with flashes of lightning and rumbles of thunder, was so heavy that he had to sprint from his car to the back door of the station, and then stop off at the gents' toilets to dry himself off.

The first thing he did when he sat down at his desk was to check the weather forecast for Sunday. The last thing they needed was heavy rainfall which would inevitably reduce the number of people attending the reconstruction. Thankfully, and much to his relief the forecast for Sunday was a return to the hot and dry conditions of the previous weeks.

Next, he asked Alan Rutherford to call into see Stacey Barnes at The Waterman's Arms on his way home, and get the necessary missing persons paperwork completed.

He was just about to pick up the phone to speak to DCI Cryer when there was a light tap on his open office door, and his boss walked in, dressed in casual clothes for once. *He must be off for a round of golf if it stops raining*, he thought to himself.

Cryer listened intently to Hardcastle, posing the odd question here and there, and when the younger man had finished the DCI began to pace around the room.

"I'm going to act as devil's advocate now, Steve," said Cryer. "Here's how I see it; you think Summers could have been involved in a paternity dispute, and that this might have been the reason he returned to live in the area. This is based on the missing photograph of a young child, and the next door neighbour saying that Summers had told her the photo was of his son."

"You also need to throw into the mix the biography of Alec Jeffreys," interrupted Hardcastle, "and the underlined sentence about DNA evidence being used to settle paternity disputes."

"OK," replied Cryer. "Now, we have had an e-fit produced by two people who say they saw someone behaving suspiciously at the cricket ground around the time that Summers was murdered. They believe the mystery man is in his mid-twenties.

"The only reply to the e-fit of any substance is from a woman in her late 60s living in Scotland who, according to her son-in-law, can actually put a name to the e-fit, despite the fact that she has only visited the area once in the last twenty-five years or so."

"Let's not forget that she says she knew Summers and that she was also born and bred around here," added Hardcastle.

"Noted," replied Cryer. "Now, what do we know about the killer, apart from the fact that we are looking for someone in their mid-twenties?"

"Unfortunately, very little other than that he is a violent and dangerous man who hasn't made any mistakes so far, other than perhaps being seen as he left the pavilion after killing Summers. Other than that, he's left us no crumbs whatsoever to feed off," replied Hardcastle.

"You mentioned that you have a gut feeling that he could be in the military?" asked Cryer. "Is there any substance to this?"

"Not really," answered Hardcastle. "Other than the lack of evidence could just suggest he might be a professional in some capacity; I have nothing else to substantiate this."

"OK. Let's move on to the murder of Neil Panton. You believe the motive for his death was blackmail, as both his sister and his estranged wife had the impression he was about to come into some money. You believe that Summers's killer was the man Panton was blackmailing?"

"That's correct, sir," answered Hardcastle. "Panton appears to have been a man totally lacking in scruples, and if he had seen the killer in some way, than he wouldn't have hesitated to take advantage of that. I also believe that once he had made contact with the killer, he was signing his own death warrant. That's what makes this man so dangerous in my book."

"And, as things stand at the moment, Kelly Heywood has been unable to provide any pathological link to the murders, and that the manner of their deaths couldn't be further apart?" enquired Cryer.

"That's also correct sir, but it could be the killer trying to muddy the waters, his way of trying to confuse us into looking for two killers rather than one," responded Hardcastle.

"Possibly," said Cryer. "Have I missed anything, or is there anything you want to add?"

"Nothing sir," replied Hardcastle, deciding that that was the best answer as he wasn't sure which way the conversation was going.

"It's interesting that you say you and the team haven't had any crumbs to feed off. That's exactly what I told the ACC this morning. I also told him that I wouldn't have done things anything different had I been the SIO from the start, and that you are still the best man to lead this investigation."

"Thank you sir, your support is very much appreciated," replied a very relieved Hardcastle.

"As far as the ACC is concerned, if we still haven't made any breakthrough after tomorrow's reconstruction, then I become the SIO. But in reality this will still be your investigation and I will be here to add whatever support you need.

"I have every confidence in you, Steve. And now, as the rain seems to have stopped, I'm off to play golf."

The pair shook hands.

Once he was alone, Hardcastle got up from his desk and went to the window to check on the weather. As he was looking out, he watched DCI Cryer get into his car and drive out of the car park.

Not for the first time did he realise he was very fortunate to have Mark Cryer as his boss. He just wished that he had as much confidence in himself as the DCI had.

Saturday 4pm

The train from Edinburgh arrived at London's Kings Cross station at 2:40pm as scheduled, and after registering at their hotel, Olivia MacDonald and her daughter Helen Stewart decided to take afternoon tea in the hotel's restaurant.

"I have to say this is all very nice," said Olivia as she poured herself a second cup of tea. "You really must thank David for me when you speak to him later."

"I certainly will, mum. Hopefully, he and the children are having a good time at the zoo," replied Helen. "I expect they'll stop off for something to eat on their way back, as David isn't much of a cook, so I probably won't ring him until after 9pm as they'll be home quite late."

"And you must let me pay for the train tickets and the hotel," said Olivia. "It must have cost you both a small fortune."

"There's no need for that, mum. The company has had a really good year, and as he's managing director, the board has voted to pay David a very substantial bonus at the end of this month."

"That's really good news, it's nice to feel appreciated," replied Olivia. "But I'm sure that he deserves it, Helen, as he seems to work very long hours."

"He certainly docs that," answered Helen, having a good look around her.

She noticed that the restaurant was virtually empty now. With her watch showing that it was almost 4:30pm, she realised that they had probably stopped serving afternoon tea, and that preparations were now underway so that they would be ready to begin serving dinner from 6pm.

With no one around, she decided that this was a good time to speak to her mum about something that had been bugging her for a while now.

"As we've made it to London mum, and we can't be overheard by anyone, can you tell me what we can expect tomorrow? I really don't want there to be any surprises when we get to Flitton."

"I can't promise you that," replied Olivia. "But when it's all over, you'll understand why we had to come down and why I needed to do things this way."

"Look mum," replied Helen. "This isn't a television police drama or a Lynda La Plante novel. This is real life. The police solve crimes by hard graft with the occasional bit of luck thrown in from time to time. The chances of someone like you suddenly pulling a rabbit out of the hat are very slim."

As soon as she'd said it, Helen regretted it and the look on her mother's face revealed the hurt she was feeling.

"I'm sorry, mum; I just don't want you to get your hopes up. I'm sure the information you've got will be a great help to the police, but the way you've spoken about this, it's almost as if you think you'll be able to go up to this murderer, tap him on the shoulder and tell the police that he's the man they've been searching for."

"But Helen, that's exactly what I'm planning to do."

Saturday 5pm

Kath Pearson arrived home just as the clock in the hallway was striking for the fifth time.

She had known that her husband was not at home as soon as she had opened the front door, since the house was deathly quiet apart from the chiming of the clock. Had Jason been there either the television would have been on full volume, or their CD player would have been blasting out music by the likes of Sam Smith and Stormzy.

Taste in music was just another one of the many things the couple disagreed on, with Kath preferring to listen to background music provided by Classic FM whenever she was at home on her own.

She had spent much of the afternoon fine tuning the running order for the following day's reconstruction, most of which she had carried out on site at the cricket ground.

She had also spoken several times to both DI Hardcastle and Phil Davison, and had factored the latest news on Danny Willard and the visitors from Edinburgh into her planning.

Pearson had asked Isha Hussein to collect Mrs MacDonald and her daughter from the railway station once the call came that their train had arrived at Dorminster. She had chosen Isha as she felt the two ladies would feel more at home chatting to another woman; even someone as young as Isha.

But more importantly, Pearson felt it would be sensible to keep their arrival low key, and away from curious eyes. Isha's VW Golf, with heavily tinted rear windows, was the best option available.

Pearson's view on Danny Willard was that the longer that he was missing, the less likely he was to resurface in time for the reconstruction. It would be disappointing if he didn't turn up after all the help he had given Steve Hardcastle and Phil Davison a week earlier.

Following the deaths of Donald Summers and Neil Panton, the Village League Cricket Committee had agreed that all fixtures scheduled for Sunday would be cancelled as a mark of respect. The Flitton Green versus Middle Ash match, which would act as the background to the police reconstruction, was the only game taking place.

Initially, some players from both teams had felt a little apprehensive about taking part, but were eventually persuaded to join in when it was explained that they had an important part to play in the ongoing hunt for the killer.

With a large number of police officers, both uniformed and plain clothes, due on site to assist with the reconstruction, Kath Pearson had arranged a briefing for all officers at midday on Sunday.

The reconstruction itself was scheduled to begin at 1pm, with the arrival of both teams. Anyone else who had visited the Village Hall or the cricket ground seven days earlier had been asked to arrive as close as possible to the same time as they had arrived on the fateful day.

At 1:50pm there would be a period of silence and the match itself would again start on the dot of 2pm.

League Secretary Richard Askell had managed to get someone with a similar build to Donald Summers to play the role of umpire and the PC playing the part of the mystery stranger was scheduled to make his appearance shortly before Summers had left the field of play due to his injury.

There was also the possibility that some people who had not been at the ground seven days earlier might turn up to watch proceedings out of idle curiosity. Pearson had made arrangements to locate any onlookers in an area as far away from the pavilion as possible, in the hope that they would soon realise that there wasn't much to see and that they were wasting their Sunday afternoon.

As Pearson was running through the reconstruction in her mind for the umpteenth time, her mobile phone bleeped. It was a text from Jason.

Should finish my last job around 7:30pm, and will be going for a curry with the lads from the pool team. Why don't you come along?

Kath Pearson let out a long sigh. Jason knew full well that she was not a fan of Indian food and not for one moment did he expect her to take up his invitation.

It would serve him right if I did take up the offer for once, she thought to herself. *That would spoil his evening.*

But that would also be cutting off her own nose to spite her face, so she sent her husband the text that he was no doubt expecting.

Thanks, but no thanks. I've got another early start tomorrow so try not to wake me up when you get home.

Not so long ago, a text from Jason saying he would be late home would have annoyed her. Now, she was totally indifferent to it. In fact she was quite pleased to have the house all to herself. She could do what she wanted, eat what she wanted, watch what she wanted and listen to what she wanted.

Bliss!

Saturday 5:30pm

Phil Davison had rung home as he was leaving the office, so he was not surprised to see his wife Sarah looking out of their lounge window and waving to him as he pulled into the driveway of their bungalow.

He gave her a little wave and a smile in return. He knew how much effort it would have taken her to get out of her chair and then walk the six steps to the lounge window.

"Hello dear," he said. "What sort of day have you had?"

This was his customary greeting to his wife; it had become almost a ritual.

"Today has been a good day," she replied. "I've made a decent start to my new book. I've written over 1,500 words, so I'll let you have a read through later. And a DVD I ordered off Amazon yesterday arrived this afternoon."

"So what are we watching this evening then?" asked Phil.

"*Witness for the Prosecution*," replied Sarah. "It was made in 1957 and stars Charles Laughton, Marlene Dietrich and Tyrone Power. I think you'll love it as it's based on an Agatha Christie story."

"Is it in colour or black and white?"

"Black and white of course," she replied. "All the best films were made in black and white."

"So, what would you like to have for dinner?" asked Phil.

"Let's have something nice and easy," said Sarah. "What about fish and chips? That'll save you having to cook, and we can eat off trays and watch the film at the same time."

"Suits me," replied Phil. "I'll whizz down to the chippy."

He was back within ten minutes, and five minutes later they were sat in the lounge, trays perched on their laps, eating cod and chips and watching the opening titles of the film.

Despite feeling fairly tired, Phil managed to keep his eyes open throughout the film, and a couple of hours later he was reaching for the DVD player remote control as the closing credits appeared on screen.

"You were right, I really enjoyed that. You can't beat a bit of Agatha Christie," he said turning towards his wife. "Now, I'll quickly wash the plates and then I can tell you about my day. Can I get you anything to drink?"

"Just a coffee will be fine."

A few minutes later Phil set down two mugs of steaming coffee on the little occasional table that was in front of Sarah, then sat down in the armchair next to her and began to tell her about his day.

Sarah was particularly interested in the impending arrival of Olivia MacDonald and her daughter Helen Stewart for the reconstruction, and asked Phil to go over everything he knew about the two ladies from Scotland.

Once Phil had told her everything that he knew about Mrs MacDonald, there was silence. This was quite normal as he knew that Sarah liked to think things through before letting him have her views.

"And what is your view on Mrs MacDonald?" asked Sarah eventually.

"As I told the boss, there might be a very outside chance that she has some information that might help us, but I wouldn't put any money on it."

"And why do you think that?"

"Because she hasn't been to the Dorminster area in ages and I don't see how she could recognise the face of the e-fit which is a man in his twenties. He might not have even been born the last time she was down here."

There was silence again whilst Sarah took this on board.

"Please don't take this as an insult, Phil, but I feel your thinking, and by 'your' I mean everyone who is involved in this investigation, is too linear. It needs to be more lateral."

"How have you arrived at that conclusion?" he asked slightly taken aback.

"Firstly, I look at things through my writer's eye, and in this instance I'm turning your facts into my fiction."

"Carry on," replied Davison.

"So, in my story, I would also have a lady in her late sixties telling the police that she recognised the identikit picture of a man in his mid-twenties, even though the last time she had visited the area was decades earlier. Now, this is where you've got to make the jump to fiction. Close your eyes and forget the face of your e-fit; clear your mind."

"Mind cleared and eyes duly closed," replied Davison, half-seriously and half-jokingly.

"In his place, think of the actor Michael Douglas."

"Seriously?" asked Davison, opening his eyes.

"Please humour me, Phil. Close your eyes and think of a picture of Michael Douglas, perhaps a Michael Douglas in his mid-twenties, before he was as famous as he is today. Who would he have reminded you of?"

"Well, obviously his dad, Kirk Douglas," he replied. And at that moment, the penny dropped. "So, what you're saying is that Olivia MacDonald may have recognised the e-fit face because, decades ago, she knew the father?"

Sarah nodded.

"And the reason we've had such a poor response to the e-fit going public is because 'Kirk Douglas' left the area long ago and there are very few people still living around here who might remember him and make the connection?"

"Exactly."

"So, all we've got to do is find Kirk Douglas and arrest Michael."

Saturday Midnight

Unable to sleep, Phil Davison got quietly out of his bed, doing his best not to disturb his wife. Because of the severity of the injuries she had suffered in the hit and run incident many years earlier, the only way that both of them could enjoy a decent night's sleep was for them to have separate beds.

He carefully closed the bedroom door behind him before making his way to the kitchen. He took out a 4-litre plastic bottle of semi-skimmed milk from the fridge freezer, half-filled a pint glass and took it into the lounge, where he sat down in the same armchair he had occupied earlier that evening.

Sarah had given him a fair amount to think about.

But how close to the truth was she?

He now felt it was possible that Olivia MacDonald did have something to contribute to the reconstruction after all, although he thought that Sarah's hypothesis was nowhere near to the truth as she had suggested.

For a start, why was Mrs MacDonald travelling down from Scotland? What did she know that she couldn't have told them over the phone? And surely the chances of the killer turning up to the reconstruction were zero.

The purpose of the reconstruction was to jog people's memories and perhaps add more substance to the identity of the killer. The best they were hoping for was that at the end of the day they might have a few more leads to follow up.

He took a long sip from his cold glass of milk, and then put it back on the coffee table.

I'm sure I'm right, he told himself. At best, the most that Mrs MacDonald could contribute was by adding another piece to the jigsaw. He decided he wouldn't mention anything to the boss, as he already had more than enough on his plate.

He looked at his watch. It was too late to call Kath Pearson. However, he would talk to her in the morning in case she felt the need to tweak her reconstruction plan in the light of Sarah's theory. And as for Sarah herself, he would do his best to make sure that she felt he was taking her views very seriously.

The odd little white lie never hurt anybody, he told himself.

Sunday 1:30am

By the time Jason Pearson arrived home, it was well after midnight and Kath had already been in a deep sleep for almost two hours.

She had thoroughly enjoyed the evening on her own.

After replying to Jason's text, she had taken a leisurely bath, after which she had microwaved a Sainsbury's ready meal, and followed this up with a generous portion of lemon cheesecake. She hadn't eaten lemon cheesecake for years, but had bought one on her way home after developing a sudden urge.

After putting the dirty plates and cutlery in the dishwasher, she had turned on the television to watch a documentary on the SKY Arts channel about the actor and dancer Gene Kelly, which was followed by one of her favourite films, *Singing in the Rain*.

Had Jason been at home, no doubt he would have asked 'what's this rubbish?' on seeing a 1950s musical on the TV. Then, without waiting for a reply, he would have grabbed the remote control and changed the channel to one that he wanted to watch.

When Jason finally arrived home, it was the sound of the front door shutting that had woken Kath up, even though, for once, he had taken care not to slam it. She hadn't been looking forward to him getting home as the last thing she felt like doing was having a conversation with him at that time of night. Thankfully, he hadn't come up to bed straight away, nor had he even looked around the bedroom door to see if she was still awake.

Instead, he had switched on the television and judging from the sound coming from the lounge he was watching one of the music channels on SKY. But for once, he didn't have the sound turned up too loud, so she hoped that she would be able to get back to sleep long before he decided to come to bed.

However, having been woken up from a deep sleep, she found herself tossing and turning, going through everything that was on her mind, and at one stage she was certain that she could hear her husband talking on his mobile phone. Curious to know who he might be chatting to at that time of night, she quietly got out of bed, opened the door and slowly walked down the stairs, her bare feet on the carpet making little or no noise.

She stopped at the lounge door that was shut.

She knew that Jason was sitting on the armchair closest to the door.

What she heard stunned her.

"Yes, I promise. I'll do it this week. It's just a matter of picking the right time."

There was silence as whoever Jason had been talking to must have been speaking.

"OK, I'll make sure I do it by then."

Once again, there was silence.

"Of course I love you. I wouldn't be leaving her if I didn't, would I?"

Sunday 6:30am

"Phil, where are you?"

Phil Davison woke up with a start. His wife was calling him from their bedroom.

He looked at his watch. It was 6:30am and he was still sitting in the lounge. It dawned on him that he must have fallen asleep in the armchair sometime around 2am, as he remembered the digital clock in the kitchen showing it was 1:45am when he'd made himself a cup of coffee. He looked at the coffee table in front of him where a half full cup of cold coffee was perched perilously close to the edge.

He went to get up, but was stopped by a searing pain coming from the left side of his neck, no doubt a consequence of sleeping in the armchair without a pillow supporting his head. Hopefully, it would wear off quickly once he was up and about.

"Phil, are you there?" came the voice again from the bedroom, this time a little louder than before.

"I'm out here, just making us a cup of tea," he replied, moving towards the kitchen. It was only a little white lie as the sight of the cold coffee had prompted him to put the kettle on.

"That's OK then," she replied. "I was beginning to worry that you had gone off to work without saying goodbye."

"Now you know I'd never do that," he answered. "I'll be with you in a jiffy."

A few minutes later he pushed open the bedroom door and put down the tray he was carrying on the table that separated the two single beds.

He leant over and gave her a kiss.

"Did you sleep OK?" he asked.

"Yes," she replied. "I went out like a light last night as I took a sleeping tablet. My back was a bit painful."

He was relieved to hear that she had slept well. It meant she had no idea he had spent the night in the armchair. He poured out the tea from the pot into two china cups and handed her one.

"Do you need some painkillers?" he asked.

Phil knew that whenever she said that some part of her body was a bit painful, it meant that she was in considerable discomfort.

"No thanks," she replied. "I'll see how I feel when I get up. What time are you leaving for work today?"

"About 9 o'clock as it's Sunday," replied her husband. "I need to pop into the office to see if anything has turned up overnight, and then I'll head off to the cricket ground. I'll probably be there for the rest of the day."

"If Mrs MacDonald does recognise the face in the e-fit, she could be in danger if the killer was to find out," said Sarah. "After all, it sounds like she is the only person who can identify him. He has already killed twice, and he might not hesitate to kill again if his freedom is at stake."

"I've been mulling things over," replied Phil, "and I'll make sure that Mrs MacDonald is well protected at all times. It's just a shame that she hasn't given us any hints as to who she thinks the murderer is. I very much doubt if the killer will be anywhere near the cricket ground today. But if for some reason he is, and she spots him, I hope she doesn't think that all she's got to do is to tap him on the shoulder."

Sunday 8am

Jason had finally come up to bed just before 2am. He had quietly opened the bedroom door and whispered, "Are you awake, Kath?" When there had been no reply, he'd quickly undressed and gotten into bed. Within ten minutes he was fast asleep.

She had pretended to be in a deep sleep and had been lying close to the edge of her side of the bed. The idea of any physical contact with her husband filled her with a deep sense of revulsion, as did the thought of him being with another woman. As far as she was concerned, Jason had broken the vow he made at their wedding when he had promised 'to be faithful only to her for as long as they both shall live.'

When he broke that vow, he broke their marriage.

For the rest of the night, she lay awake going over and over what she had heard him tell the unknown woman at the other end of his phone.

'I'll do it this week. It's just a matter of picking the right time.'

She knew that Jason would find it difficult to pick the right time, given how busy her job kept her and how little time they had been spending together of late.

She also knew that Jason lacked the moral courage to tell her that he was in love with someone else. He was more than likely to fudge it and say something like *'let's face it, things aren't great between us and perhaps we should spend a little time apart to see if we miss one another.'*

Had she not overheard his conversation with the other woman, she would probably have gone along with this. After all, it was true that things hadn't been that good between them for quite a while now.

However, it was the deceit that she could not and would not accept, and the fact that he had been carrying on with another woman behind her back. She also knew that deep down, Jason was a coward and that he would never be able to front it out with her and admit that he had been having an affair.

Because of this, she knew that she had the upper hand.

And then she remembered that she was expecting his child.

278

This was the rabbit that she could pull out of the hat, if she wanted to. It would just be a matter of timing.

She knew how desperate Jason had been to start a family for some considerable time and it was quite possible that he had decided to leave her for someone who felt the same way as he did about having kids.

But she couldn't help wondering what Jason's reaction would be if she told him that she was pregnant. Would he still want to end their marriage? Or might he want to make a go of things 'for the baby's sake'?

And what would the other woman's reaction be if she found out that Kath was pregnant and that Jason was the father? After all, she was willing to bet that he'd told her that he and Kath were no longer sleeping together as man and wife.

After much soul searching she eventually decided to say nothing to Jason and, for the time being at least, let things play out.

By that time, daylight was streaming through the curtains and the bedside clock showed it was 6:35am. She decided that she might as well get up; after all she had another busy day ahead of her. At least the weather forecasters had got it right; yesterday's rain had given way to another hot and sunny day.

Taking great care not to wake up her husband, she rolled over and put her feet on the floor. But as she went to stand up, she was immediately hit by a wave of intense nausea; her very first experience of morning sickness.

She immediately lay back down on the bed.

After twenty minutes, she tried to get up again and managed to make it to the kitchen. After half a cup of hot tea and a piece of dry toast, she began to feel better. But as she went to put the milk bottle back in the fridge, the smell of the lemon cheesecake hit her, and she began to feel nauseous again.

She went into the lounge and sat down, hoping the nausea would pass.

By the time it had subsided, it was a couple of minutes past eight, and her mobile phone began to ring. She could see that the caller was Phil Davison, the only person she felt like talking to at that precise moment. She would have ignored all other calls, even if the caller had been her mother.

"Hi Phil, how are things?"

"Fine, Kath. All OK with you?"

"I've had better starts to the day," she replied.

"Do you want to talk about it?"

"Maybe, I'm not sure at the moment."

"You know that I'm always there for you," replied Phil.

"I know that," replied Kath, "and when I feel like talking, you'll be the first person I'll turn to."

"I should hope so too! Anyway, the purpose of the call is that Sarah's come up with some thoughts about today's reconstruction, which I need to share with you before I decide whether or not to tell the boss. What time are you getting to the cricket ground?"

"I had planned to get there around 10am, but could make it 9:30am if you want?"

"No, ten will be fine," replied Phil, "I'll see you then."

As she put the phone down, she couldn't help thinking about her relationship with Phil. He was like a brother, a father and a best friend, all wrapped into one person. He was everything that Jason wasn't, and perhaps that was the real reason why her marriage was doomed to fail, and why she believed that she would never find another man who she could truly love with all her heart and soul, like she knew that, given half a chance, she could have loved Phil Davison.

Sunday 9am

Steve Hardcastle had taken his own advice for once, and had pulled into their driveway just after 4:30pm on Saturday afternoon.

Jenny and the boys were surprised and delighted when they heard the front door open, and there were whoops of delight from Thomas and Ethan when their father announced that he was taking them all to the cinema to see *Avengers: Infinity War*, the latest in the Marvel Super Heroes series of films.

Whilst the film itself was not exactly her cup of tea, Jenny was certainly up for it when Steve told them they would be going to their local Beefeater for something to eat afterwards.

With the film lasting for over two and a half hours, all four of them were ravenous by the time they sat down to eat, and they didn't get home until well after 10pm. And with the boys still a bit hyper after having enjoyed the film so much, it was almost midnight before their parents finally climbed into bed.

The family outing had done him the world of good, and for once he had been able to put all thought of work to the back of his mind while he tried to follow the complicated plot of the film.

So much so, that he hadn't woken up until just after 8am.

He'd gotten out of bed as quietly as he could so as not to disturb Jenny, and had a shower and a shave before ringing Phil Davison to tell him not to worry about calling into the office as he needed to pop in to pick up a few things, and would also check to see if there had been any messages overnight.

He had then made himself some toast and a strong cup of coffee and was just thinking about leaving when he heard the kitchen door open.

"You let me sleep in," said Jenny. "What time did you get up?"

"Just after eight," replied her husband.

"Thank you for coming home at a sensible time yesterday. It made a nice change," said Jenny, putting her arms around his waist. "It was a lovely surprise, and we all really enjoyed ourselves. We must get back into the habit of having some serious time together as a family."

She stood back, suddenly realising that he was dressed for work.

"Do you really need to leave this early? It is Sunday after all."

"I'm afraid so," replied Hardcastle, noticing that his wife was pouting her lips. "I need to swing by the office first to pick up some bits and pieces, and to check for any messages, and then I want to have a catch up with Phil and Kath before the main briefing at noon. Look Jen, I promise that when this case is over, I'll take things a bit easier and we will get that week away in August."

"Make it a fortnight, and I'm all yours," replied Jenny giving him a hug.

"It's a deal," said her husband, returning her hug and kissing her on the lips.

"I don't suppose you have any idea what time you'll be home later?"

"Not really," answered Hardcastle. "We'll have to see if the reconstruction results in any new leads. If it does we'll want to follow them up straight away. But if it doesn't, then Mr Cryer becomes the *de facto* senior investigating officer, and my chances of succeeding him when he retires won't be looking that good."

"What about that old lady coming down from Scotland you told me about on Friday evening?"

"You mean the mysterious Mrs MacDonald? I suppose there is a small chance that she knows something that might help us, but I'm not banking on it. I'd be more optimistic if I'd had a chance to have a word with her first, but for some reason, according to her son-in-law, she doesn't want to say anything until she gets to the cricket ground.

"And we had a little bit of luck yesterday when we found out that the picture Donald Summers had on display in his dining room was a photograph of his son. We're certain that the killer got into the old man's bungalow and took it away with him, and that would seem to confirm the link between killer and victim."

"See, it's not all doom and gloom, is it?" said Jenny, as her husband smiled at her.

They carried on hugging for another twenty seconds or so, before he gently eased himself away from Jenny.

"I need to get going."

"Oh well, if you must," replied Jenny. "Try and let me know how things go. Good luck, sweetheart."

I need more than luck, thought Hardcastle as he blew his wife a kiss, and shut the front door behind him.

I need a ruddy miracle.

Sunday 10am

Phil Davison turned into the Village Green car park just as the church clock began to strike ten. As he got out of his car, he could see that Kath Pearson was sat on a bench overlooking the cricket ground no more than thirty yards away.

"How do you always manage to get everywhere before me?" he asked.

"Because I always leave before you," replied Pearson turning around.

Davison was just about to come back with a suitable quip when he stopped in his tracks. Kath was quickly wiping her eyes with a tissue, but it was obvious to him that she had been crying.

"Christ almighty, Kath, what's happened?"

She could hear the deep concern in his voice.

"Why, do I look that bad? You should have seen me before I put my makeup on."

"You never look bad to me," he replied quietly. "But seriously, what's happened? Please tell me so I can do something to help you."

He sat down beside her on the bench and instinctively put his arm around her shoulder. Kath shivered instantly at the contact, and Davison quickly took his arm away, worried that he had overstepped the mark.

"I'm sorry, Kath. I shouldn't have done that."

"Don't be daft, Phil. You know you're my best friend, and if we were anywhere else other than here, I'd have been really upset if you hadn't put your arm around me—it's what best friends do. But I don't want anyone else to know I've been crying, and you being your usual kind and thoughtful self is guaranteed to start me blubbing again."

She took a deep breath, took out another tissue and began drying her eyes again.

"If anyone else notices that I've been crying, I'll tell them that I've had a bad bout of hay fever this morning. I know that the pollen count is very high today, so hopefully I'll get away with it."

"That's sorted everyone else out," answered Davison, "but what about me? I'm really worried about you, Kath. Has something happened to Jason? Has he been in an accident?"

"I wish," she replied.

"Has he hit you then?" he asked, flummoxed by her response.

"No, he knows better than that. He knows that I'd have him on his back in a flash if I ever thought he was about to hit me."

"So, what has he done?"

Kath continued to wipe her eyes, as she pondered on how to reply.

"Last night, I overheard a conversation he was having with someone on his mobile phone."

"Someone?" asked Phil. "Was it another woman?"

"You guessed it," replied Kath. "It was a woman, and I clearly heard him say that he loved her, and that he wouldn't be leaving me if he didn't. And before you think that I've probably got the wrong end of the stick Phil, I also heard him say that he'd tell me he was leaving sometime this week and that it was just a matter of picking the right time."

It was Phil's turn to think before replying.

"So what are you going to do about it?" asked Phil eventually.

"I'm not totally sure at the moment, Phil, but I don't want to force the issue with Jason. And I don't want to make it easy for him, so I'll probably just let things play out. But do you know what the funny thing is?"

He shook his head gently.

"I'm not that bothered really. I mean, I'll admit that it has come as a bit of a shock, to say the least. But then again things haven't been right between us for some time now, and they've been coming to a boil over the last few weeks."

"So, why the tears?" asked Phil.

"Well, to be honest with you, I've had a few other things on my mind lately, and I think it's just the accumulation of everything."

Kath wished she could have told Phil that she was pregnant, and because of that her emotions were all over the place. But for the time being, she felt she had told him enough.

"Let's hope we can wind up this investigation as soon as possible so you can take some time off. I'm sure that would do you the world of good," said Phil.

"I'm sure you're right," replied Kath, "but enough about me. You mentioned on the phone that Sarah had come up with some ideas about today's reconstruction, but you didn't sound that convinced. What more can you tell me?"

It took Davison just a couple of minutes to tell her the reasons why his wife believed that Mrs MacDonald might have some information which could help them identify the murderer.

"So, maybe she isn't some scatty old woman who just fancies a couple of days away from bonny Scotland," ended Davison.

"In a way, I get where Sarah is coming from," replied Pearson. "Using her analogy, knowing what 'Kirk Douglas' looked like when he was younger, made it easier for her to identify any of his offspring. So the e-fit picture is our 'Michael Douglas'.

"Like you, I don't see any way that the killer will be here for today's reconstruction, but she might be able to improve the accuracy of the e-fit. And she will be able to give us 'Kirk's' real name which ultimately should lead us to 'Michael'. But whether this 'Michael' is actually the killer is the sixty-four thousand dollar question. But it is a lead, and we're pretty short of leads at the moment."

"As always, you're spot on, Kath," replied Davison. "Do you think I should tell the boss?"

"In this instance, I agree with you and I wouldn't tell him. He has enough on his plate at the moment. Let's just make sure we keep close tabs on Mrs MacDonald all the time she is here. And then you and I can have a laugh about it, or cry on each other's shoulder's later when nothing happens."

Sunday 10:30am

Olivia MacDonald and her daughter Helen Stewart were running late. They had missed their train to Dorminster by a whisker.

The previous night they had gone for a stroll around London and unfortunately had ended up getting themselves lost. They eventually hailed a black cab to take them back to their hotel, where they had a couple of drinks in the bar before retiring to their respective rooms.

Unfortunately, the walk and a couple of wee drams had tired Olivia out more than she had realised, and she had been late coming down to breakfast. Despite a mad dash to Waterloo, they arrived at the platform only to see their train pulling slowly out of the station.

Helen Stewart looked at her watch. Missing the train meant they wouldn't be able to squeeze in some lunch before they were due at the cricket ground.

It also meant that she needed to let Detective Inspector Hardcastle know that she and her mother might not make it to the cricket ground until after the reconstruction had begun.

Telling her mother that she needed to visit the toilet, Helen walked back down the platform to find a quiet place where she could use her phone.

"DI Hardcastle."

"It's Helen Stewart, Mr Hardcastle, Olivia MacDonald's daughter. I believe you spoke to my husband on Friday?"

"That's right, Mrs Stewart, I did," replied Hardcastle.

"Unfortunately, mum and I have missed our scheduled train, and will have to catch a later one, so we won't be arriving at Dorminster until around 1:45pm. Are you still able to provide us with a lift from the station?"

"Of course," replied the DI. "You will be met by Detective Constable Isha Hussein who will be waiting for you when you arrive at the station. She will be driving her own car, a black VW Golf, rather than using a marked police car. I thought it would be better that your arrival is fairly low key, given the circumstances."

"Thank you, Mr Hardcastle. That sounds perfect. How long will it take to get to the cricket ground from the station?"

"Given it's a Sunday, the journey should take you no more than 15 minutes," replied Hardcastle. "So I look forward to seeing you and your mother around 2pm."

"Likewise, Mr Hardcastle; I hope that after all the trouble we have put you to, our visit proves to be worthwhile," answered Mrs Stewart.

"Before you go, would it be possible to speak to your mother?" asked Hardcastle. "It would help us tremendously to have some prior notice of what your mother thinks she's going to do when she gets here."

"I'm not with her at the moment," replied Mrs Stewart. "But even if she was standing next to me, I know she wouldn't talk to you. Lord knows how many times I have urged her to speak to you on the telephone, obviously without any success."

Hardcastle put his phone back in his pocket. It irritated him that this old lady refused to talk to him. Her visit would only be worthwhile if it provided them with a new lead or two to follow up on, and that sadly, was very unlikely.

Sunday Midday

By the time the hands on the pavilion clock had reached a quarter to twelve, Kath Pearson's eyes no longer looked like she'd been crying. However, just to make sure, from time to time she would sniff loudly and mutter 'bloody hay fever' under her breath, but loud enough for anyone close to her to hear.

After a while, Phil Davison wandered up to her and, with a broad grin on his face, suggested that she was in danger of overdoing it, before wishing her good luck with the briefing she was about to deliver.

As ever, Pearson had prepared extensively and the briefing went like clockwork.

Amongst those attending were DCI Cryer and Robert Lloyd, the Assistant Chief Constable (Operations), and after a brief chat with DI Hardcastle, the ACC indicated to Pearson that he wanted to have a few words with her in private.

"Well done, sergeant. That was a textbook briefing."

"Thank you, sir."

"Tell me sergeant, in your opinion how is this investigation proceeding? And please don't pull any punches."

Pearson knew she had to be careful how she replied. Lloyd was not someone to suffer fools gladly.

"As you know, sir, many investigations are like putting the pieces of a jigsaw together, and this one is no different. Each day, the investigation has progressed and whilst we are still missing some of the pieces, I believe that we are getting close sir."

The ACC gave her a piercing look.

"You have followed your textbook briefing, with a textbook reply."

"You asked me for my opinion, sir, and I have given you an honest answer," replied Pearson, holding the ACC's gaze.

Have I just ruined my career? Pearson thought to herself?

After a couple of seconds, the ACC's face broke into a smile, something which didn't happen that often.

"Both Mr Cryer and Mr Hardcastle rate you very highly, sergeant, and I can see why. I shall watch how your career progresses with interest."

And with that, he turned on heels, made his way back to the waiting unmarked car, slid into the back seat, and was gone; no doubt off to another PR event somewhere in the county. Everyone knew that Robert Lloyd was a chief constable in the making.

As the car disappeared, Kath Pearson blew out her cheeks.

"Fraternising with the enemy, I see," said a voice from behind her.

"I'm not sure that was my best ever career move, Phil," replied Pearson. "I've just told the ACC that I think we are on the verge of making a breakthrough."

"Ouch," exclaimed Davison.

"What's ouch?" came another voice from behind her.

"Did you have a nice chat with the ACC?" asked Hardcastle.

Pearson repeated what she'd just told Phil Davison.

"I do hope you're right, Kath. Pulling this one out of the bag will be good for a lot of people. Lloyd will claim all the credit and will be one step closer to the chief constable's job he's got his eye on, Mr Cryer will retire and end his career on a high note, and I might just get to hold on to my job by the skin of my teeth," joked Hardcastle.

"What about Kath and me?" complained Davison with a grin on his face.

"Kath will get the promotion she fully deserves whilst you'll be out there getting your hands dirty and solving all the crimes, while I do a Lloyd and take all the credit," replied Hardcastle.

"No change there then," replied Davison, laughing. "I'll go and get us some coffees from the chuckwagon."

They both watched as Davison made his way to the mobile food truck.

"Just how does he manage to stay so good-natured all the time?" asked Pearson.

"I've often asked myself the same question," replied Hardcastle. "I've known him for a long time now and I can honestly say that he's the most even-tempered person I've ever come across."

They carried on watching Davison for a few more seconds before Hardcastle broke the silence. "How are you feeling, Kath?"

"Not too bad thank you, sir."

"Have you told your husband about the baby?"

"No, not yet sir. I intend to have a chat with him during the week."

Hardcastle nodded, and quickly changed the subject.

"So, where do you want me today? Have you anything specific in mind?" he asked.

"I thought I would leave that to you, sir," she replied. "I do have one request, though?"

"Fire away."

"If you don't mind," replied Pearson, "I'd like to stay close to Mrs MacDonald and her daughter when they arrive."

"You're welcome to them, but any particular reason why?" asked Hardcastle.

"For the same reason we've got Isha lined up to collect the two ladies from the railway station. There's every chance that Mrs MacDonald might feel more relaxed talking to another woman. And on top of that, I've got some relatives living in Scotland, and talking about them might help break the ice," said Pearson.

She hated not being totally truthful (the aunt and uncle she had mentioned actually lived in Milton Keynes), but she had promised Phil Davison that Sarah's theory about Mrs MacDonald would stay just between the two of them for the time being.

"OK," replied Hardcastle. "I'll have a quick word with them when they arrive. After that, they're all yours. Let's keep our fingers crossed that Mrs MacDonald is not wasting our time, for all our sakes."

Sunday 1pm

The first players from the Flitton Green and Middle Ash cricket teams pulled into the village hall car park at 12:45pm, and by 1pm all of those who were expected to take part in the re-run of last Sunday's match had arrived.

There were three absentees; Neil Panton, of course, plus Alex Donahue for Flitton Green and Danny Willard for Middle Ash.

With Donahue still suffering from Post-Traumatic Stress Disorder, his father Alan had offered to take his place in the Flitton Green side, but both team captains felt it wouldn't be appropriate, preferring instead to play a nine versus ten game as the result was irrelevant.

However, Andy Hanson, the Flitton skipper, did ask Mr Donahue to join the players for the pre-match period of silence as his son's representative.

As the skippers handed out black arm bands to their respective teams, they found the mood in both dressing rooms to be very subdued. There was none of the usual pre-match banter you would normally expect to hear.

The main topic of conversation amongst the Middle Ash players was Danny Willard's absence. None of the team could explain his apparent disappearance, but the widely held view was that there must be a woman involved somewhere along the line.

The two scorers arrived at 1:10pm and were followed soon after by League Secretary Richard Askell who had given a lift to last Sunday's umpire Tony Sullivan, and to Mick Lewis, who Askell had asked to assume the role of Donald Summers for the purpose of the reconstruction.

Askell had chosen well; Lewis was a dead ringer for Summers, even though he was a couple of decades younger.

When he was introduced to Lewis, Hardcastle couldn't help thinking that someone that obese in his early forties might well struggle to live as long as Summers had.

However, when he said as much to Richard Askell, his respect for Lewis went up several notches when Askell told him that the stand-in umpire had lost over 6 stone since he began a strict diet just over a year ago.

"Basically, his doctor told him if he wanted to live long enough to see his children grow up he needed to lose at least ten stone. He's got another four to go, and he hopes to shed that by Christmas."

Hardcastle was just about to reply when he was interrupted by an ear-splitting screech from the village hall public address system, followed by someone shouting out "Testing, testing. One, two, three, four, Mary had a little lamb."

"He sounds like Corporal Jones from *Dad's Army*," remarked Hardcastle.

"That's old Ted Chambers," replied Askell. "He looks like Corporal Jones as well."

"The only difference is that Ted's a lot older," said Andy Hanson who had just joined the other two. "He's been doing the PA here for years, mainly for village fêtes and the like. It's his little baby. This is the first time he's done a cricket match and he's quite excited about it. He wanted me to ask you if there is anything you want him to announce?"

"Well, he can start off by announcing the period of silence at 1:50pm, but beyond that, if we have anything we want him to say, we will let him know," replied Hardcastle.

"As long as he knows that we don't want the PA used for anything other than what is relevant to today's reconstruction. We want today to be as accurate a replication of last Sunday's events as possible. There was no PA then, so we don't want to hear it used for anything other than what we want him to say."

At that moment, Hardcastle's mobile phone rang. It was Kath Pearson.

"Just to let you know that I checked with National Rail and Mrs MacDonald's train is on time, so Isha has just left for the station. They should be here just after 2pm."

"Thanks for that, Kath. As I said earlier, I'll have a few words with them when they get here, and then after that, she's all yours."

Hardcastle carried on walking around the ground. Even though Kath Pearson had been in charge of all the planning, and every police officer had a comprehensive running order, the DI was still the senior investigating officer, and ultimately, the buck stopped with him.

When he had reached the midway point of his walk, Hardcastle was joined by Phil Davison.

"Things seem to be going OK at the moment, boss. Kath has done a good job as usual."

"She certainly has, Phil," replied Hardcastle. "This is only a gut feeling, but one way or another I think that we might be losing her before too long."

"Funnily enough, I was thinking the same thing," replied Davison. "I would really miss her, both from a personal and a work point of view."

"Same here, Phil. The three of us make a good team."

They carried on walking around the perimeter of the ground, lost in their own thoughts.

"She would be an incredibly hard act to follow. Would you look to replace her from within?" asked Davison.

"I'd love to be able to do that, Phil, but ours is a young team, and filling Kath's boots will come just a bit too early for the likes of Paul Taylor, Alan Rutherford and Isha Hussein."

Hardcastle broke off when he noticed Davison waving to a woman in her thirties, who was waving back enthusiastically.

"Anyone I should know?" he enquired.

"That's Debra Patterson," answered Davison.

"She's very attractive. I can see why Neil Panton was smitten with her," replied Hardcastle. "I'd like to have a chat with her once we've got things moving."

They'd only gone a few paces further when the DI noticed another woman waving at Davison.

"Another one of your harem, detective sergeant?" asked Hardcastle jokingly.

"That's Christine Williams, Panton's sister."

"I ought to have a chat with her as well," replied the DI.

They had only gone a few yards further when it was Hardcastle's turn to point out some spectators.

"The woman standing by that oak tree, talking to Tanya Panton and Glen Finnemore is Stacey Barnes, the supervisor from Danny Willard's pub. Now, rumour has it that you're a detective," continued Hardcastle, turning to face Phil Davison. "So tell me, what have those three, plus Mrs Patterson and Mrs Williams all have in common?"

Before Davison could answer, a voice came from behind.

"I wondered if you might notice them, sir," said Kath Pearson, "as none of them were here last Sunday."

"Any reason that they are where they are today?" asked Hardcastle. "I thought we had agreed to keep anyone who wasn't here last week at arm's length?"

"I thought I would use a bit of discretion where those five are concerned," replied Pearson. "It seemed totally wrong to exclude Mrs Patterson, Mrs Williams and Mrs Panton. Being here might well be part of the grieving process for those three ladies. And Mrs Panton won't go anywhere without Mr Finnemore at the moment, and don't forget Finnemore knew Panton well from the days they both played for Middle Ash."

"Even though they hated each other's guts?" interrupted Hardcastle.

"Even though they hated each other's guts," replied Pearson.

"And as for Stacey Barnes, I just feel sorry for her as she seems totally lost. She told me she wanted to be here in case Danny turned up, which so far he hasn't done, and I don't think he will now."

"I think you're right, I reckon he's gone to ground somewhere," replied Hardcastle. "And you are completely right to let all five of them be here. I would have done exactly the same thing.

"But what I do find sad is that we are here for Donald Summers, and no one seems to be grieving for him."

"Well, there is Olivia MacDonald. She said she knew Summers," said Davison.

"Yes, she did, but I got the impression that that isn't why she's traipsed all the way down from Scotland. Anyway, we'll find out soon enough, one way or another," replied Hardcastle. *For better or for worse*, he thought to himself.

Sunday 2pm

The period of silence went according plan.

As Ted Chambers made the announcement over the PA system, the two teams, plus the umpires, the scorers and league secretary Richard Askell, lined up together in front of the Flitton Green pavilion, with their heads bowed as a mark of respect to the two men who had lost their lives.

Three rings on a hand bell signified the start of the period and a further three rings sixty seconds later marked the end. There was a smattering of applause from the spectators dotted around the boundary rope, led by Ellie Compton, Brian Tregunno and other family members of the Flitton Green players. There were even salutes from a couple of the uniformed police officers who were there on duty.

As soon as the bell had been rung for the second time, the Middle Ash opening batsmen trotted back to the pavilion to get their gear on, so they would be ready to face the Flitton opening bowlers when the umpire called 'play' on the dot of 2pm.

Since the two skippers had decided the game would be played as a 'friendly', neither batsman had bothered to wear a helmet.

The first ball was to be bowled by a slightly nervous Colin Sharpe. He wasn't used to having so many people watching him from the boundary, and his hands were unusually sweaty. Being well known in cricketing circles for bowling slow looping deliveries, he had decided that the first ball he bowled would be as quick as possible, so he could take the batsman by surprise.

He certainly achieved that as the ball, delivered from a sweaty right hand and travelling at around seventy five miles an hour, headed straight for the opening batsman's nose.

"No ball!" called umpire Mick Lewis.

To the amusement of his fellow Flitton Green players, Sharpey had bowled his first ever 'beamer'.

Luckily, for all concerned, the Middle Ash opener managed to duck underneath the ball just at the last moment.

The language used by the batsman might, under different circumstances, have seen him receive a hefty fine for using offensive and intimidating language in public, and there were enough coppers around who could have nicked him for the offence. Fortunately for him, the police had other matters on their mind.

While umpire Mick Lewis was giving Sharpey a warning, the batsman was calling for someone to bring out his helmet.

Despite Sharpey's profuse apologies to the batsman, they fell on deaf ears.

So Sharpey walked back to his mark, turned, ran in and bowled a gentle half volley, which the batsman promptly hit straight back over the bowler's head for six. He then launched another volley of bad language at the hapless bowler.

The Middle Ash scorer turned to his Flitton Green counterpart, "I think it's game on, old boy."

Whilst this was going on, there were hoots of laughter from the spectators, and despite it being a sombre occasion, Steve Hardcastle and Phil Davison found themselves joining in.

However, their levity suddenly stopped when Davison spotted Isha Hussein's car. He turned to Hardcastle and nodded towards the car park.

"I think our game's on now, boss."

Hardcastle's eyes narrowed as he saw what his sergeant was alluding to.

"Let's hope so Phil," he replied. "Let's bloody well hope so."

Sunday 2:10pm

Having arrived just as the train had pulled into the station, Isha Hussein had had no difficulty recognising Mrs MacDonald and Mrs Stewart from amongst the hundred or so passengers who had just got off and were now walking towards the ticket barrier.

After introducing herself, Isha had helped them with their travel bags and had suggested that both ladies got into the back of her car.

However, Olivia MacDonald had insisted that she sat in the front.

"I haven't been down here for years and I want to see how the old place has changed, and I won't see that from the back of your car," she'd said.

Isha had exchanged glances with Helen Stewart, who had given her a 'you might as well let her have her own way' look and a shrug of her shoulders, as Mrs MacDonald got in to the front passenger seat, leaving her daughter to climb into the back.

On the journey to the cricket ground, Isha had tried to engage Mrs MacDonald in conversation, but it was obvious from the old lady's single word replies that she hadn't been interested in small talk. *Perhaps she's disappointed that the DI hadn't been at the station to meet her personally*, thought Isha.

Thankfully, the traffic had been light at that time on a Sunday afternoon and as she had turned into the village hall car park, the time on her satnav had read 2:07pm.

The car park was full, but she didn't have to drive around looking for somewhere to park, as it had been prearranged that she would drive through the car park, onto the grass and park her car behind the sightscreen directly opposite the village hall. A dozen or so assorted police vehicles had already congregated in the same spot.

As she switched off the car's engine, Isha gave a silent sigh of relief when she saw DI Hardcastle and DS Davison walking towards them.

"Mrs MacDonald, I presume?" said Hardcastle as he held his hand out to the older of the two ladies. "I'm DI Steve Hardcastle and this is Detective Sergeant

Phil Davison. And I take it you are Mrs Stewart?" he said turning to Mrs MacDonald's daughter.

"Please, call me Helen," she replied.

"Helen it is, then. May I have a quick word with you, whilst DS Davison introduces your mother to Detective Sergeant Pearson who will be looking after you today."

"Of course," replied Helen Stewart, and she followed Hardcastle towards several vacant chairs that been placed on the boundary, facing the cricket pitch.

"Are you interested in cricket, Helen?" asked Hardcastle.

"My husband thinks watching cricket is perfect if you want to catch up on your sleep," replied Mrs Stewart, "but I quite enjoy the 20/20 games on the television. And I'll bet you didn't know that England once had a Scottish captain?"

"Well, you learn something new every day," said the DI with a smile. He was beginning to warm towards Olivia MacDonald's daughter.

"But I'm sure you don't want to talk to me about cricket. You want to know whether or not my mother is a raving lunatic."

"I wouldn't suggest that for one moment."

"Wouldn't you?" replied Helen. "I wouldn't blame you if you did."

"What I need to know, Helen, is whether or not you believe that your mother knows who the killer is, and if there is the slightest chance that he may be here today," asked Hardcastle.

"To answer your first question, I believe my mother is certain that she knows the identity of the man, but I have absolutely no idea whether or not that person is the man you are looking for.

"To answer your second question, my mother is also certain that he will be here today. Personally, if I was the killer, this is the last place on the earth where I'd be today."

"Has your mother mentioned any names to you?"

"None, apart from Mr Summers, and his name was mentioned in the news item which triggered all this off."

"So how did she become interested in this case?" asked the DI.

Helen explained that her son Andrew had seen a news item on his iPad about the murder of Summers, which he'd then shown his grandmother.

"Mum was really quite upset, and out of Andrew's hearing she told me that she had been sworn to secrecy by a very good friend, who had told her that

Donald Summers was the father of the child she was expecting, and not her husband. Apparently she'd had a brief affair with Mr Summers.

"This lady also told mum that she would never be able to tell her husband the truth because she was sure he would kill Summers, and would probably kill her too."

At last, thought Hardcastle. *We have the motive confirmed.*

"Has your mum kept in touch with the lady?"

"I don't think she ever saw her again," replied Helen. "Apparently, the lady's husband had always hated my mum. She thinks he resented her because she was so close to his wife.

"They continued to exchange birthday and Christmas cards for a while, but even that eventually petered out. It was probably the right thing to do, looking back. It's a very sad story, and one which my mother had never shared with anyone, until she told me last Wednesday."

Hardcastle could feel the hairs on the back of his neck begin to stand up.

"Did your mother know if her friend gave birth to a boy or a girl?" he asked.

"It was definitely a boy. According to mum, he would be around 25 years old by now."

Those hairs were now standing up even higher on the DI's neck.

"And can you remind me again what finally persuaded you to join your mother on the journey down from Scotland?"

"Because my mother is certain that the man in the identikit picture will be here today, and I don't want her to make a fool of herself," replied Mrs Stewart.

As Hardcastle watched Mrs Stewart walk back to re-join her mother, he was going over in his mind what the younger woman had just told him.

Mrs MacDonald had recognised the e-fit picture of a man in his mid-20s, he told himself, the same age as the child fathered by Donald Summers would be today. Could that child, now a young man, be the person who had murdered Summers and Neil Panton?

It now seemed increasingly likely that the person seen by Brian Tregunno and Ellie Compton last Sunday, whose likeness they subsequently turned into the e-fit, was the man they were looking for. Whether or not he was the murderer was uncertain.

Hardcastle took a good look around him. There were certainly plenty of young men in his sight, including most of the cricketers playing for the Flitton Green and Middle Ash cricket teams.

Could he be looking straight at the double murderer at this very moment, he asked himself looking around the cricket ground.

Even though he thought that highly unlikely, he couldn't help thinking that perhaps Mrs MacDonald really did hold the key to solving this case after all. One way or another, he wouldn't be letting the old lady go home without her first divulging the name of this young man.

Sunday 2:30pm

Steve Hardcastle quickly brought Phil Davison and Kath Pearson up to speed following his conversation with Helen Stewart.

"So we need to keep very close to Mrs MacDonald and her daughter at all times. Will this affect your operational plan, Kath?"

"Not at all, sir," replied Pearson. "The plan is dynamic with various contingencies built into it. Now we have identified our visitors from Scotland as a priority, I simply move them up to the top of the list."

"I should have known that you'd have all bases covered. Are you still happy to accompany our Scottish friends?" asked the DI.

"No problem sir. It's nice to be outside for once and not tied to my desk."

"And if you're OK with it, boss, I'd like to stay close to the ladies as well," asked Davison, "after all, I'm one of Kath's contingencies."

"Go for it Phil. Just keep me posted throughout the afternoon," replied Hardcastle.

As the DI walked away to speak to Olivia MacDonald, who was now talking to her daughter, the two sergeants looked at each other.

"Are you thinking what I'm thinking, Kath?"

"That Sarah might have got this spot on?"

"It is possible. Anyway, we'd better get this show on the road. All we can do now is to see how today pans out," replied Davison, and the pair moved to behind the sightscreen to join Hardcastle and the two ladies.

"So, I'll leave you two ladies in the capable hands of my two colleagues," said Hardcastle. "But before I go, I need to warn you Sergeant Davison, that you need to keep an eye on Mrs Stewart, as she seems to know more about cricket than I do."

"Is that possible, boss?" asked a slightly bemused Davison.

"So it seems, sergeant. For instance, did you know that a Scotsman once captained the England team?"

"I do as it happens," answered Davison. "His name was Mike Denness; he played for Kent and captained England in the 1970s."

"That's very impressive, sergeant. Very impressive indeed," responded Hardcastle who then proceeded to walk away in the direction of some other members of his team.

"I think you have just gone up in your Inspector's estimation," said Mrs Stewart.

"Yes, so it would seem. But please don't tell him that I heard that on *A Question of Sport* a couple of weeks ago, and it just stuck in my mind," replied Davison. "I want to savour the moment of getting one-up on my boss."

"While DS Davison is basking in the glory of a bit of one-upmanship, would you ladies like a cup of tea?" asked Pearson.

"Yes please," replied Helen.

"I'll arrange that now, and we can sit in these seats," continued Pearson, pointing to the seats where DI Hardcastle and Mrs Stewart had had their chat, "and it will give you both a chance to familiarise yourselves with the cricket ground."

"Sounds like a good idea to me," replied Helen. "Mum?"

It hadn't gone unnoticed that Olivia MacDonald had said very little since DI Hardcastle had left them.

"If you like, dear," she replied.

As the two ladies sat down, Mrs MacDonald began to rummage in the large bag she was carrying, and brought out a small pair of binoculars.

"I think I've seen those before," said Helen, "weren't they dad's?"

"They are your father's," replied Mrs MacDonald, with the emphasis on the word 'are'. "He's not dead, you know. He always kept them handy wherever we went. But he won't need them anymore. Not much use to him in the care home."

As the old lady wiped a tear away, her daughter took her mother's right hand and squeezed it a couple of times. After a few seconds, Olivia moved her hand away.

"I might as well use them; that's what I've brought them for."

Putting them up to her eyes, she panned around a full 360 degrees, before returning her gaze to the village hall and a figure carrying a tray.

"I can see that our tea is on its way," said Olivia, before continuing to scan the various people who were standing or seated around the boundary, either talking to one another or watching the cricket.

"That'll be just what the doctor ordered," replied Helen. "I'm absolutely gasping for a cuppa."

But Helen hadn't noticed that her mother had fixed her gaze on a small group of people on the far side of the ground, midway between the village hall and the pavilion.

"I think we'll have to forget about the tea for the time being, dear," said Olivia, putting the binoculars back into her bag.

"Why's that, mum?"

"Because I can see him, Helen," replied Olivia.

"See who?" enquired Helen. She asked the question, even though she was pretty sure what her mother's reply was going to be. Her stomach began to churn, and at that precise moment she wished that her husband David had been with her. He would have known what to do next.

"I can see the man who murdered Mr Summers."

"Exactly where, mum?"

"Over there," she replied, pointing in the direction group of a dozen or so young men. All of them, barring three, were wearing cricketing whites. Those in whites were obviously part of the Middle Ash cricket team.

"Sergeant Pearson," said Helen softly. "My mother thinks she has seen the man you're looking for. Apparently, he's over there, just past the pavilion."

"I know it's him, Helen. There's no doubt about it," retorted her mother.

Olivia MacDonald got up and began walking briskly towards the pavilion in a clockwise direction, with her daughter following on behind her.

"Phil," called out Pearson, "she's on the move."

"Jesus Christ. What's she up to?"

"She's just told her daughter that she's seen him."

"Who, the killer?"

"Apparently."

"Where is he?"

"He's amongst that group of lads on the far side of the pavilion, just past Mr Tregunno and Mrs Compton."

"Jesus Christ. Let's get after her. We have to be by her side by the time she gets close to any young men."

Davison and Pearson quickly caught her up the two ladies, with the former instructing Paul Taylor and Alan Rutherford over his radio where to meet them urgently.

"Please stop, Olivia," said Kath Pearson as she caught hold of Mrs MacDonald's sleeve. "Please leave everything to us. That's what we're paid to do."

However, Olivia MacDonald had no intention of taking orders from her two chaperones, and pulled her arm away from Pearson's grasp.

"Now listen to me, young lady. I've waited twenty-five years for this moment, and nobody is going to deny me now. And I mean nobody."

"Mum, please stop for heaven's sake," called out Helen.

But by now, her mother was less than thirty yards away from the group of young men.

And then, totally unexpectedly, she stopped a couple of yards short of Brian Tregunno and Ellie Compton, who were deep in conversation.

"Hello Brian," she said.

Brian Tregunno turned to see who was speaking to him. As he turned, Kath could see the shock on his face.

"You," he said in a hoarse whisper.

"Yes, it's me. Aren't you surprised to see me after all this time?"

Olivia turned towards Kath Pearson.

"DS Pearson, DS Davison, I want to introduce you to Mr Brian Tregunno, the man who killed Donald Summers. Oh, and by the way, he also happens to be my brother-in-law."

Sunday 2:45pm

There was a stunned silence as everyone tried to take in Olivia MacDonald's words. The first to respond was her daughter.

"So this is Uncle Brian?" asked Helen Stewart in disbelief. "You're telling me that Uncle Brian has murdered two people?"

"He is, and I am," replied Olivia, as calm as she could be, given the circumstances. "In fact, for all we know, he could easily have killed more than two."

"You're off your rocker, you stupid meddlesome bitch," responded Tregunno angrily. "I'm no murderer. In fact, I've been helping the police to find the killer and DS Pearson will verify that. Ask her, she'll tell you, go on ask her, you old fool."

"Brian has been very helpful, Olivia, in fact it was thanks to him and Mrs Compton that we were able to compile the e-fit in the first place," said Pearson.

However, out of the corner of her eye, she could see that Brian Tregunno was opening and clenching both fists, which she found odd, given that just a couple of days earlier he had declined to shake Steve Hardcastle's hand, telling him he was suffering from arthritis.

Whilst this exchange was going on, Phil Davison was busily texting his boss: *We have a situation here. Suggest you join us pronto.*

"That doesn't surprise me one little bit," replied Olivia. "Brian is the most manipulative person you will ever meet, and I'm afraid that he's been manipulating you and your colleagues right from the start, sergeant."

"Has this got something to do with the e-fit, mum?" asked Helen. "Is this why you said you recognised the man in the picture?"

Kath Pearson was watching Tregunno very carefully, and sensed he was close to breaking point.

"Yes, Helen. You see the man in the picture died almost 50 years ago. His name was Nicholas Tregunno, and he was Brian's elder brother."

At that point, a knife appeared in Brian Tregunno's right hand as if from nowhere, so quickly that Pearson was almost taken completely by surprise. Had she not been standing side by side with Olivia MacDonald, the old lady would have taken the full force of the blade to her upper chest. But somehow, Pearson managed to push her to one side, and by doing so she undoubtedly saved Olivia's life.

But as she was turning, Pearson took the blow to her left side. At first she thought it was just a heavy punch. But as she was falling to the ground, she heard a voice screaming 'No' before everything went black.

The scream had come from Phil Davison, who launched himself at Tregunno. But even though he was almost 20 years younger than Kath's assailant, Davison was no match for the old man.

Only the arrival of DC's Rutherford and Taylor at that precise moment saved Davison from more than the defensive wounds he suffered to his hands.

The full force of Paul Taylor's body hit Tregunno right between the shoulder blades and he couldn't stop himself from pitching forwards. Before he could respond, two more officers had joined the fray and within a matter of seconds Tregunno's hands were cuffed behind his back.

Despite blood seeping out from the cuts to both hands, Phil Davison shouted into his radio.

"Officer down, we need an ambulance. I repeat, DS Pearson is down, we need an ambulance, now."

Sunday 2:50pm

Jethro Tregunno was standing at mid-wicket when he heard the sound of raised voices. Looking to his right, where only a moment or two earlier he had noticed his father Brian speaking to Dave Compton's wife Ellie, he was amazed to see a struggle going on between two men.

Suddenly, one of the men fell to the ground, and the other bent over him with his right hand raised, as if he was about to hit him with something. Rooted to the spot, Jethro realised that the man about to strike the blow was his father.

However, that blow never happened, as a third man sent his father flying, having barged him full in the back. With him now lying face down on the ground, a fourth man got involved, and between the two of them they were able to restrain Jethro's father, with the younger man pinning him to the ground with his knee on his back, whilst the other applied a pair of restraints to his wrists.

Jethro just couldn't believe his eyes.

"Jet!" shouted out the Flitton wicketkeeper. "Isn't that your old man over there?"

That shout brought Jethro to his senses, and he began to sprint over to where all this was taking place. But when he was just a few yards away from where his father was being restrained, two fairly brawny men suddenly blocked his path.

"That's my father over there."

"And we are police officers, sir," said the larger of the two men, who pulled out his warrant card and held it up just a couple of feet away from Jethro's face.

Jethro looked at the card, and then noticed a distraught looking Ellie Compton walking towards him.

"Ellie," he called out, "what the hell's going on?"

"Oh Jet, I'm so very sorry," she replied, taking a deep breath. "It's your dad. He's just stabbed a policewoman."

Those words took the fight right out of Jethro, and he suddenly felt totally drained. It took him a few seconds to compose himself.

"Who's in charge here?"

A man, who Jethro recognised as the policeman who had taken charge of last Sunday's events, came walking towards him.

"I'm in charge, and my name is Detective Inspector Steve Hardcastle. And you are?"

"Jethro Tregunno. Is it true? My father has stabbed a policewoman?"

"I'm afraid it is true, sir."

Jethro looked at Hardcastle, and then looked to his left where he could see his father being held down by two policemen.

"In that case, stick the old bastard in jail and throw away the key."

And with that, he turned away and began to walk back towards the pavilion.

"But, Jet. I did it all for you, son," shouted out Brian Tregunno. "I did it all for you."

Jethro, ignoring his father, carried on walking without looking back.

Sunday 3:15pm

By a stroke of good fortune, an off-duty paramedic happened to be in the play area behind the village hall with his wife and children when he heard a message over the public address that a police officer was in need of urgent medical treatment.

Responding immediately, he was able to staunch the flow of blood from DS Pearson's abdominal wound until the ambulance arrived to take her to hospital.

As the ambulance left the cricket ground, a forlorn Phil Davison continued to watch it until it had disappeared out of sight. He had been desperate to travel to the hospital with Kath, but DI Hardcastle had managed to speak to her husband, and as far as he was aware Jason was already on his way to the A&E department, and might even be there before the ambulance.

"A penny for your thoughts, Phil?"

Davison turned around at the sound of his boss's voice.

"I'll need more than a penny. I just can't get it out of my mind that it's my fault Kath is on her way to hospital. I should have stayed much closer to her, but I just didn't see it coming. I assumed we were protecting Mrs MacDonald from a much younger man, not someone as old as she is."

"I don't think any of us saw it coming, Phil. But you and Kath both did your jobs and showed commendable bravery. And you should be at the hospital getting those cuts looked at. I'm sure you'll need some stitches."

Davison looked at his hands which were covered by bloodstained bandages.

"That's what the paramedic said, but I need to be here at the moment; there are too many loose ends to tie up. Anyway, the cuts are mainly superficial, and if needs be, I can always call into the A&E on my way home. By the way, how was Kath's husband when you spoke to him?"

"A bit strange actually. I think I might have woken him up because at first nothing seemed to register with him. He eventually cottoned on and said he would get down to the hospital as soon as he could.

"And talking about phone calls, have you rung Sarah yet?" continued Hardcastle. "You know how fast news travels, especially bad news, and you don't want her worrying unnecessarily."

Davison was about to say something when he noticed Ellie Compton hovering close by.

"I think you're wanted, boss."

Hardcastle turned around.

"Could I have a word with you please, Inspector?" asked Mrs Compton, somewhat sheepishly.

"Of course you can. Fire away," replied Hardcastle.

"It's about the e-fit. If the truth be known, I never really wanted to get involved. It's true that I saw someone I didn't recognise over the other side of the ground last Sunday, but to be honest with you, he was too far away for me to be able to describe what he looked like, apart from the fact he was dressed all in black.

"But then Brian came around to see me on Wednesday morning, not long after your lady sergeant had called me and asked me to help with the e-fit.

"I told him I didn't think there was much I could add to the statement I'd already made, but he was really keen that I should help. He told me that he'd gotten quite a good look at the man, but that the police would only take him seriously if someone else could back up what he told them. He said the chances of the police catching the man were really slim if I didn't do that, and how wrong it would be if the killer got away with it, just because the police hadn't taken his description seriously. He made me feel as if it would be my fault if that happened.

"So, as I couldn't see anything wrong in backing him up, I just sort of went along with it. I really can't believe that Brian attacked your sergeant, and now some people are saying that he's been arrested because he's the man who killed Neil Panton as well as the umpire. Is that true? I don't want you to think I was involved in that too."

Hardcastle could see that she was quite distressed, possibly traumatised by what she had just witnessed.

"We will need you to put what you've just told us into a statement, and I think that will be it, as far as your involvement in our enquiries is concerned. So try not to worry too much about it. As for Mr Tregunno, he has been arrested for the attack on DS Pearson. That is all I can say at the moment.

"I'll ask one of my colleagues to get in touch with you regarding a statement; and that will either be later today, or sometime tomorrow morning. But try not to worry too much, and go and get yourself a strong cup of tea."

Ellie Compton gave a nod and a little smile and began to walk back towards the village hall. Once she was out of earshot, Davison turned to Hardcastle.

"She might be a stunner to look at, boss, but she's not the sharpest tool in the box, is she?"

"It looks like she was being manipulated by Tregunno," replied Hardcastle. "I think we should have a talk to Mrs MacDonald now. After all, she's the one responsible for it all kicking off. Do you feel up to it, Phil?"

"Of course I do boss. Just try and stop me," answered Davison.

"Make sure you ring Sarah first," said Hardcastle.

"All done and dusted. I've just sent her a text to say that I'm OK. It wasn't easy with these," he said holding up his bandaged hands, "but I've told her I'll ring as soon as I can, and she'll be happy with that. I can tell her all about it when I get home.

"By the way, I haven't thanked you for getting me out of a hole, boss. I don't think I could have lasted much longer without your help. He has amazing strength for a man of his age."

"Don't thank me, Phil, thank Paul Taylor. Tregunno didn't see him coming and Paul knocked him flying; all his weight hit the bugger right between the shoulder blades. It really took the wind out of his sails."

"He's a good lad, boss; he'll go places. Where's he now, I want to thank him?"

"He, Alan Rutherford and a couple of PCs took Tregunno back to the nick to book him in. We'll join them there once we've gotten everything we need out of Olivia MacDonald. That lady has a lot of explaining to do."

Sunday 3:30pm

While they were walking over to where Olivia MacDonald and Helen Stewart were sitting, Phil Davison realised that the cricket match was still going on.

"I thought they might have called the game off after what happened to Kath."

"To be fair to them, they stopped playing as soon as they saw something was occurring," answered Hardcastle, "and when they heard that Kath had been seriously injured, they told Isha that they would call the game off. I think some of them were shell-shocked.

"However, I asked Isha to tell them that I would rather they carried on as if nothing had happened, as a lot of people had turned up for the reconstruction, and there might be someone with some important information amongst them—they just don't know that at the moment. The reconstruction is still the best way to jog the mind. I know it might sound uncaring and thoughtless given what has gone on, but I'm certain that Kath would want things to continue as planned. After all, I don't see Tregunno putting up his hands to the murders, and it's up to us to build the case against him to the point where we can be confident that it will stack up in court.

"But at the end of the day, I stressed that the decision was down to them. I believe they asked for a show of hands, and the unanimous decision was to continue the game."

Phil Davison nodded in agreement. "I'm sure that's the right decision and I've no doubt that Kath would be in favour of it continuing. So who's taking her place?"

"Billy Kiernan."

"That makes sense. I know that Billy has had quite a bit of input into Kath's operational plan."

"How is Mrs Pearson?" a distressed Olivia MacDonald asked, as soon as she saw the two officers approaching. "I hope that she isn't too badly injured."

"She is in a serious, but stable condition. Hopefully, she'll pull through," replied Hardcastle. "She is one very tough young lady."

"Oh heavens, I am so, so sorry, Mr Hardcastle. I never thought things would end the way they did. I must have pushed Brian a bit too far for him to lose his temper like that. I wish I had stayed at home now."

"Well, you didn't stay at home, did you, Mrs MacDonald, you decided to come here," replied Hardcastle, a little on the harsh side, "and DS Davison and I now have to make some sense out of what has happened, before we go back to the police station and begin interviewing your brother-in-law."

"Where would you like me to start?" asked Olivia.

"Just start at the very beginning, mum," said Helen.

Olivia MacDonald took a sip of lukewarm coffee.

"Well, I was born in 1950 and my maiden name was Sutton. My sister, Joan, came along four years later. Mum and dad loved going to the cinema and they named us Olivia and Joan after the actress sisters, Olivia de Havilland and Joan Fontaine.

"We had a fairly normal upbringing, although Joan was a bit flighty, whilst I was quite a shy child. She had quite a few boyfriends before she married her first husband, Laurence Nichols. She was just twenty years old at the time of the wedding.

"The marriage only lasted a couple of years before they separated. They divorced a year or so later. Joan said that she had married far too young and that they just fell out of love with each other, as young couples often do.

"I took my time finding a husband, and married Roderick MacDonald in 1977 when I was 27 and we've been together ever since. I have never once regretted marrying him—that is the honest truth. Unfortunately, Roderick is suffering from Alzheimer's and he is now living in a care home. I go to visit him every day, at least I do when I'm back home.

"As you can tell by his name, Roderick is Scottish and we moved to Scotland in the mid-80s. Helen here was born in 1979, and her sister Diane came along in 1982. She now lives in Perth; Australia that is, not Scotland."

"And what happened to Joan after the divorce?" asked Hardcastle, anxious to get Mrs MacDonald back on track.

"She reverted back to her maiden name, Joan Sutton, and also to her old ways. Men friends came and went at a fair rate until she met Brian Tregunno, that is."

"And when would that have been?" asked Hardcastle, who was taking down notes in shorthand. Normally, Phil Davison would have done this, but his injured hands meant that it wasn't possible on this occasion.

"Sometime around 1979 or 1980, I think. He was on leave from the army when they met up. Brian's family were living somewhere in Cornwall, and he was up this way staying with some friends. I don't think he got on that well with his parents.

"Anyway, they met while waiting in the queue at the local cinema, got chatting to one another and that was that. I know it sounds a bit corny, but Joan really did have a thing about men in uniform."

"You said that Tregunno was in the army. Any idea of the regiment, Mrs MacDonald?" asked Phil Davison.

"I believe he was in the Marines, but when the Falklands War started in 1982, Joan intimated that he had been transferred to a Special Forces regiment. She didn't say which one as it was all a bit hush-hush at the time.

"I have to be honest with you, Inspector, and say that I never liked Brian Tregunno. In the early stages of their relationship, he treated Joan OK. But as time went on his attitude towards her worsened, and when he got back from the Falklands, there were times when I prayed that Joan would see sense and break up with him.

"I tried to make allowances, bearing in mind he must have seen some pretty upsetting sights in the Falklands, but as time went on, I'm afraid he used up those allowances as far as I was concerned."

"Was he ever physically abusive towards your sister?" asked Hardcastle.

"I had my suspicions, but Joan always maintained that he never once hit her," replied Olivia. "The abuse that I witnessed was psychological and emotional. He particularly seemed to take great pleasure in humiliating her in front of her friends and family.

"Other times, he would have the sulks for no apparent reason, blaming it all on her, and would give her the silent treatment. I saw it as his way of exerting control over her. He was so very manipulative, and would be very critical of the way she dressed, or the way she wore her hair. There were times when she could do nothing right in his eyes.

"It got to the point where Roderick and I would not go out with them as a couple, and I would only go around to visit Joan when I knew that Brian wouldn't be there."

"So why, and when, did they get married?" asked Davison.

"Roderick and I moved to Scotland in 1985, when the girls were 5½ and 3, and Joan and Brian married the following year. It was almost as if they had been waiting for Roderick and me to move away. And as Joan had been married before, they had to have the wedding ceremony at the local registry office.

"We were not invited, and to be honest, we would have made up an excuse why we couldn't be there. As to why they got married, I think it got to the point where Joan was so frightened of Brian that she feared what might happen if she turned him down."

"Was Brian still in the army when they married?" enquired Davison.

"Yes. I know that he had joined the Marines in 1971 when he was 22 years old, and he left the army in 1989 after he had completed 18 years' service. Whether he was in the Marines when he left, or was still a member of the Special Forces at that time, I really don't know."

"Do you know what he did after he left the army?"

"Not specifically, no. You have to remember that by then Joan and I were living at the other end of the country from one another, and we would go months without speaking.

"However, and this may sound a bit far-fetched, I got the impression that he became some sort of mercenary. Joan said that Brian was working in the security industry, but he went away for months at a time, and when he came back home she said they would literally be rolling in cash.

"It's only in the last few years that he has been home more or less permanently."

"So, they married in 1986. What year was their son born?" asked Hardcastle.

"He was born in 1993," replied Olivia.

"That would have made Joan 39, and Brian 44, if my calculations are correct," said Hardcastle. "Why did they wait so long to have a baby—or was that out of their control?"

"I suppose one of the reasons was down to Brian being away so much," answered Olivia. "But also, Joan had problems conceiving. I know she secretly underwent fertility tests and was given the all clear, so the problem was probably Brian's.

"The next thing to do would have been for Brian to be tested, but Joan just didn't have the courage to ask him. I wouldn't like to think what his reaction would have been if he had found out that he was infertile. Imagine what a blow to his ego that would have been. So instead, he continued to blame our Joan for the lack of a baby."

"So, Olivia, let's fast forward to when Joan finds out that, at long last, she is pregnant," said Hardcastle. "When would this have been?"

"Jethro's birthday is 1 July, so he would have been conceived at the beginning of October 1992," replied Olivia.

"When did she tell you that the baby wasn't Brian's?"

"That would have been in the spring of 1993. I think it was at the beginning of April. Brian was away again fighting for someone else's king and country, and so I thought it would be a good opportunity to visit Joan and see some of my old school friends down south who I hadn't seen for donkey's years.

"Joan would have been about six months gone by then, and she was really over the moon to see me. I stayed with her for a couple of nights, and on the second night, we both had a couple of glasses of wine too many. That's when she told me that the baby wasn't Brian's.

"It took a while for me to get it out of her, but eventually she admitted that she had gone into a building society office in Dorminster the previous autumn to see about investing some of their cash that was just sitting in a bank current account, not earning any interest.

"It was there that she met Donald Summers. They got on like a house on fire and, according to Joan, she knew it was only a matter of time before they would get together, what with Donald being single, and with Brian out of the country again.

"At the time, both of them knew it was just a fling, and that it could never be any more than that. According to Joan they had only slept together a handful of times when Brian arrived back in the UK unexpectedly. With him back on the scene, Joan and Donald knew that that was the end of their little trysts. As Joan said, 'it was great fun while it lasted.'

"A few weeks later Joan found out she was pregnant. Brian, of course, assumed the baby was his. It never once entered his mind that Joan might have been unfaithful. He thought she would be far too frightened of the consequences if he found out that she had slept with another man.

"However, unexpectedly, a couple of months into her pregnancy, Joan realised that she was still carrying a torch for Donald. There was so much she missed about him; his sense of humour, his tenderness, and most importantly, she realised how safe she had felt whenever they had been together, when he held her in his arms; something she had never experienced all the time she'd been with Brian, except, perhaps, during the first few months of their relationship.

"She knew that she would be taking a huge risk if she was to meet up with Donald again, but early in 1993 she could no longer hold back her feelings towards him. She had to see him again. So, she made an appointment with the building society to meet Donald, ostensibly to discuss her investments. Joan admitted to me that she had felt like a silly teenager again, and found herself counting down the days to when she would see Donald again. And, by now, of course, her bump was beginning to show."

Olivia paused to take another sip of her coffee, which had now gone completely cold. She grimaced.

"Are you OK, mum?" asked her daughter Helen, slightly concerned.

"I'm alright, Helen, I just realise how much I miss my sister, that's all."

"Would you like a short break, Olivia?" asked Hardcastle gently.

"No thank you. It's best that I carry on."

"OK," replied Hardcastle, "when you're ready."

Olivia took a couple of deep breaths, and continued.

"Unfortunately, things didn't quite go as Joan had hoped. Before she could say anything, Donald dropped the bombshell that he had recently been promoted and would be moving to Yorkshire within a matter of weeks."

"Did she tell him about the baby?" asked Davison.

"No, not then she didn't. She couldn't bring herself to tell him as he seemed so happy. He noticed she was pregnant, of course, and offered her his congratulations and wished her and Brian good luck for the future."

"So what happened next, mum?" asked Helen.

"Well, as I mentioned earlier, Jethro was born on 1 July and of course, Brian was ecstatic. The new baby became the centre of his universe. However, he still continued to do whatever he was doing overseas; he told Joan he was doing it for Jethro so that the boy could have the best possible upbringing and education money could buy."

"And she continued to keep Donald in the dark about the paternity of the baby?" enquired Davison.

"No, she didn't. And this is where I completely disagreed with her. I felt the right thing for her to do was to forget that she had had the fling with Donald and just consign it to the past, for Jethro's sake, and for the sake of her own safety.

She knew only too well that if Brian ever found out, her life would have been in danger. And, of course, the same would apply to Donald."

"So, can I assume that she did the exact opposite and contacted Donald?" asked Hardcastle.

"It was around about a year after she had last seen him. Even with the baby, things were still very bad between her and Brian, and because of this, I think, in her mind, she had begun to resent Donald.

"She had begun to fantasise that he could have been her way out of a loveless marriage, and as time went on I think she became embittered towards Donald. It was very much a case of what might have been for Joan.

"So, she wrote to him, told him that Jethro was his son, and even enclosed a recent photo of the boy."

Hardcastle and Davison looked at each other. "The missing photograph from Donald's house," said Hardcastle.

Davison nodded.

"Please continue, Olivia," asked the DI.

"I'm not sure what she had been hoping to achieve, but I do know that she never received a reply from Donald, which she found very hurtful."

"So now we know how Donald found out that he had a son. Have you any idea how Brian found out that he wasn't Jethro's father?" asked Hardcastle.

"No, I don't," replied Olivia. "But Joan must have told him, although she would have had to have been pretty desperate to do that."

"Or perhaps she felt that she had nothing to lose," said Davison.

"Possibly," responded Hardcastle. "That's a question we need to ask Mr Tregunno when we interview him later."

"Tell me, Olivia," continued Hardcastle, "did you and Joan continue to keep in touch after Jethro had been born?"

"One of my biggest regrets is that I allowed Brian to come between us. He told Joan that she was not to speak to me, so that effectively stopped her telephoning me. And when I rang her, if he answered he would put the phone down on me. And if Joan answered, and he was there, she would say hello, ask me how I was and then say that she had to go.

"After a while we stopped speaking altogether and the only contact I had with her was the odd birthday and Christmas card, but even they dried up eventually as the years went on.

"It had been many years since we had last spoken to each other when, shortly after last Christmas, Jethro rang. As soon as I heard him say his name, my immediate thought was that something serious had happened to Joan. I feared that Brian had killed her. I was wrong about Brian for once. Jethro told me that his mother had been suffering from breast cancer and that she had passed away peacefully in a hospice on Boxing Day.

"I was devastated. I asked Jethro why someone hadn't contacted me when she had first fallen ill. He replied, inevitably, that his dad had forbidden it. I was so upset and angry that I began to take that anger out on Jethro. He listened to me ranting on for a while before quietly telling me that even he hadn't known how seriously ill his mother had been.

"He told me that he'd left home a couple of years earlier and had seen very little of his mother, because that meant having to speak to his father. It seems that by now, Brian had even managed to alienate his own son. Jethro said that the only time he saw his father was whenever he played cricket. Brian would always be there; he never missed a match, home or away. However, they never exchanged any words, nor did they acknowledge each other.

"Anyway, the main reason for his call was to let me know the funeral arrangements. I said I would do my best to get there, but explained about Roderick's Alzheimer's; he was very understanding.

"I knew that I'd never be able to get to the funeral and when I put the phone down, I burst into tears. When I had calmed down, the only thing that could console me was the thought I would never have to have any contact with Brian Tregunno again. Unfortunately, given what has happened today, I got that completely wrong.

"I would like to speak to Jethro again though, as he sounded like a really nice young man. He must have inherited Donald's genes. God knows what he would have been like if Brian had really been his father.

"And that's about the end of it. I really can't provide you with any more information about Joan and Brian after Jethro was born. I suggest you speak to the boy himself. I suspect he will be quite open and honest about his relationship with his father."

"Thank you for being so candid with us, Olivia," replied Hardcastle. "There is just one more matter which needs clarifying before we call it a day for the time being, and that's what you said that caused Tregunno to lose his temper. According to DS Davison your words were '*the man in the picture died almost*

50 years ago. His name was Nicholas Tregunno, and he was Brian's elder brother'.

"Now that sounds pretty far-fetched to me, but there must be some truth to it judging by the reaction that you got from Brian."

"When I heard that Donald Summers had been murdered, I immediately thought of Brian as the murderer," replied Olivia. "However, when the second man was killed, and the news item on the Internet said that you were now looking for a man in his mid-twenties, I just thought I had gotten it all wrong. In a way, it was a huge relief.

"But then when I saw the e-fit on Friday, I knew it was Brian who was the killer. I was 100 per cent certain. You see, Brian had an elder brother Nicholas who, according to my sister, he absolutely idolised. Nicholas joined the Royal Marines in 1964 when he was 18, but sadly was killed in Northern Ireland in 1970 in a motorbike accident.

"Apparently, his death devastated Brian, and was the reason why he decided to join the Marines a year after his brother died. He saw it as a fitting tribute to Nicholas.

"Brian kept a number of photographs of his brother, and Joan showed them to me on several occasions, when Brian wasn't around, of course. I remember them well as he was quite a good-looking man; he looked nothing like his younger brother.

"So when I saw the e-fit picture for the first time, it was Nicholas Tregunno who was looking back at me from my daughter's iPad. It was then that I realised that Brian was not only the killer of the two men, but he must also have been the person who helped you put together the e-fit. There was no other possible explanation. That was Brian all over, the eternal manipulator. This time, he was manipulating the police.

"He must have thought he was so clever when he saw his dead brother's picture in all the local newspapers and on television, knowing that nobody would recognise him. And that's about it, Inspector. I hope that helps you and your colleagues."

DI Steve Hardcastle stood up, as did Phil Davison, taking his lead from his boss.

"Until you showed up, Olivia," began Hardcastle, "Brian Tregunno must really have considered himself to be almost invincible and untouchable.

"You are quite right. The man had us chasing shadows. What are the chances of anyone recognising the face of someone who had died almost a half a century ago, who had lived in another part of Britain and who died in Northern Ireland? He must have been delighted in the way we seemed to have accepted his story of a mystery man in black.

"And then, completely out of the blue, the walls suddenly began tumbling down around him when he saw the face of the one living person who could blow a big hole in the game of charades he was playing. It's little wonder that he reacted the way he did. After all, when he looked at you he saw the biggest threat possible and he reacted in the only way he knew how to, the way he had been trained to—with violence.

"I should be taking my hat off to you, Mrs MacDonald. However, to me, this is a still a bittersweet story. You see, my biggest regret is that, for whatever reason, you didn't feel able to entrust us with this story before you confronted Tregunno, a man who you knew to be capable of extreme violence. I'm not sure why you didn't feel able to warn us. Perhaps you just wanted to look him in the eye and have your revenge for the way he treated your sister?

"Whatever your motive, you needlessly put a police officer's life in jeopardy, and for all of our sakes, and I include Brian Tregunno when I say that, I hope and pray that Detective Sergeant Kath Pearson, an outstanding officer who put herself in harm's way to protect both you and your daughter, makes a full recovery so that she is able to sit in court, not to have any revenge, but simply to see her attacker brought to justice.

"Now, we will need written statements from both of you, so it looks like you won't be getting back to London in time to catch your train back to Scotland. I suggest you make arrangements to stay locally until tomorrow."

Sunday 4:30pm

When his mobile phone had rung just before 3:15pm, Jason Pearson had been undecided whether or not to answer it. He had no idea who the caller was as the number shown on the screen was not one that was stored on his phone's SIM card.

Of late he had been receiving a lot of nuisance calls, and it was touch and go whether or not he would click on the green 'answer call' icon. In the end, curiosity, and his urge to give the caller some abuse for ringing on a Sunday, had got the better of him.

However, the caller turned out to be Steve Hardcastle, his wife's boss, and he was so surprised that at first he hadn't really taken in what the man was telling him. The fact that his new girlfriend Connie had her arms wrapped around his neck and was nibbling away at his right ear, didn't help. However, he finally got the gist of what Hardcastle was saying; his wife had been injured in an incident whilst on duty and was on her way to hospital.

After the call ended, he sat motionless on the sofa while Connie continued to work on his earlobe.

Eventually, his conscience got the better of him, and despite Connie's animated pleas to forget about the call, he got off the settee, put his tee shirt back on and picked up his phone and van keys.

Connie was really put out and close to tears, but Jason pacified her by promising to return as soon as he could. After all, he told her; with any luck the hospital might keep Kath in for a day or two, which meant he would be able to spend at least one, maybe even two nights with her.

After sharing a passionate kiss with his girlfriend, Jason drove the four miles to the hospital at a fairly leisurely pace, not wanting to arrive before the ambulance did.

He hated everything to do with hospitals; especially the long hours spent waiting at the Accident and Emergency Department. The last time he had been at the A&E he had had to wait for over 3 hours before being seen after suffering a deep cut whilst he was at work.

Trying to convince himself that he wasn't being too inconsiderate, part of him hoped that whatever injury Kath had suffered wasn't too serious, just bad enough to ensure that, being a police officer, she was seen fairly quickly, so he could get back to Connie and carry on where they'd left off.

For once, parking was easy at the hospital since it was a Sunday. On weekdays the car park was full to overflowing more often than not, and the surrounding streets were always busy with people trying to find somewhere to park.

After waiting in line at the reception for five minutes or so, he was surprised to be told that Kath had been taken to the Serious Injury Unit.

He was even more surprised when he recognised an attractive young lady also waiting at the SIU. He couldn't remember her name, but he did remember trying to chat her up at one of the rare police functions he'd attended with Kath a year or so earlier.

The young lady recognised him immediately.

"Hi, Mr Pearson," she said. "We have met before; I'm Detective Constable Frances Merrick, Franny for short."

"How's my wife? Do you know what's happened to her?" asked Jason, now beginning to feel a little guilty.

"I'm afraid she's been stabbed. I followed the ambulance from the cricket ground, and as soon as it arrived here at the hospital, your wife was whisked away for emergency surgery, so I'm really sorry, but I just don't know how she's doing. Can I get you a coffee?"

"Please."

Jason was glad to have a couple of minutes alone while he gathered his thoughts.

Despite his feelings for Connie, he had known Kath for over fifteen years, and he still loved her—but just not in the same way as he had once done. Of late, they had become more like brother and sister.

DC Merrick returned carrying two plastic cups full to the brim. Jason could see they were hot from the wisps of steam coming from them.

"How much do I owe you?" he asked.

"Don't be silly," she replied, with a sad looking smile on her face. "I was going to say, you get the next one, but let's hope we don't have to wait that long for some news on how she's doing."

They carried on making small talk for another ten minutes or so until Jason's mobile phone suddenly bleeped to indicate an incoming text.

It was from Connie:

Any news? Can't wait to see you again, please, please, please hurry back.

With no news to tell her, Jason decided not to reply. He could always say that he hadn't received her text, blaming it on a poor network service in that part of the hospital.

"It's from a mate about a job we've got on next week. It can wait," said Jason, feeling the need to explain to Merrick why he hadn't replied to the text.

They continued to talk to each other sporadically, and he was just about to ask the young detective constable if she fancied something to eat, when a middle aged man in blue scrubs came through a set of double doors to their left.

"Mr Pearson?"

"Yes."

"My name is Michaelson. I've just finished operating on your wife. Are you a relative?" he asked, looking at Franny.

"No, I'm DC Merrick, a work colleague of DS Pearson's," she replied.

"In that case, can we have a word in private please?" asked the surgeon, turning back to speak to Jason and pointing to a door a couple of yards away.

"First things first," said Michaelson once both men had sat down, "your wife is in Recovery at the moment. She has suffered an abdominal wound that thankfully missed all her vital organs. She lost a lot of blood, and it would have been much worse but for the swift actions of the paramedic who attended the scene.

"We will need to keep your wife in for a few days, and then after we discharge her, she will need a bit of looking after, so you may need to rearrange your work schedule. But we expect her to make a full recovery.

"The other good news is that we don't think that any harm has been done to the baby. We will know more when she has a scan, but I'm pretty certain all is OK."

Jason Pearson looked at the surgeon in disbelief. Kathy was pregnant?

Had he been a cartoon character, at that precise moment his jaw would have hit the floor.

Sunday 5pm

Steve Hardcastle was getting ready to return to the police station when his mobile phone rang. He saw the caller was DC Merrick. *Please let this be good news*, he thought to himself. The call lasted just a couple of minutes, and as soon as it ended he shouted out to Phil Davison, who was a dozen or so yards away from him.

"Phil, I've just spoken to Franny Merrick. It's good news; Kath's going to be alright."

"*Thank Christ for that*," said Davison under his breath, and he wiped away a tear, hoping that Hardcastle hadn't noticed. "That's terrific, boss," he called back. "I'll let all the troops know straight away."

"I'm going to go back to the nick now, Phil," answered Hardcastle, walking towards the sergeant. "Follow on when you're ready and I'll see you there. It's about time we had a word with Tregunno. Let's see what he has to say for himself."

Whilst he was driving, Hardcastle rang ACC Lloyd and DCI Cryer and gave them the good news about Kath. The ACC said that he would visit her in hospital once she was well enough to have visitors.

Before he went up to his office, Hardcastle decided to pay a quick visit to see Sergeant Patrick 'Paddy' Kennedy who was the on-duty Custody Officer.

Phil Davison had been good to his word; Kennedy had already heard the latest news about Kath Pearson.

Confirming that Tregunno had been booked in and given notice of his various rights, Kennedy told the DI that he'd been as good as gold when he'd been brought in by Paul Taylor and Alan Rutherford, and had declined his right to have a solicitor present, saying that he didn't need one.

As he was leaving to go up to his office, Hardcastle told Kennedy that he and Phil Davison hoped to begin interviewing Tregunno around 5:30pm, and would like the prisoner fed and watered by then if possible.

When he was back in his office, Hardcastle gave Billy Kiernan a call, and asked him to organise a search of Tregunno's house, and that a set of keys could be collected from Paddy Kennedy.

"I suspect my guys will be fighting each other to do this one. They all like Kath. In fact, I don't know anybody who doesn't," replied Kiernan.

Hardcastle looked at his watch. It was 5:10pm and he had just enough time to speak to Jenny and tell her that he didn't know what time he'd be home.

As it happened, Jenny was well up to speed with developments, having had a phone call from the wife of one of the coppers who'd been on duty at the reconstruction. She'd even heard the good news about Kath Pearson.

"I hoped you might ring," said Jenny. "I assumed you'd be on a late one tonight after what's happened. I'll sort out something you can heat up in the microwave in case you're hungry when you get in."

"Bless you, you're an angel," he replied. "It's been a bit of a rollercoaster, and I've no idea how things are going to end."

"But you've got him for attempted murder though, haven't you?" asked Jenny.

"Yes, of course, that's a given," he replied. "But we owe it to Summers and Panton to nail him for their murders, and I don't think he's just going to roll over. We're expecting a battle."

At that moment he noticed that Phil Davison had just arrived back.

"Got to go, love. I'll see you when I see you."

"Good luck Steve."

"Thanks, I think we'll need it."

Sunday 5:40pm

"How is Detective Sergeant Pearson?"

"She's going to be OK," replied Phil Davison. "No thanks to you."

"I'm glad she'll be alright. She is a very nice young lady. You both should be very proud of her," said Tregunno.

It was now 5:40pm, and the interview with Brian Tregunno was about to begin.

The irony that the interview was taking place almost exactly seven days to the minute since Donald Summers had been murdered was not lost on Steve Hardcastle or Phil Davison as they faced the man they now believed to have killed both Summers and Neil Panton.

"For what it's worth, I never had any intention of causing her any harm," continued Tregunno. "In the split second that I realised that she had put herself in harm's way, I was able to change the angle of the thrust so that it wouldn't hit any of her vital organs."

"You expect us to believe that?" asked Davison, incredulously.

"It's the truth. Whether you believe it or not is completely irrelevant," replied Tregunno.

"Do you normally carry a knife?" asked Davison.

"No comment."

"Was Olivia MacDonald your intended victim?"

"No comment."

"I think you've been watching too many police dramas on the television Brian," said Hardcastle. "Are you sure you don't want a solicitor? Take it from me, you need one. All this 'no comment' bullshit will do you no favours at all."

"I'm happy as I am thank you."

Hardcastle decided to change tack.

"Tell me about your brother."

Hardcastle could see that Tregunno was undecided whether or not to answer, and the room was silent for almost thirty seconds before he replied.

"Nick was three years older than me, and I couldn't have wished for a finer brother. He was always there for me when I was growing up. I absolutely idolised him.

"Our father had served in the army during the Second World War, so it was almost inevitable that Nick would join up as soon as he could. The old man was chuffed to bits when Nick joined the Royal Marines in 1964; we were all so proud of him. We were even prouder when he made corporal on his 24th birthday.

"And then came the worst day of my life when we were told that he had been killed in Northern Ireland. At first we assumed he had been killed in action. Dying for Queen and Country would have made his death a bit easier to accept. But then we were told that he had died in an accident. He had been riding pillion on the back of someone's motorbike, and was off duty at the time. The irony was that the person whose bike it was escaped with hardly a scratch.

"It just felt like it was such a waste. He had his whole life in front of him, and he was gone in an instant. We never got a chance to say goodbye. I was devastated, as were my parents and I was in a deep depression for months afterwards, before I realised what I had to do. I followed in Nick's footsteps and joined the Marines."

"How many years did you serve in the Marines?" asked Davison.

"Eighteen."

"Were all eighteen spent with the Marines?"

"I could say yes, but I'd be lying, and you'd find out anyway. I joined the Special Boat Squadron in 1980."

"Was that where you learned how to handle a knife?"

"No comment."

"Did you see action in the Falklands?" continued Hardcastle.

"Yes, I did. My unit was deployed to South Georgia. We spent most of our time operating behind enemy lines. That's all I'm prepared to say on the matter as I am still bound by the Official Secrets Act."

"Why did you make the e-fit look like your brother?" asked Davison, changing the subject again.

"Who said I did?"

"Your sister-in-law did, and you were just a couple of yards away from her at the time so don't try to pretend you didn't hear her," replied Davison.

"If you're relying on what she told you, then I'm right, I don't need a solicitor. Anyway, I'm pretty hard of hearing, due to shells exploding around me while I was in the Falklands."

"We have three witnesses who can confirm what Mrs MacDonald said to you, and we have at least a half a dozen people who saw you stab Detective Sergeant Pearson," said Hardcastle. "Let's face it Brian, your best option is to plead guilty. It might take a few years off your sentence.

"But let's get back to the e-fit. Are you denying that there is a likeness to your brother Nicholas?"

"No comment."

"OK. We'll come back to that question once we have a full report from our team of CSIs, and also from the members of my team of detectives who are going through your house with a fine tooth comb as we speak," stated Hardcastle. "According to Mrs MacDonald, you used to have a number of photographs of your brother on display. All we need is to find one of these so we can compare it with the e-fit. That will determine whether or not your sister-in-law is telling us the truth.

"If, as we expect, she is, then that begs the question why did you do it?"

"It wasn't only me involved in compiling the e-fit. If you remember correctly, I had help from Ellie Compton," answered Tregunno.

"That's interesting," said Hardcastle. "According to Mrs Compton, she felt you coerced her into supporting your description of the mystery man. She will be giving us a full statement to confirm that. So how do you feel about that?"

"No comment."

"OK," chimed in Phil Davison. "Let's park your assault on DS Pearson for the time being. How well did you know Donald Summers?"

"No comment."

"How well did you know Neil Panton? And before you answer, remember that Panton played in the same cricket team as your son."

Tregunno took a sip of the water from the plastic cup in front of him.

"We may have nodded to each other once or twice at the cricket. But that's as far as it went."

"Did you murder Donald Summers?" continued Davison.

"No comment."

"Did you murder Neil Panton?"

"No comment."

Hardcastle decided to ask one last question before calling a halt to the interview.

"When I told your son why we had arrested you, his reply was 'In that case, stick the old bastard in jail, and throw away the key'. That suggests that you and he aren't exactly on the best of terms, and before you answer the question, remember that we will be speaking to him later."

Not for the first time, Tregunno gave careful thought to how he would respond.

"I love my son to bits, Detective Inspector. Have you got any children?"

"Yes, I have two."

"Then you know what I mean. But because of my military background, I have probably been a bit too hard on the boy from time to time, but no harder than my father was on me. My work also kept me away from home for months at a time, and it was inevitable that he would grow up being closer to his mother than to me.

"My wife passed away six months or so ago, and her death has hit Jethro hard. We haven't spoken since the funeral. She died of cancer, and for some irrational reason he blames me for her death."

For a second or two, Hardcastle almost felt sorry for the man sat in front of him, but it didn't last long as he remembered that the same man had come close to killing Kath Pearson.

"We will call it a day now, Mr Tregunno. We will continue this interview tomorrow morning after I've received the full report on the search of your house. If there is any evidence there linking you to the murders of Donald Summers and Neil Panton, no matter how small, we will find it. You should have no doubt whatsoever about that.

"Even if we don't find anything incriminating, you can rest assured that you will go to prison for some considerable time for the attempted murder of Detective Sergeant Kath Pearson. If I was a betting man, I'd put some serious money on you spending the rest of your life behind bars."

The two detectives got out of their seats.

"I'll get a constable to take you back to your cell."

As he opened the door of the interview room, Hardcastle stopped and turned to face Tregunno.

"Before I go, I would like to share something with you. Whoever killed Donald Summers will almost certainly kick himself when he finds out that if he had waited just a few weeks longer, Mother Nature would almost certainly have done the job for him."

"What do you mean?" asked Tregunno. "I ask purely out of curiosity."

"Well, as it turned out, Donald Summers was suffering from an enlarged aortic aneurysm. Because of its size, it could have ruptured at any moment, possibly in a matter of days," continued Hardcastle.

"And when it ruptured, it would have caused massive internal bleeding which is fatal in 90 per cent of cases. So, not only would Summers have died from the aneurysm, but Neil Panton, of course, would still be alive today. Just think on that, Brian. Another couple of weeks and none of this would have happened.

"See you tomorrow. Sleep well, Brian."

Sunday 6pm

Jason Pearson glanced at his phone for the umpteenth time. It was 6pm, and he still hadn't been allowed in to see his wife.

To make matters more complicated, he had been receiving a text virtually every ten minutes from Connie, none of which he had answered. Inevitably, her texts were getting more and more frantic.

It was when he received a message from her that said, in no uncertain terms, that she was going to come down to the hospital if he didn't answer, he realised he couldn't ignore her any longer. The trouble was, with his mind in such a turmoil he just didn't know what he was going to say to her.

On the one hand, his feelings for Connie ran deep and there was no doubt that she had fallen in love with him. And he couldn't deny that she was much more fun to be with than Kath. Fun was not a word he would use to describe his relationship, such as it was, with his wife.

Kath had become so engrossed in her career that she seemed to have little time for anything else. Promotion to Inspector had become an obsession, and Jason felt that he had fallen some way down the pecking order of Kath's priorities.

Yet, on the other hand, the news that she was pregnant was something he had been waiting to hear for so long. He wanted a family, period. And he wanted one as soon as possible.

So many of his friends now had young families, and whenever they all got together for a lad's night out, inevitably the conversation soon got around to what the kids were up to, and he was becoming increasingly jealous of his friends.

So much so, that he had begun to make excuses whenever one of them suggested it was time they all met up again. But, at the back of his mind, he couldn't help thinking that this was the reason why he had fallen for Connie. She came from a large family where having children was a given. She had told Jason on numerous occasions that she couldn't wait to start a family with him, and that she wanted at least three children, perhaps four even.

This had been music to his ears, and life had begun to become less complicated. Kath could have her promotion and her career, and he could have the family life he craved.

"Mr Pearson?"

Startled, Jason looked up to see a young nurse smiling at him.

"Yes nurse," he replied.

"You can go and see your wife now. I'll take you through to her."

"Thank you. How is she doing by the way?"

"She's had a tough time this afternoon, and is very, very tired, so perhaps you could stay for no more than ten minutes."

The nurse led Jason through two large double doors to a corridor which had several open plan rooms on both sides with four beds in each, all of which were occupied. Half way down the corridor was a small reception area on the right with two small rooms directly opposite. The nurse stopped at the first door, which was closed.

"Your wife's in here," she indicated, "and please remember, Mr Pearson, no more than ten minutes."

Jason nodded to her, opened the door gently and looked inside.

It came as quite a shock to see Kath lying on her back, all wired up to various pieces of medical equipment. His first thought was how small and frail it made her look, and he was almost overwhelmed with an urge to pick her up, hug her and tell her that everything was going to be fine.

But of course, he couldn't.

At first, it seemed that she was fast asleep, and he thought about leaving, and coming back in the morning. Then, he noticed her eyes were beginning to open.

"Kath, it's me," he whispered.

"How long have you been here?" she asked, her voice sounding very croaky.

"I've been waiting outside for a couple of hours, and they've only just let me come and see you. I'm under strict orders from the nurse not to stay for more than ten minutes."

"If you stay that long, it'll be the longest conversation we've had for months," replied Kath.

"And whose fault is that?" asked Jason.

"We're both to blame, Jason. Look, I don't need this now. This is a conversation for another day when I feel a lot better than I do at the moment."

Jason, again, thought about leaving, but he couldn't do that. Not until he had asked her the question that had been on his mind for the last couple of hours.

"Why didn't you tell me that you're pregnant?"

Kath closed her eyes. This was turning out to be a real crap day.

"Who told you?"

"The bloke who operated on you; I think his name was Michaelson. So, come on, why didn't you tell me?"

She thought about calling for a nurse and asking her to tell Jason to leave. But she knew that that would only delay the inevitable.

"Because I haven't decided whether or not to keep the baby, that's why."

Her husband was stunned by his wife's admission.

"I can't believe you said that, Kath. Don't I get a say in the matter?"

"No Jason, you don't. I need to make this decision without interference from anybody else. And that includes you."

"Jesus, Kath, can't you see that this should be a joint decision?"

"I'm sorry Jason, but you have relinquished any right to have a say in whether or not I terminate this pregnancy."

Jason looked at Kath as though she was talking garbage.

"So, just because we haven't been getting on that well lately, you think you have the right to exclude me from one of the most important decisions either of us will ever make?"

"No Jason. You lost any right you might have had when I heard you tell your girlfriend last night that you would be leaving me sometime this week. Now, please get out of this room before I have you thrown out."

Sunday 7pm

Phil Davison switched off his car's ignition.

For the first time since he could remember, he remained sat in the driver's seat instead of bounding up the path to his front door, opening it and calling out to his wife Sarah that he was home.

Davison was shattered, both physically and emotionally. It seemed that all the energy had been drained out of his body, even though the nine hour day he had just completed was nothing in the grand scheme of things. He was used to putting in much longer shifts.

As he reached to unbuckle his seat belt, he winced. He had decided against going to A&E on his way home and was already beginning to think that he might have made the wrong decision. He knew that he would get an ear bashing from Sarah when she saw the state of his hands, but despite this, at that precise moment, he just couldn't face the inevitable prospect of waiting to be seen at A&E.

Davison looked towards the bungalow. There was no sign of Sarah at the window, so obviously she hadn't heard his car pull up outside.

"God, what a mess," he said out loud to himself.

He was feeling so desperately guilty that he hadn't been able to protect Kath. He so wished that it had been him who had taken the knife to the abdomen, and not her, and the rage he felt towards her assailant had made interviewing him an ordeal.

Every time he had looked at Tregunno in the interview room, he had had to suppress the desire to smash him in the face with his forearm.

And yet, he had also had to come to terms with the fact that he had come off worse when he had gone one to one with a man who was almost twenty years older than him, and it was quite possible that he owed his life to Paul Taylor.

"Perhaps I'm getting too old for this job," he again said out loud whilst shaking his head.

However, his overriding memory of events earlier in the day, and the one that he was finding most difficult to come to terms with, was the feeling he felt when kneeling beside Kath Pearson, when he was holding her hand and urging her to wake up.

At that moment, he had been overwhelmed by the fear and panic that she might be slipping away from him. He had never felt so desperate in his life, not even when he was at Sarah's bedside in the hospital after the hit and run incident that had changed their lives forever.

And that was when the guilt had hit him like a sledgehammer when he realised that he loved Kath Pearson like he had never loved anyone before.

Monday 6am

Steve Hardcastle was in the middle of his second slice of toast when his mobile phone rang. The caller was Billy Kiernan. *Please let this be good news*, he thought to himself. "Good morning, Billy."

"Good morning Steve. I hope I haven't gotten you out of bed?" replied the Crime Scene Manager with his tongue firmly in his cheek, as he knew that his friend was renowned for being an early riser.

"And I hope you've been too busy to have any sleep at all," came the reply. "So, have you got any news from Tregunno's house?"

"I'm afraid the house is as clean as the proverbial whistle."

"Bugger," replied Hardcastle.

"But the good news is that his car wasn't," continued the CSM.

"Now that's more like it, Billy. What have you found?"

"We took his car, a three-year-old Ford Mondeo, back to the garage because it had obviously had a good going over recently; someone had definitely carried out a full valet on the interior. After a while, having found nothing, we took out the two front seats to get a better look at the carpet underneath them and it was there that we found it."

"Found what?"

"We found something that resembles a small patch of dried blood on the underside of the passenger seat. Not much, but hopefully just enough to enable us to extract DNA. There's a chance that Tregunno might have stuffed something underneath the seat as he drove away from the cricket ground after murdering Mr Summers, and that's when it would have come into contact with the seat."

"Any idea what it might have been?"

"Not at this stage. It might have been trainers, or a jumper or something like that. It might even have been the bat mallet."

"I don't suppose you've had any luck finding that either?" asked Hardcastle.

"Afraid not," replied Kiernan. "His house is spotless, and we've tried all the usual hiding places—water tank, toilet cistern, drains, underneath the insulation in the attic and so on, and a lot of unusual places as well. The garden is well maintained, and there are no signs of any recent digging, or of anything being burnt. If I was him, I'd have washed it thoroughly and then chopped it up into several smaller pieces and then got rid of them in half a dozen different places around Flitton."

"What about photographs of the dead brother?"

"No sign of any, I'm afraid."

"And still nothing to link Tregunno to Neil Panton?"

"Sorry Steve, no luck there either. Let's face it; he had time to plan killing Panton, whereas murdering Donald Summers was done on impulse, so there was always a greater chance of us finding something to link him to the first murder."

"Fair enough, Billy. Any idea when you'll be able to confirm what it is that you've found in his car and whether it links Tregunno to Summers?"

"Hopefully, that'll be around mid-morning. I'll give you a call as soon as I've got the results of the analysis."

After he had finished talking to Kiernan, Hardcastle put another slice of bread in the toaster and then called Phil Davison, anxious to give his sergeant some good news for once.

"That's great, boss," said Davison. "But it's a shame that we can't nail him for the Panton murder yet."

"We've just got to keep plugging away," replied Hardcastle, who could tell that his friend and colleague sounded far from his normal jaunty self.

"Anyway Phil, how are you and your hands this morning?"

"The hands aren't too bad thanks. Sarah gave them a good clean up last night, although she still thinks the nurse at our GP's practice should have a look at them. I might pop in there sometime today."

"And how about you, Phil; yesterday was a traumatic day for all of us, but especially for you and Kath."

"To be honest, I'm struggling. I just can't get it out of my mind that it should be me in hospital and not Kath. I've let her down big time."

"I know what you mean, Phil. I've had similar thoughts. After all, I'm the man in charge of the investigation, so the buck stops with me."

"But I should have been closer to her, I should have seen it coming, Steve."

Crikey, thought Hardcastle, *I think that's the first time he's ever called me by my Christian name rather than 'boss'.*

"I've thought exactly the same," replied Hardcastle, "but having secret service agents close to the presidential car didn't stop JFK being assassinated, did it? And when you have a moment, have a look on YouTube at the assassination attempt on Ronald Reagan. Reagan was completely surrounded by the secret service, yet John Hinckley still managed to get off six shots in less than two seconds. And it wasn't the first bullet that wounded Reagan, it was the last one. No matter how close you might have been to Kath, you would not have been able to stop her being stabbed.

"Kath did her duty, you did your duty and so did Paul Taylor and I'm incredibly proud of the three of you, as was the ACC when I spoke to him yesterday.

"Now, I'm going to finish off my breakfast, so I'll be down to pick you up in about half an hour. God knows how many times you have been my chauffeur, so it's my turn today. In the meantime, I want you to consider this one question. Why has it taken you all these years to call me 'Steve' and not 'boss'?"

Monday 7:10am

Steve Hardcastle drew up outside the Davison's bungalow a little later than expected, and gave Phil the news that he had had a telephone call from a nurse at the hospital who said that Kath Pearson had asked to see the pair of them as soon as possible.

"I think it's best if we pop in and see her on our way to the nick in case she's got some info we might need before we re-interview Tregunno later this morning," said Hardcastle. "And, I'm sure you're just as anxious as I am to see how she's getting on."

They continued the journey in silence, both lost in their own thoughts.

When they arrived at Kath's room, they were met by Mr Michaelson, the surgeon who had operated on her.

"Mrs Pearson is doing well, but she is still fairly weak, so I suggest that you bear that in mind when you go in to see her. And please, do try not to ask her too many questions."

As they entered the room, they could see that Kath had her eyes closed and for a second or two both thought that she was fast asleep.

"Perhaps we should come back later," whispered Davison to his boss.

"I might not want to see you later," came a croaky voice from the bed. "Pull up some chairs so I can see you better."

"How are you feeling, Kath?" asked Hardcastle as he went to sit down on the chair Davison had placed closest to her.

"I'm fine apart from feeling like I've been run over by a double decker bus. Seeing you two has made me feel a whole lot better though."

"We're under orders from Mr Michaelson not to stay too long," replied Hardcastle. "By the way, both DCI Cryer and the ACC have said they want to come and see you. Would you like me to put them off for a day or two?"

"Please. I'm not that ready to make small talk. Can you tell them that I'll let you or Phil know when I'm ready to see anyone else, other than you two of course."

"And we've only come to see how you're getting on, so no talking shop," chimed in Davison.

"That's not why I wanted to see you," replied Kath, "as I owe you both an apology."

"Don't be daft, Kath. It's us who should be apologising to you."

"No, you don't understand what I mean. Let me explain to you. But, before I start, you must promise that you won't ask me any questions, and I really mean no questions."

Hardcastle and Davison looked at each other, and Davison gave a brief nod to his boss.

"Of course Kath, we promise, no questions," replied Hardcastle.

Kath took a deep breath.

"It's funny how quickly things can change," she began. "This time last week I knew exactly what I wanted from life. Promotion to inspector possibly in the not too distant future, and after that, who knows? I think you both know that my job has always been the most important thing in my life.

"Then on Monday, completely out of the blue, I discovered I was pregnant. And if that wasn't bad enough, yesterday morning I found out that Jason was having an affair and that he was planning to leave me."

"Bloody hell, Kath," exclaimed Hardcastle. "Sorry, carry on."

"I hadn't told Jason about the pregnancy because I'm not sure whether or not I want to have the baby. Unfortunately, he found out by accident yesterday afternoon.

"We had a very brief conversation. I told him that I knew he was having an affair, and that, anyway, I wasn't sure if I wanted to have the baby. We exchanged words, and then I told him to get out. As far as I'm concerned, the marriage is over.

"Hopefully, I'll be discharged from here in a few days. The surgeon has told me that I will need to rest for several weeks before I'm fit to return to work. I'm not sure where I will be staying, but going home is out of the question. I need time and space away from Jason. Once I have decided where I'll stay, I will let you both know. I'd appreciate it if you would keep that strictly between the three of us."

"That goes without saying, Kath," replied Hardcastle. "You know you are always welcome to stay with me and Jenny."

"And that applies to me and Sarah," chimed in Davison.

"I know, and I thank you both dearly for the offers, but I really need to get right away from here. I've an old school friend who I keep in touch with. She's going through a divorce at the moment, and it might be therapeutic for both of us to spend some time crying on each other's shoulders. Anyway, I'll let you know as soon as I have made up my mind."

She reached out for a plastic beaker of water and took a couple of sips, before continuing.

"Phil, I am so sorry that I didn't let you know I was pregnant. I did tell Mr Hardcastle but couldn't face telling you as I know that having a family had been so important to you and Sarah, and I felt it would be so wrong of me to tell you that I was considering an abortion."

Davison was about to jump in with a response, but Kath put a hand up to stop him.

"And sir," she began turning to Hardcastle, "I am sorry I didn't tell you that I had discovered Jason was having an affair. I did tell Phil, but decided to say nothing to you yesterday as I knew that you were snowed under with this case, and I didn't want to overload you with my petty problems."

It was Hardcastle's turn to try and butt in, but once again Kath held up her hand.

"I know I should have told you about Jason, sir, and Phil, I should have mentioned the pregnancy to you. You two are the closest friends I have, and I was wrong, and I apologise."

"If you weren't so wired up to these machines, I would reach over and give you a hug," replied Hardcastle.

"So would I," added Davison, desperately trying to hold back the tears, unsuccessfully. "You were just being that normal unselfish person that you are, always thinking of others."

"We should go now, Phil, Kath needs the rest," said Hardcastle, seeing that Kath had her eyes closed.

He took hold of her left hand and gave it a gentle squeeze, as Davison leant over and kissed her lightly on her forehead.

By the time Hardcastle went to shut the door to her room, he could see that she had already nodded off.

Monday 8:45am

Hardcastle and Davison began the journey to the Police Station in silence, each lost in his own thoughts.

It was Hardcastle who spoke first. By that time, they were only a matter of minutes away from their destination.

"Are you OK, Phil?"

"Yeah, I'm fine, boss. I'm just keen to nail Tregunno to the mast for what he did to Kath. She doesn't deserve it."

"I know what you mean. Let's have a cup of coffee, a quick update with the troops, and then get down to business."

By the time they were ready to start the interview it was approaching a quarter to nine. They strolled into Interview Room Three and dismissed the constable who had been standing at the back of the room keeping an eye on Tregunno.

Before starting the interview, Tregunno again confirmed that he was happy to be questioned without any legal representation.

"How is Sergeant Pearson?"

"Conscience getting the better of you, Brian?" asked Hardcastle.

"No, I'm just interested to hear how she's getting on. As I told you yesterday, I meant no harm to your colleague."

"As it happens, we called into the hospital this morning," replied Hardcastle, "and she's still in a lot of discomfort. The consultant said that it will be some time before she's fit enough to return to work."

For a moment, Hardcastle thought he saw genuine concern register on Tregunno's face, but if there was, it was only for a split second.

"I do have some news for you though. Our Crime Scene Investigators have found an interesting stain on the underside of the front passenger seat in your Mondeo. It's being tested for DNA as we speak, and I'm willing to bet that it will be a match for Donald Summers's."

If he was hoping to see a reaction from Tregunno, Hardcastle was disappointed. In fact, there was just the slightest hint of a smirk on his face.

"No comment."

"Given this new information, I will ask you once again, did you murder Donald Summers?"

"No comment."

As he had done the day before, Tregunno continued to reply 'no comment' to each question put to him with regards to the murders of Summers and Neil Panton.

More in hope than expectation, Hardcastle decided to change the tack of the interrogation.

"You implied yesterday that you had no intention of wounding DS Pearson, but when I asked you if Olivia MacDonald was your intended victim; you answered 'no comment'. I now ask you again, was Mrs MacDonald your intended victim?"

There was silence and Hardcastle was just about to repeat the question when, to his surprise, Tregunno suddenly replied, "Yes, she was, and with good reason."

"Care to enlighten us further?"

Tregunno took a deep breath. "You said yesterday that you have two children, Inspector."

"Yes, two boys," replied Hardcastle.

"And you would do anything for them?"

Hardcastle nodded. "Of course I would."

"There was a time when I thought I would never become a parent, never have a child of my own," continued Tregunno. "I married my wife, Joan, in 1986, and thought it would just be a matter of time before she became pregnant. Six years on, and we were still childless. Then, towards the end of 1992, Joan gave me the news I thought I might never hear—she was expecting our first child. I can't describe the joy I felt when she told me, joy which was only surpassed by the birth of the boy we named Jethro on 1 July 1993. It was a Thursday and was a day I will never forget.

"Our marriage was never the best, Inspector. I am happy to admit that. But for a while Jethro's arrival seemed to help patch things up, plaster over some of the cracks. And for once I had a reason to stay at home rather than be off working abroad.

"However, I was very good at my job, and I turned down numerous offers of work for the rest of that year, offers that would have paid me a heck of a lot of money, just so that I could spend time at home with my baby son.

"But I couldn't do that indefinitely. I had made up my mind that Jethro would have all the things I never had, as well as the best education that money could buy. So, at the beginning of 1994, I started to consider some of the work that was being put my way."

"What line of work were you in?" asked Hardcastle; already fairly certain he knew what his answer would be.

"I have a certain set of skills that I learnt during my time in the Marines and the SBS and when I left the army, I wasn't short of offers, and I began working in the security industry."

"In other words, you became a mercenary," interjected Phil Davison.

"When I left the Unit in 1989, I had a choice. Join an industry like the prison service which would have paid me around £15K a year, or become a security contractor and earn that sort of money in a month. Tell me, what would you have done, Sergeant Davison?"

"That depends on what my employers were asking me to do for that kind of money," replied Davison.

Tregunno smiled.

"I really don't care what you think, sergeant, but I am a patriot. I was, and still am, one of the good guys. And I never took on a job that I thought would see me batting for the wrong side, no matter what money was on offer.

"My work took me to some of the darkest, most conflicted areas of the world where I would train the local troops, provide security to members of the local ruling government or regime and, very occasionally, conduct missions to gain intelligence on the opposition.

"I operated under a strict code of conduct; I only returned fire if I was being fired upon."

"Did you use torture to obtain the intelligence you were after?" asked Davison.

"No comment."

"I take that as a 'yes'. Is that where you learnt the technique you used to kill Neil Panton?"

"No comment."

"How long were you a mercenary?" asked Hardcastle.

"Security contractor," corrected Tregunno.

"Sorry, how long were you a security contractor?"

"I'm not sure I ever stopped. As I got older, and my reactions became slower, I eventually moved into management."

"What do you mean by management?"

"I became a facilitator. I would visit a prospective client to find out what he wanted, and using my fairly large bank of contacts, I made sure that the client got the right men for that particular job. I never disappointed them.

"When I finally got fed up with all the travelling abroad, I only accepted work which was UK based, mainly protection related—minding footballers, pop stars, their wives, partners, children and so on."

"You must have missed a lot of your son's growing up, being abroad so much of the time," said Davison.

"That was the only real downside. But I consoled myself that I was working to provide a good life for Joan and Jethro. I can assure you, neither of them wanted for anything.

"And I did my best to have time off during the school summer holidays so I could take the boy on day trips to the seaside, or watch him play cricket, but inevitably there were times when a job offer cropped up that was just too good to turn down."

"We understand that Jethro left home two or three years ago, and that you have seen little of him since then," interjected Hardcastle.

"I still go to watch him play cricket in the summer, but unfortunately we haven't spoken since my wife died. That was a very difficult time for him. He was very close to his mother."

"I can appreciate that," replied Hardcastle. "But sometimes the death of a family member can be a time for reconciliation. Did you know that your son contacted Olivia MacDonald after your wife died in the hope that she might be able to attend the funeral?"

Tregunno pursed his lips, and shook his head.

"I didn't know that," he replied. "Thankfully, she didn't turn up. That saved me from having to tell her that she was not welcome. I would not have let that woman anywhere near the funeral, no matter what anyone might have thought at the time."

"Would you like to tell us why you have developed such antipathy towards Mrs MacDonald?" asked Hardcastle.

Tregunno took a sip of water.

"From the outset, she made it obvious that she disliked me, she told Joan that I wasn't good enough for her, that she deserved someone better. She would never come to see us when I was home on leave, and I know that she was always running me down behind my back.

"When Joan and I decided to get married, against my better judgement, I agreed, for Joan's sake, that she could invite her sister and her husband to the Registry Office. We couldn't get married in a church as she'd been married before. Anyway, Joan was really upset when her sister didn't turn up, and that was it as far as I was concerned."

"All families have spats. That doesn't explain why you still have a deep hatred for Mrs MacDonald," stated Hardcastle.

"Believe it or not, my dislike for Olivia MacDonald only turned to hatred just over six months ago, a few days before my wife passed away.

"Joan was diagnosed with stage four breast cancer towards the end of last year. The cancer was very aggressive and had spread throughout her body and she was given just weeks to live. She became very bitter as she had discovered a couple of lumps a few months earlier, but had done nothing about it. Had she gone to the doctors straight away, there is a good chance that she would still be alive. She blamed herself, and, for some reason, she blamed me. Those last few weeks were very difficult.

"A week before she died, she was admitted to the local hospice. I was sitting with her on Christmas Eve when she told me that she had something to tell me; that she couldn't go to her grave without me knowing the truth. What she told me that evening was a life changer. Two days later, she was dead."

Tregunno paused for breath.

"Can you tell us what your wife told you?" asked Hardcastle.

"She said that I was not Jethro's father. At first I just assumed that the medication they were giving her in the hospice had addled her brain and was making her ramble on. I didn't believe she was speaking the truth.

"But then she said that behind my back she had had fertility tests, and that they had showed that there was no reason why she couldn't conceive. The consultant she saw told her that the next step was to get me to have a test as there was a chance that I could be sterile. I asked her why she hadn't told me this at the time, but she just shrugged her shoulders."

"Did she give you the name of the person she believed to be Jethro's father?" asked Phil Davison.

"No comment."

"Was Donald Summers the name of the person she believed to be Jethro's father?"

"No comment."

"This still doesn't explain why your dislike for Olivia MacDonald turned into hatred though, Brian," stated Hardcastle.

"I asked my wife if she'd told anyone else. You can guess the answer."

"Olivia MacDonald," said Davison.

"It seems that she told her sister when I was away working. Apparently, Olivia had come down from Scotland and had stayed a couple of nights whilst I was abroad. According to Joan, she told her sister that she was going to tell me when I got back home, but Olivia told her not to and that she should leave home to be with Jethro's real father."

"You believed everything your wife told you?"

"I must admit that I had my doubts. As I mentioned earlier, Joan passed away a couple of days later. Once the funeral was out of the way, I went to my doctor and told him the full story. He arranged for me to have a fertility test.

"I was on tenterhooks for a few days praying that what Joan had told me was just a load of drivel, just the ramblings of a dying woman. Unfortunately, the test results confirmed that I have a very low sperm count and that it was very unlikely that I could father a child. The doctor suggested a DNA test to confirm whether or not I was Jethro's father. I felt my guts had been surgically removed by a blind butcher. When I got home, I reached for the scotch and spent the next week either drinking or sleeping.

"By the time I had sobered up, I realised that, as far as Jethro was concerned, I was still his father, and he would never need to know any different. If I decided to pursue the DNA test, Jethro would have to be tested too. That would have alerted him that there was a doubt about his parentage, and ultimately, almost certainly, would reveal I was not his father.

"I needed someone to blame. Joan was dead, so I loaded all the blame onto her sister. And that hatred grew as I came to realise that she was the only person who could tell my son that I was not his father. But as long as she stayed in Scotland, the secret was safe.

"So when I saw her yesterday afternoon, for the first time in my life I forgot my training and I panicked. I could see that the one good thing that was left in my world, Jethro's belief that I was his father, was in grave danger. For a split second, I knew I had to prevent that woman from ever spilling the beans, and on impulse...well, you know what happened next. I instantly deeply regretted my actions. I hope that the court will understand that there were mitigating circumstances surrounding my actions, and that they will grant me some leniency."

"But what about Donald Summers?" asked Hardcastle. "He was the only other person that knew the truth once your wife had died. And there we have your motive for murdering him."

"You may think you have a motive, Inspector, but I can assure you, you won't find any evidence to substantiate it."

Monday 9:30am

"Well, Phil, what did you think of that?"

Hardcastle and Davison were back in the DI's office sipping coffee.

"Well boss, I think Mr Tregunno is a clever, and a very devious man."

"There's no doubt about that," replied Hardcastle, "but, be honest, was there any point during that interview where you began to have some sympathy for him? Try and look at it from a juror's perspective."

Davison didn't respond immediately. When he did reply, he chose his words very carefully.

"As someone whose wife couldn't have children, I do know the significant pressure it can create within a marriage. So, there's always the possibility of some empathy within a jury, particularly if they or a friend or relative have found themselves in a similar situation.

"I have no experience of having a child, of becoming a parent, of forming a bond with a son or a daughter, a bond which, I can only assume, gets progressively stronger as the years go by.

"So, I have to admit, somewhat ashamedly, that even I felt a little sympathy for Tregunno when he said that his wife had told him that the boy he'd brought up as his own over all those years, was someone else's child. Particularly as she dropped this bombshell just a couple of days before she died.

"But if I felt a smidgen of sympathy, even though it lasted for no more than a second or two, you can bet that some of the jurors would feel an element of compassion. And that might influence them when they get to debating the verdict at the trial."

"I'm sure you're right," said Hardcastle. "Obviously, his barrister will concentrate on that. And I'm pretty certain that he will paint a picture of Tregunno as man who served his country with distinction when a member of the UK's Special Forces. While I'm thinking of it, can you ask Paul Taylor to pull up his military record? You never know, there might be something in it we can use to our advantage.

"So, if we are only able to nail him for the assault on Kath, the defence could treat it as a type of crime of passion, a man committing an act against someone because of a sudden strong impulse, such as sudden rage, rather than as a premeditated crime. And that Kath just happened to get in the way and was wounded by accident and not by design."

"On the other side of the fence, we have Olivia MacDonald's testimony as to what an evil bastard he was to his wife," pointed out Davison, "and that she was his intended victim, his wife's sister and a woman in her late 60s."

"We need to speak to his son today, Phil. We know he fell out with Tregunno a good two years before his mother died and we need to know how and why that came about," added Hardcastle.

"What about the DNA testing on the stain found in his car?" asked Davison. "Hopefully, that should give us the link to Donald Summers that we need, and then it will be game, set and match."

"That's worrying me a little at the moment," replied Hardcastle. "When I mentioned it to Tregunno, I saw a smirk on his face. It might have been just for a split second, but it was definitely a smirk. And do you remember what Olivia MacDonald said about him?"

"That he is a manipulator and that on this occasion he was manipulating the police?" replied Davison.

"Exactly. Hopefully, I'm worrying unnecessarily and the DNA test will give us the result we want. But as we're still struggling to put him in the frame for the Neil Panton murder, it would be a nightmare if our best lead on the Summers killing turned out to be a red herring."

There was a tap on the open door as Alan Rutherford looked into the DI's office.

"Sorry to interrupt you sir, but Jethro Tregunno is at the front desk asking to speak to you."

"Ah, that's a coincidence. Can you ask them to send him up please, Alan?"

Within a couple of minutes Jethro Tregunno was sitting in the small conference room adjacent to Hardcastle's office. The young man seemed very agitated.

"Thank you for coming in, Mr Tregunno," began Hardcastle after the initial introductions.

"Please call me Jethro, Inspector. I spoke to my Aunt Olivia last night. I'm not sure if calling me Tregunno is appropriate after what she told me. I'm hoping that you can fill in some of gaps for me."

"And that's why I was going to ring you this morning," replied Hardcastle.

"Is what she told me true, Inspector? Was Donald Summers my real father, and did the man who I grew up calling 'dad' actually murder him? And where does that leave me?" asked Jethro, gabbling somewhat. "If it's really true, it means I have lost my mother, my so called father and the man who really was my dad, all in the space of six months. I'm sorry but I just can't get my head around all this."

There were tears streaming down his face. *This young man is the real victim of this mess,* Hardcastle thought to himself. He looked at Phil Davison and nodded towards the water machine in the corner. Davison filled up a plastic cup and handed it to Jethro.

After a few seconds, and a couple of sips of water, Jethro was ready to continue.

"We do believe that your father murdered Donald Summers and that he may also have been responsible for the death of your teammate, Neil Panton. But, at this stage, the only crime we have charged him with is the attempted murder of a police officer."

"How long is he likely to go to prison for that offence alone?" asked Jethro.

"We would hope for a sentence of between 12 to 20 years," replied Hardcastle. "But he could get less if the court believes that there are mitigating circumstances, based on his age and whether or not he was provoked. If he keeps his nose clean in prison, he could be out in, say, 10 years, perhaps less."

There was silence in the room while Jethro took this on board.

"I believe your relationship with Brian Tregunno was not that good. Can you tell us how this came about?"

Jethro took another sip of water.

"When I was a young lad, like most kids I thought he was the best dad in the world, but as I got older I realised that that was just nonsense. Whenever he was at home, you could cut the atmosphere with a knife most days. My mum lived her life on the edge, in constant fear and apprehension. It was no wonder that she was on anti-depressants for much of her life. She was in tears most days.

"Yet everything changed when he was working away. Mum would be a different person. She would smile, laugh and sing; she would have friends around; she would go to the pub or to the cinema with them; she even went dancing; she would look ten years younger when he wasn't about. She could dress how she wanted, not how my dad told her to dress.

"Once when I was very young, I heard mum say to one of her friends that she often prayed that my dad wouldn't come home, that he would catch a bullet in some godforsaken country. Later, I asked her what she meant by that and she was totally distraught that I had heard what she had said. She made me promise I would never repeat that to anyone, particularly not to my dad. She was terrified of the consequences.

"Sometime later, when I had worked out that he was away working as some sort of mercenary, I shared my mum's wish that he would catch a bullet."

"Did he ever hit your mum?" asked Davison.

"I had my suspicions, but I never actually saw him do any physical harm to her. But, according to mum, he was an expert in torture techniques, so if he had hit her, I suspect I would never have seen the evidence. He was too clever for that; too clever to leave any visible signs.

"No, it was the psychological and emotional abuse that almost destroyed her."

"What form did that abuse take?" asked Hardcastle.

"He seemed to take great pleasure in humiliating her in front of family and her friends," replied Jethro.

"He would have the sulks for no apparent reason, blaming it on her, and would give her the silent treatment which would last for days, or sometimes weeks on end. No one could ever be in any doubt that he expected her to obey his every word. He was so very manipulative.

"He would be very critical of her appearance, how she dressed, the way she wore her hair, her weight. If she ever put on a couple of pounds he would call her 'fatso' or say she was looking gross. From time to time, she would go on a fasting diet, just to get a temporary respite from his abuse.

"Most of the time when he was at home she could do nothing right as far as he was concerned. How she never ended up a total emotional wreck, I'll never know.

"I shouldn't say this, but I think she was almost relieved when she became ill, she saw death as her only way out."

For the second time, they could see that Jethro was fighting back the tears.

"You said earlier that at one time you thought Brian was the best dad in the world," said Davison. "Did the way he treated you change the way you felt about him?"

"Definitely," replied Jethro. "I was 12 years old when I first began to realise he wasn't the same as other boy's dads. I had joined a local youth football club that ran sides from under 12's through to under 17's. A lot of my mates from school also joined the club at the same time.

"One Saturday morning, my dad came to watch me play. He'd been working away and had returned home the day before. I was really chuffed that he'd come to watch me as I had been playing well, and had scored quite a lot of goals. I wanted him to be proud of me.

"Halfway through the first half, one of the opposition players tripped me in the penalty box. It was a clear penalty, but one of the dads from the other side shouted out that I'd dived.

"The next thing I knew, my dad had this bloke by the throat. Some of the other dads from the opposing team tried to intervene, and in a flash, three of them were on their backs. I was stunned; it was real Bruce Lee stuff. I'd never seen anyone do anything like that before, let alone my own dad.

"After the game, some of my mates were saying it was real cool to have a dad who could handle himself like that. I didn't see it that way. I was totally embarrassed. The chap who coached the side tried to have a word with my dad, but he backed right off when it seemed like dad was going to lay into him as well.

"Three days later, he received a letter from the football club secretary saying that he was banned from watching the team play. Dad's reaction was to tell me that I was too good for that team, and that he would find me a better team to play for. What he totally ignored was the fact that my friends were playing for the side, and I didn't want to play for any other team. But he wouldn't listen to me. So effectively, that was the end of my football career.

"During the summer months, I played cricket for the school team and did pretty well. Our sports teacher played for Flitton Green and suggested I join their Colts team. Luckily, dad was away at that time. But when he returned and found out I was playing cricket, he tried to stop me, saying cricket was a game for 'Nancy' boys and 'poofs'.

"However, eventually he came along to watch a game. I scored a century and he was hooked. To be fair to him, after that first game, he came to every match he could, and that has continued ever since; even after we'd fallen out.

"As I got older, like most teenagers, I got a bit stroppy from time to time. I admit that I was a bit of a 'Kevin'. Whenever we argued, which was quite often, I threatened him that I would leave home.

"Whenever this happened, he took it out on my mum, shouting that it was all her fault for the way she'd brought me up when he wasn't around. As time went on, I got to resent him more and more for the way he treated mum. When it came to leaving school, I was offered places at a number of universities as I did pretty well at my exams. I eventually chose Durham, just to be as far away from him as possible. Inevitably, that led to another big falling out because he wanted me to go to a uni much closer to home. He wanted to control me the way he controlled mum.

"As I was 19 years old by now, he knew this was one argument he couldn't win. So off I went to uni, and I revelled in my new found freedom. Unfortunately, mum paid the price, and without me being there acting as a sort of buffer, I know he continued to treat her like dirt. I will never forget or forgive him for the way he treated her.

"After I graduated, I knew that I couldn't go back to living under the same roof as him, and within a couple of months a couple of mates and I rented a house together. I have not spoken more than a dozen words to him since the day I moved out."

"Not even at your mother's funeral?" asked Hardcastle.

"Not even at my mother's funeral," replied Jethro, with his head bowed.

"So, what does the future hold for you? I assume you don't wish to see Brian?" enquired Hardcastle.

"No, I have no desire to see him again. But what I do want is to know who my real father is, or was. I am prepared to take a DNA test. Can you please help me, inspector?"

Monday 11am

Steve Hardcastle and Phil Davison were back in the former's office sipping coffee after having organised the DNA test for Jethro Tregunno. Also sat around the DI's desk were DCs Paul Taylor, Alan Rutherford and Isha Hussein.

"You can't help feeling sorry for Jethro," remarked Davison. "He seems a really nice young man, despite having been brought up by someone as evil as Brian Tregunno. I hope for his sake that the DNA test confirms that his true father was Donald Summers."

Hardcastle was about to respond, when the telephone on his desk rang. It was Billy Kiernan.

"Good morning Billy," replied Hardcastle. "Phil is with me, as are Paul, Alan and Isha, so I'll put you on speaker phone. I hope you have some good news for us?"

"I'm afraid it's not the news I was hoping to bring you, Steve. The mark on the underside of the front passenger seat has turned out to be a mixture of what we think to be cleaning fluid and blood. The amount of blood was fairly negligible, but was enough to give us a match. Unfortunately, it matched the sample we took from Tregunno yesterday."

"Bugger," retorted Hardcastle. "Sorry Isha."

"Bollocks," added Davison. "Sorry Isha."

"We were dealing with very low levels of DNA," replied Kiernan. "And because of that, even if we'd got a match to the victim, we would have had to report that we couldn't say how and when it got to where we found it.

"A larger sample would have enabled us to say, with a degree of certainty, that there must have been contact between assailant and victim. However, when you are dealing in picograms—"

"Sorry Mr Kiernan, but what's a picogram?" interrupted Paul Taylor.

"A picogram is one trillionth of a gram," replied Kiernan. "When you are dealing with such a small amount of DNA, any decent defence lawyer worth his salt could come up with dozens of ways such a small amount of blood might

356

have attached itself to an item of Tregunno's clothing, without him and Mr Summers ever having come into contact with each other.

"For example, let's say the killer wasn't Tregunno and instead it was someone called John Smith. Mr Smith could well have had the murder weapon in his hand as he ran away from the crime scene, and drops of the victim's blood might have fallen onto the ground.

"Now, as we know, the ground round the back of the pavilion is really hard due to the lack of rain over the last few weeks, and anyone who was at the cricket match, including Tregunno, could have stepped on the victim's blood without ever knowing about it.

"The amount of blood which had attached to the sole of Tregunno's shoes would have diminished with each step as he walked back to his car, so that by the time he got there, all that would have been left was the very minute amount we found which could have been transferred from the sole of the shoe to the underside of the passenger seat if Tregunno changed his footwear before driving off, and stuffed the shoe with the blood on it under the seat.

"Given what you said about Tregunno smirking when you mentioned we had found some traces of blood on the underside of the passenger's seat, I'm willing to bet he nicked a finger, or grazed a knuckle on the seat's metal runner when he was cleaning the car. That would explain the combination of blood and cleaning fluid."

There was silence in the room whilst they all contemplated the disappointing news from the Crime Scene Manager.

"So, at the moment, the only evidence we have against Tregunno is circumstantial, and there's not even enough of that to get a green light from the CPS to charge him with murder," said Hardcastle disappointedly.

"I'm afraid so, Steve," replied Kiernan. "We have a strong motive, but little by way of fact to substantiate it. All I can say is that we'll keep plugging away at this end."

As he put the phone down, Steve Hardcastle let out a deep sigh.

"So basically, all we have on Tregunno is the charge of the attempted murder of Kath Pearson," said Hardcastle, "and, with a good brief, even that could get downgraded to causing grievous bodily harm without intent, considering the fact that Kath wasn't his intended victim.

"So, the task today, lady and gentlemen, is that we go back over everything we've got on Tregunno, and the murders of Donald Summers and Neil Panton, to see whether we have missed anything. Otherwise, I'm afraid Tregunno could well get off relatively scot-free."

Monday 7pm

Hardcastle looked at his watch. It had just turned seven o'clock.

As he had feared, a full case review had so far failed to turn up anything new, and, to make matters worse, just after lunch Paul Taylor had looked into his office to tell him that military records had unfortunately confirmed that Brian Tregunno had indeed served Queen and Country with distinction during his time with the Royal Marines and the Special Boat Service.

As Tregunno had been in police cells for nigh on twenty four hours, it had been agreed earlier in the afternoon, following discussions with the CPS, that he would be officially charged with the attempted murder of Detective Sergeant Kath Pearson. Arrangements had then been made for him to attend the Magistrates Court the following morning.

Any request for bail would be vigorously opposed, and barring a disaster, Tregunno would be held on remand in one of the local prisons, pending trial at the Crown Court at a date to be arranged.

Hardcastle looked at his watch again—it was 12 hours since he had picked up Phil Davison from his bungalow and so he decided it was time to call it a day. He had sent the rest of the team home an hour or so earlier, telling them that they needed to get a good rest as, in his words, 'We go again tomorrow. Prepare for another long day'. Now it was just him and Davison left in the office.

"I think that'll do for today, Phil. Let's surprise our wives by getting home before dark!"

"Can you drop me off at the hospital, boss?"

"I think we should give Kath some time to herself, Phil. We can always pop in to see her tomorrow," replied Hardcastle.

"I agree, boss," replied Davison. "But I've decided to take your advice and have the cuts to my hands looked at. They've been giving me a bit of pain as the day's gone on, so I think I really ought to get them looked at."

"Makes a change, you taking my advice," joked Hardcastle. "How are you going to get home from the hospital once they've sorted you out? Would you like me to wait for you?"

"No thanks boss, I could be there for ages. I'll get a cab home when they've finished with me."

Fifteen minutes later, having been dropped off by Hardcastle, Davison was standing at the A&E reception desk, explaining why he was there. Thankfully, there were only a handful of other people waiting to be seen, and when the receptionist realised that he was one of the police officers that had been injured in the incident at the cricket ground the day before, he was taken through to see a junior doctor who, to Phil Davison, looked like he should still be at school.

I thought it was only policemen who looked younger the older you get, he thought to himself.

However, young as he might have been, it didn't stop the doctor from tearing him off a strip for not having visited the hospital earlier. Half an hour later, with the wounds cleaned and stitched, he was back outside A&E debating whether he should call a cab and go straight home, or pop up to see how Kath was getting on.

Just before he'd left the office, he had called Sarah to tell her that he was going to A&E after all, and that he didn't know what time he would be home. Since his wife wouldn't be worrying where he was, he decided he had time to pay Kath a quick visit. He was glad he did as when he walked into her room he was greeted with a big smile.

"Hi Phil," she croaked. "I'm so glad you're here. I needed somebody to pour out some water."

"I've just popped in to see how you are, so no talking shop," replied Davison.

"Of course not," she said as she sipped the water. "I wouldn't dream of it. So, how's the case going?"

They grinned at each other. That was typical Kath. The job always came first.

"I'll tell you, as long as you promise not to say anything to the boss. He'll have me directing traffic if he finds out."

"Cross my heart," she replied.

It took him just a couple of minutes to give her a quick précis of the day's events.

"Well, it just goes to show that everything goes to pot when I'm not around!"

He smiled at her, and then glanced at his watch.

"I'm afraid it's time I went, Kath. Your minders outside told me I had a maximum of ten minutes with you; otherwise they would do indescribable things to me," he said jokingly. "Goodnight Kath."

"Goodnight Phil. You will call in on your way to the nick in the morning, won't you?"

"Of course I will."

Davison got up from his chair and lent over to kiss Kath on the forehead, just as he had done twelve hours earlier.

However, this time, she moved her head forward towards him, and accidentally or otherwise, their lips met. Instead of moving away from each other, they lingered in that position for a few seconds, longer than you would expect from just work colleagues.

As they pulled apart from each other and their eyes met, Davison realised he was blushing. Without another word, he turned away and walked to the door, pausing only to look back and give Kath a little wave.

As he walked down the hospital, he felt like a teenager who had just had his first kiss. But then, he stopped suddenly.

His mood changed from euphoria to guilt. He felt like he had just been unfaithful to Sarah.

Tuesday 7am

Phil Davison had endured a restless night as his conscience continued to prick away at him. At least all the tossing and turning hadn't disturbed Sarah who fortunately remained sound asleep in her bed. Had she woken up, he was ready to blame his restlessness on his injured hands. A lie perhaps, but only a little white one.

By the time he got up at 6am, he reckoned he'd slept for no more than an hour, perhaps two at best.

At least all that time awake had helped him come to a decision.

He would call in at the hospital as agreed, and act as if nothing had happened the previous evening. He would ask Kath if there was anything he could get her, perhaps a book or some magazines, tell her what he would be doing once he got to the office, and then take his leave, this time avoiding any physical contact with her.

That really wasn't what he wanted to do or say, but he thought it would be best for Kath and for Sarah. As far as he was concerned, what he really wanted didn't come into the equation. No way could he be that selfish.

Just at that point, his mobile had rung. It had been Steve Hardcastle asking if he wanted a lift to the office.

Davison had declined, telling his boss that his hands had improved and that he was ok to drive and that he would see him at the office.

After a couple of slices of toast and marmite, he said his goodbyes to Sarah, and then set off for the hospital.

It hadn't crossed his mind that the DI would also be calling in to see Kath, as neither of them had mentioned it when they had spoken earlier. So he was quite surprised when he saw Hardcastle's Range Rover parked up in the hospital car park in exactly the same spot as he'd parked it twenty four hours earlier.

As much as he wanted to see Kath, he quickly decided that what he had to do and say could only be done when they were alone, and so he did a quick about turn, and continued his journey to work.

He wasn't the first to arrive at the office as Isha Hussein was already at her desk, and with her back to him, for a split second he actually thought it was Kath.

He was just about to say something, when Paul Taylor and Alan Rutherford walked into the room.

"Morning sarge," said Taylor, "any news on DS Pearson?"

"Nothing since yesterday, Paul, but the boss may have popped in to see her on his way in. I'd say no news is good news."

Davison took off his jacket and hung it on the coat hanger and as he went to sit down at his desk, he was aware of Hardcastle walking into the main office.

"Good morning all, and before you ask, I've just come from the hospital and DS Pearson is on the mend. She was certainly better than when Phil and I saw her yesterday morning."

"Can I go in and see her yet?" asked Isha.

"I did ask her if she was happy to have visitors, but she still wants to limit it to just DS Davison and myself. I wouldn't take that personally, Isha, as she was adamant that she didn't want to see DCI Cryer or the ACC either. I'm sure that as she gets stronger, she'll be more than happy to see visitors from this office."

He walked over to Davison's desk.

"Kath said she'd like something to read and asked if you can get her a couple of magazines, and a book or two. She said you'd know her tastes better than me."

"OK boss, I'll pop into WH Smith's for some magazines and then go to the second hand book shop at lunchtime," replied Davison.

"Thanks Phil, I said that you'd sort something out and then pop in and see her later today."

Tuesday 1pm

The hearing at the Magistrate's Court was over in a matter of minutes with Brian Tregunno remanded to HMP Downsview, a prison no more than twenty miles from Dorminster.

Bail was not an issue as Tregunno had not asked for it to be admitted and the only time he had acknowledged Hardcastle and Davison was when he was being led away, when he had given the pair a nod and the vestige of a smile.

"Well, that's a start," said Davison as they left the court, on their way back to where they had parked their cars.

"By now we should have been in a position to charge him with the two murders, on top of what he did to Kath," replied Hardcastle.

"We still have a fair chance to do that boss," replied Davison. "I'm certain something will come up so we can nail the bugger for killing Summers. He must have made a mistake somewhere along the line."

"I hope you're right, Phil. But as for killing Panton, I think he's just too clever by half and the odds are stacked up against us finding any evidence that'll convict him. Anyway, fancy a bite to eat?"

"I would normally, boss, but I've got to do that bit of shopping for Kath, and it'll take me a little while to sort out a couple of books for her."

So they went their separate ways, Hardcastle to his car, Davison to the High Street.

In WH Smith, he bought several magazines including *Hello!* and *True Crime* and knowing her fascination for crimes committed in the UK during the 1950s and 60s, bought *The Curse of the Great Train Robbery*, the most recent book about the 1963 mail train robbery once dubbed '*The Crime of the Century.*'

He then went into the second hand bookshop, which was run by a local charity, and was about to buy a couple of murder mysteries when he had a change of heart. Instead he put the books back on the shelf and asked the woman behind the till if she could suggest a couple of more light-hearted reads.

"Are they for you, or for a lady?"

"For a lady," replied Davison. "She's a colleague of mine who is in hospital at the moment."

"Ah, you'll want some *Chick Lit* then," replied the assistant, who couldn't have been a day under 75.

Davison gave her a blank look.

"Do I?" he asked.

The assistant smiled at him.

"Wait here," she said, and walked towards the back of the shop.

She was back within a minute.

"Here you are," she said handing him two books which had obviously been well read.

"Someone brought a box of old books in yesterday. We haven't had time to put them out yet, but I had a quick thumb through after we closed the shop last night and noticed these two among them. I've read them both myself, and they are two of my favourites."

Davison looked at the titles; *Something Borrowed* and *Bridget Jones's Diary*.

"I'm not sure they'll be right for her."

"Trust me," said the assistant. "If she needs cheering up, she'll love them. If I'm wrong, you can always bring them back and I'll either change them or give you your money back. It's only £3 for the pair, so what have you got to lose?"

How could he refuse? He gave her the money.

Back at the office, he found everyone still hard at it.

"Anything new?" he asked out loud.

There was a mass shaking of heads, and a 'nothing sarge' from Paul Taylor.

On hearing his sergeant's voice, Steve Hardcastle came out of his office.

"How was your shopping trip? Any luck?"

"A couple of true crime magazines and a book about the Great Train Robbery," replied Davison.

He had deliberately left the books and magazines in his car. He knew he would have been too embarrassed to admit that he had bought two *Chick Lit* books as the lady in the charity shop had described them.

"Playing it safe, eh?" said Hardcastle. "It would do her good to have something a bit more light-hearted."

"So, nothing new boss, I gather," replied Davison, keen to change the subject.

"I've spoken to Billy Kiernan and he should have Jethro Tregunno's DNA test results by this evening, so that they can be compared to his dad's and to Summers's. At least we'll soon know who his real father is.

"Billy also said that his team are going to have another sweep of Panton's house to make sure that nothing was missed first time around. But knowing how thorough his guys are, I would very much doubt if they'll turn up anything new."

For the next four hours or so, everyone continued to make phone calls and go over the statements taken after each murder.

Davison flitted between his desk and Kath Pearson's, but couldn't come up with anything remotely resembling a new lead.

At six o'clock, a slightly despondent Hardcastle called time.

"That's it for the day everyone. Well done for all your efforts. Fingers crossed that we have more luck tomorrow."

He looked towards Phil Davison.

"That means you too, Phil, as you're popping in to see Kath on your way home. Give her my best, won't you."

"I certainly will. But what about you, boss? You need an early night more than anyone."

"I thought I'd hang on for another hour. Hopefully, Billy Kiernan will call me soon."

"You will let me know when you've spoken to him?"

"Of course I will. Now bugger off."

They smiled at each other. At the end of the day, they were friends as well as colleagues.

Tuesday 7pm

Phil Davison was feeling very anxious.

For the best part of the day, he had rehearsed over and over again in his mind what he was going to say to her. He was even rehearsing while walking along the long corridor that led to her room.

His main hope was that he hadn't damaged the friendship they had enjoyed for many years now. He had even begun to worry that maybe that friendship had been one-sided.

However, he needn't have worried. When he walked into her room, she greeted him with a huge smile.

"Hiya," she said. "I missed you this morning."

Davison was not sure how to reply.

"Yeah, well, when I pulled into the car park, I saw the boss's car, so I thought it would be better to leave it and go on to the office instead."

He was standing a couple of paces away from her bed.

"Look Kath, I'm really sorry about yesterday evening. I was totally out of order, and I apologise."

"Why are you apologising, Phil? It should be me apologising to you," replied Pearson.

"I know you're just being nice and thoughtful, but please hear me out," answered Davison.

"OK, you go first," replied Kath.

Davison took a deep breath.

"You are in a very vulnerable position at the moment, both physically and emotionally; but despite that I took advantage of it. I shouldn't have. I was wrong, and I apologise. I really hope that I haven't jeopardised our friendship, because it means so much to me. But I behaved inappropriately and will fully understand if you want to make a complaint to DI Hardcastle."

"Are you finished yet?" asked Kath. "It sounds like you've been rehearsing that speech."

Davison nodded, looking extremely contrite.

"That's the first time someone's tried to take advantage of me, and I didn't know anything about it," she said with a smile. "Now, before I say anything else, can you please push the door to and sit down. You're making the place look very untidy. Now it's my turn. Please listen to what I've got to say and don't interrupt."

He did as he was told.

"That kiss we shared last night was completely my fault. I guessed that you were going to kiss me on the forehead as you'd done yesterday morning, and on impulse I moved forward so that I could kiss you on the lips. It might have been on impulse, but to me, it just felt like the right thing to do.

"I realised that I might have upset you, since you left straight away, and then you didn't come in to see me this morning. I know you are a married man who is married to a wonderful person in Sarah. So, I apologise.

"I could, of course, pretend that I don't remember kissing you and blame it on the various drugs they have been pumping in me. But I would be lying. I don't regret it for one moment, and given half a chance I would do it again.

"There, I've said it. Now if you want to leave and make a complaint to Mr Hardcastle that I acted inappropriately, then I will also completely understand why."

There was a moment's silence, before the tension of the moment was broken by Phil.

"I can't leave now, Kath. Not after I've spent almost twenty quid on buying you some books and some magazines which, I've just realised, I've left in my car."

"That's more like the Phil Davison I've come to know, love and admire," replied Kath.

They looked at each other without saying a word for at least thirty seconds.

"For what it's worth, I could have pulled away from you when we kissed, but in all honesty I didn't because I didn't want it to end," said Davison finally and with just a hint of sadness. "So what happens now, Kath?"

She puffed out her cheeks.

"I have decisions to make, Phil. I have to arrange where I'm going to stay once I'm discharged from here. At the moment, I don't want to go home. If I do, it will only be long enough to pack a couple of suitcases, and make sure my husband hasn't moved his girlfriend in while I've been laying here.

"Then I have to speak to Jason. That will be over the phone and not face to face. I need to tell him that our marriage is over, and that there is no going back, despite the fact that I am expecting his baby. Once I've done that, I have to make a decision about whether or not I keep the baby, or arrange a termination. If I'm honest with you Phil, I have no idea what I'm going to do about it at the moment.

"Whatever I do about the baby will impact on another big decision I have to make. Do I come back to work, or do I call time on my career; that decision depends on whether or not I keep the baby."

"Have you any idea where you'll go when you leave here?" asked Davison.

"I have a couple of options, but whichever I choose I will let you have the address. I'll also need to give it to Mr Hardcastle so he can pass it to the HR department. I'll also need to get a second mobile phone as I won't want Jason ringing me up. You will be the only person I will give that number to. You will be the only person I want to take advice from. You are the only true friend I have."

"Won't you give it to your mum?" asked Davison.

"No. I couldn't trust her not to give it to Jason."

There was silence once again. Phil could see that that speech had been an emotional one for Kath, and that she suddenly seemed very tired.

He went to get up from the chair.

"Don't go yet, Phil."

"I'm only going to my car to get the books and magazines I'd forgotten. I won't be a minute. I'll stay with you as long as I can, but judging from the looks Matron is giving me, it won't be that long."

As he got up, his mobile phone rang. He saw that the caller was DI Hardcastle.

"I need to take this, Kath. It's the boss."

Tuesday 7:15pm

Hardcastle looked at his watch. It was 7:15pm and time to leave the office. He had told Jenny that he would be home for dinner by 8pm at the latest.

He couldn't hide his disappointment that he hadn't heard from Billy Kiernan, but there was always the hope that he would speak to him later on in the evening. He got up from his chair and was about to take his jacket off the coat hanger when his phone rang. It was Billy Kiernan at long last.

"Sorry I'm late, Steve," began Kiernan, "but you'll understand why when I give you the results. We had to make sure that none of the samples had been contaminated and I can confirm that they were all OK."

"You've got me intrigued, Billy; so what's the result?" asked Hardcastle, still standing by the coat hanger. "Was Donald Summers the biological father of Jethro Tregunno?"

Half way through the conversation with Kiernan, Hardcastle sat back down at his desk.

When the telephone call had finished, it was a full minute before he put down his phone. It was another minute before he picked it up to call Phil Davison.

Dinner would have to wait.

Tuesday 7:30pm

"Good evening, boss."

"Hi Phil. First things first, where are you at the moment?"

"I'm still at the hospital, just about to go back to my car to get the books and magazines out of the boot. I forgot to bring them to Kath's room."

"How is she?"

"She's making progress, a little bit more like her old self today."

"That's good news, give her my best wishes."

"Would you like to speak to her yourself, boss?"

He looked at Kath who was shaking her head. Obviously, she didn't feel like talking to the DI.

"No thanks, I'm sure you've been bringing her up to date with the case."

"Yes, I have, sir," admitted Davison.

"Well, I'll leave it to you to decide whether to tell her what I'm going to tell you now."

"You've heard from Billy with the DNA test results?"

"I've just got off the phone from talking to him. Are you sitting down at the moment?"

"I've just got out of the chair."

"I suggest you sit down."

"You've got me intrigued, boss," replied Davison sitting back down. "OK, I'm sat down."

For a couple of minutes, Davison just listened; he didn't say a word.

When Hardcastle had finished, there was silence.

"Are you still there, Phil?"

"Bloody hell!" replied the sergeant at last.

Tuesday 7:45pm

Kath Pearson watched Phil Davison very carefully whilst he was taking the call from DI Hardcastle.

The longer the conversation went on, the more intrigued she became. Things came to a climax when Phil shouted 'bloody hell' down the phone.

Shortly after, Hardcastle had ended the call.

"What was that all about?" asked Kath. "Have we got the evidence to charge Tregunno with murder at last?"

"Not exactly, Kath. Do you feel up to me telling you what the boss has just told me?"

"Are you kidding? No matter how tired I feel, there's no way I would be able to sleep without knowing what's going on. Come on Phil; put me out of my misery."

"OK," he replied.

A minute or so later, a wide-eyed and wide awake Kath Pearson looked at Davison incredulously.

"No bloody way!" she exclaimed.

"It's the gospel truth. That's why Billy was late calling the DI as he wanted to make sure none of the samples had been contaminated."

"So, what's the next step?"

"The boss and I are meeting at the nick at 7:30am and then we're going straight off to the prison. I think he'd like to have gone there now, but it's a bit too late for that. They'll all be banged up for the night by now."

"Promise me one thing, Phil."

"Your wish is my command."

"Come in as soon as you can tomorrow and tell me how it all went."

"Of course I will. By the way, Brown Owl out there is still giving me a glare, so I'd better get the stuff out of my boot and bring it up to you and then I'll bid you a fond farewell."

Five minutes later, he was back with the magazines and books. He put them on the little bedside table and leant across and kissed Kath on the forehead.

She was already fast asleep.

Wednesday 7:30am

Phil Davison arrived at the police station car park on the dot of 7:30am. He wasn't surprised to see the DI's Range Rover already parked up in its usual spot.

After saying good morning to the other members of the team, he made his way across to Steve Hardcastle's office.

"Good morning boss."

"Good morning Phil. You look a bit tired, my friend. Did you have trouble sleeping too?"

"Yeah, it was a bit of a restless one," replied Davison. Not only had he been thinking about the implications of his boss's phone call, he'd also spent much of the night going back over his conversation with Kath. He could, of course, chat freely to his boss about the former, but the latter would have to remain a secret between him and Kath.

"Did Kath like the magazines and books you gave her?"

"I'll let you know tomorrow. By the time I got back to her room, she was fast asleep."

"How did she react to the news about the DNA results?"

"Same as me," replied Davison. "She just couldn't believe it."

"I've spoken to DCI Cryer and the ACC to put them in the picture, and naturally they were as surprised as we were, but I want to wait until we get back from Downsview before telling the rest of the team."

"I understand, boss."

"And we will have to tell Jethro Tregunno as soon as we can. Anyway, if you're ready to go, let's get on the road."

They spent the journey in relative silence, only speaking occasionally about the amount of traffic on the road, what was on the front pages of the morning newspapers, and so on.

Once they had arrived and signed in at HMP Downsview they were shown into a small interview room where they waited for Brian Tregunno to arrive.

It wasn't long before they heard footsteps approaching, and when the door opened, Tregunno appeared in the company of a prison officer. He was dressed casually, a benefit of being a remand prisoner as they are allowed to wear their own clothes rather than prison issue.

"I'll be outside if you need me, Mr Hardcastle. Just give me a shout when you've finished with the prisoner," said the prison officer.

"Good morning gentlemen," said Tregunno once the officer had shut the door behind him. "To what do I owe this pleasure? Surely you haven't come to question me about Mr Summers and Mr Panton again? You'll be wasting your time if you have. I have nothing further to add to our previous conversations. By the way, how is DS Pearson doing?"

"She's improving," replied Hardcastle, "and we're not here to question you, Brian. Two days ago, your son Jethro asked us to take a sample of his DNA which could then be compared with the sample we took from you, and a sample taken from the body of Donald Summers. We've come to give you the result. We will be informing Jethro of the result later on this morning."

Tregunno's demeanour changed immediately. For the first time in their dealings with him, they both sensed that he was on edge.

"OK. Fire away. Let's get this over and done with."

Hardcastle opened a buff-coloured folder that was on the desk in front of him, and took out a single sheet of paper.

"A comparison of your DNA and the DNA supplied by Mr Jethro Tregunno has confirmed that you are not his father."

Hardcastle and Davison remained quiet to allow the information to sink in.

"Thank you, Mr Hardcastle," said Tregunno eventually. "I had more or less accepted that I wasn't Jethro's birth father. But I have to admit that having it conclusively confirmed is still difficult to accept.

"I think I would like to have some time to myself now, so I would appreciate it if you could tell the prison officer outside that we're finished."

"I'm afraid we aren't finished. There is something else I have to tell you."

Tregunno looked at him quizzically.

Hardcastle looked down at the sheet of paper he was holding.

"I'm afraid that a comparison between Jethro's DNA and the DNA taken from Donald Summers has revealed that Mr Summers was not Jethro's father either."

"I don't believe you," replied Tregunno. "That's just not possible. It had to be either him or me."

Hardcastle handed Tregunno the sheet of paper he had been reading from.

"Read the second paragraph, Brian."

Tregunno read and reread it.

"And there is no possibility of an error in the testing?"

"Absolutely none whatsoever. The samples were tested and retested."

Tregunno sat there, staring at the paper, and then looked up.

"Do you have any idea who Jethro's real father is?"

"We rather thought you might have some ideas on this," replied Hardcastle.

"I have no idea whatsoever, and if you have nothing else to tell me, I would like to go now please."

Phil Davison got up and opened the door.

"We've finished now. You can take the prisoner back to his cell."

As he went to leave, Tregunno turned back and looked at the two policemen.

"Thank you gentlemen; I assume you will be seeing Jethro fairly soon?"

"He's next on our list," replied Hardcastle.

"Could you pass him this message please? Tell him that I might not have been his father, but I'd like to think I was his daddy."

Wednesday 9:30am

On the way back from HMP Downsview, Hardcastle managed to speak to Jethro Tregunno. The young man pressed the DI to give him the result of the DNA test over the phone, but he was eventually persuaded that a face to face meeting would be the best way to proceed.

He told the DI that he would be able to get to the police station by 9:30am.

Hardcastle asked Phil Davison to give the rest of the team the shock news about the DNA tests while he was speaking to Jethro.

Jethro was as good as his word and just before 9:30am, he was sat in Hardcastle's office with a cup of black coffee on the desk in front of him. It was obvious that he was very much on edge.

"DS Davison and I have just got back from seeing Brian. Just so you know, he is aware of what I am about to tell you."

"OK, thank you," replied Jethro.

"There is no easy way to say this Jethro, but I have to tell you that neither Brian Tregunno nor Donald Summers is your biological father."

As Hardcastle had anticipated, Jethro was completely stunned.

"I'm sorry, could you repeat that?"

"The DNA evidence confirms that neither Brian nor Donald Summers is your father."

"But that's just not possible," stammered Jethro. "When I spoke to my aunt Olivia, she said that when my mum was expecting me, she had told her that my father was a man called Donald Summers, and not Brian Tregunno. My mum wouldn't lie about a thing like that. Are you sure you've got the right Donald Summers?"

"I'm afraid there is no doubt whatsoever about that, Jethro," replied Hardcastle gently.

"So what you are saying is that somewhere out there is a man who is completely oblivious to the fact that I am his son?"

"That would appear to be the case."

"Can you help me find him?"

"I'm sorry, Jethro, but that wouldn't be considered a prudent use of police time and resources, and to be honest, we wouldn't know where to start."

"So where do I go from here?"

"I think your best bet would be to speak to Olivia again. There's always a chance that she might remember the names of any people your mum might have been keen on back in the 1990s."

"You mean the men she might have slept with back then."

Hardcastle knew that this was an extremely difficult time for the young man, and that he needed to tread very carefully and treat him with kid gloves.

"From what I have been told, your mum was a very decent lady, who was desperate to have a child. After six years of marriage, she and Brian were still childless. The maternal instinct in a woman can be very strong, as is the amount of pressure the failure to conceive a child can put on even the strongest of marriages. So she decided to have some tests, and these confirmed that there was nothing wrong with her. So the likelihood was that Brian was infertile.

"The problem was that she couldn't talk to him about this because she was frightened of him and frightened of the consequences. The prospect of your mother conceiving was pretty slim particularly with Brian working away from home a lot of the time. However, I reckon she made up her mind to use his absence as an opportunity, and decided to use a surrogate. For her it may have been a case of it's now or never. If she didn't conceive now, perhaps she never would. It seems pretty obvious that she was desperate for a child.

"But how could she guarantee that the person she chose wasn't infertile like Brian, or that they just wouldn't click? I am only guessing here, but perhaps she decided to double her chances of success with the help of two men rather than just the one. Of course, the men concerned would have been completely unaware that they were being used for just that one purpose.

"When she learnt that at long last she was pregnant, her instinct probably told her that the father was Donald Summers. It may have been that she wanted Donald to be the father, and so blotted the second man completely out of her mind. There was no way of her knowing, of course, that it was he who was her unborn child's biological father and not Mr Summers.

"Then, unexpectedly, she found herself falling for Donald but from what I have been told, those feelings were not reciprocated. Around the same time, Summers was offered promotion by his employers which meant moving to the

North of England, an offer he couldn't refuse and, for him, that was the end of his relationship with your mother.

"Brian then returned from overseas very soon after you were conceived, and naturally, he assumed he was the father. For the next twenty-five years or so, he had no reason to think otherwise, until, that is, when your mum told him a couple of days before she died that Summers was your father and not him.

"He was devastated and angry. When your mother passed away, the focus of that anger was polarised against one person, Donald Summers. And there we have his motive for the murder of Mr Summers."

There was silence in the room while Jethro took this in.

"Will you be charging him for the murder of Mr Summers?"

"We will when we have compiled sufficient evidence," replied Hardcastle. "And the same applies to your teammate, Neil Panton."

Jethro seemed lost for words, but Hardcastle decided to keep quiet to allow the young man time to gather his thoughts.

"It's difficult to understand why my dad, Brian that is, couldn't sort the problem out without resorting to violence. I'll never understand why he did what he did."

"Why don't you go and see him?" asked Hardcastle. "It can't do you any harm. At worst, you might come away no better off, but there is always a chance that he will explain what was going through his mind when he committed those crimes, why he treated your mum the way he did, why he treated you the way he did. It might give you the chance to get some things off your chest. You don't have anything to lose."

"I'm not sure I can do that, Mr Hardcastle. Too much has happened too quickly."

"He did ask me to give you a message," said Hardcastle.

"And what was that?" asked Jethro.

"That he might not be your father, but he is still your daddy."

Wednesday 10:30am

"How did the team take the news about the DNA results?" asked Steve Hardcastle, as Phil Davison sat down in the chair that Jethro Tregunno had vacated just a few minutes earlier.

"At first they were all gob-smacked," replied Davison, "but then it sunk in that it doesn't change things where we're concerned. Tregunno is still guilty of two murders and it's still our job to get enough evidence so he can be charged. By the way, how was Jethro Tregunno, boss?"

"In a bit of a mess mentally," replied Hardcastle. "I did my best to treat him with kid gloves, but the lad needs more than that. The problem is, he doesn't have a shoulder to cry on at the moment. He recently split up with his girlfriend and the only relatives he has are his Aunt Olivia, and the Stewart family back in Scotland.

"I'm sure Olivia would be sympathetic but I don't think she can add much more to what she's already told him. I'm going to call her anyway and tell her about the latest developments and to let her know that Jethro may be in touch with her.

"But I think he's going to need some serious counselling; after all, he's recently lost his mother; he's found out the man he thought was his dad has killed two men; including the man he'd just been told was his real father, who now turns out not to be. And nobody has a clue who his real dad is."

"To be honest, boss, I don't think I'd have been able to cope with all that at his age. I'd have been in bits," replied Davison.

"I'm sure I would have been too."

"But what can we do?"

"That's what worries me, Phil. I was thinking about calling Andy Hanson, to tell him Jethro could do with his mates from the cricket team rallying around him. That might help a bit.

"I also suggested he visit Brian in prison, as he might be able to answer some of his questions, but that didn't seem to go down too well."

"Isn't he Jethro's stepdad now?" asked Davison.

"I suppose he is, I hadn't thought about it that way."

There was a light tap on the door and Alan Rutherford walked in.

"Sorry to disturb you, sir, but I just took a call from Downsview. It was Brian Tregunno. I was going to transfer him to you, but he said not to bother you."

"Did he leave any message?"

"He did," said Rutherford looking at his notebook, "and he asked me to take it down word for word. He said, 'I just want to tell you that after the meeting we had this morning, I have decided to engage a solicitor to represent me. He will be present at any future interviews, should you decide to have any more that is'."

"Was that it?" asked Hardcastle.

"Yes sir. That was what he said, word for word."

"How did he sound, Alan?"

"I was surprised sir, because he sounded pretty jaunty. Not what I expected after Mr Davison told us about your meeting with him at the prison this morning."

"That's very interesting, thank you Alan."

Hardcastle and Davison looked at each other.

"Well, that's a bit of a turn up," said Davison. "What do you think that means? It's a bit late to engage a brief now."

"Better late than never I suppose," said Hardcastle rubbing his eyes with his right hand. He was suddenly feeling very tired, as if everything was catching up on him.

"I think it means he's going to do his level best to mitigate the sentence he might get for wounding Kath, so that he can get out of prison whilst he's still got a bit of life left in him.

"I reckon that he might actually have an idea who Jethro's father could be, Phil. And I think he still wants his revenge."

Wednesday 11:30am

After finishing his conversation with Phil Davison, Hardcastle thought hard and long about who he should make contact with. In the end, he decided to make the two calls he had mentioned to Davison.

The first was to Olivia MacDonald.

She sounded a bit prickly over the phone; no doubt a result of the dressing down Hardcastle had given her on Sunday afternoon for not having revealed her intentions earlier. She felt that he had blamed her for the injury suffered by the police woman.

As he had expected, she was as stunned as everyone else had been to learn that Donald Summers was not Jethro Tregunno's biological father.

And she reiterated that her sister Joan had never mentioned anyone apart from Summers when it came to who the father of her unborn child might be.

"As I told you before, after she divorced her first husband, and before she met Brian, men friends came and went at a fair rate of knots. That all stopped when she got together with Brian. She would be far too frightened of the consequences if he found out that she had slept with another man. I was utterly amazed that Joan had the courage to sleep with one man, let alone a second, from what you tell me. So, I'm sorry but I can't help you any more than that."

She had been on the verge of putting the phone down when Hardcastle mentioned that Jethro, her nephew, was struggling to come to terms with the events of the last 10 days.

"I'm sorry to hear that, Mr Hardcastle. He seems a very nice young man, and certainly doesn't deserve all these trials and tribulations. I will ring him this evening. Goodbye."

The second call was to Andy Hanson, the skipper of Flitton Green CC.

He didn't mention the DNA tests to Hanson as that was still confidential and, anyway, that would be best coming from Jethro himself.

But he did say that the young man was going through some tough times, and support from the members of the cricket team might be helpful.

Hanson, reading between the lines, promised that he and the rest of the team would do what they could to support Jethro.

And that was the best Hardcastle could do.

He felt it wasn't enough.

He was very concerned about the young man's well-being.

Wednesday 6:30pm

The rest of the day was spent the same way as the previous two, checking and rechecking witness statements and making phone calls to anyone who might have been in the vicinity of either murder when it had been committed.

During the middle of the afternoon, Hardcastle sensed that the morale amongst the team had begun to sag, and so he took the opportunity to pass on his theory that Brian Tregunno might have his own idea who Jethro's biological father could be, now that Donald Summers had been ruled out by the DNA evidence.

Should that be the case, he told them, then the earlier Tregunno was released from prison, the greater the odds were of him committing a third murder. The only way they could stop that from happening was to secure a conviction for one or both murders.

That appeared to do the trick and everyone seemed to get a second wind. Shortly before 6pm Hardcastle gave them a 'well done' and told them it was time to go home.

He and Phil Davison stayed on for another half an hour, until they too decided to call it a day. Hardcastle went straight home and Davison went to the hospital after telling Sarah he would be home around 8pm.

When he arrived at Kath's room, he was gently chastised for not having been to see her sooner as she was dying to find out what had happened when he and the DI had visited Tregunno in prison.

She was not disappointed, and Phil then went on to tell her about the boss's meeting with Jethro, his telephone conversation with Olivia MacDonald, and the DI's theory that Tregunno might have an idea who Jethro's real father could be, with Summers now out of that frame.

"Do you know, Phil, I must be getting better as I'm actually really disappointed that I'm not part of all this."

"Any idea when they might discharge you?" asked Davison.

"Possibly at the weekend, if I keep progressing," she replied.

"I'll pick you up and take you to wherever you want to go, if you like," offered Davison.

"I know you will," she replied, "but what would Sarah say?"

"She wouldn't mind at all. She knows that you would do the same if the roles were reversed. How's the book going?" asked Davison, nodding towards *Bridget Jones's Diary* that was lying open on the bedside table.

"That was an inspired choice," replied Kath. "I'm really enjoying it. It's not the sort of book I would have chosen. Thanks, you did well."

"I did have some help to be honest. The lady in the charity shop I bought it from said you'd really like it. I was a bit sceptical, but she obviously knew what she was talking about."

She smiled, and then Davison noticed that the smile had turned to a frown.

"What's up?" he asked.

"My mother came in to see me today. She knew about the baby because Jason had been to see her."

She looked at Davison expecting a reaction from him.

"Don't you want to know what she said?" she asked.

"Of course I do, but I'm not sure if it's any of my business."

"I'd like you to make it your business," she replied.

"OK. What did she say?"

"After asking me how I was, she spent the next ten minutes telling me that I should make it up with Jason, leave the job and have the baby."

"And what did you say?"

"I won't go in to all the detail, but I left her in no doubt that she should mind her own business."

"How did she react?"

"Not a lot she could say really, she knows how stubborn I can be. Anyway, I told her I was feeling very tired and needed to sleep."

"Sounds like it all went well then," replied Davison.

"You could say that," she said with a broad grin.

At that moment the staff nurse came in.

"I'm afraid I must ask you to leave. You've had ten minutes more than I would normally permit."

And she made it obvious that she wasn't going to move until Davison had said his goodbye. With her watching his every move, he bent over and kissed Kath on the forehead.

As he pulled away, Kath rolled her eyes and pursed her lips and simulated a kiss, knowing that Phil's body was blocking the nurse's view.

"Goodnight DS Pearson."

"Goodnight DS Davison."

Wednesday 7:30pm

Brian Tregunno was lying on his bed in the single cell. He had had a fruitful afternoon writing two fairly long letters. He was not much of a letter writer, but on this occasion he was very satisfied with his efforts.

He was surprised how quickly and easily he had settled in at HMP Downsview. Being a remand prisoner meant that he could wear his own clothes and the prison regime was not quite as draconian as it was for convicted prisoners.

Sometime earlier, a prison officer had looked in on him, and then shut the cell door where he would remain until the door was unlocked early in the morning.

Having spent much of his army career as a member of the UK's Special Forces, Tregunno was used to spending time in the most austere and uncomfortable conditions imaginable. In his opinion, prison life was a doddle.

As for his fellow inmates, there were plenty who were swaggering around as if they owned the place. Within the prison hierarchy someone of his age and build would be considered of little or no threat to those that had spent much of their life doing porridge, and they would normally waste no time in letting the newcomer know that he was no more than a drone or a grunt at best. He had soon put a stop to that.

Earlier on in the day, whilst he was still struggling to come to terms with the results of the DNA tests, his way back to his cell had been blocked by three fairly well built cons who thought they would show the newbie who was boss. Tregunno had looked around, and as there wasn't a prison officer in sight, decided he would have a bit of fun with them.

"I wouldn't do that if I was you boys. This is your first and only warning," he had told them.

"What are you going to do about it, grandad?" asked one of them.

Within a matter of seconds, all three of them were down on the floor, holding various parts of their anatomy.

"I did warn you," replied Tregunno, stepping over them.

A short time later, a prison officer had walked into his cell.

"A little birdie tells me that you flattened three of your fellow inmates. When I asked the three of them what had happened, they all said that they'd slipped on a wet patch."

"So what has that got to do with me?" he had asked the officer.

"Officially, it has nothing to do with you whatsoever. Unofficially, this is a friendly warning. You've made your point; no-one will dare touch you now, so I don't want to hear of any more accidents on this wing."

"I wouldn't worry about that," he'd replied. "I don't plan to be here that long."

Thursday 6:40am

Steve Hardcastle had had a fitful night and had got up at 5:45am, without waking Jenny. He had showered and dressed leisurely and was now watching the news on the kitchen television while waiting for his toast to pop up. It was while he was waiting that his mobile phone rang. He saw that the caller was Sergeant Kennedy.

"Good morning Paddy, what can I do for you?"

"Good morning sir, sorry to bother you, but I've just taken a call from Downsview. Brian Tregunno is dead."

Hardcastle felt like he had been punched in the stomach.

"Do they have any idea of the cause?"

"Apparently there are no visible signs so it could be natural causes. That's all I know at the moment. I've got a contact number which I'm sending you now."

"OK Paddy. Thanks for the call. I'll ring the prison and then I'll let Phil Davison know."

His mobile buzzed as the phone number came through.

He was about to call it, when the phone rang again.

This time the caller was pathologist Kelly Heywood.

"Good morning Kelly."

"Good morning Steve. Have you heard from the prison?"

"I've just had a call from the nick. Where are you?"

"I'm on my way to the prison. They hope and think it could be natural causes, but they've found two letters in the cell, so it could point to suicide. Both letters are marked 'strictly private and confidential'."

"Who are they addressed to?" asked Hardcastle.

"One is to you and the other is to Jethro Tregunno. If they haven't already steamed them open by the time I get there, can you give me the authority to open the one addressed to you?"

"Of course you can," replied Hardcastle. "By the sound of things, this probably isn't a criminal matter, so there's little point in me driving to the prison unless you tell me otherwise."

"I agree. Anyway, they'll want me to get the body taken away as soon as possible. As long as I think we're not dealing with a crime scene, I'll get the body removed and do the post mortem as soon as I can. I'll call you when I've opened the letter."

Kelly ended the call, and Hardcastle remembered his toast. Both slices had popped up, and were now cold. He hated cold toast and he would have to throw them out into the garden for the birds before he left for work.

He put another two slices into the toaster, and decided to give Phil Davison a quick call.

Davison was as stunned as he had been.

"I've no sympathy for Tregunno, but once again, it's Jethro I feel sorry for," said Hardcastle. "How much more can this guy take?"

Hardcastle then gave Davison a quick précis of his conversation with Kelly Heywood, and they agreed to meet up at the nick at 7:30am. He ended the call and then remembered his toast. Both slices had popped up and were now cold like the other two. They would also end up on the lawn.

He looked at his watch, decided he couldn't be bothered to put more toast in the toaster and grabbed a Wagon Wheel out of the cupboard instead. He picked up his car keys and quietly shut the front door.

In his haste, he had forgotten to throw the cold toast out for the birds.

Thursday 8am

The news that Brian Tregunno was dead created a monumental stir around the office; news that was passed on to each member of the team as they arrived for work.

"So, what do we do now?" was the question on hearing the news for the first time.

"Carry on as normal until you're told otherwise," was the answer.

Steve Hardcastle and Phil Davison were sat in the former's office, waiting to hear from Kelly Heywood.

"I suppose it's too much to hope that this letter he's written is some sort of deathbed statement, owning up to killing both Summers and Panton?" asked Davison.

"Knowing the way my luck's going at the moment, he's probably asking me to settle up his overdue phone bill," replied Hardcastle.

"By the way, when you get a moment Phil, can you ring the prison to make sure that someone there has been in contact with Jethro? Brian died while he was in their custody, so it's their responsibility to inform next of kin."

And then, his mobile rang. He was relieved to see that it was Kelly Heywood calling.

"Hi Kelly, what's the latest?"

"Hi Steve, I'm back at the mortuary. Tregunno's body will be here soon. I've opened his letter to you, and your luck's in on two counts."

"Hang on, Kelly, Phil's with me. I'll put the speaker on. OK, go ahead."

"Good morning Phil. I just said to Steve that your luck's in. Not only was his death suicide, but in his letter he also confesses to both murders."

"Bingo!" shouted out Davison.

"I'll scan the letter and then email it to you, Steve. It'll be with you in a couple of minutes."

"Thanks Kelly, I'll come over and collect the original if you can let me know when you're going to do the post mortem."

While he waited for the email to arrive, Davison went into the main office and told the team that Tregunno had confessed to both murders. There was a loud cheer; handshakes were exchanged, and backs were slapped.

Hardcastle's computer pinged. The email had been delivered.

"It's here, Phil," called out the DI.

He opened the attachment and with Tregunno's letter now on his screen, the pair began to read:

To Detective Inspector Steven Hardcastle

Mr Hardcastle

You are probably wondering how and why I decided to end my life now. The how is simple.

As a mercenary, I was involved in numerous highly dangerous missions overseas for various employers, and on each mission part of the essential equipment I took with me was what is colloquially known as a 'suicide pill'. I'm sure your pathologist will be able to confirm the content of the pill I have taken. I personally have no idea and couldn't care less.

Had I been captured by some of those I was fighting, I would not have hesitated to use one; a quick death being far more preferable to hours or perhaps even days of slow torture.

As a remand prisoner permitted to wear his own clothes, it was fairly simple to hide one of these in the waistband of my tracksuit bottoms.

The why is far more complicated.

Many years ago, my wife and I made wills where Jethro is the sole beneficiary. On my death, he inherits my house, conservatively valued at £750,000 and the contents of two safety deposit boxes, which have a combined worth around £1million, all legitimately earned. The letter I have written to Jethro gives him all the necessary details of how to access these boxes.

Jethro has now become a fairly wealthy young man, the very least I could do for him by way of some compensation for all the pain he has had to endure, particularly these last few months. Even though he is not my son, I still love him like nothing else on this earth.

When my dying wife told me that I was not Jethro's father, I thought this was just a dying woman's revenge. But the more I thought about it, the more I

392

realised that it was a distinct possibility, particularly as she had named Donald Summers as Jethro's real father. Unbeknown to Summers, I found out that he had recently moved back to the area, and quickly discovered where he was living. Soon after, when he was out, I broke into his bungalow and in one of the rooms I found a photograph of Jethro when he was a baby. It seemed to confirm that my wife had been telling me the truth about the boy's parentage.

Hardcastle and Davison looked at each other.

"That explains the mystery of the photograph," said Hardcastle. "Tregunno saw the picture when he broke in, but couldn't take it away with him as Summers would have known that someone had been in his bungalow. But after he'd killed him, he knew that he had to go back and remove it, as that was the only thing that could link him to Summers."

They continued to read the letter.

But to then find out from you that Jethro's true father was someone else, whose identity is a complete mystery, was more than I could take.

Had she deliberately lied when she named Summers as Jethro's father? Did she even know who Jethro's real father was? Had Summers upset her in some way? She knew by giving me his name that I would go looking for him.

But, in the end, I didn't have to. He fell into my lap. As you know, I went to watch Jethro play cricket Sunday before last, and who should be umpiring? None other than Summers himself.

And yes, I did kill him. Everything fell into place. He went off injured, someone had left a bat mallet around the back of the pavilion and it was over in a matter of seconds. I can't tell you how much pleasure I got at the sound of his skull cracking in two. Just like shelling a soft-boiled egg.

I now know that Summers wasn't Jethro's father, but I have no remorse. He shouldn't have slept with my wife in the first place.

By the way, you never had a chance of finding any evidence. I had plenty of time to erase any trace of DNA to link me to his murder. It wasn't as if it was the first time I had done something like this. Now that's got you thinking, hasn't it?

And then there was Panton, an odious character disliked by anyone who came into contact with him. His fate was sealed the minute he picked up the phone and tried to blackmail me. Once you give in to someone like him, they always come back for more. They just get more and more greedy.

I really enjoyed killing him. Watching the life disappear from his eyes gave me so much pleasure. He got what he deserved.

My only regret is injuring Detective Sergeant Pearson. She is a brave woman. It wasn't really my fault that she got stabbed. Blame it on my wife's sister. If she'd have kept her nose out of it, you would never have had a chance to catch me. May she rot in hell.

So, there you have it, Inspector. Both of your murders solved. I hope they give you a raise.

Brian Tregunno

Phil Davison was the first to speak.

"Well, I'd say that that's pretty comprehensive."

"Yeah," replied Hardcastle. "It more or less confirms what we thought, but couldn't prove."

The pair shook hands.

"Well done, Phil."

"Well done, Steve," replied Davison. "Would you mind if I pop over and see Kath later this morning? I'd like to give her the news. It might give her some closure, and I'm sure she will be relieved to know that she won't have to go to court now."

"Of course you can. She deserves everybody's thanks for all the hours she put in, and you and I know the pressure she's been under in her personal life. And make sure you take some flowers with you."

"I'll have a whip round amongst the team," said Davison. "She'll be dead chuffed."

Thursday 11am

After all the self-congratulating had ended, Phil Davison picked up his phone and dialled Jethro Tregunno's mobile number.

The phone was answered on the second ring.

Davison was relieved to hear from Jethro that the Governor of HMP Downsview had already been in touch.

"I'm really sorry, Jethro, you have my deepest sympathies."

"Thank you, I appreciate that," replied Jethro, "but I can't help thinking that maybe it is for the best. And I understand that as well as writing a letter to me, he also wrote one to DI Hardcastle in which he confessed to killing Mr Summers and Neil Panton. Is that true?"

"Yes it is. If you don't mind me asking, how are you doing?"

"Better than I thought I would be," replied Jethro. "I am keen to pick up the letter from the prison though, and I've decided I'd like to see his body. I think it might help me with some sort of closure."

"Perhaps I can help you there," said Davison. "I'd be happy to get one of my colleagues to collect the letter from Downsview and then pick you up and take you to the mortuary as soon as the pathologist says that she is free to see you. Then when you've finished, my colleague will take you back home."

"That would be really great. Thank you so much, that's a load off my mind."

"OK. My colleague's name is Isha Hussein and she'll give you a call as soon as she's sorted out the detail."

As soon as the call ended, Davison spoke to Isha who, understandably, was a little apprehensive.

"You'll be fine, and it will be good experience for you. And you're closer to Jethro's age so he might feel more relaxed talking to you rather than to an old fart like me."

His next stop was the local florist who put together a beautiful bouquet while he waited, and shortly after midday he walked into Kath's room with his arms full of roses, carnations and numerous other colourful blooms.

"They're lovely Phil, thank you."

"They're not just from me, everyone in the office contributed. And I've got a lot to tell you. You are in for a big surprise."

He sat down and started from the beginning. By the time he had finished a quarter of an hour later, Kath didn't know whether to laugh or cry.

"I'm glad it's you who told me Phil, I feel a bit tearful and I don't mind having a little weep in front of you. I'm pleased we can close the file on this case, and of course I'm relieved I won't have to go to court now.

"But there are no winners in this case. If Joan Tregunno hadn't made that death bed confession to Brian, three people would still be alive."

"I'm sure she felt that it was her last opportunity for some payback for the way he'd treated her for most of their married life," replied Davison.

"I still think she did it on the spur of the moment," replied Kath. "If she had thought it through thoroughly, she would have realised that it was going to have some massive consequences for her son."

"You're right, of course," replied Davison. "But what's done is done. Anyway, have you any news on a discharge?"

"Yes, I have. Mr Michaelson, the consultant, said that I could be out over the weekend if I continue to improve."

"That would be fantastic," replied Davison. "So where do you want me to take you?"

"I'm not sure at the moment. I made some calls earlier and have a couple of options, but they're both over 100 miles away, and Mr Michaelson wants me to remain local as the dressing on the wound will need changing, and that's best done by the district nurse. Still, at least I've got a couple of days to sort something out."

"Well, whatever you decide, I'll be your taxi."

"I know Phil, thank you."

Phil looked at his watch.

"I better go now. We've still got some loose ends to tie up back at the office."

"You'll come back later?"

"Of course I will."

He looked through the window from where he could see a couple of nurses with their backs turned away. He leant towards Kath, and their lips met for just a couple of seconds, before he pulled away at the sound of a chair scraping the floor outside.

Thursday 5pm

Back in the office, it had the feel of a last day of term and Hardcastle and Davison decided to have a quick catch up before allowing the bulk of the team to have an early finish.

"Kath's doing OK," reported Davison. "There's a chance that she could be discharged at the weekend. She'll need some time recuperating, so it'll probably be a few weeks before we see her back in the office. And she sends her thanks for the lovely flowers, by the way."

"Is she going to go back home?" asked Hardcastle. "It could be awkward if her husband's going to be there at the same time."

"She's undecided. She has to stay locally so the District Nurse can change the dressing on her wound from time to time, but there's no way that she's going to share the house with Jason. At least she's got a couple of days to think things over."

"Keep me posted, Phil. How did Isha get on with Jethro Tregunno? That was an inspired choice of yours, by the way. The experience will have done her good."

"She just got back. She was pretty apprehensive when I asked her to pick him up," replied Davison, "but she said everything went really well. In fact it was far better than she thought it would be.

"By the sound of it they got on like a house on fire and they even had a coffee at Starbucks after they'd finished at the mortuary. Speaking of the mortuary, has Kelly done the post mortem yet?"

"No, not yet," replied Hardcastle. "I think it's going to be tomorrow morning now, but Kelly is pretty certain that the pill he took contained potassium cyanide. He would have been dead within a couple of minutes."

There was the sound of laughter coming from the main office and both men turned to look.

"I'll tell them they can knock off early so they can go down the pub and celebrate if they want. Do you fancy a drink with them?" asked Hardcastle.

"No, I don't think so; I don't want to cramp their style. I'll hang on here for a while. I've got some calls to make. What about you, boss?"

"I've got a quick meeting with the ACC, DCI Cryer and Alex Till at 5:30pm," he said looking at his watch. "And there's a press conference arranged for 6pm. I'll head off home after that. I could do with an early night."

"Well, it's Friday tomorrow," replied Davison, "We've all put in a lot of hours these last eleven days or so, so fingers crossed we can all look forward to a quiet weekend."

"Amen to that," replied Hardcastle.

Friday 6:30am

Jenny Hardcastle turned over in bed. She was surprised to see that her husband was lying next to her, still asleep. He would normally be up and ready to leave for work by now.

"Steve," she said nudging him, "your phone is buzzing."

Hardcastle, yawned, rubbed his eyes and looked at the bedside clock. He realised that he had overslept. He reached for his phone, still half asleep.

"Hardcastle."

"Sorry to bother you sir, it's Sergeant Kennedy."

"Good morning Paddy, this is beginning to get a bit of a habit. What can I do for you?"

"I'm sorry to bother you sir, but we've got another body."

Hardcastle was immediately fully awake.

"Where?"

"The Golf Club. The Head Greenkeeper was doing his rounds before any of the members turned up for an early game, and unfortunately for him, he found a body in a bunker in front of the third green. Right put him off his breakfast by the sound of it."

"Have we got anyone there yet?"

"PCs Anderson and Henry are on site now. They were just a couple of minutes away when the call came in."

"Suspicious?"

"I'm afraid so, sir. It seems the gentleman has been shot, right between his eyes."

"Jesus," he replied, getting out of bed. "I'll be there as quick as I can. Could you call DS Davison for me and ask him to meet me at the Golf Club as soon as he can?"

"I will sir, but there is something else I need to tell you."

"Go ahead," replied Hardcastle, phone to his ear and walking into the en-suite.

"From the description, it sounds like the victim is our misper; I think we might have found Mr Willard."

Epilogue
Three Weeks Later

He stopped and looked at his iPhone.

It was a quarter past one in the morning. The sky was clear and there was a gentle breeze keeping the temperature down to a pleasant 15C.

The previous day had been yet another warm one, with temperatures just below 30C. It was now almost a fortnight since any rain had fallen in that part of the country, and there was talk of the local water authority imposing restrictions in the coming weeks.

Tonight's little escapade was the result of several weeks of meticulous planning and he had visited the target several times, both by day and by night. The only difference this time was that he was carrying a holdall. Occasionally, he was changing hands due to its weight.

As he approached the large wooden two-storey building, he heard a noise. A sudden surge in adrenaline caused his heart to skip a beat. He stood perfectly still. Almost certainly, it had been a fox or a badger.

After a minute or so, he carried on walking until he had reached his destination.

He tapped a window at the front of the building with the rock hammer he'd taken from the holdall, and on the third tap, he heard the window crack. Another tap and he was through. With a gloved hand, he picked away at the glass until there was a hole large enough to shove a hose through.

He then walked around to the right hand side of the building and did the same again. This time, the window cracked on the second tap.

In no time at all, he had poured petrol through both windows from the jerry can that had been in the holdall. After putting the can and the hammer back into the holdall, he lit two cigarettes and put one through each window.

In an instant, the petrol had ignited and he knew the building would be completely engulfed in flames in no time at all.

He turned on his heels and began to walk quickly back to where he had left his car, feeling satisfied with his night's work.

This time it was not the thrill of the fire that gave him pleasure.

It was the thrill of revenge.

A shock was in store for the cricketers of Middle Ash Cricket Club.